AN INSPECTOR SARALKAR MYSTERY

206 BONES

SALIL DESAI

Published by Westland Books, a division of Nasadiya Technologies Private Limited, in 2025

No. 269/2B, First Floor, 'Irai Arul', Vimalraj Street, Nethaji Nagar, Alapakkam Main Road, Maduravoyal, Chennai 600095

Westland and the Westland logo are the trademarks of Nasadiya Technologies Private Limited, or its affiliates.

ISBN: 9789371977869

10 9 8 7 6 5 4 3 2 1

This is a work of fiction. Names, characters, organisations, places, events and incidents are either products of the author's imagination or used fictitiously.

Typeset by Mukul

Printed at Manipal Technologies Limited, Manipal

206 BONES

Salil Desai is one of India's leading crime fiction writers and the creator of the much-acclaimed Inspector Saralkar mystery series. *206 Bones* is the sixth book in the series and his tenth fiction title overall. His short fiction has also been published in popular anthologies published by Westland, Hachette, Unisun and Penguin.

Screen rights of several of his books and stories have been acquired by leading production houses and studios, including his Inspector Saralkar series novels, which are currently being adapted into a web series by Jio Studios.

An alumnus of Film & Television Institute of India (FTII), Salil Desai is also a screenwriter, having scripted a web series, *Kalsutra*, that awaits release on JioHotstar, as well as a feature film that has recently been green-lit.

He is a seasoned newspaper columnist, with over 400 articles, op-ed pieces, features and travelogues in leading dailies. His books have been reviewed in *The Hindu*, *New Indian Express*, *The Pioneer*, *Bangalore Mirror*, *DNA*, *First City* and *The Tribune*, among others. His work has been praised by veteran authors Dr Shashi Tharoor and Shobhaa De, and film-makers Sriram Raghavan, Sujoy Ghosh and Sandeep Modi.

Salil was one of the four international authors worldwide selected for the HALD International Writers' Residency in Denmark, hosted by the Danish Centre for Writers & Translators in June 2016. He was also invited to Gullkistan Centre for Creativity, Iceland and spent the month of May 2023 there as a Resident.

Know more about him at http://www.salildesai.com.

OTHER TITLES BY SALIL DESAI

The Grudges of Gajanan Godbole (2024)
The Kid Killer (2023)
Murder Milestone (2020)
The Sane Psychopath (2018)
3 and a Half Murders (2017)
The Murder of Sonia Raikkonen (2015)
Lost Libido and Other Gulp Fiction (2012)
Murder on a Side Street (2011)

1

'Is that deep enough?' The digger paused to catch his breath and wiped the sweat running down his face. It was a cool night but the dig had been tough.

The digger received a terse reply. 'The pit needs to be deeper!'

'But I'm standing almost waist-deep. That's almost three feet …'

'It's got to be at least neck deep.'

'Neck deep? Why? That'll take me at least two more hours …'

'You can rest for ten minutes if you are tired.'

'It's double the work. I need to be paid more …' the digger replied morosely.

A long, tense beat followed. 'How much?'

The digger quoted a figure, expecting some haggling.

'OK. Dig!' the reply came promptly.

The digger was surprised. Should he have asked for more? Later perhaps. 'And, I can't do it all alone. I'm going to need help …'

He received a preoccupied glare. 'Hmm … OK. I'll fetch someone. But no more complaints then …'

The digger nodded. 'Just pass me some water to drink,' he said, took the bottle handed to him and gulped down half of it.

Thirst and greed satiated for the moment, the digger began scooping up the earth again. Ten minutes later, he was joined in the pit by a familiar face with a spade in hand. The two men glanced at each other distastefully, then barely exchanged words as they began digging away.

'It's a small scheme. Sixteen flats in all. The bungalow owners get four flats,' Rajat Mali said to his prospective father-in-law whom he had brought along specifically to impress.

The young architect was excited about the redevelopment deal he had clinched as his first independent construction project. 'Shanti Villa', the original bungalow, had been demolished and the foundations were now being excavated to make way for the construction of a swanky new building of bespoke apartments, loftily named 'Crest Condos'.

The prospective father-in-law, Suresh Sarnaik, nodded approvingly. 'So, you can sell twelve units. It's a great locality. In fact, why don't you design the top floor as duplexes or … or … what do they call it … penthouses?'

Rajat Mali beamed. 'Yes, yes, Sarnaik uncle. I've just now got the plan approved for sixteen equisized apartments, but hopefully we'll manage to convert the top units into duplexes.'

He hoped his prospective father-in-law could hear him over the din of the bulldozer, which was in full swing, excavating the foundations of the plot. Rajat was relieved when the machine seemed to stop for a bit.

'Hmm. This Shanti Villa—whose bungalow is this?' Sarnaik asked.

'It's the property of two siblings, Sunit Welde and his sister, Niharika Das. They inherited it from their parents, both of whom passed away last year within a few months of each other,' Rajat replied. 'Since Sunit stays abroad and Niharika in Goa, they decided to give the property for redevelopment.'

'Oh, so their father had built this bungalow.'

'Yes, it's about forty years old and the old man, Shashank Welde, and his wife lived here till—'

Rajat's sentence was cut short when his site supervisor uncharacteristically barged into the conversation.

'Sir …' the supervisor began, an anxious expression on his face. 'There's something you need to see.'

'What?' Rajat asked with a frown.

The supervisor licked his lips and struggled to articulate. 'It … it looks like a dead body, sir.'

'What?' Rajat's eyes and blood pressure shot up. 'Dead body?'

'I … I mean … a skeleton, sir, it got dug up when we were excavating the patch of lawn, under … under a granite sitting platform,' the supervisor explained.

Rajat Mali stared at the supervisor. 'Are you sure?' he hissed, throwing a quick sideways glance at his prospective father-in-law, Suresh Sarnaik, who he knew had been a police officer once.

'I … I … what else could it be, sir?' the harried supervisor asked.

'Show me,' Suresh Sarnaik, the retired cop spoke, assuming charge almost naturally. 'Come, Rajat.'

He beckoned the young architect and gestured at the supervisor, who started walking back towards the location of the find.

The JCB operator and a couple of workmen were standing around, peering at the pit-like formation in the ground. One man had dropped into the cavity and was holding what looked like an assembly of bones in his hands.

'Hey, leave that alone,' Sarnaik barked. 'Don't touch it. And get out of there.'

The man in the pit instantly dropped the bones, as if he'd been slapped, and scrambled out.

Rajat Mali and Suresh Sarnaik gazed at what looked like a full skeleton that had disintegrated, probably because of being scooped up by the JCB.

Rajat gasped. His prospective father-in-law remarked, 'We've got to call the police ...'

Before Rajat could say another word, Sarnaik had started dialling.

'Do you have photos of the bungalow, before you began the demolition?' Saralkar asked, as he finished examining the skeleton and the pit-like cavity from which it had been unearthed.

'Yes, sir,' Rajat Mali said quickly, unlocking his phone and scrolling through the photo gallery to identify the relevant pics.

'How come you are here, Sarnaik saheb? Buying a flat in this scheme?' Saralkar said turning to the ex-policeman, with whom he had had a nodding acquaintance when Sarnaik was in the force.

'No, no. I wish I could afford a flat in this locality,' Sarnaik replied, wondering whether he should reveal that Mali was his prospective son-in-law. 'Rajat ... Rajat is a family friend ... ' he continued after a pause, much to the dismay of the young architect, who had just found the photos and was about to show them to Saralkar.

'I see … ' Saralkar said. He took the phone from Rajat Mali and began flicking through the pics of the recently demolished two-storey bungalow.

Shanti Villa hadn't been an architectural marvel but it hadn't been indifferently designed either. The owner and architect had striven for style and individuality. Moreover, the bungalow seemed to have been well-maintained. It had a porch and an elegant staircase on one side, going up to the upper storey. A rectangular patch of lawn had been bordered by fruit-bearing guava and mango trees, as well as a gulmohar tree, with its flaming red flowers.

On the other side of the lawn was a small tiled pathway, next to covered parking space for two cars. At the edge of the lawns at both ends were granite-topped sitting platforms. The bungalow itself was nicely painted and next to the terrace a roof sloped down, both at the front and back.

Saralkar tapped on the phone and looked at Rajat and his supervisor. 'So, is this the granite platform under which you found the skeleton?'

'Yes, sir … ' the supervisor replied before Rajat could.

The sound of a police car pulling up at the gate of the site made Saralkar turn around. Doors opened and slammed in quick succession as PSI Motkar, two constables and two forensic technicians walked over.

'Morning, sir,' the new arrivals chimed together, and Saralkar nodded back in acknowledgement.

'What's with the goggles, Motkar? You turning into Tom Cruise? *Mission Impossible*?'

PSI Motkar wished he had the panache to reply, *No, sir, Salman Khan from* Dabangg*!*

Instead, without making any effort to remove his goggles, he replied awkwardly, 'No, sir … Conjunctivitis.'

'What?' Saralkar grimaced, as did almost all the others who voluntarily took a step back. 'How in the world did you contract conjunctivitis? Why didn't you tell me on phone earlier? You can go back home if you wish to … '

'It's much better today, sir. The goggles are just a precaution,' Motkar replied.

'Is that why you were on sick leave for the last three days?' Saralkar remarked, refusing to get off the matter. 'But you told me you had a viral …'

'Viral conjunctivitis, sir. But it's not exactly a badge of honour,' PSI Motkar said sheepishly.

Saralkar regarded him dubiously. 'So the doctor prescribed eye drops or something?'

'Yes, sir,' Motkar said, wishing his boss would get off the topic. 'Is that the skeleton, sir?' he asked, pointing at the pit.

'Yes, more like a bag of bones,' Saralkar replied. 'You sure you are not infectious? Do I need to wear goggles around you?'

Motkar sighed. 'No, sir. But if it puts your mind at ease, then please do … '

Suresh Sarnaik seemed to take the cue and put his goggles on.

Saralkar grunted. 'Ah well, I'll take my chances, I guess.'

He turned to the two forensic technicians. 'Any of you boys know how to determine how long the skeleton's been lying here buried?'

The two technicians looked at each other. 'It's a specialised task, sir,' one of them responded. 'It will have to be done at the lab.'

Saralkar had thought as much. 'I see. So, is there anything you can tell me here—whether it's a male or a female, probable age … cause of death?' he asked.

Another exchange of glances. Then the senior of the two, Arvind Tambat, said, 'I … I could try, sir … once I examine … but I can't promise … '

'Well, see if you find anything to ascertain if we have stumbled upon a murder victim,' Saralkar said, waving all the others away from the pit, so that the two forensic technicians could get on with their job.

He turned to Rajat Mali. 'We will need details of the previous owners of this bungalow.'

'Yes, sir. The bungalow owners are …'

'Give the information to PSI Motkar,' Saralkar delegated the task to his subordinate with a sideways gesture.

He turned around to take a good look at the plot where Shanti Villa had stood and the surrounding neighbourhood. It was an enclave of old elites—retired bureaucrats who'd managed to get prime plots, army officers, well-off businessmen of the 1970s/80s, and others who had money and connections. People who built bungalows when Pune still managed to pass off as a pensioner's paradise.

Now, many of the erstwhile bungalows had been sold or redevelopment deals had been struck by the heirs, given the wonderfully lucrative offers made by builders who were keen to construct tony 3 BHK/4 BHK apartments for the new elite in these prime localities.

There were two similar-sized plots on both sides of Shanti Villa. On one stood another tastefully designed bungalow of similar vintage, while the other plot was empty. Saralkar wondered how a forty- to fifty-year-old bungalow plot would still be lying vacant.

He walked out of the gate towards the empty plot, overgrown with grass and shrubs. Two rusted metal boards at different spots claimed that the property belonged to two different claimants—probably siblings—and that it was under litigation. It never ceased to amaze Saralkar how legal disputes continued interminably in the country. If there was legal hell, it was here in India. He wondered what the story behind this plot was, and whether the rival claimants were fighting all the way up to the Supreme Court.

Saralkar retraced his steps and regarded the bungalow on the other side of Shanti Villa. It was an elegantly designed dwelling, again two-storeyed, but more compact. It had a lawn with a small fountain-like structure in the middle. Two swings, mounted on a metal frame, stood at the far end of the lawn. A house with kids, most likely, Saralkar thought to himself. In the porch hung a hammock. But the bungalow didn't seem to be occupied at the moment.

He looked at the name on the gate-stone. 'Sethi Cottage' was inscribed neatly on the white marble, and below it was 1986, presumably the year the bungalow was built. Thirty-eight years ago. So, the owners of Shanti Villa and Sethi Cottage must have known each other for a long, long time.

Saralkar beckoned one of the constables towards him. 'Ahir, just check if there is anyone next door. If not, ask around and get contact details of the owners.'

Ahir nodded, opened the gate of Sethi Cottage and stepped inside. Saralkar strolled back to the Shanti Villa site.

'Got the owner's information, sir,' Motkar said, appearing at his side. He quickly briefed Saralkar, then asked, 'Do you want me to set up a call with Sunit Welde and his sister, Niharika Das?'

Before answering, Saralkar looked at Rajat Mali. 'I presume you signed the deal quite recently. Do you have any idea if Sunit Welde is still in India, or has flown back to the US?'

'We signed it when he was here about two months ago, sir. I was a little delayed in starting the demolition,' the young architect replied. 'He must've flown back weeks ago. I messaged him on WhatsApp about ten days ago to let him know we had commenced work on the site.'

Saralkar nodded, then turned to Motkar. 'Let's talk to the sister first after we get back to the office. In any case, if the brother is back in the US, it would be the middle of the night right now.'

Motkar nodded, then addressed Mali. 'Don't message or inform either before we talk to them.'

Rajat Mali agreed hastily, then craned his neck towards his prospective father-in-law, who cleared his throat and spoke, 'Saralkar saheb, I hope Rajat will not have to stop work on the site for more than a couple of days.'

Saralkar made a face. 'Let's hope so. Unless, of course, more bodies are found.'

His words seemed to send shock waves all around, as Suresh Sarnaik gaped, Rajat Mali gasped and the supervisor's eyes goggled. Even Motkar couldn't believe his ears, and it was only when Saralkar snorted that everyone seemed to realise that the senior inspector was just being fatuous.

Many faces broke into nervous grins. 'Please don't say that, saheb!' Rajat Mali said wretchedly. 'It's my first project.'

But Saralkar, having said his throwaway line, was now peering at the two forensic technicians down in the pit. 'Yes, Tambat, any initial impressions?'

Tambat looked up. Hesitation was writ large on his face. 'Sir, it might be better to wait for a lab analysis. As I said, I am no specialist and don't want to … er …'

'That's OK, Tambat. I'd like to know what you think,' Saralkar reassured him. 'If you are wrong, I won't hold it against you.'

Arvind Tambat looked uncomfortable, as if reluctant to opine. 'Sir … I … I think the skeleton has been buried here for long …'

'How long? Take a guess.'

'Sir, I'd say at least fifteen to twenty years … Maybe more …'

Saralkar regarded him grimly. 'What else?'

'I … I think it's the skeleton of a male, from the appearance of the pelvic area, sir …' Tambat said, then hastened to add, 'But as I said, sir, I could be terribly wrong.'

'I see. It's not a female, you think?' Saralkar murmured, 'What else? How did he die? At what age?'

'That … that is beyond me, sir. I won't even think of taking a guess,' Tambat said, as if he'd already committed blasphemy and wasn't prepared to sin again.

'Alright,' Saralkar grunted. 'Go through the pit carefully. See if you find anything that was buried with the body. Any clothes, belongings, anything worth analysing forensically.'

'Yes, sir.'

Saralkar glanced at the lone constable, since Ahir hadn't returned from his inquiry about the owners of Sethi Cottage. 'Help the technicians. Come, Motkar, let's get moving. Unless, of course, you want to go back to your house to nurse your eyes back to health.'

'No, sir, I'm OK. I've got the eye drops with me, so …' Motkar said.

Saralkar eyed him suspiciously. 'OK. You damn well make sure you don't pass on the conjunctivitis to me.'

He then turned to Rajat Mali and Suresh Sarnaik. 'Too bad something like this had to happen. I'll let you know as soon as possible when you can resume work.'

What he had avoided using was the word 'if' in place of 'when'.

'Sir …' Mali spoke, 'Can … can this at least be kept from the media? My project will be doomed if news of a skeleton being found on the plot gets splashed all over …'

Saralkar felt sorry for the young man. 'We'll try our best, but it's very difficult, Rajat.'

2

Niharika Das nee Welde often felt life had gone by in a whirl. Hadn't she been twenty-two just yesterday, so how come the mirror showed a woman past fifty today?

She didn't have any regrets though, not many anyway. A fairly normal childhood had been followed by a fun-filled college life. She completed her MBA by the time she was twenty-two, with a placement in a good company. Two years of corporate life ensued. Then she met Anshuman Das, a new colleague. She'd made up her mind about him in just six months.

'Why a Bengali?' her mother had asked.

'What do you mean, Aai?' she'd shot back, indignant and yet not sure what her mother had implied.

'I mean they are so different from us,' her mother had said.

'Oh, come on, Aai! Their language is different, that's all …'

'They eat fish, probably every day. How are you going to live with a fish-eater?'

'So what?'

'Well, either you'll have to become a fish-eater yourself or at the very least learn to cook for him, which isn't a pleasant experience. Trust me,' her mother had persisted.

'Aai, what kind of an absurd objection is this? Maybe Anshuman will give up fish instead,' Niharika had replied angrily.

'For how long, Niharika?' her mother had asked sagely.

Well, Anshuman hadn't given up fish, and Niharika had neither become a fish-eater nor learnt to cook it. But their marriage had endured. It wasn't gloriously happy. But then, which marriage was? They had two sons and no sooner did they stop needing looking after, Niharika got caught up in taking care of her mom-in-law on the one hand and her ageing parents in Pune, on the other.

Five years of constantly shuttling between Pune and Panaji ended when her mother-in-law passed away just before COVID-19 struck and then the demise of her parents one after the other last year.

That had been, in short, the summary of her life so far. Her husband Anshuman had just been fired from his company and had received a handsome severance package. There wasn't much to worry about since both their sons were now grown up and were doing well—Ripujit was with one of the best hotel chains in India and Shatrujit was studying to become a product designer.

Also, both Niharika and Anshuman had inherited enough from their parents, so financial security wasn't weighing on their minds. What instead had cropped up in the empty nest was a different issue altogether.

'Anshuman, I have been a wife, a mother and a daughter for twenty-six years now,' Niharika said angrily. 'I think I have earned the right to do what I want.'

'Of all the things you want to do this? Acting?' her husband asked, incredulity competing with fury within him.

'Yes, I see nothing wrong with it,' Niharika replied stubbornly. 'It was an open casting call. I applied ...'

'Are you mad, Niharika? What's got into you at this age?' Anshuman screamed.

Niharika's phone rang right then. She glanced at the screen and saw that it was a call from an unknown number, but decided to take it all the same. Anshuman could fume all he wanted but she was not going to let this degenerate into a shouting match.

'Hello,' she said, taking the call.

'Hullo, am I talking to Mrs Niharika Das?'

'Yes,' Niharika said, almost unconsciously taking note of the Marathi accent of the caller. 'Who's calling?'

From the corner of her eye, she could see Anshuman staring at her grimly, as if waiting for the call to end to start haranguing her.

'I am PSI Motkar from Pune Police. You and your brother recently entered into a redevelopment deal with Mr Rajat Mali for your inherited bungalow, right?'

'Yes,' Niharika said, frowning. 'What about it … er … Mr Motkar?'

'We need to speak to you. Are you in Pune? Can you come and meet us?'

Niharika's eyes shot towards Anshuman, who after twenty-eight years of togetherness could immediately sense her discomfort. 'Who is it?' he asked.

She held up her hand and said, 'I don't understand Mr … er … Inspector Motkar. What inquiries? I … I stay in Goa. I can't come and meet.'

Anshuman's eyes shot up on hearing the word Inspector.

'Oh! So can I ask you a few questions over the phone right now? Then we can decide whether you need to come over to Pune.'

'Right now?'

'Yes, madam.'

'OK, Inspector, my husband Anshuman is here with me. Can I put the phone on speaker? Because he would know what to do …'

'Sure, please do,' Motkar replied.

'Just give me a second, Inspector,' Niharika said hastily. She then put the phone on mute and turned to Anshuman. 'It's an officer called Inspector Motkar from Pune Police. Says he wants to talk to me about the redevelopment deal.'

'What?' Anshuman scowled. 'Are you sure, it's not a crank call? Lots of mobile scams these days.'

'How should I know, Anshuman? That's why I said, I'll put it on speaker.'

'OK, go ahead,' Anshuman replied.

Niharika unmuted the phone and put it on speaker. 'Hello, Inspector, my husband Anshuman is also listening in.'

'Hello. This is Anshuman Das,' her husband said. 'Could you please repeat what this is about?'

'Pune Police is conducting some inquiries. We have some questions about your in-laws' bungalow, which is undergoing redevelopment, Mr Das,' Motkar replied.

A look of anxiety passed between Anshuman and Niharika.

'Oh, I see. Inspector … how do we … we know this is genuinely the Pune Police? I'm sorry. Would it be possible to have a WhatsApp video call so that we can be sure? If you don't mind,' Anshuman said with a slightly dry throat.

'I understand, Mr Das. Sure, I'll call back in a few minutes so you can see me,' Motkar said. As soon as he disconnected, he immediately regretted agreeing to the video call. Wouldn't he look both suspicious and ridiculous with his goggles on? But it was too late now.

Meanwhile, at the Das residence, the husband and wife regarded each other uneasily.

'Could it be about that clause in the will?' Anshuman said gingerly.

'Oh god … I hope not,' Niharika, said looking worried.

Her phone sprang to life again, showing an incoming video call on WhatsApp.

Anshuman signalled her to take it. Niharika composed herself and swiped on the screen. A most un-policeman-like cop appeared. PSI Motkar had never quite fitted into the stock image of a cop. He wasn't tough-looking, hard of face, cynical or shrewd of appearance, nor physically robust.

He had always looked like a mild-mannered accountant or someone with a white-collar job. He had decided to discard the goggles, after having checked quickly that his eyes were almost back to normal.

'Hullo, Mr and Mrs Das,' Motkar said. 'As I mentioned, I am PSI Motkar. Should I begin with my questions?'

The couple nodded.

'Well, I'd like to know a little bit about Shanti Villa. I understand your father built it, Mrs Das. Can you confirm that?'

'Yes, my father Mr Shashank Welde built it. We shifted into the house on Diwali in 1982. I was in the third standard then,' Niharika replied.

'OK. Any idea when he purchased the plot?' Motkar asked.

'That I am not sure. My brother Sunit would know exactly, but I'd think around five or six years earlier.'

'I see. And the bungalow was fully constructed as it was when handed over for redevelopment, or was there some subsequent construction done after 1982?'

'No, the second storey with two separate flats was added later. I was working in Mumbai at the time,' Niharika replied. 'So, that means about fourteen to fifteen years later.'

'OK. And were the platforms in the lawn area also built at the same time?'

'Lawn platforms?' Niharika asked, confused.

'Yes, there were two granite-topped sitting platforms with concrete bases on the lawns.'

'Oh, those. No, no, I think those were built even later. I don't remember when exactly. Why?' Niharika asked.

'Would your brother know when they were added?'

'I'm not sure. Are you going to talk to him too?'

'Yes, we might,' PSI Motkar said shortly.

Anshuman Das, who hadn't had a chance to speak so far now, interjected.

'Er … Inspector Motkar … I think my older son, Ripujit, was just one or two years old when my father-in-law put up those platforms. I remember because I mentioned to him that Ripujit might hurt himself on the granite corners, which were sharp, while playing in the lawns.'

'OK, good. So, when must that have been, Mr Das?'

'Ripujit is twenty-five now, so let's say the platforms were installed about twenty-three or twenty-four years ago,' Anshuman said.

'Yes, yes, I remember now,' Niharika chimed in. 'You had told me too. Then, Baba got the corners rounded.'

'So 2000 or 2001, is it?' Motkar asked to confirm.

'Yes,' Anshuman said. 'But er … inspector, may I ask what exactly are you investigating? I mean … your question about when what was built in the bungalow …'

A golden rule of policing was to extract maximum information from people relevant to an inquiry while imparting none or bare minimum facts. PSI Motkar's reply was in keeping with that rule.

'Something has been found, during demolition and excavation work at Shanti Villa,' Motkar said.

'What has been found?' Niharika asked even before Anshuman could respond.

'This is a preliminary conversation, Mrs Das, so I can't talk about that right now,' PSI Motkar replied. 'However, we'll let you know soon. Meanwhile, let me ask a few more questions.'

If Motkar thought that would be enough to stop Niharika Das, he was mistaken.

'But unless you tell me what you have found why should I even answer your questions. I have a right to know what the inquiry is about, Inspector,' she blurted out.

'Mrs Das, I would request you to be patient and answer my questions.'

'Of course, Inspector, but why aren't you telling me what exactly you've found? With all this secrecy you make it sound as if you have found some buried treasure or some contraband or an ancient temple or maybe a dead body,' Niharika Das continued feistily, making her husband wince.

There was a moment of silence as PSI Motkar himself seemed at a loss. Anshuman Das hastened to make amends on observing his silence.

'I'm sorry, Inspector, but police means crime … and naturally my wife is upset because she has such an emotional connection with Shanti Villa. So, please don't mind. But it would be really good if you can tell us what the matter is.'

He hoped his wife wouldn't open her mouth again and gave her a warning look to wait for Motkar to speak.

PSI Motkar was again quiet for a few seconds, then spoke. 'Madam, why did you say "dead body"?'

Niharika Das blanched, hesitated then said, 'I … I was just saying anything that came to my mind … '

'Are you sure?'

'Of course, Inspector! Come on … now you are scaring me,' Niharika Das said, her voice suddenly shaky.

'Well, Mrs Das, then do you have any explanation for the fact that a human skeleton was discovered in a pit under a granite sitting platform in the lawn area?' PSI Motkar asked.

It took Niharika or Anshuman Das a while to react.

3

'TENANTS? FOR OVER TWENTY-FIVE YEARS?' SARALKAR EXCLAIMED.

'Yes, sir, the old couple added the upper storey nearabout twenty-eight years ago and constructed two 2BHK apartments on top, one each for their two children,' Motkar explained. 'Mrs Das told me that it was decided to rent both apartments so that it would generate rent as well as provide company for the parents, who were getting on in age.'

'Because the children were not living in Pune?'

'Yes, sir. The idea was that in case the son and family decided to shift back to India or Mrs Das's husband ever took a job in Pune and decided to settle here, the accommodations were ready. But while they were away, the apartments could be rented out.'

'Hmm,' Saralkar said. It was thinking quite typical of that generation of well-off, upper-middle–class Indians. 'You know what that means, Motkar?'

'Yes, sir. That if it is indeed foul play, then we'll have to trace all the tenants who'd stayed here over the years too,' Motkar replied. He knew it would be a time-consuming and monumental task.

'Unless, of course, the skeleton turns out to be of some pre-historic ancestor of mankind,' Saralkar said dryly.

'Quite unlikely, isn't it, sir?'

'What's the harm in hoping, Motkar! Anyway, I had asked Ahir to check who the owners of the bungalow next door are. Turns out, the house belongs to some rich Mumbai family who visit three to four times a year. They've got a part-time caretaker who is supposed to get the place aired and cleaned, and to water the lawns and flower beds once a week. Just get someone to dig up more details.'

'And what about the tenants, sir? Should I ask Mrs Das if they have any rental agreement records or something?' Motkar asked, adjusting his goggles. He wondered if Saralkar would freak out if he removed the goggles.

'No, let's get after that once we have confirmation on the skeleton,' Saralkar said. 'Instead, ask Mrs Das if she can put us in touch with some of the people who worked at the bungalow in her parents' lifetime, particularly old-timers such as maids, cooks, drivers and gardeners.'

'From thirty-five to forty years ago, sir?' Motkar said, sceptically.

'Well, if this does turn into a murder investigation, we have to find people who had access to the bungalow on a regular basis. Say even when the old couple were not in town or had gone visiting one of their children. Or somebody who might remember if something unusual had occurred many years ago. Anything that can give us a hint of where to begin.'

PSI Motkar made a note. He looked at his watch. 'I have to call Sunit Welde in about an hour's time, sir. I have already sent a WhatsApp message intimating him. Would you like to join the call?'

'No, you talk to him first,' Saralkar said. 'By the way, what was the occupation of the father? Did you ask his daughter?'

'Yes, sir. Mr Shashank Welde retired from a senior position in a public sector petroleum company,' Motkar replied.

'I see. That's probably why he managed to bag a plot in such a prime residential area in those times,' Saralkar remarked. 'You should try interrogating suspects with goggles on, Motkar. Gives you a sinister air.'

Sir, you don't have to rub it in. I know it looks silly, Motkar felt like saying. Instead, he gave a thin smile as he got up to leave, and said, 'Will try it, sir …'

He was almost half-way out of the cabin door when Saralkar said, 'Did you see the pit in which the skeleton was found? It was done by someone who knew how to dig one. It was trench-like, and the depth was also right.'

Motkar turned to look at his boss. 'Sir, you mean it was done by someone who regularly did that type of work?'

'Correct. Also, I have been thinking. Just because the skeleton was found directly below the lawn platform, can we assume it was done to ensure that the spot was never again dug up by anyone, or that no one accidentally discovered the pit and thus the skeleton?' Saralkar reflected.

'Well, sir, that's how it appears. The natural reaction is to do your best so that your crime is not discovered,' Motkar said.

'If you presume that the lawn platform was deliberately constructed on top of the pit, then it could only be the owners who could have committed the crime,' Saralkar observed. 'Not tenants or anybody else, for no one but the owners could have got a platform installed on their property.'

Motkar nodded slowly. His boss's logic was correct. 'Yes, sir. But that would also eliminate both Mrs Das and Mr Welde. Because if either of them was involved, they wouldn't have let the bungalow be redeveloped, knowing the skeleton would inevitably be unearthed.'

'Now you are thinking, Motkar! That would leave only the old couple as murder suspects. But what if the sitting platform being located over the pit is sheer coincidence? Then, we have to look at many more suspects, including the tenants. Worse, then it's also possible the murder took place earlier, practically any time after the bungalow was built.'

Motkar gave a shudder. 'Yes, sir. I wonder who the poor victim is. I mean how unfortunate can a person's fate be—to have disappeared from the face of the earth, then get discovered in these circumstances so many years later, and yet probably remain unidentified.'

'Hmm, but you are not thinking of the poor murderer at all, Motkar!' Saralkar said with a cynical chuckle.

'Sir?'

'Think of what a nasty surprise they are in for, if they're still alive! To have been lulled into believing that one has got away and then to suddenly find that one's crime has been discovered.'

—

PSI Motkar felt the momentary sting of the eye drops in his two eyes, one after the other. He shut his eyelids and tilted his head further back for about thirty seconds, then dabbed his eyes with his handkerchief, before opening them.

He turned his phone camera to the selfie mode and checked his eyes. They seemed almost normal now. He had not felt any sticky discharge during the day, and neither had he experienced that slight prickly sensation in his eyes. His conjunctivitis was probably gone by now, although the only way he could be completely sure would be if he woke up the next morning without irritability and that unwelcome stickiness.

He looked at his watch. It was almost time to make the video call to Sunit Welde. He hadn't used the goggles during the call with Niharika and Anshuman Das. He wouldn't use them while calling Sunit Welde either.

Philadelphia—that's where the man had made his home now, 12,751 kilometres away from Pune, ten and a half hours behind. It was evening in Pune and morning there.

Sunit Welde belonged to a generation of middle-class, upper-caste Indians who had the brains and parents' resources to make the most of education and career opportunities abroad in the last two decades of the past century. They had had a kind of first-mover advantage and now, thirty to thirty-five years later, most of them had prospered—they had become citizens of the first world, while enjoying a unique status in India.

Most contemporaries envied them, even those who had been far more successful in India itself, simply because India, for all its progress and material prosperity, still didn't offer anywhere near the quality of life, ambience and conditions of the developed world.

To Motkar, however, NRIs were simply another category of privileged Indians with chips on their shoulders. He called Sunit Welde's number now, and soon a clean-shaven man with salt-and-pepper hair appeared on screen. He was wearing a blue round-necked T-shirt and looked younger than the fifty-six he was supposed to be.

'Hello, good morning, Mr Sunit Welde,' PSI Motkar began, wondering why in the hell he had felt the need to wish the man good morning. Would he have done it to an Indian in India?

'Good morning … er … Inspector Motkar, right?' Sunit Welde replied in a rather hoarse voice. 'Sorry, I have a sore throat. Can't talk much, but what is this I hear from my sister?'

He broke off and coughed. 'Sorry …'

Motkar could not detect any hint of an accent, either put on or naturally acquired.

'When did you talk to Mrs Das?' PSI Motkar asked.

'Just ten minutes ago …' Sunit Welde said recovering from his bout of coughing. 'She'd left a couple of urgent messages on phone.'

'I see. So, what did she say?'

A woman's hand suddenly seemed to enter the screen holding a mug full of some hot liquid. Sunit Welde took it. 'Thanks,' he said off the camera, then turned to Motkar on screen. 'I hope you don't mind me sipping on this kadha for my throat, Inspector.'

'That's alright,' PSI Motkar said, suddenly filled with the urge to put eye drops into his eyes in response. 'Tell me about your conversation with your sister.'

'Actually, my brother-in-law Anshuman did most of the explaining. And I was horrified to know that … that apparently a body—I mean, a skeleton—was found in the lawn of our bungalow, when the developer started demolishing and digging up the foundation.'

He paused, coughed a couple of times, then took a sip of the kadha.

'Yes. The developer, Rajat Mali, informed us about it this morning. Our team visited the spot, and the skeleton has been taken for forensic analysis,' Motkar said. 'I spoke to your sister this morning, and I'd also like to hear your thoughts on the matter.'

'My thoughts, Inspector?' Sunit Welde said, wrinkling his face—because of the taste of the kadha or the matter they were discussing, Motkar couldn't be sure. 'I … I am speechless. I … I can't believe or imagine something like this … I mean, such things happen in movies …'

He paused and broke into a bout of prolonged coughing. When he recovered, he spoke again, 'I know it's a long shot, but the only possibility I could think of is, could it be one of the workers of the contractor who built our bungalow? I mean, I remember hearing conversations between my parents and some family friends about how the workers caused incessant trouble and delay, how they'd argue between themselves and how they would often get drunk and fight and curse. I was just a child then …'

'You mean one of the contractor's men was killed during the construction and the others buried him there?' Motkar asked.

'Yes … who knows? How else could a skeleton have got deep underneath and remained there all these years?' Sunit Welde said, sipping his concoction.

What he had suggested wasn't all that far-fetched, Motkar thought, and was as probable—or not—as other such theories. 'Do you know the contractor hired by your father hired for the construction of the bungalow?' he asked.

'The architect was my father's friend, Subhash Atre. He died about ten years ago. I think we got the contractor through him. I remember his first name for some strange reason—Sarjerao. If I am not mistaken, Mr Atre's son, Yashodhan, runs the architectural firm his father set up. I can find out his coordinates, if that helps,' Sunit Welde said.

'Please do. We can at least explore that possibility,' PSI Motkar said. 'When did you shift to Shanti Villa?'

'Let me see …' Sunit Welde said, tilting his head back and running his fingers down his throat. 'Diwali of 1981 or 1982. The construction of the bungalow started when I was in the sixth standard, and we went to stay there when I was in the eighth standard.'

'I see. So, for the next ten to twelve years you stayed in Shanti Villa before you left for the US?' PSI Motkar asked.

'Yes and no. I was away doing my engineering in Belgaum for about four years—from 1987 to 1991—then returned to stay with my parents for about two years when I was working in a manufacturing company in Pune. Then, in 1994, I left for America to pursue my MS,' Sunit Welde clarified.

'OK. In all this time, from 1982 onwards when your family shifted to the bungalow, can you think of extended periods of time when Shanti Villa was unoccupied—when the family was away for long and perhaps someone had access to the house or could trespass?'

Sunit Welde frowned. 'You mean like no one from our family was there for weeks or months?'

'Yes, not short periods of time like a couple of days or a week, but something much longer … when possibly it was known no one was going to be at home for some time …' Motkar emphasised.

'I'll really have to rack my brain to remember stuff from thirty to forty years ago,' Sunit Welde said. He was clearing his throat much more frequently, but his cough seemed to have subsided. 'Of course, beginning late 1990s till around 2015, my parents would come over to stay with me in the US every year or two for about two or three months at a time. At those times, the bungalow would be unoccupied, but of course the tenants would still be there … so Shanti Villa wouldn't be completely empty or deserted …'

'I'm glad you mentioned tenants. Now, did your parents make registered leave and licence agreements with various tenants over the years, Mr Welde?'

'Yes, I think so, at least for the last ten to twelve years certainly. I am not sure of the period before that, because things like leave and licence agreements became quite stringent and mandatory only from 2010, I think,' Sunit Welde said.

This was true. Even fifteen to twenty years ago, often landlords just got notarised agreements made, or sometimes just made agreements on hundred-rupee stamp paper without getting them notarised or registered. This was done mainly to avoid reporting rental income or to evade higher property tax payments, apart from eliminating registration expenses and legal fees.

'So did your father maintain a file of such leave and licence or rental agreements, which can be made available to us?'

'Well, I cleared a lot of my father's papers after his death and I faintly remember seeing such a file. We put all important documents in a few boxes, and I think my sister has it,' Sunit Welde said, then suddenly his face changed as if something had just struck him. 'Actually, Inspector, why don't you first check with my father's property broker, who generally got him tenants, for as long as I can remember. His name is Uttam Padwal. I'll send you his number. He probably would have all agreement copies and other details of the tenants over the years.'

'Yes, that would certainly help, Mr Welde.'

Sunit Welde nodded, then took a sip of the kadha again. His face seemed to become grim. 'Inspector Motkar, does it mean you suspect one of the tenants could have … er … murdered someone and buried the body in our lawns many years ago, when my parents were away?'

'It's difficult to speculate at the moment, Mr Welde, but I'll get in touch with you again in a day or two when we have more information,' Motkar parried.

'Sure. But I hope the police are not entertaining any suspicion that our family … or my father had anything to do with the buried skeleton?' Sunit Welde asked, his anxiety finally spilling over.

Motkar wasn't sure how exactly to respond to that question. He wondered what his boss Saralkar would have said. Inspiration came almost instantly. 'It's less than twelve hours since we were called in, Mr Welde. Our entire focus right now is on gathering facts and background. OK? Do send me the contact details of the property broker, Uttam Padwal, and also the architect's son, Mr Yashodhan Atre,' he said. 'Also, if you think of anything else that you recollect, please feel free to call me.'

'Sure,' Sunit Welde said, and Motkar cut the call, nipping in the bud any possibility of Sunil Welde repeating his question about suspicions on the Welde family.

He glanced at his watch and decided to call it a day. If it indeed turned out to be a murder, the victim had lain dead and buried for many years. Was there a realistic chance of solving a case like that?

He had recently read of a murderer who was nabbed in Ahmednagar district forty-nine years after he had killed his landlady in Ahmedabad, circa 1973. But there, the suspect had been identified almost immediately after the crime, including by eyewitnesses who had named him. However, the suspect had fled and never been found, until some officer dusted the old case files again in 2023, wondering if the suspect could have returned to his home town, assuming he was safe now and perhaps even got an Aadhaar card issued in his original name.

And surprise of surprises, this hunch actually turned out to be true, leading the police straight to the murderer's doorstep.

In the Shanti Villa case, not only the suspect but even the victim was unknown. It would be the blindest of all blind cases, even in Saralkar's career, Motkar reckoned.

But for now, it was time to go home.

4

'DO YOU THINK HALF THE MURDERS IN THIS WORLD WOULD HAVE occurred if the killer had paused to think what they were going to do with the body?' Saralkar asked, cracking his fingers.

Motkar had just finished briefing him on his call with Sunit Welde the previous evening and given other updates. 'Perhaps not, sir, but aren't most murders spontaneous, heat-of-the-moment actions?'

'True. Still a considerable number are premeditated,' Saralkar remarked. 'Yet, most such murderers only plan to dispose of the person, not their bodies, which is strange. The body and the mess around it are the evidence that often points to the murderer. Whereas, the cardinal principle of law is corpus delicti—no body means no murder, because there is no evidence to support the claim of murder.'

Motkar looked at him confused. 'I am not sure I understand the point you are driving at, sir ...'

Saralkar cast an annoyed look at him. 'I am saying that the idea of killing is so powerful and deceptively gratifying to murderers as a solution to their problems that many may summon the motivation to kill. But after they have committed the act, what do most murderers do? They just leave the body where it is and run—or make a clumsy effort to hide or get rid of it! Correct?'

'That's right, sir,' Motkar said, still wondering what Saralkar was leading to.

'Why is that?'

'Because they panic or just want to get as far away from it as possible?'

'Yes! And what is the reason for that? Because they don't know what to do with the body,' Saralkar emphasised, like some professor teaching his class. 'Again, why? Because they have no experience. And second, their mind stops working. Now contrast this with murderers who manage to successfully get rid of the bodies of their victims. Who might such individuals be?'

'I would say somebody who has killed before or even a serial killer.'

'Or? Who else?'

Motkar thought carefully. 'Or individuals who have some experience with human bodies? You know, flesh and blood ...'

'Exactly! Doctors, hospital workers, policemen, defence personnel, firemen, professionals who handle accidents or rescue operations, morgue workers. All kinds of individuals who have to handle dead bodies, flesh and blood, as you put it, as part of their jobs,' Saralkar remarked.

It finally began to dawn on Motkar what Saralkar was perhaps hinting at. 'Are you saying, sir, that in the Shanti Villa case, we ought to look for someone with such a background?' he asked doubtfully.

Saralkar gave a grim chuckle. 'Whoever managed to keep a dead body hidden in the middle of the city for twenty, maybe thirty or even forty years, in all likelihood, had a good idea of how it could be accomplished, apart from possessing nerve and cold-bloodedness. So, we need to be doubly suspicious of someone with such a background, since we might be dealing with a lot of people once we start digging into the Shanti Villa case.'

Motkar had to concede that it was a good filter.

'Yes, sir. Niharika Das has given me a list of a few servants and others who worked for her parents in some capacity or the other. She said she'll add to the list as she recalls some of the older servants, who were employed in the 1980s and '90s,' Motkar said. 'Should we start tracking down the names we already have and summon them for questioning? Or, are we waiting for confirmation on the skeleton being a murder victim, before we officially proceed?'

'I talked to Forensics this morning, and it's going to take much longer to get a definitive confirmation on that,' Saralkar said matter-of-factly. 'It might have to go to a more advanced lab facility, which has experienced specialists in forensic anthropology to determine sex and age of the person whose skeleton it is, the cause of death, and—most importantly—how long the body has lain buried.'

'How long before we get the results, sir?' Motkar asked.

'A fortnight, maybe even a month,' Saralkar replied. 'No point waiting for their conclusions. Let's go by common sense and assume it's a suspicious death of person unknown, probably murder, and commence the investigation. I'll brief the CP.'

'So, I'll start with the list of servants that Niharika Das has shared,' Motkar said. 'But what should the line of questioning be, sir?'

He had loads of experience in conducting inquiries but in most investigations, Motkar had had some idea and context of what or who exactly they were looking for, or the specifics of what information needed to be teased out of the people he questioned. In this case, however, everything was rather vague, with no reference point to use for setting the compass.

Saralkar grunted. 'Keep it simple. Ascertain, as far as possible, the exact period during which the maid or the cook or driver, or whoever you are speaking to, was associated with the Welde family. The kind of relations they had—long, short, harmonious, acrimonious; any disturbing incidents in the household during their tenure, or any conflict with any outsider the family had—neighbours, visitors, relatives, strangers, or even among themselves; anything odd they had observed while working there or anything they'd like to narrate that happened during their association with the Weldes. That's it for now. Then we'll see if anything relevant emerges.'

'OK, sir,' Motkar said. 'And how about …'

'When is Zirpe going to be back from her training module?' Saralkar interjected.

He was referring to ASI Sanika Zirpe, who was inducted as a Homicide Squad member after Saralkar was impressed by her work in the Pranjal Bhatti case.[1]

'Tomorrow is the last day of the training module, sir.'

Saralkar scowled. 'Ask her if she can skip the last day. We need her here, unless it's too important to skip.'

It was an order to be framed as a request, Motkar knew too well. 'OK, sir, I'll talk to Zirpe. Should I pass on the inquiries related to the contractor, the architect and the property broker to her, if she gets back tomorrow?'

Saralkar looked indecisive for a moment, then shook his head. 'No, you form the team to start the process of tracking the servants today, but let Zirpe take over all that from you tomorrow. I want you to fully focus on the architect, contractor and broker and see if those leads get us anywhere,' he said.

Motkar nodded.

---

[1] Read *The Kid Killer*.

'By the way, why aren't you wearing your goggles, damn it?' Saralkar asked, as if suddenly remembering Motkar's malady.

'I'm OK now, sir,' Motkar replied. He had been wondering how Saralkar hadn't noticed earlier.

Saralkar scrutinised him sceptically. 'Are you sure you are no longer a threat to public safety, Motkar?'

'Absolutely sure, sir!'

'How do you know?'

'The doctor said so, sir. I went for a quick check-up this morning.'

There was doubt writ large on his boss's face, but eventually he said, 'Ah well! Got to take your word for it. Anyway, do you know how many bones there are in the human body?'

Motkar was startled by the question. 'No, sir. Why?'

'Two hundred and six in an adult, it seems, the Forensics people told me this morning, when I inquired,' Saralkar replied laconically, 'Only babies and infants have around three hundred.'

Motkar waited for him to elaborate, perhaps mention the count of bones in the skeleton they found.

Instead, the senior inspector shrugged. 'Do you realise that most human advancement has been based on macabre curiosity? I mean whoever first wondered how many bones human beings have and then took the trouble of counting them in different skeletons and categorising them. Thirst for knowledge, of course, but tinged with ghoulishness, I guess.'

'Right, sir,' Motkar said, not sure if it was an apt response, but his general knowledge thus enriched, he took Saralkar's leave and set off on the tricky tasks that lay before him.

ASI Sanika Zirpe did not seem to have minded skipping the last day of the course. She had cheerfully taken over the tedious and uninspiring task of tracking down various servants and odd-job men and women who had worked for the Weldes.

'Motkar, sir, the case sounds straight out of a movie,' she said with grim amusement. 'All we need now are reports of the bungalow being haunted by the ghost of whoever was killed.'

PSI Motkar gave a dry laugh. 'Well, no such spooky tales floating around so far, but if you believe in ghosts, let's hope the victim's spirit helps us find some clues double quick.'

He paused then glanced at his watch. 'I've got to get going now, Zirpe. Boss wants an update around 4 p.m.'

She nodded as PSI Motkar scrambled away. He was in two minds whether to start with the architecture firm that had built the bungalow or with the property agent who had arranged tenants. But finally, it just boiled down to who picked up his call first.

The call to Uttam Padwal, the property agent, had remained unanswered after several rings, whereas the call to the office of Atre and Associates had been answered promptly and he had been connected to Yashodhan Atre as soon as the receptionist learnt a policeman was on the line.

Yashodhan Atre had seemed puzzled but had shown no hesitation in agreeing to meet. And so, Motkar now found himself at Atre's office on Fergusson College Road. Atre and Associates gave the feel of a successful firm—plush, elegant, air-conditioned. Yashodhan Atre did not keep him waiting either.

He was a cheerful, fit man who appeared to be in his early sixties. Yet, his hair was fully white—moustache and eyebrows included. He was in jeans and a collared T-shirt. They shook hands and even before they were seated, Yashodhan Atre asked the receptionist who'd shown Motkar in to send in tea.

Motkar noted that unlike most people, Atre hadn't even asked or offered the option of coffee or a cold drink as a formality.

'Yes, Motkar saheb. What would you probably want with me?' he asked with a smile. 'You were quite vague on the phone but I was so intrigued to get a call from a policeman. I guess I watch too much *Crime Patrol* ...'

PSI Motkar couldn't think of another person he'd met in his entire career who looked so thrilled and eager to meet a cop. 'Mr Atre, I understand your father was a close friend of Mr Shashank Welde and also the architect of their bungalow, Shanti Villa.'

Yashodhan Atre's eyes narrowed, as if even more puzzled. 'Yes, that's right! We were family friends with the Weldes. My father and Shashank uncle were childhood pals. I remember my father designed the bungalow,' he replied without hesitation. 'What about it, Inspector?'

'Had you joined your father's firm by then?'

Yashodhan Atre grinned. 'Don't go by the colour of my hair. I am not that old. I think I was in tenth class around the time the bungalow was being built, and had no clue I was eventually going to follow in my father's footsteps and become an architect,' he said. 'I thought I was going to be the next Sunil Gavaskar back then. Forget India, I didn't even play Ranji Trophy for Maharashtra!' He chuckled and winked as if his life was one long mirthful odyssey.

'Oh, I see! So, I understand your father not only designed the bungalow but also got it built for Shashank Welde?' Motkar asked.

Yashodhan Atre looked away and up, as if trying hard to recollect. 'Yes, I think so. Constructing a bungalow back then was quite a headache for middle-class folk. Cement supply was controlled, contractors were unreliable, permissions were a problem. That's why Welde uncle told my father to get it built for him.'

'I presume your father must have engaged one of his regular contractors to do the job, right?'

'I guess so. That's the way it works even today,' Yashodhan Atre said. 'You are making me very curious with all these questions, Inspector.'

Motkar kept a poker face. There was a knock on the door and a peon came in with two cups of tea and a bowl of sugar cubes on a tray, which he laid on the table.

'Any recollection of the contractor engaged by your father?' Motkar asked after the peon had left the cabin.

Yashodhan Atre slurped at his tea and nodded approvingly. 'This boy makes better tea than my wife. How I wish I could add a cube of sugar. But what to do? Diabetes! And I don't like that sugar-free stuff.'

PSI Motkar gave him a slight smile, almost feeling guilty when he dropped two lumps of sugar into his tea. He took a sip and repeated his question since Atre seemed to not have heard it.

'I am afraid I have no idea. Nor do I think we have retained records going all the way back to forty years,' Yashodhan Atre said. 'Why, what's so important about who the contractor was?'

'Does the name Sarjerao strike a bell? Do you remember if your father engaged a contractor with that name on any of his projects?' Motkar asked.

'Sarjerao Bhoir!' Yashodhan Atre exclaimed. 'That old codger?'

Motkar felt his hopes rise. 'We don't have a confirmation on the surname, but was this Sarjerao Bhoir a contractor your father would employ often? Could he have worked on Shashank Welde's bungalow?'

Yashodhan Atre's face no longer had an amused look. A frown had replaced it. 'Quite possible. Reliable fellow, when most other contractors were prone to cutting corners or cheating on the material,' he said. 'In fact, I worked with him on a couple of projects, but that was before his conviction and imprisonment.'

Motkar experienced a flutter of excitement. 'You mean this Sarjerao Bhoir went to prison for a crime?'

'Yes, he was accused and found guilty of murder,' Yashodhan Atre said. 'Last I heard, he was serving life imprisonment.'

'When was this?'

'Around 1998, I think, but I'm not exactly sure.'

PSI Motkar made a quick calculation. Chances were that the man had already served his full sentence and been released.

'Do you remember any more details of the case, Mr Atre? Who did Sarjerao kill and what was the motive?' he asked earnestly.

Yashodhan Atre took a few moments to speak, once again scrunching his face as if squeezing out facts from memory. 'Pretty sordid stuff, from what I remember. Sarjerao killed a man who owed him money and with whose wife he had sexual relations … something like that …'

'I see. By any chance would you have contact details—his address or phone number—since Sarjerao worked for your father?'

The white-haired architect puckered his lips. 'Well, it's easily been over twenty-five years since he last worked for us. But I could try and find out from my father's secretary, although she's very old. But won't you be able to track Sarjerao through police records? He was a convict, after all.'

PSI Motkar nearly blushed. 'Of course, Mr Atre, but sometimes it's just faster this way …'

The grin was back on Yashodhan Atre's face. 'Then why don't you bribe me, Inspector, by telling me what your investigation is all about? Welde uncle's bungalow, your interest in Sarjerao—what's the big mystery?' he asked with naked curiosity.

PSI Motkar demurred. There probably was no harm in telling the man in front of him. It could well be in the news any time now. Yet, as a policeman, it had become second nature to reveal nothing or as little as possible. Just as he was wondering how to respond, he was saved the trouble by a call on his mobile. He glanced at the screen and saw it was Uttam Padwal returning his call.

Motkar took the call. 'Hello, this is PSI Motkar from Pune Police. I will call you back in a few minutes,' he said. Then, he turned to Yashodhan Atre and said, 'Thank you for your time and the tea, Mr Atre. I have to leave now. Do send the address or contact details of Sarjerao Bhoir, if you can get it from your father's secretary.'

He shook hands with the disappointed architect and left. Outside, Motkar quickly dialled Uttam Padwal's number. The call was promptly answered.

'Yes, Motkar saheb, tell me how I can help Pune Police?'

The man sounded wary and anxious to please.

'Where is your office?' Motkar asked.

'I have a small shop space at Deep Bungalow Chowk, sir. It's called Saibaba Real Estate Agency. What is this about, sir?' Uttam Padwal inquired deferentially.

'Send me your location. I'll be there in about ten minutes.'

'But … but, sir, I am in Shirdi right now, for darshan and some work.'

Motkar sighed to himself. One of the most revered pilgrimage centres in western India, the temple town of Shirdi is about 185 kilometres from Pune and visited by people of all faiths. Devotees believe that Saibaba's blessings bring about miraculous turns in their fates and fortunes.

'When are you back, Padwal?'

'This evening, sir … I can come straight to your chowki …' Uttam Padwal replied eagerly. 'Which police chowki should I come to, sir?'

'Come over to my office at Pune Homicide Unit, 10 a.m. tomorrow morning,' Motkar replied.

'Homicide? Sir?' Uttam's voice suddenly sounded apprehensive now. 'What exactly is the matter, sir? I … I have nothing to do with any murder case …'

PSI Motkar was impressed that Uttam Padwal knew the meaning of homicide. 'We just need to ask you some questions about a few tenants who'd rented a house through you. That's all!'

'I … I always get police verification of tenants done, sir. Beside that, I … I don't know anything about tenants who approach me,' Uttam said defensively.

'That's alright. You come over tomorrow,' Motkar said and disconnected.

Uttam Padwal was about to spend the rest of the day and night nervous and restless. He couldn't really help that, Motkar knew. It was a good thing the man was in Shirdi. Saibaba would provide him much-needed spiritual comfort and strength.

5

'OF THE FIRST TWELVE NAMES ON THE LIST, WE HAVE MANAGED to make contact with only two persons,' ASI Zirpe said. 'Tayabai Mahisal, who did sweeping and mopping work for the Weldes for a period of about two years, and Namdev Phutane, who washed the Welde family's cars and scooters as well as other vehicles in the neighbourhood for several years. I'll question them soon at their homes, rather than scare them by calling them here …'

Saralkar grunted. 'What about the rest of the names?'

'Sir, we just started this morning. We have managed to track down a couple more people who worked for the Weldes at some point in time: Manabai Parit, Datta Kadam and Hirabai Landge. But they're no longer alive. Two of them died during the pandemic and one of the women died of uterine cancer,' Sanika Zirpe explained. 'As for the other names, we still have no idea about their whereabouts, but it's early days still.'

'You started with those who worked for the Weldes long ago, not the ones who were employed by them just a few years prior to their deaths?' Saralkar asked.

'Yes, sir. I thought that's the way you wanted it,' ASI Zirpe said. 'Given that the skeletal remains appear to be very old …'

'Well, always start with the low-hanging fruit first. Get the recent past out of the way, before delving into the remote past.

You never know you might get a quicker connection to the past that way.'

'Sir, you mean someone working for the Weldes recently could be related to the earlier generation of servants?' ASI Zirpe asked.

'Something like that, especially because the family has been staying at the same location for decades. And maybe the servants working in the neighbourhood too come from the nearest slums or working-class colonies,' Saralkar elaborated. 'Familiarity leads to references.'

Zirpe nodded. Her boss had a point.

There were a couple of raps on the door. It swung open and PSI Motkar entered.

'Ah, Motkar!' Saralkar greeted him wryly. 'Do you realise your knocks are sharp and vigorous when you are on to something, and soft and subdued when that isn't the case? Plus, you always look as if you are walking on your toes when excited.'

Motkar's face seemed ready to turn beetroot red. 'Nothing like that, sir. But you are not going to believe the information I received from Yashodhan Atre, the son of Shashank Welde's architect friend, Subhash Atre, who designed and got Shanti Villa built for him.'

'What?'

'I asked him if a contractor named Sarjerao was engaged by his father to construct the Welde bungalow. He promptly replied that a person called Sarjerao Bhoir had indeed been one of his father's most reliable contractors back then, so it was quite possible,' Motkar said. 'But astonishingly, this Sarjerao Bhoir was later convicted and sentenced to life on a murder charge in the late 1990s.'

Saralkar's usually sluggish eyebrows shot up. 'That's bloody interesting, though it could always be a coincidence that a body was found in the premises of a bungalow built by a contractor later convicted for murder.'

Motkar nodded. 'Of course, sir, I have not yet checked out the facts. Of Sarjerao's conviction and the exact circumstances of the case, or if it is indeed the same Sarjerao who built Shanti Villa. But it does point us towards one violent individual capable of murder, who might be connected to our case.'

'Hmm, I can well understand your excitement, Motkar, but stop levitating, will you?'

ASI Sanika Zirpe couldn't stop a giggle from escaping her lips.

Motkar threw his boss a reproachful look, as if taking potshots at him in front of a female colleague were a low blow. 'There's at least a fifty per cent chance it might be the opening we have been looking for in the case, sir,' he said defensively. 'I am going to scan the court, prison and police records for Sarjerao Bhoir to see if he's served his sentence and been released, or is still in prison.'

Saralkar figured he needed to make amends. 'Go ahead. It's certainly worth digging around further. Let's just hope this Sarjerao character is still alive. Half the servants Zirpe is looking up seem to have kicked the bucket.'

'Is that so?' Motkar asked glancing at Sanika Zirpe.

She nodded. 'Out of the first list of twelve, three are dead and whereabouts of five or six are unknown. We've managed to contact only two so far,' she summarised.

'Not unexpected, considering the overall life expectancy in our country is sixty-seven years. I guess, it must be far lower for those less privileged,' Saralkar observed.

'And even lower for those who have spent years in prison,' Motkar said gloomily. 'I read somewhere that for every year spent in prison, life expectancy of convicts reduces by two years.'

'Thankfully, we are policemen and not sociologists, Motkar. There's a good chance we might find that the people we are looking for have beaten the odds and survived,' Saralkar said, before returning to his trademark snappy manner. 'What else? Did you get a word in with the real estate agent?'

'He is in Shirdi today, sir. Will be back by tonight. I've called him here tomorrow morning,' Motkar said. 'I haven't told him what it is regarding yet.'

'Hmm. Are you a devotee of Saibaba, Motkar?' Saralkar asked out of the blue.

'I am not devotee material, sir,' he responded.

Saralkar grinned, then turned to Zirpe. 'How about you, Zirpe?'

'Me neither, sir.'

Saralkar's grin grew wider. 'What a bunch of agnostics we have gathered in this department,' he chuckled. 'Anyway, I got a call from Forensics.'

'They have some news on the skeleton, sir?' Motkar asked eagerly.

'No, no, that's still going to take time,' Saralkar said. 'But what they seem to have discovered among the bones is one of those cheap and tiny brass amulets that many people wear with a black thread. It had probably gone undiscovered before because it is tinier than an old five-paisa coin and was stuck to the inside of a bone.'

He tapped on his phone and slid it across the table, between Motkar and Zirpe. Both saw the photo of an oval-shaped, discoloured and chipped piece of cheap, malleable brass amulet.

Its bottom half had eroded considerably but the top portion showed traces of imagery that appeared Saibaba like— something most Indians could easily recognise because of the familiarity of the outlines and the motifs that are generally seen on such amulets.

'What do you think? That's definitely a Saibaba amulet, right?' Saralkar asked.

Motkar enlarged the photograph of the amulet on the phone. 'I think so too, sir, but wouldn't bet on it. It could well be some other god.'

'Like who?'

'I am not sure, sir.'

'What's your take, Zirpe?'

'It's the kind of amulet we used to get at fairs at my maternal grandparents' village,' Zirpe said. 'Saibaba, Datta Guru, Hanuman … can't be absolutely sure of the image, sir …'

'But what about that cloth wrapped around the forehead? Isn't that the clincher?' Saralkar said, turning the mobile and pointing to the spot on the photo.

'You might be right, sir, but there's no way one can be sure until one can recreate or match the full image,' PSI Motkar said apologetically.

Saralkar gave him a bleak look. 'It's Saibaba, alright,' he grumbled.

Even if it was a Saibaba amulet, Motkar wondered how it really helped.

'But what does that really tell us, sir?' Zirpe put into words what Motkar was merely thinking.

'Come on, Zirpe. Why are policemen trained to note down ornaments, lockets, amulets and other personal items, in missing person's cases?' Saralkar snapped. 'Somewhere in some police record in Pune city, chances are this skeleton was listed as a missing person, many years ago. The Saibaba amulet is another such small piece in the jigsaw we might need while ascertaining identity, isn't it?'

Zirpe clearly hadn't expected a rebuke of such force. She reddened. PSI Motkar was glad he had only thought of the question. Of course, the counter-argument could simply be that it was too commonplace an amulet to be a piece of definitive evidence of anyone's identity. Yet, one could never be certain of what mattered and what didn't in any police case.

But Saralkar was not finished. 'Which reminds me of another thing you could do, Zirpe. Check if any of the people in the servants list have a police record for a serious crime.'

'Yes, sir,' Zirpe replied a little stiffly.

She was generally unfazed by Saralkar, but Motkar knew only too well that his boss had a knack for getting under one's skin unexpectedly.

'One more thing. Do you think putting the photo of this amulet on social media might help us in any way?'

Both Zirpe and Motkar said nothing. Motkar shrugged and Zirpe looked away as if she didn't think the question was being addressed to her.

'Well?' Saralkar glared.

Motkar said, 'It might … or it might not, sir …'

'What the hell does that mean, Motkar?'

'Well, sir, it's too commonplace to provide any meaningful leads through social media. All it will do is trigger thousands of people to send in useless information that we will have to trawl through.'

Saralkar scowled. For a moment it looked as if he would brush aside Motkar's objections. Instead, he blinked, then shrugged.

'So social media isn't magic after all. I thought it was the solution to every damn thing on earth.'

Both his subordinates steadfastly refused to join issue. Saralkar waited a few seconds as if challenging them to counter him, then changed tack. 'There's one thing we haven't dwelled upon. Not a stitch of cloth was found with the body or in the pit. That can mean only one thing. The corpse was stripped and buried naked.'

He paused, then gave an involuntary shudder. 'Could one person have been able to accomplish all this all alone physically—murdering someone, digging the pit, stripping the corpse, burying it, then filling up the pit?'

—

Uttam Padwal was short, portly, ingratiating and surprisingly dapper for a real estate agent. He came wearing a smart cream-coloured half-shirt, a pair of well-ironed black trousers and admirably polished black leather shoes. His hair was dyed, as was his neatly trimmed moustache. He wore just one gold ring and his spectacles made him look almost scholarly.

There was a kind of earthy trustworthiness in his face, which was probably why Shashank had continued a long association with him, confident that he could be relied upon to supply the right kind of tenants.

To Motkar, he had appeared pretty jumpy and fidgety at the beginning, but once Padwal realised he wasn't a suspect or a person of interest, he had visibly relaxed. 'Welde saheb was a grand old man ...' Uttam said when Motkar asked him how long he'd known Shashank Welde.

'Grand old man,' he repeated, as if Motkar should be impressed too. 'They don't make men like that anymore. I think the first time I got tenants for his house was in 1997. He had wagged his finger at me and said, "Don't get me any riff-raff. People from good families only."'

'I see. But isn't that what most landlords must be telling you anyway?' Motkar asked.

'Correct, sir … correct! But Welde saheb was very, very particular. He didn't mind non-vegetarians, or Muslims or Christians, or any caste for that matter, but he had his own way of gauging and grilling a tenant. It could be very daunting, and not all prospective tenants would like it …'

'OK. I understand he had asked you to keep and maintain the copies of agreements with all tenants,' Motkar said.

'Yes, sir. He was particular about documentation. He told me that it was imperative to keep papers related to each and every tenant who stayed in his houses.' Uttam Padwal said. 'To start with, I thought it was a bit of a nuisance. I mean I was just a broker. My job was to show tenants the houses and then get all formalities completed, including the leave and licence agreements. But to keep meticulous files for years seemed too much trouble. However, I realised that every two years or so, new tenants would be required for Welde saheb's houses. It was sure-shot business for me for years on end, since his son and daughter were settled elsewhere. It would add up to be quite a sum, so I maintained all records as a part of my services, especially because the old man had also helped me once early on by putting in a word with a government official when I was in er … a bit of a jam …'

'So, you have a file of all the tenant agreements of the Weldes from 1997?'

'Yes, luckily I didn't throw the files away even after I heard about the redevelopment deal of the bungalow,' Uttam Padwal said. 'Although I was a little put off that Welde sir's son and daughter did not use my services in the process.'

A pained look appeared on his face. 'I mean … after all these years of bringing them tenants every single time, the least I had expected was they'd involve me in at least getting them proposals from various builders. I am sure I could've got them a much better deal …'

PSI Motkar didn't want to hear his sob story. What he wanted was his hands on the files at the earliest. 'Well, I need those files. When can you get it?' he said interrupting the broker's tale of woe.

Padwal seemed hurt at Motkar's palpable lack of sympathy. 'It's somewhere in my office, sir, but … but … in between for one to two years, Welde saheb had shifted to another broker.'

'Why and when?'

'Around 2002. Er … because … because there had been trouble with the tenants of one of the houses … and for no reason at all he held me responsible,' Uttam Padwal explained. 'So he took on another broker for a while, then realised I was far better and called for me again when the house fell vacant in 2005.'

'So, what are you saying, Padwal? That you threw away the records prior to 2002 and now only have subsequent documents?' Motkar asked, spouting disappointment.

'No … no, sir. I only don't have documents from 2002 to 2005 … when Welde saheb used another broker,' Uttam Padwal clarified.

Motkar heaved a sigh of relief in his mind. 'Ah, OK! So, he switched back to you because he had problems with the other broker?'

'Yes, I guess so. He didn't like it that the tenants brought by the other broker caused many problems and then vacated much earlier than the agreement period of two years. Something like that.'

'What happened with them?'

'I remember only vaguely but he told me the couple used to fight often and loudly too, then some incident happened … I don't quite recollect exactly what, sir …'

'I see. But obviously you would know who the other broker was, right? Being in the same business and area?' Motkar asked.

'I did but he's not around anymore—for several years now, sir. At least I haven't heard about him. Guy called Sawant …'

'First name?'

'I don't recall, sir. I can try and find out. I'll ask someone who knew him back then …'

'And what was the reason Welde senior was displeased with you in the first place?'

'I was really not to blame, sir, but the old man got annoyed with me. Two young working professionals had been staying in one of the flats since 1999. Usually, Welde saheb would change tenants every two years, so they were due to vacate in 2001. But these boys were shortly expecting their company to transfer them elsewhere, so they asked me to persuade Welde saheb to extend the tenancy for just three to four months. Welde saheb was very reluctant, but grudgingly agreed,' Padwal replied. 'Actually, both boys were quite decent, well-behaved, etc., and there had been no problems till then. Unfortunately, just a month or two after the extension, when Welde saheb and his wife were abroad, the boys got involved in some fracas—a brawl and a police complaint and all! The old man was furious with me because I had talked him into giving them an extension for a few months, contrary to his usual practice.'

'Police complaints?' Motkar had sat up. 'What exactly was the incident and which year did this happen?'

Uttam Padwal cleared his throat, 'The boys got drunk and it led to an altercation with the watchman of a nearby society, who they said had burgled money from the house. They had thrashed him up … he had lodged a police complaint … then they lodged a counter-complaint for burglary. A few nights later there was another ruckus … so one of the neighbours called the police. The matter eventually simmered down, but old man Welde asked the boys to vacate immediately … like overnight … and wanted me to make that happen …'

Padwal paused and made a face inviting sympathy, 'Now, sir, you tell me, how was I to do that? I reasoned with Welde saheb that I could only try and persuade the boys, but not force them. It was not my house nor was I into strong-arming … They left after about two weeks but the old man was angry with me nevertheless for all that had happened …'

'I see. You have their papers in one of your files, right?'

'Yes, sir.'

'Good! Now which year was this? The police complaint?'

'Probably 2002, sir.'

'OK. Now, Uttam, let's go straight to your office and recover those files of Welde's tenants right away,' Motkar said, getting up from his seat and expecting the dapper broker to follow suit.

But Padwal didn't mirror his movements. He got up from the chair hesitantly. 'Sir, please just give me a day or two. Some renovation is going on at my office, so I packed up all my files and papers in various boxes. I don't particularly remember which box has the Welde files, because it was no longer important to keep near at hand for the old man. I need to search for it … which I can only do once the renovation work is over.'

Motkar knew there was no point fretting over the delay. 'You are sure it's there? Don't tell me later you had thrown them away.'

'Trust me, sir!' Uttam Padwal said solemnly.

6

'SARALKAR,' CP ARUNDHATI KOTWAL ALWAYS SOUNDED BRUSQUE, as if it were her default setting. 'Do you know DCP Kuldeep Khalap?'

'Only by reputation, madam,' a sleepy Saralkar replied while trying to regain his bearings. It was unlike the CP to call at indecent hours in the night.

'Well, he appears to have just shot his wife and himself. I want you to go to his house in Sainik Society, Wakad, immediately and take charge of the case. It's sensitive. As you may or may not know, Khalap was being investigated on rape charges, not to speak of the custodial torture matter last year.'

'But if it's a straightforward case, then …' Saralkar began.

'Just do it, Saralkar. There are reasons,' Arundhati Kotwal said testily.

Saralkar grunted his agreement as the CP disconnected the call, then let out a groan as he started heaving himself out of bed.

Jyoti, who too had woken up because of the call, remarked, 'You are leaving me in the middle of the night at the instance of another woman?'

'Keep your wisecracks to yourself, Jyoti. I should've resigned on the phone. Getting too old for these midnight bloodbaths,' Saralkar grumbled. 'Why couldn't the bugger shoot himself and his wife at a decent hour?'

Jyoti heard him shut the bathroom door, still griping. She had often wondered how human beings managed to kill another—especially someone they knew, and had loved and lived with for years. What level of anger or hate or distress enabled people to do it? Even more unbelievable—how did an individual readily commit violence against one's own self? One's being and body that one probably loved above all else.

She drifted back to sleep—an option her husband didn't have.

Motkar looked no less bleary-eyed than Saralkar when he arrived at DCP Khalap's house, which already had dozens of policemen from Wakad Police Station swarming around.

'DCP Khalap's son called in around 1.30 a.m., sir. He said that he had heard shots from his parents' bedroom. And that the door was locked from inside,' Inspector Rajguru, who had been the first to arrive at the scene, explained.

'How old is the boy?' Saralkar asked.

'Early twenties, sir. Just finished his engineering and is pursuing an MBA now.'

'Have you taken his complete statement?'

'One of the constables is doing that now, sir, but briefly, he narrated that his father had been drinking and there was some unpleasantness between husband and wife over dinner. DCP Khalap had then raised his hand as if to strike his wife, when the son, Aditya, intervened. Father and son then had a brief argument, after which DCP Khalap stormed away to his room and locked the door behind him,' Rajguru said. 'The boy, Aditya, his sister and their mother sat watching TV and discussing matters, including the DCP's mental state, given the inquiry he was facing. After about an hour, Khalap saheb's wife got up and knocked on the bedroom door, imploring her husband to open it. After fifteen minutes or so, he relented. His wife went in but the brother and sister sat outside anxiously, instead of going to their respective rooms. They didn't hear raised voices or anything alarming coming from their parents' room. In fact, they felt their parents were having a normal conversation and seem to have even heard their father sob.

'Finally, the siblings retired to bed. But around 1.15 a.m., the boy was woken up by a loud argument between his parents. He says he heard his mother hollering at his father, calling him a rapist and a depraved man. There were more angry exchanges along these lines, and then Aditya heard two shots. That's when he frantically began banging the bedroom door and calling out to his parents to open it.'

'Two shots? I see. So what does it look like? Khalap shot his wife first and then himself in quick succession?' Saralkar asked. 'Let's take a look at the bodies.'

'Actually, sir, both were rushed to hospital. DCP Khalap and his wife were both breathing when we arrived,' Inspector Rajguru said. 'But Mrs Khalap passed away in the ambulance. The DCP is still critical. He might also not survive.'

'I presume he used his service weapon?'

'Yes, sir.'

'Anything else that I need to know? Any sensitive information that you have uncovered?' Saralkar asked.

Inspector Rajguru's facial muscles twitched. 'You mean the note he left, sir?'

'DCP Khalap left a suicide note? Where's it?' Saralkar asked.

'Not an actual physical note, sir. It's in the form of a WhatsApp message which we found he had sent to his wife's phone,' Inspector Rajguru replied.

'Show me,' Saralkar demanded.

Inspector Rajguru fished out his phone and showed Saralkar a screenshot. 'The phones have been handed over to the Cyber Forensics team, sir, so I took this screenshot of the WhatsApp message.'

Saralkar clicked his tongue. 'Get the phones back before the items are logged in for forensic analysis. Also, every single item of evidence is to go only through Homicide. PSI Motkar will handle it. Brief him.'

Inspector Rajguru's mouth half opened, as if to raise an objection.

'CP madam's orders. You can check with your Zone ACP or directly with CP,' Saralkar said, then began reading Khalap's suicide message.

'Shobha, I did not rape the woman. I did not force myself on her. Yes, I went to bed with her a couple of times, but you are as much to blame for it as I am. I am not proud of it but I had my needs like any normal man, which you have refused to fulfil for many years now. Anyway, I am tired of things and all the problems. Either I'll kill her or myself. Tell me what do you want me to do, or I'll shoot myself tonight. I am tired of your taunts and harangues.'

Saralkar glanced at Rajguru. 'This is the screenshot from Mrs Khalap's phone, right?'

Rajguru nodded.

'According to the timestamp, she received this message at 10.28 p.m. That's probably when she started knocking on the bedroom door, asking Khalap to open it, as the boy said. Khalap opened it fifteen minutes later, so we can assume she went in around 10.45 p.m.'

'Yes, sir. It tallies with the siblings' account,' Inspector Rajguru said.

'Do the siblings know about the message?' It was Motkar who had spoken, as if waking up fully for the first time since they arrived at the crime scene.

'No. They didn't know about it,' Rajguru replied. 'Both were near hysterical when we arrived, and once they saw the parents in that state, they were shell-shocked.'

'OK, where are they both now?'

'They wanted to be at the hospital with their parents, so we just got their brief verbal accounts and my constable escorted them to the hospital,' Inspector Rajguru said. 'That's where he's taking their statements.'

Saralkar nodded. 'Let's take a look at the couple's bedroom.'

Inspector Rajguru led the way in, and Saralkar and Motkar followed. The very fact that an officer of DCP level had this kind of a bungalow, in a fairly high-priced locality, hinted at many possibilities. No honest cop could afford such luxuries unless he came from a wealthy background.

The bedroom door showed signs of having been broken open. There were also hacking and blow marks on the surface of the door. Blood was omnipresent—on the floor, spattered on the walls, on the bed and wardrobes, and at a few spots on the ceiling too. Even without the presence of the bodies, Saralkar was struck by the all-too-familiar nausea he always felt.

'I suppose, since they were both alive and had to be rushed to hospital, no photographs were taken where they lay,' Saralkar said.

'Actually, sir … I … I did take a couple of quick shots on my phone camera, although technically they were not dead,' Rajguru replied almost apologetically, as if he had somehow desecrated the victims. 'There was no question of waiting for the police photographer since they needed immediate medical attention.'

'Of course,' Saralkar replied gruffly. 'Can I take a look at the pics you clicked?'

Inspector Rajguru showed him the photos he had taken using his phone. The woman lay on the floor, her back by the side of the bed on the floor, her arms splayed behind her. Her face had snarled up in agony. She was wearing a nightgown, typically worn by middle-class women from conservative backgrounds. There was no jewellery on her; she'd probably removed it all as part of a regular habit, before settling in to sleep.

Blood had soaked the entire area between her breasts and waist. She had taken a bullet in the abdomen. 'Two bullets or one?' Saralkar asked.

'Going by the size of the entry wound, I feel both bullets hit her, sir,' Inspector Rajguru said. 'Like the shots were fired in quick succession at nearabout the same spot.'

Saralkar shook his head. 'Unlikely to have hit the same exact spot unless the barrel were pressed right against her stomach. And even then, there is usually a minute shift in the second entry wound.'

'The fact that she's lying on the floor next to the bed means he didn't shoot her in her sleep,' PSI Motkar remarked. 'Looks more like a struggle ensued, resulting in the discharge of the bullets.'

Saralkar nodded, then moved to the photos of DCP Khalap. His body lay at an awkward angle by the wardrobe and dressing table, bent at the knees and lying side on. It looked as if he had slumped off the cushioned stool placed in front of the dressing table. Prima facie, it looked as if he had put his service weapon to his right temple and shot himself. Blood had pooled under his head and face, and the entry hole looked hideous. The blood that spurted from the wound had smudged most of his visage and trickled down his ear and neck. His hand had fallen back on his side, still clutching the weapon.

His eyes were half-open and he looked quite dead. It was a miracle that he and his wife had still been breathing when the police arrived.

'How much time had elapsed between the son's call and your breaking open the door?' Saralkar asked Rajguru.

'About twenty-five minutes, sir, give or take,' Rajguru replied.

'Hmm,' Saralkar grunted, then took another look around the room. 'By then, they ought to have been dead ordinarily.'

PSI Motkar was surveying the bedroom door and the broken latch. 'There seem to be signs that the siblings tried to force the door open,' he remarked to Rajguru, pointing to the chipped and hacked portion, away from the broken latch area.

'Yes, the boy had tried unsuccessfully to break the door with a car jack,' Rajguru said. 'We've taken the car jack for forensic analysis.'

'That was after he called you?' Saralkar asked.

Rajguru hesitated. 'I am not sure, sir.'

'OK, just gather the entire team in the drawing room, including the Forensics guys,' he said to Rajguru, as they walked out of the bedroom.

Inspector Rajguru went off to summon the team.

'Were you dreaming of something nice when I called you, Motkar?' Saralkar asked his subordinate in his usual mildly mocking tone.

'I don't usually dream, sir,' Motkar replied. 'Seen too many nightmares like this, I guess.'

Saralkar gave a sad, knowing grunt. 'You know I hate to see anyone sleeping. Almost always, their napping postures remind me of some dead body I have seen at some point in time. Those images just superimpose themselves on the person I have just seen sleeping.'

Motkar wished his boss hadn't mentioned it. Now there was a chance he too might get similarly affected by the random sight of someone sleeping—in trains and buses, at home, on the footpath.

Both officers stood in silence for a few seconds before Rajguru returned with his squad members. Saralkar cast a glance at the team of constables, forensic technicians and a lady ASI.

'This is a case involving a senior officer of our department. Not a single piece of information regarding what you have seen, what you know, what you have gathered as evidence is to leak out. These are CP madam's clear instructions,' Saralkar said in a measured tone of authority that seemed to come naturally to him. His eyes tracked each face. 'All evidence gathered will be vetted by Homicide, and we'll decide what is to be done with it. Is that understood?'

The team members nodded back, some also mouthing agreement. 'Need I warn you about the consequences if anyone is indiscreet?'

There was silence. The message had hit home. He dismissed them all with a curt nod.

'Any update from the hospital, Rajguru?'

'Yes, sir. They are operating on DCP Khalap. It's the only chance of saving him, although the possibility of fatality is extremely high,' Rajguru replied.

Saralkar clicked his tongue. 'I wonder if the only thing worse than suicide is a failed suicide attempt.'

7

ASI Sanika Zirpe scanned the two-room tenement. A twenty-four-inch flat TV occupied pride of place on a wall that sported a sickly green colour and was in urgent need of repainting. A refrigerator stood in the corner, its top stacked with assorted stuff—dishes and glasses, chipped showpieces, a clock, a mixer, a mobile charger, a packet of biscuits, small toys and someone's spectacles—as if it were Noah's Ark , with everything jostling for dear life atop it.

The furniture in the room included two diwans, two plastic chairs, some shelves and a steel cupboard that had seen better days. Assorted photos of gods and family members hung on two walls and a small wooden table stood in one corner, with a school bag and books on it.

On one of the diwans sat Tayabai Mhaisal, thin as a reed, almost shrivelled, dressed in a simple, faded saree. She was peeling potatoes. These were her worldly possessions after fifty-seven years of life on earth. A life spent trying to make ends meet as a maidservant, living just above the poverty line and probably weary, yet grateful that she at least had that much.

It was quite clear she had grown-up children who weren't faring much better in the world than she had. Grandchildren too, going by the school bag on the table, although the child who owned it seemed nowhere around.

'To be honest, madam, I don't remember much. It was so long ago …' Tayabai began. She was talking about the Weldes. 'They were like any other family I worked for all those years. The lady had a sharp, Brahminical tongue, but never raised her voice. She'd just make me sweep or mop again if she felt some corner had not been cleaned properly. But that's what they all did …' her voice trailed off.

'What was the atmosphere like in the house? Do you remember any unfortunate or disturbing incidents?' Sanika Zirpe asked, feeling curiously out of depth, as if she was desperately trying to find excitement in what was boringly mundane.

Tayabai looked at her, somewhat perplexed. 'I … I don't know what you mean, madam. The atmosphere in the house was normal … I don't recollect any disturbing incident of any kind.'

'Do you remember the exact years you worked for them?' Sanika Zirpe persisted.

'Before I got married. In fact, I left their work because I was to get married the following month,' Tayabai replied.

'Which year was it, Tayabai?'

'The year after Indira Gandhi was assassinated,' Tayabai replied promptly. 'I had just turned eighteen …'

Prime Minister Indira Gandhi had been assassinated in October 1984, which meant Tayabai had probably been married off in 1985. This meant she had been a minor when she worked for the Weldes.

'I see. You left because you shifted to another part of the city or what?'

'No, no. My husband and mother-in-law didn't want me to work. And then by the time I got around to convincing them, I was pregnant with my first child,' Tayabai replied without lament.

'Did you bump into the Weldes again?'

'Yes. Some years later, when I started working again, I had approached Welde madam but she already had maids,' Tayabai said. 'Then a year later she called me to do sweeping and mopping work at her place. But the timings didn't work for me, and she didn't agree to pay the wages I was asking for.'

'OK,' ASI Zirpe said, coming around to the view that there wasn't anything useful to be had out of Tayabai. As a last question she asked, 'When you worked for them, their daughter, Niharika, must have been very young ...'

'Yes, she was in school, about four or five years younger than me,' Tayabai said. 'Now that you mention her, I remember a strange incident about her. The family had a pet parrot and their daughter would often feed it. One day, it bit her rather badly for some reason and she had to be taken to a doctor. Poor girl! The family then decided to release the parrot, but she wouldn't allow it. Then a few days later, the parrot was found dead in its cage. Their cook and gardener later gossiped that the parrot had been poisoned. Perhaps by the girl ... Of course, these were just rumours.'

'Oh, I see,' ASI Zirpe's interest was piqued. She made a note of the information without trying to read too much into it. 'Are you in touch with anyone who worked for the Welde family back then or later?'

Tayabai sighed. 'After we shifted to this house, I lost touch with most of the people from my earlier neighbourhood. My parents and brother also passed away, so there has been no real reason to go back there in the last few years ...'

'Tell me if you know any of these persons,' PSI Zirpe said, and began reading out the names on her list.

Predictably, Tayabai recognised the names of Namdev Phutane and Manabai Parit, even Hirabai Rakshe. Of the rest of the names, she recognised two more—Baidabai Ladkat and Rajendra Gawli.

'Baidabai used to wash their utensils a couple of years after I left. I think her husband and she then started a vegetable vending business and later they moved to the Katraj area. She must be around still— she's only a couple of years older than me,' Tayabai told Zirpe.

'OK,' Zirpe said and jotted down the information. 'Anything else you know about this Baidabai from back then?'

'Well, she had a reputation for picking up items lying around in houses and was dismissed from some jobs. Somebody later explained to me that it is not theft but a kind of illness,' Tayabai said. 'I think, that's also why she and her husband became vegetable vendors. She probably couldn't get any work in homes, after word spread about her reputation.'

Zirpe was impressed Tayabai knew about the condition, despite not knowing the word kleptomania.

'And what about Rajendra Gawli?'

A sudden smile lit up Tayabai's face and it was withdrawn equally quickly. 'He drove an auto-rickshaw and I think dropped one of the Welde children to school. I am not sure which of the siblings.'

'How do you know him?'

'That Rajendra Gawli was from a nearby "wasti" only. He would try and flirt with me and the other young maids … thought of himself as some kind of hero …' Tayabai said almost fondly, then suddenly began laughing. 'You won't believe it, but he would offer to drop me to work or back home in his auto.'

PSI Zirpe had seen her face come to life and her eyes twinkle. She wondered how this frail, reed-thin, buck-toothed woman must have looked as a young girl and what hopes she must have had from life.

'Do you have any idea where he lives now or may be some acquaintance through whom we can get in touch with him?' she asked hopefully.

Tayabai shook her head. 'Last I heard he had sold his auto-rickshaw and had left for Mumbai to try his luck. But after that, I don't know. His auto had turned turtle and a few children had got injured. He believed it was Providence that no one had died or been seriously injured, so he decided to stop the work of plying schoolchildren.'

Sanika Zirpe knew only too well how till only a few years ago, auto-rickshaws crammed with children would ply to and from school. Things had got a little stricter over time but such mishaps still continued to happen once in a while.

'So, any other names you can help me with—maids, cooks, driver, gardener, watchmen, anyone who worked for the Welde family?' Zirpe asked.

Tayabai had finished peeling and cutting her potatoes. She paused, thought some more and then reeled off three to four names and the possible whereabouts of these people. Zirpe took it all down gratefully, then began readying to take her leave.

'Madam ...' Tayabai said hesitantly.

'Yes?'

'You say Welde saheb and his wife are no more, so what crime are you making all these inquiries for?' Tayabai asked, sounding genuinely puzzled.

Zirpe could not tell her. But before she could answer, Tayabai spoke again, 'And since you are asking about maids and other domestic help, is it because something has come up now?'

This old lady was sharp if nothing else, Zirpe thought. 'Tayabai, if you remember anything else, please contact me,' she replied. 'Just remember, it's important but I can't tell you anything.'

Tayabai nodded, her face halfway between puzzlement and amusement. 'I wish they allowed women to join the police in my time … ' she responded with a woeful smile. 'I would have definitely joined.'

For no reason at all, Sanika Zirpe felt a lump rise in her throat—life for the woman before her could have been so different if only she had been born in a different time, place or circumstances. Women were already being recruited in the Maharashtra Police Force when Tayabai had been young, but in such minuscule numbers that hardly anyone from the general public had been aware of it, let alone try and aspire to be a woman cop.

The young police officer did not know how to respond, so ASI Zirpe just returned Tayabai's smile.

'Why exactly are we saddled with the DCP Khalap case, sir?' PSI Motkar asked, with not a little degree of indignation. 'It's pretty straightforward, not much of a mystery. Anyone can handle it.'

Saralkar threw him an oblique glance. 'Ours not to question why …' he drawled.

The visit to the hospital had meant another couple of sleepless hours, at the end of which they had conferred for a few minutes with the operating surgeon, Dr Kaushal.

'Fairly good chance of survival with minimal brain function impairment, I'd like to believe,' the surgeon had said. 'Unless complications set in … we will have to wait and watch.'

'You are sure it was a self-inflicted shot?' Saralkar had asked.

Dr Kaushal had looked at him, surprised. 'I'm no forensic specialist, but yes, it very much looks like that from the angle of the entry wound. Why? Is there some doubt?'

'No. Two people were in the room and no eyewitnesses, so all possibilities need to be considered as to what might have actually happened.'

'I see. Then I'd like to offer my opinion after re-evaluating and discussing with some colleagues who have experience in forensic or medico-legal cases, just to be absolutely sure.'

Prior to the conversation, while they had been waiting for the surgery to get over, Saralkar and Motkar had had a brief interaction with DCP Khalap's children. Grieving over the death of their mother and anxiety-ridden at the prospect of losing their father too, Aditya and Pallavi looked distressed and their responses weren't too coherent. So Saralkar had decided that it was best to talk to them when they were more composed.

'That's never been your attitude, sir,' PSI Motkar said. 'You have always refused to do anyone's bidding.'

Saralkar smirked. 'I am gratified you think so highly of me, Motkar. But over the years I have learnt that refusing to do the bidding of your superior or the system or anyone in power can be done in two ways—foolishly and tactfully,' he said. 'For most of my life I have done it with defiant foolishness and got away with it, but it always came at a price—mostly stress, anger and hypertension. So perhaps it's time to give tact a try.'

PSI Motkar had rarely seen his boss being self-deprecating or even less than frank. Was he turning into someone who had learnt the hard way to only pick some battles, not all?

'Does CP madam expect a big stink to rise in the case?' he asked gingerly. 'And has Homicide been deployed to put a lid on it?'

Saralkar's eyes flashed at him. 'I am not a showcase honest cop that CP madam intends to use to whitewash DCP Khalap's sins, uphold the department's reputation and do damage control. They have others who can do that.'

'But then why bring in Homicide at all, sir?' Motkar asked.

'I suspect it's got something to do with my credibility, Motkar. Perhaps it's my vanity speaking, but I reckon CP madam was trying to forestall any attempt to pressurise her into handing over the probe to a more pliable team,' Saralkar replied. 'By quickly bringing Homicide into the picture, there's hardly any scope to sweep things under the carpet, since our credibility is high. It now makes it very difficult for her superiors or other powers that be to transfer the case to another team, since it would cause an uproar!'

PSI Motkar hadn't thought of this angle. Yes, the police force was increasingly susceptible to becoming complicit in helping powerful people at different levels in whatever their objectives were—political, personal or professional. That's why honest and upright officers too needed to be shrewd and crafty in their moves.

'So does the Shanti Villa case go on the back burner?' he asked.

'Hardly! Haven't we handled multiple cases before, Motkar?' Saralkar said dismissively. 'Let's try to put together all the basic facts and sequence of events in the DCP Khalap case, maybe recreate the crime to establish exactly what might have occurred in the room and how. Once it is also borne out by Forensics team and witness testimonies, we will then turn to all that led up to this event—starting with the inquiry against Khalap and other related developments.'

'I was rather hoping to follow the Sarjerao lead,' Motkar said wistfully. 'I've already finished questioning Uttam Padwal, the agent. Hopefully we might get somewhere in tracking down all the tenants who lived in the bungalow …'

'Do I hear a complaint underneath all this?' Saralkar snapped. 'I mean, we aren't private detectives, you know? We can't choose to pursue only the cases we are interested in.'

Motkar glanced at him sheepishly, but there was also an element of resentment. 'Sorry about the grumbling, sir, but it somehow feels like prioritising someone's death over that of an unknown, inconsequential person's equally ghastly fate.'

Saralkar opened his mouth as if ready to shoot a stinging retort, then seemed to think better of it. 'I know!' he finally said. 'All I can say is that the skeleton has waited very long. A few more days won't do much harm, will it?'

Motkar didn't agree with his boss but refrained from reacting. He had made his point.

8

Namdev Phutane was one of those hardy, cheerful men whom life appeared not to have broken. He lived in relative prosperity compared to Tayabai, but by no stretch could he be called well-off either. He still belonged to what was politely referred to as India's lower middle class—people who had jumped clear of poverty and ensured their next generation could look forward to a much brighter future but who were still a long way from leading a comfortable, secure existence.

'You know what the rate for washing vehicles was back then, madam? A hundred rupees per month for cars and fifty rupees for two-wheelers ...' Namdev Phutane remarked with a chuckle. 'But I was young and strong. Mornings, I washed vehicles and after that, I worked in a small shop ... God has been kind. My sons don't have to wash vehicles for a living. One is now in the municipal corporation and the other joined a private company in Bhosari Industrial Estate.'

He did not elaborate further, but there was a contented expression on his face, as if he had achieved more in his life than he had set out to.

'For how long did you work for the Welde family?' ASI Sanika Zirpe asked.

'I think I washed their vehicles for nearly five years. First, they owned a white Fiat, and then some years later they bought a Maruti 1000,' Namdev Phutane said, screwing up his eyes. 'They also had a Kinetic Honda scooter, I remember, and then their son got a Hero Honda motorcycle.'

'I see. And what kind of people were the Weldes? Five years is a long time. You must have known them pretty well. Heard any good or bad things about them?' Sanika Zirpe asked.

'Welde saheb had a personality. You couldn't trifle with him. If the vehicles were not cleaned to his satisfaction, he'd give me an earful, but he wasn't fretful,' Namdev Phutane said. 'You didn't have to ever ask him for wages. He'd pay me without fail on his own on the first or second of every month. I never heard any negative things about him in the five years I washed vehicles in that area. His son was also nice, but I think he was away for at least two to three years, studying elsewhere ...'

'What period did you wash vehicles for them—what year to what year?'

'I think 1987 to 1992 ... or a year here or there.'

'OK, do you remember any kind of disturbing or unusual incident involving the Welde family, in their house or with neighbours or something like that—during the time you worked there?' Zirpe asked that vague but key question again.

Namdev Phutane frowned, as if scratching his head, even if not physically. 'I am not sure what kind of incident you are referring to, madam.'

How was it even possible for people to remember something that didn't personally affect them, after all these years, Sanika Zirpe wondered.

'Like something serious or odd or surprising. It could be anything—trouble of some kind, perhaps ...' she tried to explain.

Namdev Phutane was quiet for some time, trying to recollect.

'I don't know. Can't remember anything of the sort. It was all so long ago.'

'I know. Just try and see if you can remember something … anything …'

He cleared his throat, then spoke with some hesitation. 'I don't know if this answers the question you are asking, madam, but I … I … remember one day I turned up to clean the vehicles, only to find that the car had already been washed—like thoroughly. I was taken aback because it was the rainy season and usually Welde saheb's car would have some amount of mud spray and sludge sticking to it, which happens when cars are driven during monsoons. But the car was spick and clean, as if it hadn't been used at all the previous day. Now, I had seen Welde saheb drive away the previous morning, when I was cleaning another car in the neighbourhood. So, it had definitely been used. That's why I was puzzled to find it all clean, as if it had just been washed by someone else …'

Namdev paused as if emphasising the bewilderment that he had felt all these years earlier, then continued, 'Still, I had my usual job to do. I picked up the bucket from the garage, but found that the washing cloth was missing. I rang the doorbell and madam answered. I asked her if someone had picked up the cloth I used for cleaning the car. She told me to wait and then returned with a new wiping cloth for me to use. Then, when I started wiping the vehicle, I noticed a large dent on the front bumper and the front light also seemed to be smashed. There were other scratches and dents above the wheel on one side …'

Sanika Zirpe's pulse quickened. 'Go on …'

'Since I cleaned the car every day, I knew the dent, broken headlight and scratches had not been present the previous day

… so in all probability, the car had bumped into something or there had been a collision,' Namdev Phutane reasoned.

'And you say the car had already been cleaned?'

'Yes, I wondered whether I should enquire with Welde saheb. So after cleaning the vehicles, I hung around. Welde saheb usually returned from his morning walk around the time I finished cleaning the car. But that day there was no sign of him. So I concluded he hadn't gone for his walk that morning. I rang the bell again and once again it was madam who answered. When I asked to speak with Welde saheb, she said he was bathing. Hesitantly, I mentioned the bumps and broken headlight to her. She said she knew nothing about it and would inform saheb. After that I left …' Namdev Phutane said.

'I see. And you are saying the regular cleaning cloth was missing and Mrs Welde gave you another one?'

'Yes.'

'Did you notice any dried blood on the bumper or the dent?'

'Blood?'

'Yes?'

Namdev Phutane shook his head. 'Oh, you mean from a dog that the car might have hit, which caused the dent? I actually assumed that and eventually asked Welde saheb about it the next day. He denied hitting a dog. He said, in the heavy rain, his car had run into a deep pothole full of water and that had caused the dent and the broken headlight.'

'A pothole?' PSI Zirpe remarked with disbelief. 'And you believed him?'

Namdev Phutane seemed to be taken aback. 'Why would I not believe him, madam? If Welde saheb's car had hit a dog, why would he lie that he hadn't? He had no reason to.'

'What was the size and shape of the dent?'

Namdev Phutane scowled. 'I would say it was about the size of a football ... Welde saheb said it had been a big pothole filled with water. You should have seen the kind of craters on some Pune roads back then, madam.'

Not that they were any different now, ASI Zirpe mused. 'OK, Phutane kaka, do you remember when this had happened?'

Namdev Phutane scratched his head. 'Let me see ... Can't say I remember ...'

'Wait, you said, they first had a Fiat and then bought a Maruti 1000, correct?'

Namdev Phutane's face lit up, then turned sheepish. 'How could I be so absent-minded? This incident happened about a year after they bought their brand new Maruti 1000. More's the pity! Oh, and one more thing ... They appointed a driver a few weeks later.'

'Interesting. A driver was appointed soon after the incident?' Zirpe observed.

'Yes. Total rogue. North Indian ...' Namdev Phutane said in a tone loaded with disapproval. 'Imagine, madam, the fellow had the cheek to find fault with my cleaning, when Welde saheb himself never did. I had a couple of run-ins with him. Finally, seven or eight months later, I told Welde saheb I couldn't continue if that low-life, foul-mouthed driver was going to hassle me every other day. Welde saheb told me to ignore him and also admonished the fellow, but I could see he wasn't going to replace the driver, so I quit.'

'Do you remember the driver's name or where he was from?'

'His name was Bansi Vishwakarma. I don't know where he was from. UP, Bihar somewhere ...' Namdev Phutane said with distaste. 'The fellow was cunning. He ingratiated himself with Welde saheb and his family. Apart from driving the car, he did all kinds of odd jobs for the Welde household. In a few months, even their gardener got fed up with this driver's interference. What would that rogue driver know about gardening! But he would tell Mrs Welde this or that could be grown in the garden and when the gardener tried to reason with madam, she would not believe him. And then she'd blame the poor gardener if the plants she fancied didn't survive.'

'Hmm … what was the name of the gardener? Would you know if he's still around?' Zirpe asked, clutching at straws.

'I should think so. That guy was different from the rest of us. Hard to forget a chap like him. You see, he was studying for an agriculture degree then. Later, I heard he got a very good job.'

'Where? Do you remember?'

'In some seed company. State-owned, if I remember correctly.'

'And his name?'

'His name was Rohidas Phule. He came from the gardener community only,' Namdev Phutane asserted.

As usual, Zirpe made a note, then asked as an afterthought. 'So, Phutane kaka, when you were working there, at that time the bungalow was only single-storeyed, and the Welde family's four members were the only ones who stayed there, right?'

'Yes, it was single-storey. When I visited the area a few years later, I saw they had built another floor on top. Unfortunately, they were outside the country at that time or I would have dropped in to meet Welde saheb for sure to pay my regards.'

Then, sounding apologetic, Phutane asked, 'What was your second question, madam?'

'Whether all the four members of the Welde family were staying there at the same time?' Sanika Zirpe repeated.

'I told you about the son. He was studying elsewhere at first and would be home every now and then, but the Welde couple and their daughter were here throughout,' Phutane replied. 'And … oh … how could I forget Welde saheb's sister was staying with them too.'

'Sister?'

'Yes. I am not sure whether she was unmarried or a widow. No one really knew. She worked in some bank, I think. Very serious, stern lady … never saw her smiling …'

This was news for ASI Zirpe that the Welde family had also included another adult—Shashank Welde's sister. 'What was her name?'

'Everyone referred to her as Urmilatai …'

'Was she older than Welde saheb or younger?'

'She looked like his younger sister, because I heard him address her as Urmila a few times. I think she was the same age as Sheetal madam …'

ASI Zirpe took a few seconds to digest the wealth of information she had received from Namdev Phutane.

Her silence prompted the old man to speak again, 'Come to think of it, I remember another odd thing now. A few days after the pothole dent, I was supposed to clean the car interiors, which I usually did twice a month. For that I required the car keys to unlock the car. But quite unusually, Welde saheb kept putting it off for almost ten to twelve days. That was very unlike him because he was very finicky that the car be thoroughly cleaned from inside every fortnight. In fact, he would often hand over the keys to me earlier than the usual fortnight. That is why it was puzzling that he kept delaying the cleaning, especially because during the monsoons, car interiors get dirty very soon, what with muck and wet feet.'

Sanika Zirpe wondered at the marvels of human memory—the nooks and crannies of the brain into which incidents and related details lodged themselves and how they surfaced unexpectedly. 'Phutane kaka, you have been a lot of help. If you remember anything else, give me a call,' she said, deciding to conclude the interaction.

Namdev Phutane broke into a grin. 'But I don't know what exactly have I helped with madam, or why it is important to remember something unusual that happened thirty to thirty-five years ago …'

For no reason at all, ASI Zirpe felt the itch to be sarcastic. 'You know how the police is, kaka! We just like to waste our own time and of others!' she replied and left.

9

Saralkar regarded the disconsolate young man sitting in front of him. There was deep anger somewhere below the surface, caked by disbelief and grief. The enormity of the events had clearly bushwhacked him.

'Aditya, we need to go over all that happened again. It's important,' Saralkar said without any preamble.

'When will I get my mother's body?' Aditya responded without making eye contact.

'The autopsy is going to take some time but not too long,' Saralkar replied. He hadn't expected the boy to throw back a question at him.

'Why? He shot her. She's dead. What more is an autopsy going to tell you? Why desecrate my mother's body?' Aditya asked with quiet vehemence.

'All this is necessary legal procedure. You know that. Your father was … is … a police officer,' Saralkar replied, trying to sound matter-of-fact. Sympathy would only further derail the questioning.

'Why didn't they take away his service weapon if he was under suspension?' Aditya demanded.

It was a fair and relevant question. Saralkar didn't know if DCP Khalap had ever fired his gun on a criminal or even in the air during the course of his career as a police officer, but he had ended up using it on himself and his wife. What an irony!

'Look, Aditya, there are no eyewitnesses to what exactly transpired inside your parents' room. So we will have to reconstruct it based on forensic evidence, and your sister's and your testimonies. Right now, your father is still critical and not in the condition to talk,' Saralkar said. 'We cannot go only by conjectures and assumptions.'

'But I've already told everything to the inspector who was the first to arrive,' Aditya said with agitation. 'What more do you expect? It's common sense, isn't it? My father shot my mother, then turned the gun on himself. What else could have happened inside? Surely, you don't think there is any doubt about that? You think they made some kind of suicide pact because my father had been disgraced? Or do you think my mother shot at my father, then managed to kill herself?'

His bitterness and rage were understandable but Saralkar knew better than to look away from it. 'Are you furious with yourself that you couldn't stop it from happening?' he said, looking straight into the blazing eyes of the young man.

The remark seemed to act like a lit fuse. Aditya's face seemed to explode with emotion. 'How could I have stopped it? What could I have done?' he growled at the top of his voice before collapsing into a spate of tears and sobs a moment later, like a balloon pricked.

Saralkar let him cry his heart out, without saying a word. He felt sorry for this poor young man who would carry the burden of the event all his life. But offering soothing words to someone who was seething had never been Saralkar's strong point.

'Of course, you couldn't have stopped it from happening,' he said when the boy had finally quietened a little. 'Stop blaming yourself. We need to get as close to the truth as possible. It will help you too. The truth often has many wrinkles, which need to be ironed out.'

Aditya nodded, then was overcome by tears once again. 'Who are you?' he finally asked.

It was a long time since someone had asked Saralkar this question. 'I am Senior Inspector Saralkar from the Pune Homicide Unit,' he replied.

'Did you know my father personally?'

'No. We never worked together or met.'

'But you know about him? The inquiries, the allegations?' Aditya asked sharply.

Saralkar nodded. It seemed like their roles had been reversed and it was he being interrogated by the boy. Saralkar needed to wrest back his role but waited for Aditya to run out of questions. The next question from the young man was even more unexpected.

'Have there been any inquiries instituted against you?'

'No,' Saralkar said. All departmental inquiries were not the same. There was no equivalence between DCP Khalap and him.

The boy was quiet for a few seconds, then said, 'Please ask me your questions.'

Saralkar felt relieved that his hostility and defence mechanism had been disarmed, at least for the moment. 'Aditya, you said your father had an altercation with your mother over dinner. What was it about and how did it start?'

Aditya blinked. 'There had been tension at home ever since the woman's rape accusations against my father and the inquiry against him …' he said. 'My father and mother had had several arguments … my mother was heartbroken and enraged … My father denied everything and drank almost through the day, raging or retreating into silence by turns. My mother had …'

He paused as if embarrassed at what he had just begun saying.

'You don't have to watch your words. Tell me everything. Don't be ashamed or embarrassed,' Saralkar quickly said, surprised at how gentle he sounded.

Aditya nodded and cleared his throat. 'Mum had also told Papa not to enter their bedroom … You could say she had locked him out, and he had been sleeping in the spare room for the past several days. He took that very badly. She also stopped talking to him, despite him trying to initiate a conversation with her many times. It was an intolerable situation …'

'Would your parents talk to you about the situation, or did you try to engage them in conversation?' Saralkar asked.

'Yes, but these were mostly long, self-righteous speeches from their side. My father would rave against senior officers, the woman who had accused him and also against my mother. She would rant against my father. What could we say? And on what basis? I knew what kind of officer my father was, but it was hard to believe the worst of him. Yet, how could I tell my mother not to behave the way she was with him, with the kind of accusations he faced?'

'So what exact argument did your parents have at dinnertime that night?'

'My sister, Pallavi, went to call my father for dinner. He had already been drinking. Since he didn't come for almost fifteen to twenty minutes, my sister and I helped ourselves. My mother had already eaten. Finally, when my father appeared, Pallavi and I were just finishing. This seemed to anger him.'

'What angered him?'

'He said that now he was being served leftovers in his own house … that none of his family members thought it necessary to even wait for him any longer and that he was supposed to eat all alone like a bloody servant.'

'What happened after that?'

'Pallavi and I tried to pacify him, saying we were hungry and thought he would take time. But he was actually needling my mother. Then, when he began checking out what was made for dinner, he was incensed to see brinjal and some dal. There were also no sweets on the table and the food wasn't warm any longer. He started shouting at my mother, accusing her of deliberately cooking dishes he hated, and about how everything had gone cold … and that after throwing him out of his own bedroom, he was not even being served proper meals. He said how dare she do something like that … that she enjoyed all the luxuries of life only because of him and was an ungrateful, undeserving and useless wife …'

Aditya halted as if stung by the memory of the ugly scene.

'Go on,' Saralkar prompted.

'He then began throwing the plates. He overturned the serving bowls which had food. All this while, he kept hurling out abuses … he'd totally lost control. My mother, who had been quiet till then, got provoked and lashed out at him. She called him all sorts of insulting names and said he was a characterless man who ought to be ashamed of himself … It was really, really ugly … the things they said to each other and the way they said them …'

'Did you or your sister intervene? Did you try to calm down your parents?' Saralkar asked.

The young man's eyes suddenly flashed at him in anger. 'Do you tolerate your children intervening when you are arguing with your wife?'

It was a barb that cut deep, especially because Saralkar had never found himself on the receiving end of something like this from anyone he'd interrogated. And it offended him but he held back any sharp retort.

'I don't have any children,' he said to Aditya with a quietness that chastened the young man.

Aditya quickly lowered his eyes and looked away. He didn't apologise for his remark, just picked up the narrative again. 'Then my mother said she hoped they sent my father to jail, so that our lives would be free of his malign shadow. That's when my father said that it was his house and if she despised him so much, she should get out, not him. With that he stomped off into his bedroom and banged the door shut.'

'What time was this?'

'Around 9 p.m., I think … I don't know for sure …'

'OK, you said he threw dishes and overturned utensils. That must have made quite a mess. But we didn't see any that night?' Saralkar asked.

'Pallavi and I cleaned it up,' Aditya replied.

'When?'

'After my father went in, we sat for a while with my mother. She was in bad shape but eventually regained her composure …' Aditya said. 'Then Pallavi and I began cleaning up, while my mother just lay down on the sofa in the drawing room. I put on the TV for her … An hour later, my mother suddenly got up looking agitated … I don't know what happened but she rushed to their bedroom and began knocking on the door urgently, calling out to my father to let her in. A few minutes later, we heard the door open and she went in. That's the last time I saw her alive ...'

He gave a little shudder and for a moment his face crumpled as if he would burst into tears again.

Saralkar let a beat pass. 'What happened after she went in?'

'The door was slammed shut and we heard their raised and harsh voices at first, but soon they were lowered ... and I ... we thought my parents were talking in a normal, regular tone without shouting and screaming. After about half an hour, we couldn't even hear murmurs and all was quiet. That's when we thought things had calmed down, so we went into our respective rooms ...'

'What time did your mother go into the bedroom?' Saralkar asked.

'I am not sure, but I'd think it was around 10.30 p.m.'

'And what time did you go into your rooms?'

'That I am sure of, it was 11.35 p.m.,' Aditya replied.

'I see. Did you see the light go off in their room, when you said things had quietened down?'

'Yes, I think so.'

'You think so or are you sure?'

'I am sure it was off when I went into my room.'

'Alright, you said earlier that when your mother went in at first, you could hear your parents' loud voices. Could you hear what was being said?'

The young man pursed his lips and closed his eyes as if focusing. 'She was saying things like—are you mad, are you crazy ... we could hear only snippets, even when we strained our ears. Something like adding to his sins and punishing us for a lifetime ... and to not be a fool ... that she was begging him not to do anything insane ...'

He stopped, opened his eyes and stared at Saralkar, aghast. 'Do you think she was … she realised he was in a dangerous mood … and understood his intentions?' Aditya asked.

'Maybe,' Saralkar replied.

So far it didn't seem likely that Aditya knew about the suicide message DCP Khalap had sent his wife on WhatsApp, which was probably the reason why she had suddenly got up from the sofa and knocked on the bedroom door, calling out to her husband frantically.

'Why do you think your mother suddenly got agitated and went inside to the bedroom a mere hour after such an ugly fight?' he asked Aditya.

'I have no idea … I have been thinking about it,' Aditya said, his voice cracking. 'Why did she have to go in? If she hadn't, she would have been alive still. He had locked her out … Why did she have to go in and try and pacify him? And invite her death!'

There was an answer to his question, but Saralkar didn't think it would serve any purpose telling him about the message, till there was a clearer picture about what had happened inside. 'Did you fall asleep as soon as you went to your room?'

'More or less … I just scrolled through my Instagram feed, checked my WhatsApp messages, then fell asleep,' Aditya said.

'What exactly woke you up again?'

'I … I don't know. I just woke up with a little start … I had this odd feeling that something was happening … that something was wrong … I can't explain how and why I felt propelled to get up and take a look. And as soon as I opened my bedroom door, I could hear my parents. They were both screaming at each other at the top of their voices … I could also hear thuds, as if they were having a physical scuffle.'

'Did you do anything—call out, bang on the door, anything?'

'Well, before I could gather my senses and decide what to do, I heard a loud sound like crackers had gone off and I heard my mother scream—a sound I can never forget in this lifetime … There was so much pain and fear in it … it curdled my blood … ' Aditya paused, breathing heavily as if distress had just got the better of him.

'Where was your sister when all this was happening?'

'Pallavi had also rushed out of her room … I began pounding on my parents' bedroom door … pleading with them to open up … I wasn't sure what had happened … whether my father had shot himself or my mother? Whether either of them was injured or killed … All I could hear was my mother half-moaning, half-crying, as if in extreme agony. At first there was no response from inside and I was terrified … so I dialled the police helpline from my mobile and told them to send help immediately. Then I called up a colleague of my father's, ACP Shekhar Sandbhor, but he didn't take the call. So I also called up Wakad Police Station and repeated what I had said on the helpline number …'

'On both calls you said you had just heard shots from your parents' room and that you thought your father had killed your mother or had attempted suicide,' Saralkar said with emphasis. 'Now, I want you to think carefully, was there anything that you heard or sensed that made you jump to these conclusions?'

Aditya looked at him bewildered and shook his head, as if he was trying to make sense of the cluttered memories of the day. 'I … I just thought the worst had happened. My heart was pounding. I wanted the police to get there quickly and stop what was happening … save my parents … somehow … I … I …'

Words failed him. Saralkar was watching him carefully. 'I see. You didn't, for instance, hear your father's voice or your mother speak words to that effect?' he asked.

'That ... that was later ... after I had made the calls ... I ... I could just hear my mother's groans at first, but nothing from my father,' Aditya said. 'I was frantic ... I didn't know what to do next ... Pallavi suggested we should try and break down the door without waiting for the police ... so ... I looked around for something, then thought of the car jack and got it from the car. I began trying to somehow break open the door with it ... That's when Pallavi said she could hear father's voice ...'

'What did you hear?'

Spasms of emotion rippled across Aditya's face. 'He ... my father ... he seemed to be sobbing ... sniffling by turns. It really sent a shiver down my spine ... to hear my mother's groans and my father's sobs. My heart was sinking ... Pallavi and I called out to my father several times ... banged on the door asking him to open it ... I even told him I would break it down. I said that if mum was injured, we needed to get her to the hospital ... to please open the door ...'

He stopped, suddenly overcome with grief.

Saralkar waited for Aditya to compose himself. 'Did your father respond?' he eventually asked.

Aditya nodded. 'After several minutes he replied. He told us not to try and come in, then repeated it a couple of times when we kept pounding the door ... then when I wouldn't listen, he threatened that he would shoot himself. I immediately stopped ... I swear I did, and instead started to try and dissuade him. We told him not to harm himself or mum ... that we loved him ... that ... that we did not believe the allegations against him ... that everything would be alright ... that he should open the door and come out. We kept saying that over and over again ... but he was just silent ... sobbing ... I thought he was calming down a little. We just hoped the police would get there soon ... It was almost fifteen or twenty minutes since I had called. Suddenly, we heard another shot … and we feared he had turned on himself …' The young man paused. 'Can I please have some water?'

'Sure. Do you want anything else? Tea?'

'No … no … just water …'

Saralkar heaved himself from his seat and walked out of his cabin into the corridor outside. He could well have summoned a constable with a bell, but decided he himself needed a two-minute breather. It had mostly to do with the nagging feeling he had that he was missing something—something rather basic, on which he wasn't able to put a finger.

At first, he had toyed with the idea of interrogating Aditya and his sister at their home, given the sensitive circumstances and their loss. It would have also helped in understanding their movements that night and what occurred at what spot in their house. But he had found that often witnesses improvised their testimonies when they were questioned at the scene or at the place where they had themselves been at the time of the crime, because it offered visual reference.

However, there were often gaps and inconsistencies in their statements that did not fit the actual physical layout or the actions described when the testimonies were collected away from the crime scene. These contradictions often threw a better light on matters.

And this was why he had decided to meet Aditya in his office first and then conduct a second round at their house if need be.

He returned to his cabin now. A constable had already given Aditya water, which he seemed to have gulped down. Saralkar settled back into his seat, no wiser about what basic fact was eluding him. The break had not provided the flashbulb moment. Well, there was time at hand still. But before he could resume the questioning, Aditya spoke. 'Sir, does the fact that my father tried to shoot himself indicate he was guilty of the allegations against him? Of raping that woman?'

Saralkar found himself caught off-guard yet again by this twenty-three-year-old son of a cop!

10

ASI Sanika Zirpe glanced through the notes she had taken down while questioning Namdev Phutane and Tayabai. Two things had emerged from her conversations with them: one, the names of some other domestic staff who had worked for the Weldes in some capacity and two, curious incidents that needed further probing.

But perhaps the most significant discovery she had made was that Shashank Welde's widowed or unmarried younger sister had also lived with the family at some point. The first thing she needed to do was to find out whether this Urmilatai was dead or alive.

Sanika Zirpe flipped through some of the jottings PSI Motkar had made earlier on his notepad. There, she found the number of Welde's daughter, living in Goa. She dialled Niharika Das's number. Several rings passed before the call was taken. 'Hello? Yes?' a woman's impatient voice answered.

'Mrs Niharika Das, this is ASI Sanika Zirpe from Pune Homicide.'

'Who?'

'ASI Sanika Zirpe. My colleague PSI Motkar had spoken to you earlier.'

'Yes … yes. I had sent him the list of domestic staff and servants that I remembered …'

'I know. But I need to talk to you about something else,' Zirpe said.

'Now?'

'Yes!' ASI Sanika Zirpe said firmly.

'But now's not convenient! I am busy. Later perhaps …' Niharika Das said quickly as if Sanika Zirpe was just some pesky telecaller.

Sanika Zirpe found her tone rather peremptory. 'I am afraid you will have to make time, Mrs Das. It's important.'

'But … but … I am working … auditioning! I can't answer questions right now. I need to concentrate …' Niharika Das said, her voice becoming shrill.

'Auditioning, did you say?' Sanika Zirpe asked, surprised.

'Yes … yes …'

'You mean auditioning like an actress or something …?'

'Yes … yes … it's important … I need to focus … '

'Oh,' Sanika Zirpe said, 'So, when will you be free?' Before she could get an answer, she heard the click of the phone being disconnected by Niharika Das.

For an instant, ASI Sanika Zirpe's angry instinct was to call up again but she decided against it. Perhaps Niharika Das was really not in a position to take calls right now. Zirpe didn't remember PSI Motkar mentioning that Niharika Das was a professional in a field that required auditioning of any sort. But who knew nowadays what with YouTube, Instagram, TikTok and WhatsApp? Everybody was an artist—real or self-proclaimed.

Of course, her investigation couldn't wait, so instead of calling again she sent a short text message to Niharika Das: 'Send me the contact number of your aunt, Urmila Welde.'

She had paused a second before adding the surname, Welde, for she was not sure of the marital status of the woman in question. But she reckoned, Niharika Das would correct her if her aunt was married and had a different surname.

Zirpe's phone pinged a minute later: 'Why?'

She was surprised at the speed of Niharika Das's reply given her claim of being busy auditioning. Moreover, it was an odd reaction, hinting at a certain reluctance to part with the information, but at least it indirectly confirmed one thing—that the aunt was most likely alive.

'Investigation formalities. Procedure,' ASI Zirpe responded cryptically and waited for a reply.

This time, it took a while before Niharika Das replied, as if she had pondered over her response. 'She can't be disturbed. Medical condition. Unfit.'

ASI Zirpe had had enough of this WhatsApp exchange. She messaged back tersely: 'Send contact details or call immediately.'

After a few beats, she received Niharika Das's response. 'OK. Ten minutes.'

ASI Zirpe turned to Constable Khot, who had just walked in and raised her eyebrows. 'What's it, Khot?'

'Madam, the domestic staff list you had given … no one seems to have a police record,' Khot replied.

Zirpe had expected exactly that but still felt disappointed. 'Just no convictions, or not even accused in any crime?'

'No record of conviction or as accused in heinous crimes, madam,' Khot replied. 'Petty crime records are only for the last fifteen years. To go further we will have to check prison and court records …'

'Hmm …' Zirpe said thoughtfully, 'I should like to think that if their names have not shown up in crime records for the last fifteen years, they are unlikely to have committed any crimes. So how do we trace them? None of them is an accused so we cannot put in requests for Aadhaar data. We don't have their last known addresses and it's possible some of them are even dead.'

Constable Khot was an old hand and his reply was matter-of-fact. 'We can confirm who is deceased from the death certificate database with the Municipal Corporation. The living could be the real problem, madam.'

'Good idea. Get someone to trawl the death certificate database. But first look up police records for these new names,' Zirpe replied, handing over the list of fresh names she had received from Tayabai and Namdev Phutane.

Constable Khot glanced at the list of names and nodded. 'OK. And madam, Ahir is working on putting together a list of all domestic staff who worked for the Weldes in the five years prior to the death of the old couple.'

'Alright,' ASI Zirpe said and looked at her wristwatch.

Niharika Das had still not called back. Annoyed, Zirpe dialled Niharika's number. Her irritation increased further when she got a recorded message as a response: 'The number you have dialled has been switched off.'

How dare Niharika Das pull this stunt? Why would she do that? ASI Zirpe's curiosity about Urmila Welde went up a notch. Could it be that indeed there was some medical reason behind Niharika Das protecting an elderly family member? Or did some other intent lie behind it? If there really was a medical reason, Niharika Das could simply have called back and explained the nature of the problem, instead of playing hide-and-seek. Or was she being hasty in judging the woman's reactions so far? Didn't Senior Inspector Saralkar always say that people usually had numerous reasons to be nervous around the police?

Zirpe tried Niharika Das's number once again and the same 'switched off' message played back. The police officer sat chafing for a few minutes and then consulted her watch again. It would probably be the early hours of the morning in the USA, but what did she care. If Sunit Welde cared about not being disturbed by phone calls while asleep, he would have put his mobile on silent. If not, too bad for him. He was going to have his sleep disturbed.

She could claim the matter was urgent, if he expressed any annoyance at being woken up by her phone call. Hell, she could say she had miscalculated the time it would be now in the US.

ASI Zirpe dialled Sunit Welde's number on WhatsApp. Rings passed and the call went unanswered. She disconnected the call. She would probably have to wait for Urmila Welde's contact information until Sunit called back when he woke up in the morning, or in case Niharika stopped playing truant.

Sanika quickly typed a message to Sunit Welde, introducing herself. While she was typing in a text requesting him to forward his aunt's details, she was surprised to see the incoming WhatsApp call. It was Sunit Welde.

'Hello, Mr Welde.'

'ASI Sanika Zirpe, are you aware it's the middle of the night here in the US?' Sunit Welde asked in a voice that sounded more intrigued than exasperated.

Zirpe, having already prepared for this question, replied, 'Oh, what time is it? I thought it would be early morning.' She didn't apologise—Indian cops were not expected to do so or, for that matter, be courteous to anyone.

'It's actually 4 a.m., not even dawn yet. Fortunately for me and you, I happen to suffer from insomnia every now and then,' Sunit Welde said. 'Anyway, tell me what is it?'

'Well, I need the contact details of your aunt, Urmila Welde.'

'My aunt? Why?'

'I understand that she too was a part of your family and stayed with all of you for several years in your bungalow. We need to talk to her,' Zirpe replied.

'I see. Well, she was with us in Shanti Villa for about ten to fifteen years but shifted to her own place afterwards,' Sunit Welde said. 'How exactly would talking to her help?'

'We need to speak with her as part of our procedure,' Sanika Zirpe said simply. 'Do you have any objection to it?'

'Objection? No, no … she's just old and does not keep too well from what I understand,' Sunit Welde explained.

'So please give me her contact number,' Sanika Zirpe said patiently.

'Actually, she doesn't have a phone.'

'What?'

'No … I mean, she has caretakers, who keep changing! I don't know who her latest caretaker is. Niharika will have the caretaker's number. Why don't you ask her?'

'What about your aunt's address? I am sure you have that,' Zirpe persisted.

She heard Sunit Welde sigh. 'So sorry, you will have to ask Niharika the address too. I don't know where my aunt lives these days. You see, I have not been a particularly good nephew. Actually, I haven't even gone to meet her for many years now.'

'I see. Why is that? I would have thought she stayed with you when you were much younger so there would be a bond?' PSI Zirpe asked.

There was a silence for a few seconds. 'Well, Inspector, I don't see how that is any of your business, but I … I never got along with my aunt. As I said, please get in touch with Niharika.'

There was something about his tone that suggested he found talking about the subject of his aunt distasteful.

'Well, everything is our business when a skeleton is found buried in a bungalow co-owned by you, Mr Welde,' PSI Zirpe reminded him sharply of Indian Police's perspective. 'Anyway, one last thing. What is your aunt suffering from that she requires a caretaker?'

Sunit Welde gave a noisy yawn. 'Sorry, talking to you seems to have made me sleepy finally. To answer your question, well, it seems old age has brought upon dementia or Alzheimer's or something like that … so she needs constant looking after. This is what Niharika told me. We are the only next of kin but can't really do that on our own, so we have this arrangement of caretakers.'

His reply meant Niharika Das hadn't lied after all. Her aunt did indeed have a malady that might make it difficult to interview her.

'OK, Mr Welde. Next time I will make sure to call you later in the day,' Zirpe said and disconnected. Indian Police never thanked anyone either!

11

'Does the evidence corroborate what it looks like prima facie?' CP Arundhati Kotwal asked in her usual clipped manner. Her voice on the phone always sounded more abrupt than when she spoke in person.

'Broadly,' Saralkar replied after a pause. 'But he might survive or at least regain consciousness to give a statement, so I wouldn't like to jump the gun.'

'That's a rather unfortunate turn of phrase, Saralkar,' the CP remarked. 'It might be days before DCP Khalap is actually in a position to give a statement. What are the chances of survival?'

'Fairly good chances, unless fresh complications set in.'

'How about the possibility of brain impairment or him sinking into a coma?' the CP asked.

'The doctors say he might be very lucky to escape with minimum brain function damage, but he's still not out of danger.'

'OK. Report to me again tomorrow morning, Saralkar,' the CP said and seemed all set to end the call.

'Madam, I need to know if the inquiry into the rape charges has reached any conclusions,' Saralkar got a word in before she could hang up.

There was the briefest of pauses before the CP replied, 'Appears to have been consensual. Rape looks unlikely. The complainant hasn't been particularly forthcoming or cooperative.

But that's a separate inquiry which will progress independently from your investigation.'

'I might have to question the lady too for the investigation,' Saralkar said.

'Why? Don't be disingenuous and try to establish abetment to Khalap's suicide, just because she made allegations against him,' CP Kotwal rebuked sharply.

'Khalap's WhatsApp message to his wife hours before the incident can be interpreted as that,' Saralkar replied.

'That's not enough to drag her into the suicide investigation …'

'It appears she was in touch with him in the last few days,' Saralkar retorted. 'Isn't that reason enough for me to question her?'

He heard the CP draw in her breath, but she didn't speak for a few seconds, as if turning what he had just said over in her mind. 'It will be bad optics, Saralkar. Might appear as if the police department is being vengeful and trying to implicate a victim, because she made rape allegations against an officer,' Arundhati Kotwal finally said.

Saralkar felt his hackles rise and even as Motkar walked into his cabin that very moment, it didn't stop him from falling back on the trademark tactlessness he had recently forsworn against. 'Are we looking for the truth, madam, or only the politically correct, sanitised truth?'

Motkar's mouth fell open to hear his boss's words while the CP's rejoinder was immediate. 'What are you trying to insinuate, Saralkar? If I didn't want the truth, I wouldn't have put you, of all people, on the case!'

Saralkar did not respond. He did not feel the need to retract, apologise or reframe what he had already said. He just glared defiantly at Motkar instead, as if he were the CP.

'Are you at all capable of finesse and subtlety, Saralkar?' Arundhati Kotwal railed forth.

This time Saralkar replied. 'I am, madam, provided you don't forestall or prompt me! Homicide merely questioning the complainant lady can by no means be construed as trying to implicate her.'

'Don't be naïve, Saralkar! What stops her from claiming that to the media?' the CP said. 'She's already gone to the press with her rape allegations. No, you keep off her till I give you the go-ahead.'

Several rebellious responses rose to Saralkar's lips but the sight of Motkar's face watching him keenly brought him back from the brink of rashness. He didn't know why exactly his subordinate's presence did that to him, but he just replied, 'OK, madam,' as his own boss rang off.

Perhaps because it would have been an open act of insubordination—an example he wouldn't like to set for his own subordinate. He grunted as he kept the mobile then stared back at Motkar, as if considering snapping at him for no reason at all.

Motkar deadpanned awkwardly for a few seconds, then almost without precedent, his face broke into a grin. 'Having trouble with tactfulness, sir?'

To his surprise, Saralkar found himself smiling a little too. 'It's like starting fitness exercises late in life. Aches all over!' he replied. 'Anyway, update me with what you got.'

PSI Motkar briefed him in detail on all the items of evidence vetted and sent for forensic and ballistic analysis in the Khalap case—firearm, bullet shells, blood spatter and crime scene photos. 'We haven't sent in their phones for analysis. What is to be done?'

'Hang on to them. Apart from the list of the last ten calls made and received, which you gave me, we need complete call data for the last one month of both phones—DCP Khalap and his wife's,' Saralkar said.

'What about the woman who levelled allegations against him? When do we call her in for questioning?' Motkar asked.

Saralkar smirked. 'What do you think the pleasantries I exchanged with the CP were about? We have to lay off her, till the CP gives us the go-ahead.'

Motkar frowned. 'But, sir ...'

Saralkar raised his hand as if to pre-empt him, 'We will wait for forty-eight hours. By then, I'll think of something to tackle the issue. Meanwhile, nothing stops us from getting her call data. It might help strengthen our case for questioning her.'

Motkar nodded. 'OK, sir. As you said, we also need to recreate the crime, with all elements including the gunshots and conversation sounds, to be absolutely sure.'

'That's right! Which brings me to the questioning of the Khalap siblings. We need to match and compare notes, so brief me on what Khalap's daughter recounted to you.'

PSI Motkar referred to his notes, then meticulously relayed to Saralkar what Pallavi had told him about the events that evening. He punctuated it with some of his own observations and comments about Pallavi's answers and assertions.

'Hmm,' Saralkar said. 'As far as I can make out, their testimonies match. Too closely perhaps.'

'Yes, sir, I too got the feeling ... like she was speaking almost mechanically—as if she remembered everything minute-by-minute. For most people who experience them, such situations are a blur and there are several contradictions in the accounts of different witnesses.'

Saralkar sucked his lower lip in and chewed on it thoughtfully. 'You think the brother and sister sort of rehearsed what to say?'

'Hard to say, sir,' Motkar said, scratching his forehead. 'Pallavi refused to make eye contact throughout, even with the lady constable who was with me. She would tense up after every question, blink for a couple of seconds and then shoot out the answer as if she'd learnt it by heart. If I asked a follow-up question, she'd pause for a few seconds and repeat a part of the answer in nearly the same exact words, without the clarification I had asked for … Or she would say she couldn't remember and suggest I ask her brother about it.'

'Hmm. If the siblings did decide to match their stories perfectly, the question is why did they do so?' Saralkar asked, more to himself.

Motkar didn't have an answer or a conjecture. He just shook his head.

'How old is the girl?' Saralkar asked.

'She said she's eighteen,' Motkar replied.

'Maybe we can ask Zirpe to question her again,' Saralkar said.

'Zirpe?' Motkar said. 'It might help but wouldn't it be better if she just focused on the Shanti Villa case, sir?'

Saralkar looked at him vexedly. 'Oh, come on, Motkar! She's good at multitasking.'

But another thought had struck Motkar meanwhile. 'Sir … or why don't Zirpe and I switch places. Now that I am more or less done with the most critical aspects you wanted me to deal with on the DCP Khalap case, I could go back to pursuing the leads on the Shanti Villa case and Zirpe could assist you with the Khalap case?'

Saralkar opened his mouth to dismiss Motkar's suggestion, then took a moment to mull over it. 'You've really got a bee in your bonnet about the Shanti Villa case, haven't you, Motkar?' he grumbled.

Motkar kept a straight face. 'You are the boss, sir!'

Saralkar grunted. 'Well then, first complete the crime recreation on the DCP Khalap case and then go chasing clues on the Shanti Villa investigation.'

Motkar cursed himself for having brought up the crime recreation in the conversation a while ago. He was stuck with it now. 'OK, sir,' he nodded unenthusiastically. 'Let's at least get an update on the Shanti Villa case from Zirpe.'

'Stop sulking,' Saralkar snapped, familiar with Motkar's manner when he wasn't happy doing something. He then picked up the intercom and dialled. 'Zirpe, come over and update us on the Shanti Villa investigation.'

They sat waiting in silence like a couple that had run out of things to say to one another. Fortunately, ASI Sanika Zirpe arrived in less than a minute.

'Ah, Zirpe, tell me you have solved the case for us already,' Saralkar said, greeting her with fatuous seriousness.

'Sir!' Sanika exclaimed, shaking her head, unable to think of an apt repartee that was neither cheeky nor suitably witty.

'Not even a major breakthrough?' Saralkar continued in the same vein.

'No, sir, but I've discovered a family member of the Weldes we didn't know about till now. Someone who stayed with them in the bungalow for years,' Zirpe said.

'Who's that?' Motkar asked with interest.

'Old man Welde's younger sister—Urmila Welde. She's still alive, it seems, but probably suffering from dementia or Alzheimer's,' Zirpe replied.

She narrated the details, including her conversations with Namdev Phutane as well as Sunit Welde. 'But Niharika Das hasn't got in touch with me as yet. In fact, her phone's been switched off since this afternoon,' ASI Sanika Zirpe concluded. 'I'm really starting to wonder why she's avoiding me.'

'That is rather suspicious,' Motkar chimed in.

Saralkar, however, had still said nothing. He was quiet for a few more seconds. 'Did you get the same feeling with Sunit Welde?' he asked finally.

'No, he told me quite frankly he never got along much with their aunt and hadn't really kept in touch or even seen her in years,' Zirpe said.

'That didn't seem like a clever dodge to you, did it?' Saralkar asked.

'No, sir. There was no reason for him to say his sister knew but he didn't. He could simply have said that neither he nor his sister had kept in touch with their aunt if he wanted to make it difficult for us to find her,' Sunita Zirpe reasoned.

'Hmm. And Niharika Das is not contactable since how long?'

'It's been at least four to five hours.'

Saralkar turned to Motkar, 'Do you have her husband's contact number, Motkar?'

Motkar shook his head. 'I have their address in Goa.'

'Well, then Zirpe, just message her that she'll have to appear in person in Pune for questioning by the day after tomorrow if she does not get in touch immediately,' Saralkar said. 'That should do the trick.'

Zirpe nodded, as if she had been waiting for his go-ahead. Saralkar was surprised at how quickly she typed in a message on her mobile and sent it. He would have taken at least a few minutes to compose and send a text message.

'How about the servants?' Motkar was asking her now. 'Has it thrown up any interesting facts that we should be looking at?'

Sanika Zirpe briefed them on her interactions with Tayabai and Namdev Phutane, then said, 'Except for the incidents of parrot poisoning and their car possibly having been involved in some kind of an accident, which throw up probabilities, nothing else struck me in their recounting as odd.'

'Did you ask Sunit Welde about either of these incidents?' Saralkar inquired.

'No, sir, I haven't. I thought I'll discuss it with you first,' Zirpe replied.

'Hmm. Well, it certainly is worth asking about and observing their reactions,' Saralkar said. 'But only when they are sitting right across from you, not on the phone or video call. What else?'

'Oh yes, one more thing, sir. None of the older servants seem to have a police record for heinous crimes at least. Constable Khot is also checking out the death certificate database with the municipal corporation to confirm those on the list who might be dead. Besides that, there are fresh names I have got that are being checked out.'

'OK. Let's hope it yields something concrete. Meanwhile, Motkar is getting back on the case soon while I am going to require your assistance in the DCP Khalap case, Zirpe,' Saralkar said. 'I'll brief you when, and on what.'

Zirpe's mobile suddenly started ringing. Her face lit up. 'Your gambit worked, sir. It's Niharika Das calling. Can I go outside and take the call?'

'Take it right here and put it on speaker,' Saralkar replied.

ASI Zirpe did as instructed.

'Hello … Inspector Sonia?' Niharika Das's flustered voice came through.

'It's ASI Sanika Zirpe.'

'Yes … yes … Inspector Sanika! I couldn't, er … call earlier. I had no … range …' Niharika Das said.

'I don't believe you, madam,' ASI Zirpe retorted, looking at her two senior colleagues for their reactions to her tone too. 'You deliberately switched off the phone …'

Obviously, Niharika Das hadn't expected to be called a liar. 'What? What? No … no … why would I do that? I … I already told you I was auditioning when … when you called … and the range was not good where I was …' she replied hurriedly.

She was clearly on the defensive. So, ASI Zirpe turned the screws further. 'You think the police are fools, madam?'

'No … no … I … Why don't you believe me, Inspector Sanika? I … I called you just now, didn't I? In fact I tried calling you earlier too … but your phone was busy …'

'Well then, without wasting any more time, please give me your aunt's contact number and address,' Sanika Zirpe said.

'Yes, actually I wanted to talk to you about that …' Nikharika Das said cagily. 'You see … as I told you … my aunt is really in no condition … health-wise … to … er … undergo police questioning. So, my request is … why … why do you wish to …? I mean can't you spare the old lady from interrogation …'

'Mrs Das, please stop stalling and give us her contact details. We will make our own assessment as to her health and whether she is unfit in any way to undergo questioning,' Sanika Zirpe replied. 'Also give us her doctor's details, and we will take his advice, if need be.'

'Why don't you understand? She's got dementia ... She is not mentally fit ... ' Niharika Das said shrilly.

'We know that. Your brother Sunit told me about it. Now, if you don't give us the details, it will be considered obstruction and non-cooperation with the police,' ASI Zirpe said.

Saralkar exchanged a glance with Motkar. Zirpe was doing a fine job.

'Oh, this is just harassment! You are arm-twisting me,' Niharika Das screeched.

It was time to intervene, Saralkar decided. 'Mrs Das, this is Senior Inspector Saralkar. Please share the contact details of your aunt immediately, or appear before us in person, day after tomorrow, before 11 a.m. The choice is yours,' he said curtly.

There was a long pause and the sound of heavy breathing for a few seconds. Then Niharika Das sighed. 'You cops are just cruel. You only know how to torture and trouble others,' she remarked and disconnected the call, stunning all three of them.

But a few seconds later, Zirpe's mobile pinged again. Niharika Das had sent her Urmila Welde's address and her caretaker's name and phone number.

12

Having been dragged by Saralkar into the DCP Khalap case all of a sudden, PSI Motkar had not been able to set into motion the search for Sarjerao Bhoir, the ex-convict who had been sentenced for murder. He did so now, deputing Constable Pol to forage through prison and court records, to check if Sarjerao had already served his prison sentence and been discharged. And then of course, his current whereabouts.

Motkar had also called up the agent, Uttam Padwal, demanding why the tenant files had still not been delivered to him as promised.

'But, sir, I have already delivered the files to your office yesterday,' Uttam pleaded. 'You were not available, so I left them with Constable Angre. He said he would make sure you got them …'

'I see. You should have informed me about it, no?' Motkar grumbled. 'Hang on, let me check.'

He first threw a look around his desk to see if he had failed to notice the files, already placed on the table somewhere by Constable Angre. It was unlikely, though always possible, that he had grown absent-minded.

Motkar then walked out of his cabin and almost bumped into the very man he was searching for, carrying the very files he had been anxious about.

'Sir, a person called Uttam Padwal ...' Constable Angre began. He was a young, untested, rookie constable, recently assigned to Homicide.

'You certainly took your time delivering it to me, Angre,' Motkar said with mild irritation. He then spoke into the phone, informed Padwal he had received the files and disconnected.

'Sorry, sir ... I ... I ...' the young constable spluttered to Motkar. He knew he had no good reason for the delay except sloppiness. Motkar couldn't help imagining that if it had been Saralkar in his place, Constable Angre would have had his head bitten off, after which he would never have dared to be tardy again.

But he wasn't Saralkar and yelling at Constable Angre wasn't his style. Still, something resembling a rap on the knuckles was in order. But Motkar had an even better idea.

'This kind of casualness won't do, Angre,' he said, mustering up all the sternness he could. 'So here is what I need you to do for me now.'

He beckoned Angre to follow him to his table, opened the files and tapped on the tenant agreements inside. 'These are separate tenant agreements over the last twenty-five years or so. I want you to note down the names, ages, addresses, contact details and any other relevant information of each tenant. In some cases, it could be more than one tenant in the agreement. Also, I want the information tabulated in chronological order with agreement date and the period for which it was made, so that we know which tenant stayed for how long. Is that clear?'

Constable Angre looked at him as if he had been given the worst task he had ever imagined. 'Both files, sir?'

'Yes, I want it done by the end of the day. No mistakes. Wherever photos or scanned images of tenants have been affixed, probably 2010 onwards, I want you to mention it,' PSI Motkar said. 'If there are details like PAN card and Aadhaar card numbers, take note and add that information too. Last but not the least, if the witnesses to the agreement appear to be friends or relatives of the tenant, take down their details too. OK?'

Constable Angre's expression suggested he'd prefer to say 'no', but of course he had no choice. He nodded and picked up the files. Policing was a tough task and an unbelievable amount of paperwork was a part and parcel of it. Something that most recruits took time getting used to. Not everyone had the flair or patience for it.

'Get going then,' PSI Motkar said and Constable Angre left with his burden. Motkar's thoughts turned to his forthcoming interaction with Urmila Welde.

After much deliberation the previous evening, it had been decided that he would meet and talk to the old lady, while Sanika Zirpe would question DCP Khalap's daughter this time around. Saralkar had decided to oversee the recreation of the murder-cum-suicide himself, inside the bedroom of the Khalaps.

In the course of his career, PSI Motkar had questioned and interrogated people with different psychological and mental conditions, even criminally insane individuals. But interviewing an old lady possibly afflicted by dementia was probably going to be a first for him.

When he had called Urmila Welde's caretaker, Pushpa Sonawane, the woman had confirmed to him that the old lady suffered from memory loss and frequent erratic behaviour bordering on the aggressive. She could be even hysterical sometimes and also displayed many other minor eccentricities.

An LPC (lady police constable), Shreya Patil, accompanied him now as they rang the bell of a flat on the ground floor of a dilapidated building. Motkar was surprised that Urmila Welde resided in a locality that could be at best described as lower-middle class.

The gate of the building was broken, the premises were shabby, old and rundown with small mounds of rotting garbage in different corners of the compound that had not been cleaned for days. The door to the house was opened by a middle-aged woman whose face had that resigned, long-suffering look of people who knew they were stuck in jobs they did not really wish to do.

Sonawane let them in. 'You will have to give me some time,' she said. 'She's just had her bath and is … er … refusing to wear clothes. It will require some persuasion before she agrees.'

Motkar and Shreya Patil were too shocked to respond, as the caretaker scurried back into a room. 'Is the woman we are going to talk to a mental case, sir?' LPC Shreya Patil, who was the first to recover, asked Motkar in a whisper.

Motkar shrugged, unsure if he had even a rudimentary understanding of exactly what the difference between dementia and psychiatric problems was. They waited in silence. Motkar could hear voices from the inside room, although the door was closed and bolted. He looked around the room they were sitting in.

Every item in the house seemed to have a decrepit, untidy and outdated look and feel. A musty, damp smell pervaded. He wondered how the old lady had ended up in a dump like this. From what he had heard, she had worked as an officer at a bank. Would a lifetime of savings, provident fund, gratuity and perhaps even post-retirement pension have amounted to only this much?

'Sir, should I go in and help the caretaker get the old lady dressed, if she's not listening?' LPC Shreya Patil offered.

Motkar frowned. 'She might react badly or get frightened to see a stranger. Let's wait for a while longer.'

LPC Patil looked disappointed, as if itching to discipline the recalcitrant old lady.

A few more minutes passed before they heard the door open and Pushpa Sonawane walked out, followed by a tall and fair old woman, who was admonishing the caretaker. 'It's hot I told you … I am sweating! Why can't you just mind your own business …'

The caretaker nodded indifferently. 'Look, Ajji, here are the guests who have come to see you,' she said, pointing at the two cops.

Urmila Welde squinted sharply at the newcomers and appeared to study them. First LPC Patil then PSI Motkar. 'Who are you?'

The horns of a dilemma presented itself to Motkar. How would the old lady react if he told her they were the police? He had taken the precaution of dressing in plain clothes and instructed LPC Patil to follow suit. Yet, would it be right to conceal their identities from Urmila Welde, now that she had asked a direct question?

'We are here to only ask a few questions, madam,' Motkar said, settling for ambiguity.

Urmila Welde kept gazing at him quizzically, her expression unchanged. 'Who are you?' she repeated in the exact same tone she had used earlier.

He had no choice but to provide a direct answer now. 'I am PSI Motkar and this is my colleague, LPC Shreya Patil.'

The old lady's eyes remained transfixed on his and her expression too didn't change. Then her eyes turned to Shreya Patil.

'You are police?' the old lady asked in a clarificatory tone.

'Yes, madam.'

A few moments of silence passed, during which Urmila Welde's eyes darted between Motkar and Patil a few times. Then she turned to her caretaker. 'I told you they would find me,' she said as if aggrieved with Pushpa Sonawane.

'You told me? I … I don't know what you are saying, Ajji!' the caretaker exclaimed, glancing at Motkar nervously as if she was being accused of abetting a criminal.

Urmila Welde turned to face Motkar. 'Are you going to arrest me and put me in Yerawada jail?'

Motkar's skin seemed to crawl. What exactly was this old woman hinting at? Why would she ask such a question? LPC Patil was looking at him eagerly, as if urging him to go for the kill and demand a confession from the old lady.

'We need to first hear what you have to say, madam,' he said.

Urmila Welde stared at him. 'I am going to tell the truth,' she said in a steady voice. 'It was me … I did it.'

Motkar felt a sense of disbelief, sitting in front of this old lady who seemed to be on the brink of some confession. 'You did what, madam?' he asked gingerly.

Urmila Welde gave him a stern frown, which then gave way to a rapid blinking of eyelids. 'I … I can't remember …' she said. 'It's those pills they give me … They make me forget …'

Before Motkar could speak, the caretaker quickly said, 'I … I just give her the prescribed medicines … Here is the prescription, saheb … nothing else. And … and I have been here only for a month …'

Pushpa Sonawane thrust a small plastic folder towards Motkar. He looked at the prescription given by a neurologist. It was dated over a year ago.

He nodded at the caretaker. 'OK,' he said, cryptically assuring her she was under no immediate suspicion, then turned to Urmila Welde. 'Have you remembered it now, madam?' he asked gently.

Urmila Welde stared at him thoughtfully. 'I … will not sleep with you again … You … you cannot force me to …'

Her words knocked the breath out of Motkar. The other two women, Pushpa Sonawane and LPC Patil, were regarding him like a villain who had just been unmasked.

'I have never met you before, madam …' he said with as much calm and dignity he could summon.

The old woman continued looking at him without hostility or suspicion. Then she hissed, 'Who betrayed me then? Who told you everything?'

PSI Motkar wasn't sure what response would help him make some headway. Only a professional neurologist might help unravel the ramblings, he reckoned. He decided to try and make one last effort. 'Do you miss your brother?'

The old woman's face seemed to come alive with conflicting emotions. Motkar couldn't quite read her expression as she glared at him silently. Then suddenly she spat out, 'No one should have a brother like him …'

She stopped, then turned to her caretaker, now appearing completely agitated. 'It's hot … I told you it's hot! You … you made me wear this gown. I refuse to sweat to death …'

And then, Urmila Welde began tugging and clawing at her gown as if frantically trying to remove it.

Saralkar stood in a corner of DCP Khalap's bedroom and watched the preparations underway for the crime recreation. It was always a tricky exercise—a kind of interpreted enactment based on conjectures arrived at from witness statements and material evidence gathered.

Crime recreation was sometimes invaluable in understanding what might have happened and what could be ruled out. It could check out a set of hypotheses while unequivocally striking down the testimony of some witness or the impression sought to be left behind by a perpetrator. Most times, it helped by simply confirming what the evidence seemed to indicate, or throw up so many contradictions that the crime needed looking at from a different lens altogether.

A majority of crimes were straightforward and didn't really require the exercise. Crime scene recreation was mainly done in cases that presented complications or doubts, or in high-profile cases where precaution had to be taken to ensure that the investigation was foolproof.

'We have to also verify whether sounds and conversations carry into the rooms of both the brother and the sister, even when their doors are shut,' Saralkar instructed the team.

Two constables—a man and a woman—had been selected to perform the enactment. They had also been asked to rehearse and carry out a conversation at different pitches and volumes. A police videographer was going to shoot the proceedings.

Saralkar threw his gaze around the room, trying hard to remember his first observations and impressions when he had entered the room that night. 'Rajguru,' he said to the officer standing beside him, who had been the first man to arrive at the crime scene. 'Anything out of place, or is this how you recall it?'

They had just one photo that gave a view of the full room, clicked on Rajguru's mobile camera by his constable. To Saralkar's eyes, the positions of different objects now matched with their appearance in the photo, including the positions of the bodies of DCP Khalap and his wife.

Inspector Rajguru nodded. 'That's just the way I remember it sir, except …' He paused and hesitated. 'Except I think the curtains were not fully drawn …'

Saralkar quickly held up the reference photo. Sure enough, he could see a gap between the curtains. At a guess, the gap between the two curtains was about one foot apart. 'You are absolutely right,' he said to Rajguru in a gruff tone. He instructed a constable to push the curtains apart slightly, then frowned. In subsequent photographs, taken after both the victims had been moved to the hospital, the curtains appeared fully drawn, as if someone had pulled them together to close the gap.

It could have happened naturally of course; sometimes, the breeze was strong enough to push the folds of a curtain together or apart, but if only the windows were open in the first place. Saralkar stepped gingerly towards the curtains and gently pulled the curtains apart again. Right behind the curtains stood full, ceiling-to-floor sliding windows, secured by a panel of two grille doors that opened on the outside, into a small patch of lawned space, bordered by a flower bed. Beyond it was the five-feet-high compound wall that separated the bungalow from the next plot.

'Had your team checked that night if both the glass windows and grille doors were fastened or bolted from inside?' Saralkar turned his head and asked Rajguru.

Inspector Rajguru looked discomfited, opened his mouth, then licked his lips. 'Actually, sir … I am not sure we checked that when we arrived here. Later on, yes, we did … and they were bolted if my memory serves me right …'

Saralkar growled inwardly. It was always the small, basic things that got skipped—sometimes inadvertently, sometimes out of sheer indifference and laziness, and sometimes because of the ghastly situations that confronted cops. Come to think of it, even he hadn't bothered to check behind the curtain that night. Shouldn't it have occurred to him, as an experienced cop, that it was a bungalow, in which bedrooms tended to open up into patios or lawns, thus providing another possible entrance into the room?

This also raised a series of other serious questions. Had the glass windows been closed that night? And what about the grille doors outside it? What explained the fact that the curtains had been drawn apart at first and then pulled together?

'You need to check with your team if someone had noticed or checked the glass windows and grille doors,' Saralkar said to Rajguru. 'And do you recollect if the air conditioner in the room had been on when you came in?'

'Yes, sir. The air conditioner was on when we broke in through the door,' Inspector Rajguru asserted.

'And when did you switch it off?' Saralkar asked.

'A while later, after the bodies … I mean both DCP Khalap and his wife were shifted out to hospital in their injured state,' Rajguru replied.

'Hmm … I presume their son, Aditya, was with you in this room all along, while you called the ambulance and took stock of the situation?'

'Yes, sir … the son was with us. Although, after a while, I asked him to wait outside with a constable, since I didn't want him to contaminate the crime scene, with his movements or by touching things …'

'And what about their daughter? Was she in here too?'

'No, sir, she remained outside. I don't think she even attempted to see the condition of her parents …' Rajguru said.

Saralkar chewed over the facts for a moment, then said, 'OK, you can start with the crime reconstruction now …'

He went back across the room to his original position and began watching the proceedings thoroughly. Meanwhile, his brain had started on another round of rumination—puzzling and pondering over why a son who claimed to have tried breaking down the wooden door of the room had not thought of trying to go to the back of the bungalow and breaking the glass window through the space between the grille bars?

Or, if nothing else, at least tried to peep inside through the glass to see what was happening inside and pleaded with his father? Or had he?

13

'WHY ARE YOU ASKING ME THE SAME QUESTIONS THE OTHER inspector had asked?' Pallavi Khalap said to ASI Sanika Zirpe. Her tone was resentful and her expressions furtive.

'Am I?' Zirpe said feigning surprise.

'Yes. Hasn't the other inspector told you what questions he put to me and what answers I gave?' the girl said, fidgeting with the two rings on her fingers, sliding them up and down. She was referring to PSI Motkar who had interviewed her just two days before.

Zirpe regarded the teenager thoughtfully, neither confirming nor answering her question, just observing her reactions. Pauses and silences always ruffled most people being questioned. It built up tension.

'Some of your replies were a little confusing and they contradicted what your brother Aditya told us,' Zirpe finally said.

Alertness and anxiety leapt into the girl's eyes afresh. 'What? I … I already said that I was in a daze! I … I don't remember everything accurately, so … so my brother's answers would be right …'

Sanika Zirpe waited for Pallavi to continue. There was no reason to rush the next question.

Sure enough, the girl spoke again. 'If something like this had happened to you … in your home … to your parents … would you have remembered everything properly?' she demanded shakily.

It was not an unfair question and Sanika Zirpe had the difficult task of separating the grain from the chaff. 'You told my colleague, Inspector Motkar, that Aditya woke you up after midnight because he heard your parents quarrelling loudly and then both of you heard the first gunshot?' she asked the girl.

'Yes … yes …' the girl said.

'But your brother told us that you rushed out of your room after hearing the first gun shot,' ASI Zirpe continued. 'This is contradictory. Did you wake up due to the gunshot sound or did your brother wake you up first and then you both heard the gunshot?'

Pallavi's face had gone pale. 'I … I don't remember clearly now. Maybe what my brother said was right … It … it all happened so fast …'

She gave a little start and stuttered to a halt as Saralkar walked into the room and sat next to Sanika Zirpe. Pallavi gazed at him nervously.

'Carry on, Zirpe,' Saralkar said to his colleague.

'So, Pallavi, if your brother is right, you were in your room when you heard the gunshot. Was the door of your room shut?' Zirpe asked.

The girl was still staring uneasily at Saralkar. 'Yes … yes, as my brother said, the noise woke me up … and I got up and opened the door to check …'

'And when you opened the door of your room, your brother was already outside?'

'Yes, I think he had also been awoken by the same sound …'

'How did you realise what you had heard was a gunshot?' Zirpe asked.

Pallavi looked at her baffled, then said, 'I … I think my brother told me it was …'

'I see. So, you only think so because Aditya told you so …'

Perhaps the manner in which Zirpe spoke seemed to suddenly trigger Pallavi. 'Why are you harassing me with such questions? What difference does it make if the gunshot woke me up or my brother did? How does it change the fact that my father shot my mother and then himself, inside their room?' Her voice had turned shrill and hysterical.

'Calm down, Pallavi!' ASI Zirpe said quickly. 'I have just a couple of questions more.'

Pallavi groaned and lowered her face into her palms. 'You think my brother and I are lying or hiding something! You have no right to make us feel like that …'

Sanika Zirpe ignored her outburst. 'While your brother was trying to break your parents' bedroom door, what were you doing?' She asked the question Saralkar had just whispered to her.

Pallavi slid her rings up and down for the umpteenth time. 'I … I …' she began to stutter. 'I don't know … I was kind of in a funk … that something dreadful had happened inside …'

It seemed like a genuine answer to Zirpe's ears. 'So, you just stood watching …'

'Yes, my mind wasn't working …'

'Did Aditya give you any instructions? To fetch something or to do something?'

Pallavi shook her head.

'Tell me,' Saralkar spoke for the first time. 'Didn't your brother or you think of going to the back of the bungalow and looking inside your parents' bedroom, through the grille and glass doors?'

Pallavi appeared to freeze and no reply escaped her mouth for almost a whole minute. 'No …' she croaked weakly at last, breaking eye contact and staring fixedly at the floor.

'You are sure your brother didn't do that when he went to get the car jack?' Saralkar asked again.

Pallavi was quiet for a few more seconds, then shook her head.

Both Saralkar and Zirpe sensed something was amiss. Saralkar briefly considered whether to grill the girl further on the point, then decided against it because she was still a minor, not eighteen as she had claimed.

Instead, he asked, 'How close are Aditya and you?'

Pallavi's eyes lifted in his direction and Saralkar was intrigued to see an indescribable expression on her face. 'What do you mean? We are brother … and sister …' she stuttered.

There was an abjectness in her tone that sounded odd. Why had she answered a simple question in this manner? Why not just 'We are close' or 'Not very close' or 'We get along well' or something like that?

It set Saralkar thinking dark and sordid thoughts—if anything could be darker and murkier than what had already happened in the house. Perhaps it was time to confront Aditya again …

Angre was hard at work on the tenants list when PSI Motkar returned after the meeting with Urmila Welde. The young constable looked miserable and out of depth. Motkar threw a glance at the tabular format he had prepared to note down various details asked for.

'What's with your handwriting, Angre? Can you even read it back?' the PSI remarked with a frown.

Angre looked up at him defensively, 'It's … it's not that bad, sir.'

Motkar sighed. 'Look, if I have a problem reading it, I'll make you write it all over again or feed it into the computer.'

Constable Angre squirmed, then nodded.

'Sir,' another voice called out from behind Motkar.

'Yes, Pol.' Motkar turned around and was surprised to find the constable there.

'I got Sarjerao Bhoir's address, sir. He was released from jail in 2015,' Pol replied.

'That was quick, Pol. Is it a Pune address?'

'Actually, it's a Chinchwad address, sir, so I can go right away,' Pol replied. 'Since I saw you I thought I'll ask if you wished to come too …'

Pimpri-Chinchwad was Pune's twin city. Once a suburb in which major Pune industries were located in the 1970s, it had metamorphosed into a city of its own as automobile and engineering firms proliferated in the succeeding decades. Many outsiders and even Punekars still considered it a part of the Pune metropolis and in a sense it was. But for all practical purposes, Pune and Pimpri-Chinchwad were two independent, administrative units, including a separate police commissionerate.

'Good thinking, I'll come along. But are you sure this really is Sarjerao Bhoir's current address?' Motkar asked.

'It's the address he also gave for his paroles and furloughs during his sentence,' Pol replied. 'It seems his sons stay here. It was also his release address.'

Motkar considered. It was likely the family had shifted in the interim between 2015 and now, or that Sarjerao himself was dead. But on the other hand, it could well be that he was indeed alive and this is where he stayed, even now.

'Come on then,' he said to Pol, then turned to Angre who seemed to be more interested in their conversation than his own work. 'You aren't going off duty before you are done with this.'

Constable Angre looked like a boy put on detention after school.

—

The cabin was quiet and so were its occupants. It had been a long, hot day and each of them was dog tired and weary, as always. The trio had exchanged information and insights gained in the course of their respective day-long toils.

And now, like disciples with their guru, Motkar and Zirpe awaited Saralkar's final thoughts so that all of them could go to their respective homes, grab a bite and hit the pillow for the night, to begin afresh the next day.

Sanika Zirpe surreptitiously glanced at her watch. Saralkar had sat lost in thought without uttering a word for close to ten minutes now.

'Getting late, Zirpe?' the senior inspector asked, breaking the silence.

ASI Zirpe wasn't sure if she had detected sarcasm in his tone or consideration. 'Just a little hungry, sir …' she replied—an answer that she reckoned was more acceptable than confirming to her boss that she thought it was getting late.

Saralkar's reaction was unexpected. 'Ah!' he said and proceeded to open the top drawer of his desk, then pulled a small packet of Bourbon biscuits and another one of wafers. 'Here,' he said, pushing both items across the table to his subordinates.

Both Motkar and Zirpe looked astonished and crestfallen at the same time. Astonished because neither knew their boss had started maintaining a secret larder of snacks, and crestfallen because it meant they weren't going home anytime soon.

'Thank you, sir,' Zirpe said, moaning inwardly and looked at Motkar, as if offering him the first choice.

'Want some tea to go with it?' Saralkar asked, as he dialled the canteen on his intercom and ordered three cups.

His two subordinates opened both the packets and offered the contents to each other and to their boss. For a few minutes, the only noise was of hungry humans crunching on wafers and biscuits.

'So … ' Saralkar began and was interrupted by the rings of his mobile.

He frowned, squinting at the caller ID, almost certain it would probably be the CP. But it wasn't, Motkar deduced, from the way his boss took the call and answered.

'Yes, Sarnaik?' he said, then listened for a while. 'Well, I suppose he can resume work now. Hold on a minute.'

He glanced at Motkar. 'It's that retired cop, Sarnaik, calling on behalf of the architect and builder, Rajat Mali, who is redeveloping Shanti Villa. No reason not to let him resume work on the site, right?'

Motkar nodded. 'We have got all we need, sir. No harm if the chap starts work again.'

'OK, then,' Saralkar said and spoke into the phone again. 'Yes, Sarnaik, you can tell him he can resume work day after. I'll just get the formalities done tomorrow. No, no, that's OK. There is no need to thank me.'

He hung up, then said to Motkar, 'Issue him formal clearance.'

'But, sir, I have to go to Narayangaon tomorrow.'

'Hmm. Then Zirpe can do it,' Saralkar replied. Zirpe nodded.

A canteen boy chose that moment to arrive and served them tea in paper cups. Saralkar scowled. 'What's the matter with you? Are you serving tea on the railway platform? Get proper mugs, damn it.'

The canteen lad didn't seem intimidated at all. 'At night time there is no one to wash, so we use only paper cups.'

Saralkar grunted. 'But you don't serve snacks and food in paper plates, do you, smarty-pants?'

The lad still showed no signs of perturbance or embarrassment. 'True, saheb. So, you want me to take the tea back and return with the same tea in normal mugs?'

Motkar marvelled at the canteen boy's nonchalance.

'Yes,' Saralkar smirked. 'Or just go back and get the mugs. We'll do the rest ourselves.'

'Either way, the tea will turn lukewarm, saheb …'

This was pure daredevilry. Saralkar gave him a withering look—a kind of glance equivalent to third degree. 'Forget it. But next time, don't you dare get tea in a paper cup for me.'

'OK, saheb,' the boy nodded before walking away.

Zirpe and Motkar heaved a sigh of relief and reached out for tea. Saralkar picked up his paper cup with a look of disapproval and sipped. 'At least the tea is good. Nincompoops!' he remarked, then looked at Motkar. 'I would have liked to accompany you to Narayangaon too, but I have got to be here. DCP Khalap might regain consciousness any time and the CP might skin me alive if I am not around. You said Sarjerao Bhoir now has a farm in Narayangaon, right?'

'Yes, sir. He grows grapes on it and supplies most of his output to the winery nearby,' Motkar replied.

His dash to the Chinchwad address had led Constable Pol and him to Sarjerao's son, who after much hesitation told them that after being released from jail, Sarjerao had decided to go back to his native village on the outskirts of Narayangaon, a town about 80 kilometres from Pune. There, on his ancestral farmland, Sarjerao had joined his older brother in growing grapes. A couple of years later, his brother, a widower who had had no children, passed away, leaving Sarjerao the sole owner.

The grape yard was doing well and Sarjerao, in a sense, had successfully rehabilitated himself. Motkar had just a little earlier briefed Saralkar and Zirpe about it.

'Winery! Yes, they've got some world-class set-ups there,' Saralkar said. 'I have never understood why people like wine and go gaga over it. It tastes like ghastly syrup …'

'Don't all spirits taste like that, sir?' Zirpe remarked.

'Yes, most liquors do, but wine masquerades as some kind of manna from heaven,' Saralkar observed. 'But wasn't Sarjerao's son uneasy wondering why the police were looking for his father, after all these years?'

'Yes, sir, but I told him there was nothing to worry. The Police department was just looking for released convicts who had assimilated into normal life for a kind of research project,' Motkar explained.

'And he bought it?'

'Yes, sir. I even told him to inform his father that we were coming over to Narayangaon tomorrow, to allay any suspicion,' Motkar replied.

Saralkar took the last sip of his tea, crumpled the paper cup but, to his dismay, found his dustbin missing. He clicked his tongue in annoyance, then said, 'Let's see if your gut feeling about Sarjerao gets us anywhere.'

He paused briefly, then turned to Zirpe. 'I am going to need you again on the DCP Khalap case. Till then, you can go back to working on the Shanti Villa case.'

'Yes, sir,' Zirpe replied, hoping the session was coming to an end.

For once she was right. Saralkar looked at both and made a gesture waving them away. 'Off you two go now. I need to do some thinking.'

'You are staying back for some more time, sir?' Motkar asked surprised, even as he got up.

'Yes, Motkar. I need to run through what you told me about Urmila Welde's answers. That, and what the demeanour and replies of DCP Khalap's daughter signifies. It's triggered something in my mind and I need to figure out if it makes any sense and decipher if it adds up to any plausible conjectures that one can draw.'

Motkar and Zirpe looked at each other, a little perplexed. 'You want me to wait, sir?' Motkar offered half-heartedly.

'No, no, I need to do this alone,' Saralkar replied, much to Motkar's relief.

14

Sarjerao Bhoir possessed one of those weather-beaten, hard faces that instinctively conveyed to people that he was not a man to be trifled with. He stood straight at five feet ten, his still sturdy frame belying his age. His eyes were unblinking and challenging; his close cropped hair white with patches of grey and black—a sort of tricolour combination that one did not often see. His thick moustache, however, was fully white. It didn't curl at the ends nor did it need to, for Sarjerao's vanity marker was a scar that ran across the left side of his jaw, as if his barber had slashed him over an argument while shaving.

Prison fight, Motkar wondered, feeling rather puny in front of Sarjerao, although the man was no giant.

'What makes you feel I have the time to speak to you?' he asked Motkar in a throaty voice. Dressed in a half-sleeved shirt, loose trousers and sandals, Sarjerao stood with his still muscular arms and rugged hands on his hips.

'We had already informed your son yesterday,' Motkar replied.

'So what?' Sarjerao said. 'The police don't have any right on an ex-convict's time.'

PSI Motkar wasn't irked by his demeanour, but he hadn't expected the belligerence. It, however, raised Constable Pol's hackles.

'Talk properly with Motkar saheb,' he said to Sarjerao with the hint of a warning.

Sarjerao's eyes turned to him. 'Or what? I don't have to waste my breath on lowly constables.'

It riled Pol further. 'Don't you have a decent tongue in that old mouth?'

Before the exchange could escalate, PSI Motkar spoke. 'Sarjerao, your name has cropped up in connection with another case. That's why we are here.'

It had just the salutary effect, Motkar had expected. Alertness and anxiety sprang into Sarjerao's features and body language at once. 'What case?' he remarked gruffly, but there was no incredulity in his tone. 'I have committed no other crime.'

'Can we sit somewhere and talk?' Motkar said quickly.

Sarjerao nodded and led them towards the veranda of his modest house, from the gate where they had been standing so far. It was a short walk. He offered Motkar a steel folding chair and sat down in another, but ignored Constable Pol as if it was beneath him to get the man anything to sit on.

'Constable Pol is not going to keep standing, Sarjerao,' PSI Motkar said pointedly.

Sarjerao threw a hostile glance at Pol. 'There is a moda in the corner,' he said and pointed towards a low cane stool. The message was clear. Pol was to fetch it himself, which the constable did because it was futile to take offence.

Sarjerao offered them neither water nor tea. 'What's all this about? What am I being accused of now?'

'I'll come to that,' Motkar said. 'First, I would like to talk about the murder for which you have already served your sentence, Sarjerao.'

'Why?' Sarjerao snarled. 'Everybody knows about that. It's ancient history. Done and dusted. Haven't you read the case records?'

Motkar had indeed gone through a quick summary of the case, just before leaving for Narayangaon that morning. 'I know you killed a man called Laxman Kore, who owed you one lakh rupees and whose wife, Chaya, you had sexual relations with. It seems you got into a drunken brawl at his house over the delay in him returning your money and your relations with his wife. You then struck him repeated blows with a brick that killed Laxman.'

'No,' Sarjerao reacted.

'What do you mean, no?' Motkar asked, surprised.

'I wasn't drunk. I was stone-cold sober …' Sarjerao replied. 'My lawyer told me that it would be better to claim I did it under the influence of alcohol.'

PSI Motkar had always marvelled at the things criminals admitted to sometimes. 'I see. So, if you were sober, was it premeditated?'

'Nah!' Sarjerao said dismissively and looked at Motkar contemptuously. 'You haven't read the file properly, saheb, have you?'

Motkar said nothing.

'A murder is an accident really,' Sarjerao said. 'One false move, one momentary rage-filled reaction that goes too far …'

'What are you saying? That you didn't intend to kill him? The report said you struck him several blows with the brick.'

'The prosecution lawyer painted that picture of multiple blows. I just hit him twice with the brick, and he was dead. Maybe he had a thin skull, or perhaps it hit a vulnerable spot,' Sarjerao said. 'My lawyer objected and pointed out to the judge that there weren't multiple blows. But the judge held that technically there was more than one blow, while none of the experts were willing to testify that there were no more than two blows.'

Sarjerao's face was flushed, as if it still mattered a great deal to him that he hadn't clobbered the victim but just struck him twice.

'Sarjerao, even if what you are saying is true—that you weren't drunk and that you only hit him twice with the brick—what can't be denied is that you had a strong motive to get rid of him. The money he owed you and your trysts with his wife …'

Sarjerao's throaty voice rose and his expressions hardened, 'At least I haven't denied killing him, like most murderers do. And that sick bastard Laxman was no saint. He had begged me to supply him with building material on credit. But even a year later, he hadn't paid me back. Then when he saw I was furious, he offered me his wife, saying I could have relations with her in lieu of the money. Women were my weakness, I admit, and I fell for it. I slept with his wife a couple of times but it just made me feel terrible because the woman would keep crying and snivelling. So, I just let it go and told Laxman to return my money.'

He paused and glared at Pol, as if the constable was Laxman reincarnated. 'But the shameless arsehole asked me what my problem was when he had offered his wife to me. I told him how miserable the woman was. The slimeball then beat up his wife and sent her to me again. I got fed up and sent her home. He then invited me to his home the next day, saying he would settle the matter satisfactorily over a drink.

I went, and there Laxman offered me some cheap liquor, which I just had a sip or two of. It tasted foul so I pushed it away. He then started saying he wasn't going to return my money and if I tried to demand it back again, he would go to the police and lodge a complaint that I had raped his wife.

That is when I lost my temper and began slapping him. He, in turn, picked up this brick and came at me. It struck me on my hand, as I shielded my head. I knocked it out of his hand, picked it up, and landed two blows on him. That's it. He just dropped dead. That's how the whole thing happened. A bloody accident—that's what it was.'

He stopped and glowered at Motkar and Pol indignantly.

'So why didn't you report to the police immediately? Instead, you and his wife put Laxman's body in his rickshaw-tempo, then drove into the woods about 5 kilometres away, dug a grave and buried his body,' Constable Pol suddenly spoke, before Motkar could respond. 'And that's not all, two days later you went back to the place in the night, poured petrol and rock-oil over it and burnt his corpse.'

Sarjerao's face went red with rage and his eyes flashed in Pol's direction, but he looked away as if trying his best to regain his composure. 'Yes, that was the real crime I got sentenced for … for the gory act of first burying, then burning the body. Not for the murder,' he muttered.

PSI Motkar was suddenly struck by what Saralkar had said to him only a few days before—that murder could well be the job of a novice, but not the disposal of a body.

'I … I should have gone to the police instead of trying to hide the body and my crime … I shouldn't have listened to his wife, who later turned approver against me …' Sarjerao said.

Motkar let a couple of beats pass, then said, 'Well, Sarjerao, it's interesting you killed the man, then dug his grave all by yourself in a few hours and buried the body. Single-handedly. Almost as if you had some practice of having done it before?'

His eyes were observing Sarjerao carefully as the old man's face leaked varied emotions—first startled, then hardened and finally turning guarded.

'What the hell are you accusing me of, Inspector saheb?' Sarjerao asked, a dangerous edge to his voice.

Motkar wondered whether it was his imagination that the man suddenly looked wound up, or was it normal anger and apprehension playing out at the possibility of being accused of a heinous crime.

'I understand you worked as a building and bungalow contractor in Pune prior to being sentenced?'

'Yes, what about it?'

'You worked for an architect called Atre quite a few times, correct?'

'Yes …' Sarjerao's tough face twitched.

'And under his supervision, you also built a bungalow for his friend, Shashank Welde, around 1980–82, correct?'

This time Sarjerao did not open his mouth, just nodded in acknowledgement.

'Do you have any thoughts on how a skeleton seems to have been found buried under the lawns in the premises of that bungalow?' PSI Motkar asked, keenly choosing his words, his eyes rivetted on the convicted murderer sitting in front of him.

Sarjerao Bhoir's face, he noticed, appeared to have turned into a stony scowl!

'Why didn't you have dinner last night? I had left it all on the table,' Jyoti asked as they sipped the morning tea.

Saralkar looked at her distractedly, wondering whether a lie would work better than the truth. The problem with both lies and truth was that one never knew at the moment of choosing either, which would be the lazier or easier option. Sometimes, both could be incredibly hard work, depending on the buttons they pushed of the person you told it to.

For instance, he could simply tell Jyoti he had eaten out, with no questions asked. On the other hand, it might rile her up and start an argument. Conversely, if he told her the truth that he had just been too tired and sleepy to bother eating, it might not go down well with her either. A white lie that he'd eaten dinner before returning home seemed the easier option, with chances of it likely to go unchallenged.

'I'd had something at the canteen,' he replied, dipping his Parle G biscuit in the tea.

'What did you have?' Jyoti asked casually.

Saralkar grunted. So, it hadn't been the lazier and easier option after all. Now he had to think up a dish. 'Idli-vada,' he lied.

'But don't you hate the canteen chutney?'

More work. 'It was late. Not much choice really,' he replied laconically. 'The tea is good …'

'Why can't you have a thali or something filling?' his wife continued harping on the subject.

Saralkar clicked his tongue. 'I hate that even more. Actually, Jyoti I didn't even have idli …'

She frowned, then gave a little knowing smile. 'The truth always comes out, Saralkar saheb! Let me guess. You couldn't be bothered to heat up dinner when you got home and didn't want to wake me up?'

'Something like that,' Saralkar said, going for the second biscuit.

Jyoti gazed at this man she had been married to for over two decades. 'How come you have become so considerate these days? You having an affair or something?'

'Yes,' snapped Saralkar.

'With Sanika Zirpe?' his wife teased.

'No, with the CP Arundhati Kotwal, don't you know?'

Jyoti gave a gurgling laugh. 'Why, has she been making life difficult for you over that DCP Khalap case?'

'Hmm,' Saralkar said and grabbed his third biscuit, something he rarely did.

'Is the case bothering you that much?' his wife asked.

Saralkar finished his tea. 'It's never the case. It's always the sordid scenarios my mind thinks up that bother me, Jyoti. Unfortunately, many of the possibilities turn out to be true in the end, although some don't.'

'I know that,' she said. 'What is it this time?'

'Absolute taboo stuff. Relationships that are frowned upon. I hope I am wrong,' he replied. 'I need to get going.'

He got up. Jyoti knew he didn't want to discuss his cases, or his theories about them, with her. It was as if he was protecting her from the darkness of the world he witnessed almost daily.

'OK. I'll get your breakfast ready,' she replied.

An hour later, Saralkar was back at his desk. It was just as he had left it barely seven hours ago after a marathon bout of thinking. It seemed to have been dusted by the cleaner and the room had also been swept. But there was an additional object on his table that hadn't been there the previous night—a light brown A4-size envelope from the local forensic unit.

Usually, all forensic reports and other paperwork found their way to Motkar's desk first. This one seemed to have been hand-delivered and marked in his name specifically. He quickly slit it open and was glad to see that it was the long-awaited report on the Shanti Villa skeletal remains, prepared by the central specialised laboratory and forwarded to the local forensic unit.

Saralkar began running through the reports and his brow furrowed. Whatever he had been expecting, he hadn't anticipated these findings. There had of course been no reason not to, for the conclusions were obviously in the realm of possibilities. There was no way he could decipher the technical jargon and scientific reasoning given, so he immediately called up the local forensic unit.

Ten minutes later, he disconnected, having received a confirmation of the conclusions and an explanation of the reasons. The skeletal remains were that of an eleven- to twelve-year-old boy, not that of an adult. The boy had been dead and buried for approximately twenty-five to thirty-five years now.

Saralkar, for all his years of experience, felt a chill run down his spine. Somehow, they had never factored in that the victim could be a child. For some reason, it completely altered the nature and gravity of the crime.

15

'You sound down, Niharika!' her brother remarked.

They still talked on phone the old-fashioned way—voice calls mostly. Smartphones and WhatsApp had turned long-distance calls into video chats but the siblings did not feel any compulsive need to gaze at each other while conversing on the phone. In fact, there was something oddly comforting about only hearing each other's voice without visual overload.

'No ... no. I'm OK,' Niharika replied without much conviction.

'Sure? Is this bungalow matter disturbing you?' Sunit asked.

'Yes, it's all very upsetting and scary,' Niharika replied.

'I ... I can't get my head around it. How do you think a skeleton got there, below our lawn in the first place?' Sunit said.

'How would I know, Sunit?' Niharika's response was sharper than usual. 'It makes me shudder to even think of it.'

There was an awkward silence for a few seconds, then Sunit spoke. 'Why do you think Baba put that clause in his will?'

'Shhh ... Sunit! What do you mean? What's that got to do with anything?'

'Does it not seem strange to you that he wanted to prevent us ...' Sunit began speaking.

'Hush … not over phone, Sunit, please!' Niharika interrupted him quickly. 'And it's crazy you seem to be drawing a connection between Baba's will and this unfortunate discovery.'

'Maybe we should have just followed the condition in his will and waited,' Sunit remarked. 'But since you said you and Anshuman needed the money …'

'Of course, I needed the money, Sunit. Not just that, I deserved it,' Niharika snapped. 'I was the one who looked after them all these years, while you didn't have to do a thing. And who was going to look after the maintenance and repairs of the bungalow, and keep searching for tenants otherwise?'

'Yaar Niku, why do you have to keep flying off the handle like that?' Sunit said.

'Because I am over fifty, menopausal and tired of living life for everyone but myself—husband, children, parents, in-laws, even Urmila Attya! And my responsibilities never seem to end …' Niharika raged. 'And now this. You know the police threatened me that if I refused to give them Urmila Attya's contact details, I would have to present myself before them in Pune within forty-eight hours! Just my rotten luck that this … horrible, eerie matter had to surface just now.'

'I know, it must be bad for you, Niku, and I am very sorry the police keep bothering you because you are in India, unlike me … but … but tell me, why were you reluctant to give them Urmila Attya's contact details?' Sunit asked.

'Because you have no idea what she's become as the dementia has progressed,' Niharika said. 'She says all kinds of weird things … about everyone … about Baba and Aai, about you and me too … I didn't know what shocking things she would tell the police. Even now I am scared … what she might have told them about us, about our family.'

'Oh! Exactly what kind of things does she blabber about, Niku?'

'I don't want to talk about it Sunit … she says all kinds of creepy and senseless stuff. It's scary,' Niharika replied. 'Sometimes I wish she passes away soon …'

'Come on, Niku … watch your words,' Sunit chided her.

'As if you care whether she dies or lives, Sunit,' Niharika lashed out at him. 'Don't I know how much you dislike her …'

'Niku, do we have to go into all that? All I am saying is why are you saying things like you hope she dies …'

'Because you don't know what it's like to deal with her condition … or even arrange for her care! Her caretakers keep leaving almost every one or two months … it's so much trouble getting a new caretaker and instructing them about various things,' Niharika replied. 'I go crazy … so what I have done is I told another spinster, Pramilabai, in her neighbourhood to take care of her in case the caretaker suddenly quits or takes leave. The agency always takes a day or two before they can send a new caretaker. Till then, the neighbourhood woman looks after her, and I pay her but it's all such a flimsy and temporary arrangement. Puts me under a lot of unnecessary stress …'

'Hmm. It always beats me why Baba made a provision for Urmila Attya, despite her behaviour with him and why did Aai allow him to?' Sunit said. 'Just as I don't know why you have taken her responsibility on yourself at all?'

'Because Baba and Aai both made me promise, Sunit.'

'What? Aai too? But she and Urmila Attya never got along! They were always daggers drawn,' Sunit said with incredulity.

'I was surprised too, but Aai said … I … I should keep in touch with Urmila Attya and look after her. She said it was very important for our well-being,' Niharika replied.

'Important for our well-being? Yours and mine? I don't understand. Whatever did Aai mean?'

'I never could get to the bottom of that. Aai wasn't keeping too well in the last few months when she told me this, and although I broached the topic once or twice, she avoided any discussion and would not elaborate on what she had meant.'

'You never told me this before, Niku, and … Aai didn't mention anything like that about Urmila Attya to me either,' Sunit said.

'How would she? She knew you didn't like Urmila Attya at all and weren't even on talking terms.'

'I guess,' Sunit said thoughtfully. 'Did Urmila Attya ever come to visit Aai when she was dying?'

'No. In fact, I did inform her, but she wouldn't react,' Niharika said. 'Then several weeks after Aai's death, Urmila Attya called me one day and told me she had been suffering from dementia, and it had now started deteriorating rapidly. She said she wanted to meet me and asked me if I could accompany her on her next visit to her neurologist.'

'Yes, you told me you visited her neurologist, who explained her condition to you.'

'She did. Then Urmila Attya told me she needed my help to sell her flat, move into a smaller, cheaper place and use the extra money to help fund her caretaker, medication and household expenses. She said she wanted to get everything done before her mental faculties eroded further,' Niharika said. 'So I arranged all that for her.'

'Well, you certainly have been a good niece, Niku. I suppose she'll leave the house and whatever money she has to you eventually,' Sunit said.

'If there is anything left to leave, Sunit. And you are welcome to have the house she stays in now. The locality and this flat are a dump! She chose this ramshackle place where she could just live out her remaining days with a caretaker looking after her.'

'Hmmm. Do you think the Pune Police questioned her about the skeleton?' Sunit asked.

'I have no clue, Sunit. They haven't got in touch with me again, although I expect their call every day. I can only say, anybody who spends a few minutes with Urmila Attya will notice her incoherence and bizarre behaviour. They are bound to realise there is no point in questioning her because there's no likelihood of getting any credible information,' Niharika said. 'Yet, I shudder to think what she might have said about our family because I know she says all kinds of disturbing and shocking things.'

'Come on, Niharika. What's the worst she can say, even in her present state?'

'You won't be able to bear hearing it Sunit,' Niharika replied. 'Do you really want me to tell you?

'Yes.'

'Very well …' Niharika said harshly and told him the ramblings her aunt had hurled at her on more than one occasion.

Her words seemed to rob Sunit of speech. When he spoke again it was a hiss of fury. 'How dare she say such filthy things … I'll kill her …'

ASI Sanika Zirpe had finished jotting down her tasks for the day in her notepad. Since she had been sure she would forget it later, Zirpe had first taken up the paperwork necessary to permit resumption of work on the Shanti Villa site by the redevelopers, as Saralkar had instructed.

Next on her list had been to take an update from Khot and then feed in the status of different lines of inquiry in her daily report. She sat back now, reviewing the names on the list of domestic help who had worked for the Weldes in various capacities. It struck her that perhaps she should try a social media search of one particular name, even though the other names were unlikely to yield any traces on the internet.

But Rohidas Phule, the gardener who had been named by Namdev Phutane, might well throw up some links on social media sites like Facebook, LinkedIn or Instagram. Hadn't Phutane said the young gardener had bagged a degree in agriculture? Not just that, according to Phutane, Rohidas Phule had joined a seeds company and done well for himself.

Surely such a person was likely to have basic social media presence at least, as a professional on LinkedIn or some organisational website? She punched in his name and ten minutes later had shortlisted a man who might just be the Rohidas Phule she was looking for. If the man whose profile she was looking at was indeed the same person, then his rise had indeed been impressive. Not only had his first job been at a state-owned seeds company, but thereafter he had moved to a private sector organisation in the field, collected an MBA along the way and was now the President of the Agriculture Division of a leading multinational company in India.

For a moment, ASI Zirpe was assailed by doubt. It was the story of a meteoric rise—a true, humble beginnings to high-achiever tale. What certainly matched with Phutane's description was that this Rohidas Phule had studied at Pune's Agriculture

College in the late 1980s and early '90s, then joined a state seed company.

She dialled Namdev Phutane's number. 'Hello, Namdev Kaka, do you use WhatsApp?'

'I don't know what that is, madam,' Phutane replied.

'Is there anyone else at home now?' PSI Zirpe asked.

'Yes, my son is here.'

'Give him the phone and tell him who I am,' Zirpe instructed him.

As soon as Phutane's son came on line, Zirpe asked him if he used WhatsApp. When he replied in the affirmative, Zirpe asked for his number and told him she was sending him a photo, which he needed to show his father and then call her back promptly. She then sent him two pictures taken from the LinkedIn profile of the Rohidas Phule she'd zeroed in on.

A few minutes later, her phone buzzed. It was Namdev Phutane. 'Did you recognise the man in the photos, Phutane kaka?' she asked the old man.

'He looks vaguely familiar, madam, but I am not sure who it is. Do I know him?' Namdev Phutane asked.

It was often difficult to recognise an older photo of someone who you knew when you were much younger, ASI Zirpe was well aware of this.

'Kaka, please look at the photos again carefully. Could this be the gardener, Rohidas Phule, you once knew?' she asked, trying to keep a neutral tone, for she also knew sometimes people simply gave police officers the answers they thought the cops wanted to hear.

'Oh! Let me take another look, madam,' the old man said. Several seconds passed before Phutane came back on the line. 'The man in the photo certainly resembles the Rohidas Phule

I remember … I mean many decades have passed since I last set my eyes on him … and … he also looks well-to-do and different now.'

'I understand that, Kaka. Thank you. I just wanted to check whether the person you remember is anything like this photo,' ASI Zirpe said and disconnected.

So, there was a 50:50 chance this was the Rohidas Phule she had hoped to find. She looked up if his contact email or information was available anywhere, then dialled the landline number of his company's office in Gurgaon.

'Hello,' said the cool voice of a corporate receptionist—a breed Zirpe thought would soon disappear as redundant, as so many human occupations had over time.

'Hullo, I'm ASI Sanika Zirpe from Pune Police,' Zirpe said, rather self-consciously. 'I'd like to know if Mr Rohidas Phule is still employed with your company.'

A pause greeted her, then the receptionist asked, 'I am sorry, could you please repeat that?'

Zirpe repeated her request slowly, wondering whether the woman hadn't been able to hear or was just checking if she had heard right.

'Yes, Mr Phule is the President of India Operations, but what is this regarding?' the receptionist asked in a cautious tone.

'I need to contact Mr Phule in connection with an ongoing investigation,' PSI Zirpe replied.

'An investigation, did you say?' the receptionist repeated, as if in disbelief.

'Yes. Can I speak to Mr Phule? Or can you give me his mobile number?' Zirpe asked, patiently.

'Oh, let me check if Mr Phule's secretary is available. You are from Pune Police you said, right, madam?'

'Yes.'

'Let me put you on hold,' the receptionist said. For the next two minutes, Zirpe was treated to saxophone music, which was soothing no doubt, but she'd heard it before.

Another woman's voice came on the line. She identified herself as Mr Rohidas Phule's secretary and ASI Zirpe had to repeat herself all over again.

'I see. Mr Phule is busy in some meetings right now. Could I take your number and ask him to call back a little later?' the secretary said.

Zirpe gave her number. The secretary had some problem getting her surname right, but eventually managed to.

'May I please get details of the case so that I can brief Mr Phule about it?' she asked.

'No, I can discuss that only with Mr Phule,' ASI Zirpe told her matter-of-factly. 'Please tell Mr Phule to definitely get in touch right away, and can I have his mobile number and email ID?'

It was the secretary's turn to decline. 'Sorry, madam, I can't do so without his permission, but I will definitely give him your message.'

Zirpe called off, then began to check Rohidas Phule's posts, first on LinkedIn, then on Facebook. There was nothing out of the ordinary on either platform. The professional photos were with colleagues at conferences, trade fairs and other company events. There were other on-field photos with farmers and others at various locations. There were also a few news items and video clips in which Rohidas Phule came across as a knowledgeable man, who spoke fluently in English and Hindi, with an emphatically Marathi accent.

His personal photos on Facebook were with family—wife and two kids of high school and college-going ages—at holiday locations, both in India and abroad, at family functions and so on. There was also a throwback photo of a much younger Phule, with a rather rustic-looking old couple, probably his parents. Zirpe downloaded it with a mind to send it to Phutane. Maybe that would help him identify if it was indeed the same Rohidas Phule he had spoken about.

Zirpe also began browsing Phule's friend list and then entered a couple of names from the servant list she had, to check if they happened to be in touch with him, although she knew it was highly unlikely. How many people who came from humble backgrounds and had risen to be successful would want to keep in touch with their casual acquaintances from much humbler days? That simply wasn't in the nature of human beings.

Her phone rang. It was an unknown mobile number. Could it be Rohidas Phule, calling back in less than thirty minutes since she had spoken to his secretary? She was pleasantly surprised to find it was.

'Hullo, Rohidas Phule speaking. I believe you had called for me, ASI Zirpe?' It was the same voice she had heard in the LinkedIn video clips a little while ago.

'Yes, that's right, Mr Phule. This is ASI Sanika Zirpe.'

'Please tell me what this is regarding. I am a little puzzled why Pune Police has felt the need to contact me,' Rohidas Phule said, the Marathi accent quite prominent in his speech. 'I hail from Pune, alright, but as far as I know I am not remotely involved as a complainant or witness or anything in any police case.'

ASI Zirpe suddenly became conscious that she was speaking to a man who had distinguished himself and it was essential to be absolutely certain of his identity. 'Mr Phule, I'd first like to verify whether you are the same Rohidas Phule we are looking for,' she said.

'Excuse me?' Phule responded, sounding a trifle offended.

'What I mean is that I want to confirm it's not a case of mistaken identity arising out of sharing the same name with someone else,' Zirpe hastened to add. 'So, let me ask you a couple of preliminary questions. You passed out of College of Agriculture, Pune, in 1991, I believe?'

'Yes, I did.'

'While you were pursuing your course, were you also … er … working?'

'Yes,' came the curt reply.

'As a gardener?'

A couple of beats followed before Phule replied, 'Yes.'

He was not denying it, but clearly he did not seem to relish being reminded of his humble past.

'I see. Mr Phule, do you remember having worked at Mr Shashank Welde's bungalow at that time?'

There was a longer silence this time. 'Surely, you don't expect me to recollect the names of people I worked for over thirty years ago, Inspector!'

'We were given to understand you worked for them for a few years,' Zirpe said. 'The name of the bungalow was Shanti Villa.'

'Who said that I worked at this bungalow?' Rohidas Phule asked irritably.

'Another person who used to work there—one Mr Namdev Phutane. He used to wash vehicles for a living.'

Again, there was silence. 'I … I don't remember who that is. Anyway, how is it relevant? What is this all about, ASI Zirpe?'

'Perhaps I can jog your memory with another name. It seems the Weldes appointed a driver named Bansi Vishwakarma, who started interfering in your gardening activities and, we are told, you then decided to stop working for the Weldes,' Sanika Zirpe said.

'This is ridiculous and very awkward, ASI Zirpe! I don't remember any such person,' Phule said. 'Look, I have to get back to an important meeting. Let me try and see if I can remember any of these names, and I will get back to you.'

'Mr Phule, please understand it's very important to us. What we are investigating is a possible murder that probably happened around the time you were working there, and the body of the victim has just been found in a skeletal state,' Sanika Zirpe remarked somewhat impulsively.

'What? What's all that got to do with me?' Rohidas Phule spoke, sounding more excitable than before. 'I mean … even if I did work for this family … how … how do I come into the picture if somebody had murdered someone and buried a body under that bungalow?'

'I didn't say anything about a buried body, Mr Phule,' PSI Zirpe pounced on his remark.

'Didn't you just say the skeleton of the victim was found?' Rohidas Phule fumbled. 'So I assumed it was a buried body …'

He was right, Zirpe reckoned. Phule was an intelligent man, and it was quite possible that he had made the assumption that a buried body had been found when she mentioned skeletal remains. 'OK, Mr Phule, do think back and try to recall whether you worked for Mr Shashank Welde. If you want, I can send you photos of the bungalow and that of Mr Welde, even of Mr Namdev Phutane, who recognised your photo when I showed it to him,' Zirpe said. 'It would be of great help to us.'

'Sure, I will,' Rohidas Phule said tentatively, then disconnected.

ASI Zirpe knew human memory was both malleable and fallible. It was quite possible Rohidas Phule had chosen to blur out memories of the days he'd worked as a humble gardener now that he had such a successful career—a far cry from his roots. Perhaps those days embarrassed him and there really hadn't been anything worthwhile or memorable enough.

Yet, she couldn't believe human minds forgot inconvenient memories altogether. Could it be that Rohidas Phule was reluctant to admit he had worked for the Weldes or known Namdev Phutane and Bansi Vishwakarma because he knew of a piece of the skeleton puzzle either advertently or inadvertently?

16

'Alright, you had a hunch about Sarjerao Bhoir since he's a convicted murderer. More so because he also buried his victim in a grave he dug all by himself,' Saralkar said. 'But what exactly has strengthened your suspicions after meeting him?'

PSI Motkar struggled to articulate a convincing answer. 'Sir, it was his overall demeanour, his abrasive cockiness. But mainly because of one particular thing ...'

'What?' Saralkar asked sceptically.

'Sir, I had asked him if he had also built the second storey of Welde's bungalow for them, later on,' Motkar said. 'In response, he denied doing so, but then told me that he had done only one more minor job for Welde a few years afterwards. I asked him what it had been and he sort of mocked me and said that it was up to me to find that out ... So I asked him if that meant he had built the two lawn platforms for the Weldes ... And just for a few moments he seemed to freeze as if he knew exactly what I was talking about. Then he replied that it was something else—and none of our business.'

'Hmm,' said Saralkar, still not enthused by what he had heard. 'The problem with hunches and gut feelings, Motkar, is that once a police officer gets them, they are difficult to shake off. We look for the flimsiest of reasons to hold on to them.'

'It's not become my hobby horse, sir. I genuinely feel Sarjerao Bhoir is involved in some way,' Motkar said, adamant.

'How, Motkar? How? The initial basis for suspecting Sarjerao was that since he was a convicted murderer, he had perhaps killed someone earlier too, right? Perhaps a labourer or someone who worked for him, while the Welde bungalow had been under construction.'

'Yes, sir.'

'Well, the bottom falls out of that theory now because the skeleton is not of a man but of a child—a boy of about eleven or twelve.'

'What? A child?' Motkar asked, genuinely flummoxed by the revelation.

'Yes! The report came in this morning and I was as startled as you are,' Saralkar replied. 'The fact that the victim was a child completely alters the approach we have had to this case. And as you can see, the theory about Sarjerao gets thrown out of the window because he couldn't have employed a boy of eleven or twelve as a labourer.'

'Why not, sir? Surely child labour, and that too thirty or forty years ago, cannot have been an impossibility ...'

'No, Motkar. Very unlikely even back then. Even basic tasks in the construction industry require too much strength for children to be viably employed. It's just not practical. So, why should Sarjerao or any other contractor employ a boy and, worse still, kill him?' Saralkar reasoned. 'The reasons for anyone killing a child are very different from why adults are murdered.'

Motkar was silent for a few seconds, a deep frown adorning his face. Then he grudgingly said, 'I agree, sir, and I see your point. My God, sir! We probably need to start again from scratch. Have you told Zirpe too?'

'Not yet. Call her.'

Motkar quickly stepped out of Saralkar's cabin. A few minutes later, he returned with Zirpe.

'Anything to report, Zirpe?' Saralkar asked her. He knew she had given him two missed calls in the late afternoon, so there had to be something.

'Sir, I have traced another person who worked for the Weldes for a couple of years. A gardener named Rohidas Phule. I spoke to him this afternoon,' Zirpe replied.

'Is he in Pune?'

'No, sir. In Gurgaon. He is a big shot now—the head of India operations of a leading agri-seeds multinational,' Zirpe said, and briefed them on her conversation with Rohidas Phule.

'Interesting! But even if he is pretending not to remember having worked for the Weldes, it could simply be to avoid the hassle of being involved in a police investigation,' Saralkar observed. 'Or because it's inconvenient and awkward to have memories of a humble background dug out. His motive for claiming he does not recollect need not be sinister.'

'That might be true, sir,' Zirpe said. 'All I am saying is that perhaps if you were to speak to him, he might be less evasive and more forthcoming.'

'Hmm. Let me think about it,' Saralkar said. 'Meanwhile, there is a more critical fact that has come to light. The skeletal remains found have turned out to be that of a child—an eleven to twelve year old boy.'

ASI Zirpe reacted on anticipated lines—her eyes shot up, then dived back as her face settled into a baffled frown. 'Could the Forensics team have made a mistake, sir?' she said. 'I mean, maybe the skeleton is that of a short man or someone who was of small build …'

'No, Zirpe. They don't make mistakes like that. I have already offended the Forensics chaps this morning by making all these layman's insinuations and conjectures,' Saralkar said. 'In fact, I received a fifteen-minute lecture on how the distinction between an adolescent's skeleton and that of a fully grown male is made.'

Zirpe suddenly shuddered. 'We are hunting down a child killer[2] yet again, sir?'

Saralkar gave her a grim nod, then said, 'As I was just saying to Motkar, the motive and circumstances for killing a child are very different from those for murdering adults. So, we need to re-orient our approach and line of inquiry—the what and the why we now need to look for. The first thing we need to find out is who this child could be. How was he connected to the Weldes—directly or indirectly, through their servants or acquaintances or family or tenants? Because the bungalow couldn't have been chosen just randomly by some stranger to bury the body under.'

'But that would be true even for an adult victim, sir,' Motkar said. 'Also, we have so far been looking for clues among the same set of people—servants, family, tenants.'

'Yes, but a child narrows down the possible victims considerably. There cannot be many eleven- or twelve-year-old children that the Weldes would have been connected to, directly or indirectly. That too boys,' Saralkar replied. 'Second, till now we were shooting in the dark, looking for some lead either to an adult victim or possible murderer. Now we can focus our efforts on identifying an eleven- or twelve-year-old boy who went missing at some point in time. Unlike in the case of an adult, the disappearance of a child is very alarming and it is likely to

---

2 Read *The Kid Killer*.

be noticed and remembered. In fact, if we are lucky, there's a chance there might be a missing person report.'

He paused and looked at his subordinates eagerly.

Motkar nodded slowly. 'Suddenly the case seems darker and more sinister, sir. And just like we didn't know about Urmila Welde at first, could there have been a young family member of the Weldes who we are not aware of?'

'Hmm. Maybe it's time to call in Niharika Das for questioning anyway,' Saralkar said. 'Perhaps we need not give the Welde family the benefit of the doubt any longer. All this while we were going by the logic that the Welde siblings—Sunit and Niharika—would not have given the bungalow for redevelopment if they knew a body was buried in the lawns.'

'Sure, sir, I'll summon her to Pune,' Motkar replied.

'Good. Now let's brainstorm on the motives why children are usually killed, and keep these in mind henceforth as we investigate this case further,' Saralkar said. 'Yes, Sanika, your turn first.'

'Kidnapping gone wrong, sir,' Sanika Zirpe said.

'True. Seen a lot of that. About five per cent of kidnapped children get killed,' Saralkar said.

Motkar gave him a quick glance. Saralkar had revealed to him a couple of years ago that he had been kidnapped as a child and had been lucky to have survived the ordeal. Of course, Sanika Zirpe had no reason to know about this.

'So, we check if Shashank Welde, his family, tenants or acquaintances had even a remote connection with anybody whose child was kidnapped for ransom,' Saralkar explained. 'Next motive, Motkar?'

'A grudge against the family or parents, sir. One of the oldest reasons children get killed,' Motkar added.

'Yes. Much too often. Murderers kill a child of the family, because it's easier than harming an adult,' Saralkar conceded. 'So, did a child go missing in this locality or neighbourhood and was never found? Moreover, what is the possible link to the Weldes or their bungalow? What next?'

'Human sacrifice, sir! Superstition!' Sanika Zirpe hazarded.

'Yes, a disproportionate number of children are victims of that kind of crime too. But for the moment, I think we can rule it out. Human sacrifice often involves horrible mutilation of the victim. The skeleton doesn't seem to have any such signs.'

'Were they able to figure out the cause of the death, sir?' Motkar asked.

'Their preliminary opinion is that death was caused by an injury to the skull, but they can't say for sure whether it's because of a blow to the head or because the head struck something. For instance, one of the experts told me it reminded him of a rare injury to the skull he'd seen of a man, on whom a coconut fell from a tree.'

'Really, sir? I thought coconuts never dropped when people are standing underneath,' Sanika Zirpe said.

'Who told you that? You think coconut trees have sensors to detect human movement underneath them?' Saralkar retorted.

ASI Sanika Zirpe grinned. 'Sorry for deviating from the main discussion, sir.'

'Anyway, let's keep aside human sacrifice as a possible motive. What other motives can be attributed?'

'Sexual crimes, sir. Paedophiles,' Motkar replied.

'Yes, but it's a more modern-age crime—a phenomenon of recent times, I dare say,' Saralkar said thoughtfully. 'I rarely remember children so young being victims of sexual or predatory crimes when I joined the force. It's increased exponentially in the last decade or so. I am not saying paedophilia did not exist earlier, but I think criminals too are a product of their times, and I doubt thirty to forty years ago an adolescent boy was looked upon as a possible sexual object, as is quite unnervingly common these days. In a sense, it's a new-age perversion.'

'All the more reason why we need to consider it a possible motive, sir. Because back then it was uncommon. No one might have suspected something like this or imagined individuals capable of such crimes,' Motkar reasoned.

'You mean no one might have reckoned a sexual crime could be behind the disappearance of a child and probably thought the child had just run away or something?'

'Yes, sir.'

'OK, fair enough. Anything else we can think of?'

'Sir, lots of children can be inadvertent victims of parental conflicts—divorce, separation. Sometimes, the husband or the wife may kill their own child because of extreme possessiveness or jealousy,' Sanika Zirpe suggested. 'Like that woman who killed her own child in a Goa hotel last year because she was going to lose the child's custody ...'

'Or the man who killed a child because he thought the boy was not his but a result of his wife's adultery,' Motkar added. 'It happens all the time.'

'Not out of bounds, but then who had the opportunity to be able to bury the boy in Weldes' bungalow and what exactly is the Shanti Villa connection?' Saralkar said.

Silence prevailed for a few seconds as the three cops reflected over all the points that had been made so far. 'Alright, one last possibility. Some parents get rid of children who are mentally challenged or physically handicapped or suffer from incurable congenital defects that make them a complete burden,' Saralkar said. 'It can be done from weariness or compassion or total frustration. Again, we need to see if anyone in Weldes' circle had such a child.'

'Those who do it think they are putting the child out of its misery, don't they, sir?' ASI Sanika Zirpe asked grimly.

Saralkar smirked sadly, 'Yes, sometimes, but often people do it just to free themselves from the onerous responsibility of looking after the child in this state.' He paused momentarily, then said, 'OK, enough of brainstorming. Let's get to work on the basis of what we have run through just now.'

As Motkar and Zirpe nodded in agreement and got to their feet, Saralkar's mobile pinged.

Their boss looked at the text, then turned to Sanika Zirpe. 'Zirpe, you and I need to go and meet someone tomorrow morning,' he said.

'Yes, sir! Who … ?' Zirpe said, and began framing a question.

But her boss had already started speaking again, this time to Motkar, 'The CP has consented to the questioning of the rape complainant in the DCP Khalap case. What do you say to that, Motkar?'

It cannot have been your charm, sir … That is what Motkar would have liked to say. Instead, he just smiled tactfully at his boss.

Urmila Welde knew she was losing her mind when the fog lifted and there were moments of lucidity. When, by some freak realignment of her faculties, she regained normalcy suddenly, for a brief while as if to remind her that the self she had known, still existed, behind all the strange confusion and bafflement she experienced daily.

She remembered what her doctor had said. Dementia was the process of becoming a stranger to oneself, little by little—a creeping alienation where you woke up a person who was slightly altered from yesterday, not because you had really changed but because irreversible processes in the brain told you so.

And yet, sometimes, one's consciousness of one's original self surfaced, like the sighting of a mythical or extinct creature. The clarity almost always vanished as suddenly as it made an appearance. Urmila Welde knew it would be gone soon. Wasn't it important then to record the most critical truth of her life? The truth she had suffered for, carrying the improbable burden of lies and cruelty and self-denial and, above all, of terrible sin?

Before she passed over into the next world, wasn't it time to lay down the truth in all its starkness—about her and others—even if it was unforgivable? Because even if it didn't matter, it actually did.

Quick! Her mind told her, before the fog descended again. Quick! She needed a pen and paper. Quick! Before she became someone else.

17

Komal Raina was a bundle of nerves and yet her demeanour was defiant. 'Are you also here to intimidate me?' she asked as soon as Senior Inspector Saralkar and ASI Zirpe were seated.

There was something about her—a combination of angst, honesty and vulnerability that struck Saralkar. She was fair and reasonably alluring. She also looked her age, which was in the mid-forties—over a decade younger than DCP Khalap.

'Who tried to intimidate you, Mrs Raina?' Saralkar asked.

She scoffed. 'As if you don't know your colleagues haven't tried their best to get me to withdraw the rape allegations against Khalap ...'

'We have no connection with the inquiry team looking into your allegations, madam. We are from a different team, which is investigating DCP Khalap's suicide attempt and his wife's death,' ASI Zirpe replied.

Komal Raina gave her a sullen look. 'It's just another way to pressurise me, isn't it—suggesting I was responsible for triggering what he did to himself and his wife!'

'Why are you presuming our intentions, Mrs Raina, if you don't want us to presume your guilt?' Saralkar responded.

'I am not guilty of anything, except refusing to take rape lying down,' Komal Raina said without flourish. 'DCP Khalap raped me, right here in my house, when I refused to continue being his mistress.'

'Would you mind giving us the background to what transpired between DCP Khalap and you?' Saralkar said gently. 'We are not privy to what you have told the officers conducting the inquiry into your allegations.'

'Haven't you read the newspaper reports from about two to three weeks ago? The media carried all my allegations in great detail,' Komal Raina said.

'I have, but I would like to get an authentic account from you, please,' Saralkar replied.

'You just want to check for inconsistencies in what I have said previously,' she said resignedly. 'Whether I am changing my story? Whether I am lying?'

Saralkar decided not to respond. He just waited. Zirpe too said nothing, taking the cue from her boss. Komal Raina had not expected her assertions to be met with silence.

'Suppose I don't wish to repeat what I have already narrated several times already?' she spoke again, with defiance creeping into her tone once more.

'Then we will come straight to our questions,' Saralkar said simply.

'I would prefer that,' she replied.

'Very well,' Saralkar said and glanced at Zirpe, who promptly put the first question. 'Madam, you said you refused to continue being DCP Khalap's mistress. Without going into how long both of you were in a relationship, was there a specific reason you decided to end it?'

There was no hesitation in Komal Raina's reply. 'I had had enough of being sexually and emotionally exploited by him. I thought I had done enough to repay my debt to him. I did not want Khalap in my life any longer.'

'What debt?' Saralkar asked.

She looked at him coldly. 'Nothing that portrays either me or him in good light. He helped me escape imprisonment and extracted a price. That's who he was … is … It was time to stop being grateful … '

'Can you give us more details of what this case was in which DCP Khalap helped you escape imprisonment?' ASI Zirpe asked.

She smiled a bitter smile. 'I would be foolish to tell you that, wouldn't I? But I was not the only one who was indebted to him … he bragged of others too.'

'I see. How often did you meet, prior to your decision to stop it?' Saralkar added.

'Too often. Twice or thrice a week, whenever he needed … you know …' Komal Raina said.

'Did you also go out together? Maybe for a movie or dinner or on a trip? Zirpe asked.

Komal Raina looked at the woman officer and again emitted a scoffing laugh. 'He took me to Mahabaleshwar and Goa once. Look, there was no love or romance. It was give and take. I didn't mind it for a couple of years, but then it really began grating on me—his drinking, his rough treatment of me, his forcing himself on me without regard for my …'

She seemed to choke over the sentence, then continued after a pause, 'I … I also had some gynaecological issues, but he wouldn't listen. When I finally told him I was done, he reacted with absolute fury. He was abusive, behaved like a brute … raped me violently, turned me into an absolute wreck.'

Her voice had gone so low, it was as if she was whispering a secret to herself. Saralkar glanced at Zirpe. His young colleague appeared to be affected by Komal Raina's account. 'Is that when you decided to file a complaint against him and go public?' Zirpe asked her.

Komal Raina seemed to be somewhere far away. Just as Zirpe was about to repeat her question, she shook her head. 'No, he came back again a week later—first trying to appear sorry, then pleading with me. But I told him point blank it was over and that he was no better than an animal for what he had done to me the previous week. I told him I would file a complaint against him,' Komal Raina said. 'This provoked him further and he … he raped me again and told me nothing I did would get him into trouble but would certainly get me killed.'

A muffled sob escaped her lips and her eyes filled with tears, that didn't trickle down her face. 'I realised he wouldn't stop this brutish behaviour and I would never be free of him if I didn't do something. That's why I immediately went and got myself medically examined by my gynaecologist … pleaded with her to put in writing my condition and that there was evidence of rape. Then I promptly sent a written complaint to the Commissioner's office. I also contacted the media through an acquaintance.'

In his long experience, Saralkar knew that there was no completely reliable indicator to differentiate between lies and truth—body language, facial expressions, tone of voice, pauses, hesitation, tears, anger, defiance, denial—nothing. Nor were a police officer's well-developed instincts or hunches always right. In fact, hunches were as likely to go wrong as being proved right.

Yet, going by all parameters—objective and subjective—he had the uncanny feeling this woman was telling the truth.

'DCP Khalap's call records show that even after you filed your complaint against him and an inquiry was set up, he tried to call you and you received his calls, Mrs Raina,' Saralkar said. 'We can see you also made calls to him.'

'He tried to call me using different numbers immediately after I filed the complaint. He would call me in the middle of the night threatening of dire consequences. I told him, he could do the worst he wanted and I would record and report his threats to the inquiry committee,' Komal Raina said. 'Then he stopped calling for a while. A few days later, he called from some other number and spoke in a different tone. This time he said his career and family life would be destroyed. He begged me to withdraw the complaint, and said he would leave me alone, never harass me again. When I refused to relent, he tried to remind me that he had saved me from imprisonment and for that reason, I should remain grateful.'

'Did you record any of the calls and report them?' Zirpe asked.

'Yes, I recorded a few calls but the inquiry officer said I would have to submit my original device—my mobile—for forensic evidence. That they would have to conduct various tests to ascertain authenticity and to verify if it was really DCP Khalap,' Komal Raina said. 'I refused to hand over my phone because I suspected I would lose all the evidence and be left with nothing. I still have the recordings, if you wish to hear them. I have downloaded them all on my laptop.'

'But then why did you call DCP Khalap on his mobile?' Saralkar asked. 'What explains that? It can be alleged that as the complainant you were blackmailing him, or that you pushed him to take his own life and that of his wife, Mrs Raina.'

She went pale and her eyes darkened. 'On what basis are you jumping to this conclusion and making these allegations, Inspector?'

'Answer my question, madam. Do understand, DCP Khalap has left a note behind. If he dies, it will be considered a dying declaration, to which courts tend to give weightage,' Saralkar said without harshness.

ASI Zirpe realised he was playing the classic bluff. Nowhere in DCP Khalap's WhatsApp message had there been a reference of Komal Raina blackmailing or pressurising him. How would Komal Raina react? She watched the woman closely for any sign of anxiety on her face, or for the slightest change in her expression.

'I have recordings of my phone calls to him too, Inspector. I can play them for you,' Komal Raina said without wavering. 'I only called on his number twice. Once because Khalap's wife had got hold of my number and called me, heaping abuse. I did it to inform him to keep her from calling me again.'

'And the second call?'

'To tell him that if I got any more threats from gangsters at his behest, I would spill some of his other wrongdoings that he had shared with me,' Komal Raina said. 'That's not blackmail, it's self-preservation, Inspector.'

'You were getting threats from gangsters asking you to withdraw allegations against DCP Khalap?' Zirpe asked.

'Yes, from unknown callers who claimed to be gangsters. I have saved the numbers and recorded some threats I received,' Komal replied simply.

Whatever else she was, Komal Raina seemed to have steeled herself well for the ordeal—from getting herself promptly examined by her gynaecologist after the rape, to recording calls from Khalap and other strangers. Being brave wasn't easy, Saralkar knew.

She looked at him. 'It is I who should have been on the brink of suicide, Inspector, not DCP Khalap,' she said, her eyes again brimming with tears that didn't stream down her face. 'You are accusing me of pushing him to suicide … But I didn't do that. I didn't even wish it upon him … I just wanted him to leave me alone …'

'But, it is a fact, Mrs Raina, that DCP Khalap took this step following your allegations in the media and complaint to the Commissioner, which led to the inquiry,' Saralkar said.

The tears finally rolled down her cheeks, but she quickly wiped them. 'It's sad that he shot his wife and himself, but as I said, I am not guilty of anything. What he did to me, he has done to others. Maybe all his sins overwhelmed him.'

'If you know about others, why don't you share that information?'

She shook her head. 'That's not my funeral, Inspector … It's none of my business. That's all you will get from me.'

She looked at both Saralkar and Zirpe resolutely, as if she would not answer any further questions, no matter how hard they tried.

Saralkar nodded. 'If DCP Khalap does not survive, you might have to disclose some of the information you have refused to give just now.'

Komal Raina said nothing.

Saralkar and Zirpe got up from the sofa they were seated on, and just as they started to leave, the senior inspector spoke, 'Mrs Raina, are you separated from your husband?'

She blinked and her face flickered with emotion. 'No. He died seven years ago in a rock-climbing accident. His hobby killed Nishant.'

Zirpe felt a twinge. 'Oh, I see,' Saralkar said. 'And you don't have any children?'

A spasm rippled across her face. 'My son Ashit passed away two years later. He was haemophilic and succumbed eventually.'

Another great tide of emotion seemed to rise in her eyes, as if she would burst out sobbing.

'So sorry for your loss,' Saralkar murmured clumsily. He paused a few awkward beats, then said, 'Can we take copies of the call recordings you have made of your conversations with DCP Khalap and the gangster threats you received, Mrs Raina?'

She looked at him for a long minute, then nodded.

18

The rookie constable Angre hadn't done a bad job of listing and segregating detailed information of most tenants, who had stayed at Shanti Villa between 1997 and 2023, from the files provided by Uttam Padwal.

PSI Motkar had immediately put him and Constable Pol to work on finding their current whereabouts. 'Contact each of them and get confirmation that they had stayed as Shashank Welde's tenants. Also get an update on where they reside and work currently, as well as a summary of their lives after they left Shanti Villa. Most importantly, don't forget to ask them the two most critical questions—do they remember any strange or abnormal incidents during their stay and ask about their kids. Check their reactions and if you find something odd, jot it down so we can call them over for questioning,' he instructed his men.

'Yes, sir,' Pol said, raring to go as ever.

'And, Pol, get Khot or someone to dig out undetected missing boys' cases from 1985 to 2000, registered at the police station under which Shanti Villa falls. Remember, it might have been under a different station or chowki back then. Also, look for unsolved kidnapping cases of boys in the age group of ten to fourteen years, for the same period.'

'But, sir, I doubt the records will be easy to locate, because it's unlikely manual records of that period would have been digitised,' Pol said.

Motkar knew he was right. Digitisation of police station records was a project initiated in 2020 in Pune and it was a long-drawn process, oriented towards the present and future. Legacy data of the immediate past beginning 2015 had also been undertaken but it would be a long time before the project reached back to digitising manual records that were twenty-five to forty years old.

'Nothing about this case is easy, Pol, but we now know the buried skeleton is that of an eleven- to twelve-year-old boy. That's a fate no boy deserves,' PSI Motkar said. 'We owe it to this unknown child. Let's try our best.'

About ninety thousand children went missing in India every year. Less than half were traced. Those who remained missing probably ended up as victims of trafficking—as labour, beggars or, in the case of girls, as prostitutes.

It was a dismal scenario that these were just official statistics of those reported missing. Motkar reckoned, unreported cases could add at least another twenty-five per cent to the figures. Thirty-five to forty years ago the scenario had been bleaker still in terms of retrieving missing children. Systems, tools, priorities and, most importantly, reporting of cases back then were more skewed towards failure than success.

As Pol and Angre left for their assignments, Motkar wished his boss's attention was not divided between two cases. If they were to make any headway in the Shanti Villa case, they desperately needed a concrete lead—something specific—the identity of the victim, a witness, an established fact, or a particular incident or a peculiar set of circumstances that shed light on a possible motive.

As Saralkar had said, it was time to put the Welde siblings under the scanner, starting with Niharika Das. PSI Motkar dialled her number. Several rings passed, and just when Motkar was about to disconnect the call was answered.

'Yes, Inspector,' Niharika Das answered in a voice that sounded groggy.

'Madam, we need you to come to Pune within the next two days,' Motkar said straight away.

'Now what, Inspector? I gave you Urmila Attya's contact address. Come on!' she whined.

'We need to ask more questions to you in detail,' Motkar replied.

'Why can't you do it over a video call, Inspector?' Niharika Das asked. 'Anyway, I have answered your questions. I know nothing more about the matter, for heaven's sake. I have given you all the information—details of servants and all that you asked for …'

'It can't be done on video call, madam. You will have to appear in person.'

'What is this? A police state? I can't come now … I am unwell, Niharika Das remonstrated.

Motkar had had enough of her shrill protestations. 'Unless you are hospitalised with a life-threatening illness, for which I will require evidence, you will have to appear before us within seventy-two hours. You may bring along your husband to accompany you if you wish.'

'And who is going to pay for my travel? Pune Police?' she responded with helpless spite.

Motkar ignored her jibe. 'Please also get photograph albums you may have of your family, pertaining to the period between 1980 and 2000,' he slipped in the instruction deftly.

It had just struck him that one effective way of tracing the child who might have been connected with the Welde family was to simply look through family albums. There was a fairly good chance the boy might have been photographed with the Welde family on some occasion.

'What? Our family photos? Why do you need them?' Niharika Das demanded, sounding quite offended.

'Calm down, madam. Old photographs are a good tool to jog one's memory about people, events and places from long back. They act as a stimulus,' Motkar replied.

'But?'

'Trust me, madam. It will also make it easier for you to answer our questions. Let me know which date you will be here on,' Motkar said in a tone of finality and hung up.

He was relieved that Niharika Das hadn't protested further and he didn't have to reveal that the skeleton had turned out to be of an adolescent boy. That would be the ace up his sleeve when he questioned her. It would be interesting to see her reaction face to face.

'Have you personally listened to Komal Raina's call recordings?' CP Arundhati Kotwal asked Saralkar, seated across the table from her.

'Only certain excerpts that ASI Zirpe wanted me to hear and opine on,' Saralkar replied. 'But she has heard every word and we are making transcripts, if you would like to go through them.'

'But are you sure the recordings are not edited or manipulated?'

'I don't think so, but the call recordings have not been forensically examined. Komal Raina is not willing to submit the original device on which it was recorded because she does not trust the Pune Police, given her experience with the allegations inquiry team,' Saralkar said without mincing words.

CP Arundhati Kotwal gave an imperceptible nod. 'I will keep in mind her remarks about the inquiry team, which you have already reported to me. But that is not the point here. I am asking you whether we can rely on the recordings to conclusively rule out that she had any role in triggering DCP Khalap's actions in shooting his wife and himself?'

'There is nothing incriminating in these recordings. But it is she who has made those recordings. Maybe there is a call between Khalap and her that we do not know about yet, although that's highly unlikely. I will get that checked out,' Saralkar replied, 'I would also like to dig out which case DCP Khalap had helped Komal Raina with, to escape imprisonment.'

Arundhati Kotwal rolled her eyes over and nearly gritted her teeth. 'Stick to the present, Saralkar. To the case I have assigned you! Why do you want to go digging up dirt in the past?'

'Just to make sure that Komal Raina has not got away with anything heinous,' Saralkar replied.

The CP gave him a steady, unpleasant glance. 'Look, it's clear from the two inquiries instituted against Khalap—this rape, inquiry and the earlier custodial death inquiry—that he is thoroughly rotten. The more we go looking, the more dirt we will find. And all that dirt is going to stick to the Pune Police by association. Incidentally, I have checked out and found that his father, who rose to the post of Senior Inspector in his career, was equally rotten. So, rottenness seems to run in his genes.'

'Then what exactly are you asking me to do, madam?' Saralkar said, bristling.

'There you go again, Saralkar,' CP Kotwal rebuked him. 'I am not asking you to bury the body you have found. All I am asking you is to not go looking for more corpses. Contain the damage. The woman, Komal Raina, has accused DCP Khalap of rape, and it is good you have found nothing incriminating against her to suggest abetment of suicide. Leave it at that. A senior cop facing an inquiry kills his wife and turns his gun on himself is enough indictment of him as well as Pune Police. Now let us not complicate matters by digging up more murky stuff and advertising just how rotten he was.'

Saralkar shifted in his chair and counted up to five in his mind as CP Kotwal waited for his response with a mild glare. She wasn't asking him to scuttle his findings with regard to the investigation into Khalap's shooting. She was just telling him not to delve further into the background because it was not relevant to the current case.

The question was whether Komal Raina had directly driven, blackmailed or had been in any way responsible for Khalap pulling the trigger on his wife and himself. That was the scope of the investigation in the context of Khalap's shooting, which Kotwal had not asked him to suppress. Then, why was he chafing because the CP had asked him to leave well alone the purported crime of Komal Raina that Khalap had covered up years ago?

'OK, madam,' he replied finally. 'If DCP Khalap succumbs, I won't probe any further, but things might be different if he lives.'

CP Kotwal smirked. 'DCP Khalap will have bigger problems on his hands if he survives. He will be charged with murder, in addition to allegations of rape and custodial death.'

ASI Sanika Zirpe had spent the first half of the day transcribing the recordings made by Komal Raina. Thereafter, she had played certain excerpts for Saralkar, which she felt it was important for him to hear, before his meeting with the CP.

Once that was done, she had treated herself to lunch at a nearby restaurant with a colleague. It was a break from the usual canteen food. Sometimes, Sanika Zirpe wished she had a boyfriend. A year ago, she had parted ways with her beau of three years. He had been a nice, normal young man, doing well in his chosen career as a catering contractor, besides being a volleyball coach.

In fact, it had been volleyball that had brought them together, since Sanika Zirpe herself had played state and nationals, just as her boyfriend had. But she had never been in love with him, nor he with her. And then she had realised he had started feeling awkward that she was a policewoman. It had come through in little ways, and from the fact that he had not even proposed they get engaged or married, even after three years together.

Then, one day, he had hesitantly told her that his parents were not comfortable with the idea of their daughter-in-law being a policewoman. What she had read between the lines was that he too was not kicked about the notion of his wife being a cop.

She had stopped seeing him, then told him forthrightly that she had no intention of leaving her job in the police force and that he better look for someone else. Inevitably they had parted ways. Yet she missed his company sometimes, even now—going to movies, spending evenings together, chatting, holding hands and just doing something else in life other than police work.

Today was just the kind of afternoon when she would have liked to take half a day off and spend it lazing around, chatting with a boyfriend—a welcome break from work, from the disillusioning wretchedness that murder cases often triggered. And from the numbing tediousness and frustration of crime investigation, the relentless grind, in the hope that the insipidity would give way to excitement.

Sanika Zirpe had been loath to return to work, but where else could she go? And so, she had returned to her desk. She had plenty of threads to pick up. Of that there was no dearth, but she just wasn't in the mood. Maybe she ought to go home and take a nap, then go to the police sports complex and play volleyball. There was always some team practising in the evening and she could join in. That would cheer her up perhaps.

Of course, it was possible Saralkar or Motkar would look for her and find her missing. So be it, she decided. What's the worst that could happen? She got up to leave.

Her phone rang just that very moment. Sanika looked irritably at her mobile, surprised to see that it was from Rajat Mali, the architect who was redeveloping Shanti Villa. She had already handed him over the paperwork to resume work on the site the previous day, as Saralkar had instructed. Why was he calling now? She had half a mind to ignore his call, but then decided to take it anyway.

'Yes?' she said.

'Zirpe madam, this is Rajat Mali. I am trying to get in touch with Saralkar saheb, but he is not reachable,' a high-pitched, jittery voice fell on her ears.

'He must be busy. What is it? I will pass on your message,' Sanika Zirpe replied curtly.

'Oh!' Rajat Mali said, as if unsure what to do next. 'Madam, the thing is … we … we resumed work this morning … and … found another one!'

'You found another what?'

'Another … another skeleton, madam … under the other lawn platform …' Rajat Mali replied as if confessing to murder.

In that moment, all the ennui ASI Sanika Zirpe had felt flew out of the window!

19

Senior Inspector Saralkar was not prone to being alarmist, but sirens were going off in his head as he watched the Forensics team conduct a careful search in and around the pit, where the second skeleton had been unearthed. It was almost dark, and the excavation would have to be called off for the day.

'Could there be more bodies?' he finally gave voice to the alarm sounding in his brain.

Both Motkar and Zirpe, who had been flanking him, were startled by his remark. 'Is that what you suspect, sir?' Motkar asked.

'We hadn't expected a second skeleton. Now, who knows what we are dealing with?' Saralkar said. 'Maybe there are more. Why wait for more unpleasant surprises? Let's get the remaining portion of the plot excavated.'

It was a sensible idea but a scary thought. 'You are right, sir, but I really hope we don't find any other skeletons,' Motkar remarked.

'Neither do I, Motkar,' Saralkar snapped. 'I just want to ascertain the nature of the crime and the criminal we need to go looking for. Two bodies could be a double murder, but more bodies may suggest multiple crimes and perhaps a particular type of crime.'

'Do you mean like the Nithari killings, sir?' Zirpe asked with a shudder.

She was referring to the infamous 2006 case in which decomposed remains of several children who had gone missing over the last few years were found in a house in Nithari village, Noida, in the state of Uttar Pradesh. The house belonged to Maninder Singh Pandher, a Chandigarh-based businessman, and he, along with his resident servant, Surinder Koli, were initially convicted and even sentenced to death.

The case had caused quite a stir. Pandher and Koli were suspected to have killed thirty-one children in all. Among the many allegations they faced were murder, sexual crimes against the children, cannibalism and organ trade.

Amidst the public frenzy, the case had first been investigated by the local Noida Police and then by India's premier investigative agency, the Central Bureau of Investigation. But side by side, there had been a vigorous and lurid media trial, constantly building pressure on all the authorities.

The condemned men were declared guilty much before the courts did. There had been twists and turns galore. In fact, Surinder Koli had received a last-minute reprieve, just days before he was scheduled to be hanged, not once but twice.

'Let's hope there is nothing half as awful that we find here, Zirpe,' Saralkar said curtly. 'And by the way, do you know Pandher and Koli were acquitted by the Allahabad High Court in 2023, after having their convictions upheld earlier even by the Supreme Court of India?'

'What?'

'Yes. The Allahabad High Court found there was no credible evidence against them in some cases, except for their confessional statements. Imagine, what if they had been hanged many years earlier?'

ASI Zirpe looked bewildered. 'Sir, you mean they were not guilty of killing those children?' she asked.

Saralkar shrugged. 'If they weren't, then it means the Nithari killings cases still remains unsolved. Because someone killed those children, didn't they? Anyway, let's focus on our case and make sure it does not remain undetected.'

'So, should I ask the team to dig up the entire unexcavated area of the plot?' PSI Motkar asked.

Saralkar nodded gravely. 'Yes, we need to get it all done tomorrow. Meanwhile, I will speak to the Forensics unit to get cracking on the second set of remains. The sooner we get the analysis, the better.'

'What are we going to do now, Aditya?' Pallavi Khalap said to her brother.

'It depends ...' Aditya replied.

They had cremated their mother two days before and conducted the other rituals. There had just been a handful of relatives and neighbours in attendance. Most acquaintances had kept away, given the circumstances of the death.

Their mother had one surviving brother, who was settled abroad with his family. They had chosen not to come. DCP Khalap had two sisters, both of whom had snapped ties with him many years ago after Khalap had deprived them of a share in their father's property. His colleagues had not attended either.

'Depends on what?' she asked.

Their eyes met and said things they dared not speak of.

'I am scared Aditya …' Pallavi said with soft dread. 'I am so scared …'

He moved closer to her and clasped her hands. 'Why are you afraid? I am there, no? I will take care of you, Pallavi … of everything …'

'But what will people …'

'Shh … Pallavi, we haven't done anything wrong! OK? It's not our fault …'

'Mum's gone and Dad is going to hate us,' Pallavi said, her voice cracking.

Aditya's face and voice both turned harsh. 'We will worry about that when the time comes. He has his own sins to answer for, first.'

'What do you think Dad will tell them when he regains consciousness?' Pallavi asked, putting her head on Aditya's shoulder.

'Even the doctors don't know what state he will be in if he regains consciousness,' Aditya remarked. 'They don't know if he will be able to talk, walk or do anything at all.'

They sat quietly for a few minutes, contemplating the complicated future they were faced with and what they had done.

'The police know that we have something to hide, Aditya. I can feel their suspicions like a huge spider crawling over me. I can't bear this entire situation anymore,' Pallavi suddenly said, holding him tighter.

He put his arms around her, then kissed her on her forehead, then on her cheek …

The Shanti Villa skeletons case exploded in the media at prime time on the very evening the second set of bones were found. Saturation coverage continued the next day, reinforced by front-page headlines in newspapers. The news went viral on social media too.

It had been a minor miracle that the discovery of the first skeleton had remained under wraps, possibly because the coverage of a political scandal had peaked around the time and then because of the DCP Khalap case. This was due to the nature of the crime and the involvement of a Pune cop, who had been in the news just two weeks earlier, facing a rape inquiry.

But as the DCP Khalap story began running out of steam, mainly because the Pune Police had managed the herculean task of ensuring no leaks happened, the media had gleefully pounced on initially unconfirmed reports of a skeleton having been found in a posh neighbourhood and swarmed to the spot.

Soon, given the scale of the police activity, the Shanti Villa surroundings had turned into a media circus, despite the cops neither confirming nor denying any details. Resourceful reporters had soon dug out the bare bones of the goings-on, and the very fact that the site was going to be excavated to look for more corpses, had further fed the media frenzy.

Two individuals who had so far remained unaware of the discoveries at Shanti Villa like the rest of the general public suddenly had the fact brought home to them. One of them who had lived his life fearing this very moment. He felt his blood run cold, as if ice would start forming in his veins any moment. He choked on the morsel of food he had just put in his mouth and was seized by a prolonged bout of coughing and gagging. Such was the violence of his shock that he half expected to die, vomiting out his lungs and intestines. His name was Adinath Khubba.

The other individual felt a terrific jolt, even though he had been anticipating that the chickens would come home to roost someday. It had already remained hidden far longer than he had imagined. All the accumulated wisdom of mankind, of religions, of philosophies warned that no crime would go unpunished. The perpetrator always paid—with constant torment of the soul, with unexpected consequences, with sins visiting upon self or someone close!

Navnath Shinde had experienced it. Wasn't the cancer diagnosis a manifestation of exactly that? And now, this double shock in the last few weeks, just like a bad omen! Surely, it couldn't all be a coincidence.

'What do you mean you are not hungry?' Jyoti looked at her husband, more than usually puzzled. She had never known him to refuse the dish she had made for dinner—ragda patties.

Saralkar did not stir from his sprawled position on the sofa, his legs resting on the handrest of the single-seater next to it. 'I'll have it after a while,' he said. 'But you go ahead.'

Jyoti watched the slight frown on his face and the clenching on one side of his jaw. 'You can talk to me sometimes about your cases, you know ...'

He squinted at her. 'What does that mean? I am not disturbed or anything. I am just not hungry yet.'

'That is your fourth peg,' she observed. 'On an empty stomach with no munchies.'

'So?' Saralkar grunted. 'Don't try your amateur psychoanalysis on me!'

'Must you always try to be all macho?' Jyoti asked him in a tone calculated to rile him.

Saralkar sat up and gave her an annoyed look. 'I am not being macho. I am just being myself, Jyoti … I have been a policeman for over half my life. It'll take more than a few skeletons to bother me.'

He took a sip of his rum and coke, as if to make a point.

'I'll eat when I am hungry.'

Jyoti had helped herself and started eating. 'It's nice and hot. You should have it right away. Will drive away your blues faster than all the Old Monk in the world.'

'I don't drink to drive away my blues or cope with stress,' he replied, bristling a bit.

'I seem to remember you did once upon a time, didn't you?' Jyoti replied evenly.

Saralkar scowled at the reminder of a phase about eight to nine years ago when he had started binge drinking.[3] But he had stopped that the moment he realised what a fool he was being. Now he drank perhaps a few times a month, that too only when he felt like it. It was rare to be the kind of drinker he was—neither regular nor social, but completely random.

'That was to cope with you, not work,' he retorted.

'Really! If I had turned to drinking to cope with you, I'd have liver cirrhosis by now, you know,' Jyoti said smugly.

Saralkar narrowed his eyes, took another sip, yet could not come up with a cutting rejoinder. 'All right! Stop chewing my

---

3 Read *The Murder of Sonia Raikkonen*.

brain. I'll join you for ragda patties right away!' he said, then heaved himself up and ambled over to the dining table.

'That's like a good boy,' Jyoti said, mighty pleased with herself. She quickly prepared a plate for him.

Saralkar took his first spoonful and immediately felt better. His wife was right. Sometimes a morsel of food did far more in elevating the mood than an entire bottle of liquor.

'How is it?' Jyoti asked, wiggling her eyebrows a few times.

'Too soon to dish out compliments. Let me have a few more bites first,' Saralkar said, relishing the taste.

'As if you ever compliment without being prompted!' Jyoti ribbed him.

'Nice,' he said, licking his lips.

'Oh, come on, it's better than nice. It's delicious, isn't it?'

Saralkar nodded with his mouth full. 'Can't deny that ...' he began saying, and just then the phone rang.

He grunted, then clicked his tongue and reached out for his mobile, half expecting it to be the CP or some journalist wanting to get an inside scoop on the Shanti Villa skeletons. But it was neither.

'Yes, Shaikh,' he said, taking the call from the constable posted at the hospital.

'Sir, DCP Khalap saheb regained consciousness about fifteen minutes ago. The nurses have informed the junior doctors on duty. The senior doctor is also on the way,' Constable Shaikh informed him.

'Good. I'll be there soon. Tell the senior doctor to call me as soon as they finish examining DCP Khalap,' Saralkar said. 'And you call Inspector Rajguru and tell him that I am reaching the hospital shortly and need him there too.'

He disconnected and threw a glance at Jyoti, who was eyeing him vexedly. 'Don't tell me the call of duty is stronger than the taste of my ragda patties!'

Saralkar hurriedly began gobbling up the contents of his plate and said between bites, 'I have to leave pronto, Jyoti. What if DCP Khalap sinks back into unconsciousness. Damn it!'

Jyoti made a face. 'I really ought to divorce you, you unappreciative man,' she said. 'Want me to pack some for Khalap? I guarantee you that'll keep him from losing consciousness.'

Saralkar was too busy finishing the food to respond. He had to get dressed and leave. Why was he made this way, he wondered. Why couldn't he be like one of those people who felt no need to scramble; who didn't go around carrying the feeling that the world depended solely on them doing their jobs?

'I am going to have some more when I get back. Don't tuck them into the fridge,' he said and rushed inside to change. Jyoti didn't seem placated in the least.

A few minutes later, just as he was putting on his shoes, she remarked, 'I am going to call 100 and report you for drinking and driving the moment you leave.'

Saralkar grinned. 'Stop sulking. Does not suit you.' Then he did something he rarely ever did before leaving the house. He kissed his wife. Before Jyoti could recover from this pleasant surprise, he had left.

Twenty minutes later, Saralkar was at the hospital. The senior doctor had called about ten minutes earlier, while he had been driving.

'I am about to reach. Don't leave,' Saralkar had told him and disconnected the call. Now, they were face to face. Inspector Rajguru had also arrived.

'What's his condition, doctor?' Saralkar asked Dr Kaushal, the senior neurosurgeon in attendance.

'Still critical but I think he'll pull through now,' Dr Kaushal replied.

'Preliminary assessment of his faculties?' Saralkar asked.

'The patient is responding to visual and verbal stimulus but his answers are in gestures or monosyllables with some slurring. About his motor functions, I suspect there is some impairment, but whether it is temporary or permanent will be clear only after a few days,' the doctor replied.

'Is there a danger of him slipping back into unconsciousness?' Saralkar queried.

'It does not look likely but cannot be ruled out altogether,' Dr Kaushal said, looking at his watch.

'Well, then I must make haste and ask the patient a few urgent questions,' Saralkar said and turned to enter the ICU from which the doctor had emerged.

Dr Kaushal hesitated, then said, 'Can't it wait till the morning, Inspector? I'd like to keep the patient under observation for a few hours since he has just regained consciousness.'

'It is a sensitive case, Dr Kaushal. I can't afford not to do my job right away, if there is even a slight chance that DCP Khalap might succumb. Unless you can guarantee me that no complications will arise and he won't suddenly take a turn for the worse.'

Dr Kaushal shook his head unhappily. 'Even the best doctor cannot say that for sure. But please, the patient is not yet in a condition to undergo any sustained questioning. So just five to ten minutes is what I would advise,' he said. 'Also, it is quite likely that at the moment he has no memory of the incident. It happens sometimes after brain injury, so please don't pressurise him.'

It irritated Saralkar. 'Of course I won't, doctor! You can join me if you wish,' he replied, although he hoped the doctor wouldn't volunteer to accompany him.

'No, no, Inspector, no offence meant. I am just striking a note of caution,' Dr Kaushal replied defensively.

Saralkar gave him a curt nod and began walking towards the ICU, then stopped. 'One more thing, Dr Kaushal. Please tell your entire staff that DCP Khalap's son and daughter are not to be intimated that he has regained consciousness without clearing it with me first. Even if they happen to call the hospital and ask.'

Dr Kaushal frowned. 'But for how long, Inspector? They are his family. Won't it be unethical?'

Saralkar's eyes flashed at him. He struggled to keep his temper. 'Dr Kaushal, I respect your ethics, but let me ask you this—did the patient ask for his family or request you to inform them?'

'No, he didn't ...'

'Is his condition so critical that he might die any minute?'

'No, I already told you.'

'Correct! It's almost midnight now, so will it make a big difference if his family is informed tomorrow morning, instead of right now?'

The doctor shuffled uneasily. 'Well, I guess that's OK but usually we inform the patient's family immediately ...'

'He is anything but a usual patient, doctor. He is accused of rape, custodial death and murdering his wife. And even if his guilt has not been established, neither has been his innocence,' Saralkar said and strode towards the ICU.

20

Even the most despicable human being or hardened criminal appeared pitiable and deserving of compassion when they lay suffering, writhing or defenceless on a hospital bed. That was the first thought that crossed Saralkar's mind as his eyes fell on DCP Khalap.

He lay with his eyes closed, his head draped in bandages. The opening and closing of the door when Saralkar and Rajguru entered didn't elicit any reflex reaction. The patient's eyes didn't open, nor was there any other hint of awareness. It was an ordinary, round face, wheatish complexion, with a longer-than-normal bulbous, fleshy nose. Although there was a stubble, it appeared as if Khalap did not sport a moustache or beard regularly. The officer was a few years older than Saralkar and closer to retirement, but he didn't look it.

'DCP Khalap,' Saralkar called out softly.

There was no response. There were three policemen in the room at that moment—Khalap, Rajguru and Saralkar—but a strange silence ensued for several seconds before Saralkar spoke again. 'DCP Khalap,' he said in a louder voice.

The patient stirred slightly, but his eyes remained shut.

Saralkar gently put his hand on the man's arm and shook him. 'DCP Khalap,' he called out for a third time.

This time Khalap's eyes opened halfway and he stared with a disoriented gaze for a couple of seconds. Then his eyelids began drooping again.

'DCP Khalap, I am Senior Inspector Saralkar and this is my colleague, Inspector Rajguru,' Saralkar quickly said to nudge him into wakefulness.

Khalap's eyes opened wider, but his demeanour didn't change. There was no acknowledgement or any sign that Khalap had registered what Saralkar had said. Saralkar repeated himself, trying to figure out if anything was getting through. He also looked out for any sign that suggested pretence, but Khalap's eyes refused to focus, as if he was in a stupor.

'How are you feeling?' Saralkar asked neutrally.

No response.

'DCP Khalap,' Saralkar persisted. 'Are you aware you are in hospital?'

The patient's eyelids moved in a manner that felt like a nod.

Saralkar repeated the question just to be sure. This time, he heard a grunt-like sound from Khalap and again the eyelids made a nod-like movement.

'Can you hear me properly?'

Khalap's lips moved as if mouthing a silent yes.

'And can you speak alright?'

Khalap's eyes closed and there was a slight shake of the head. 'No …' he said in a barely audible whisper.

Saralkar glanced at Inspector Rajguru to see his reaction to the conversation so far. He was surprised to see scepticism on his junior colleague's face.

'I see. Do you know why you are in the hospital and why we are here?' Saralkar asked, turning to Khalap again.

The eyes were still shut and Khalap did not respond. Saralkar was closely observing for reactions as also any slight movement from the patient. He let the seconds tick by, wondering if the silence would make Khalap uneasy enough to fidget or open his eyes.

'DCP Khalap?' he said after a couple of minutes.

Khalap's face twitched and he shook his head with palpable weariness.

'How is that possible?' Saralkar asked, his tone a little sharper than what he had used so far.

Khalap did not open his eyes but mumbled something.

Saralkar moved closer. 'Can you please repeat what you said?'

'I … am … blank …' DCP Khalap whispered as if it required all his energy to do so.

His speech sounded slurred to Saralkar's ears. Was it his imagination that the first time Khalap had replied, uttering the single word 'No', there hadn't been any slurring?

Saralkar wondered whether he should ask the senior policeman if he remembered that he had shot his wife or that she was dead? Instead, a better idea struck him and he framed the question differently. 'Do you wish to meet your wife?'

DCP Khalap's eyes suddenly fluttered open and a ripple seemed to run across his facial muscles. Saralkar watched with satisfaction as Khalap struggled to exercise control over the spontaneous reflexes of his mind and body. He glanced at Rajguru, who gave a nod of appreciation.

Clearly, DCP Khalap was not as blank as he had claimed to be a few minutes ago. Either the question had suddenly triggered a recollection of the incident, piercing through the trauma sustained, or DCP Khalap knew exactly what he had done but hadn't expected his wife to be alive—which had been implied in Saralkar's question.

'Doctor … please …' the patient mumbled, but this time his whisper was loud enough to be heard, although the slurring was still audible.

'Sure, DCP Khalap, I'll get the doctor. Please take rest. I will be back tomorrow,' Saralkar said, before walking out of the room with Rajguru.

'Dr Kaushal,' Saralkar said, rushing to the surgeon, once outside the ICU. 'You can inform his family if you wish to, but I have another request …'

'What is it, Inspector?' the doctor asked apprehensively.

'DCP Khalap is not to be told about his wife's death, even if he asks,' Saralkar said with emphasis. 'Please tell all your staff. I am sure you agree that the shock might be too much for the patient in his condition. Just in case the question of ethics troubles you again, doctor.'

'Yes, it might not be advisable,' Dr Kaushal agreed sheepishly.

'Also, I would like an early assessment of DCP Khalap's condition because I need to question him quite intensively in a day or two. I want to be sure he is not using his brain injury to stall us,' Saralkar said.

Dr Kaushal nodded. 'Yes, we will be putting him through brain scans and tests once we are sure he has stabilised in the next twenty-four hours. Till then he will be under observation.'

'Good,' Saralkar said and walked off. When they were some distance away in the corridor, he turned to Inspector Rajguru. 'Apart from Shaikh, get one more constable on duty. Make sure DCP Khalap's children are not permitted to meet him in the next twenty-four hours and there are no leaks to the media.'

'Yes, sir,' Rajguru replied.

'OK, I am leaving now,' Saralkar said, suddenly tired.

'Sir,' Inspector Rajguru said. 'Just one more thing …' He paused, as if hesitating.

'Yes, Rajguru.'

'I was going to call you up and inform you tomorrow. We received an anonymous tip this afternoon,' Rajguru said.

'About this case?' Saralkar asked, all ears.

'Yes, sir. I am not sure how credible it is but the letter we received claims that there is … something hanky-panky going on between DCP Khalap's son, Aditya, and daughter, Pallavi,' Rajguru said rather gingerly, as if he found it distasteful.

Saralkar felt his hair stand on end. This was the exact niggling suspicion, the spectre of which his own mind had raised, and which he had hesitated to entertain. 'By hanky-panky, do you … do you mean of a sexual nature?' he asked.

'Yes, sir …'

'Incest? Is that what the letter has suggested?' Saralkar asked.

Inspector Rajguru nodded. 'Yes, sir. It hints at incest.'

'Where is the letter?'

'I'll send it across, sir, but I can brief you about the exact contents right away,' Rajguru said.

'Go ahead!' Saralkar replied, with a feeling of curious squalidness and sordidness.

'Niharika!' Anshuman Das called out to his wife, who was showering in the bathroom. The couple had reached Pune around seven in the evening and checked into a hotel.

'Niharika!' Anshuman shouted again, a little louder, as he watched the news coverage on the television.

'What is it, Anshuman? Can't I even shower in peace?' Niharika replied, having finally heard him as she had just turned the shower off.

'You have to see this. Come out, right away … My God!' her husband's voice came through.

'For heaven's sake, I can't … I'll need another five minutes at least.'

Her husband came to the bathroom door and hollered. 'It's a news item, damn it. It won't wait for you … Come out … You have got to see this for yourself, urgently.'

Something in his tone prompted Niharika to quickly slip on a bathing gown and step out of the bathroom.

Anshuman was sitting on the edge of the bed and staring at the television. He turned around as he heard the bathroom door open. 'Look, they … they found another skeleton under the Shanti Villa lawns,' he said excitably. 'What the hell is going on?'

Niharika felt her legs wobble beneath her and her heart felt as if it had ceased functioning. She sank into the single-seater sofa and gaped, dumbstruck at the television.

'They are saying the bodies are of kids,' Anshuman said, in a voice filled with horror. 'Kids, dammit, kids. Who? How? Niharika?'

A cold dread engulfed Niharika. 'They'll arrest me tomorrow, Anshuman! They'll throw me in jail the moment I … I go for questioning. Let's go back to Goa. Let's go into hiding. I … I don't know anything. Please, Anshuman, I can't face this.'

She started trembling, as if she would crumble right there.

Her husband quickly went to her and held her close. This is the girl he had fallen in love with, and although the years had created fissures that were inevitable, there still was a residual glue of belonging that held them together.

'Tell me, Niharika, do … do you know something? Some terrible secret that has been impossible to share, even with me?' he asked his wife, his mind beginning to imagine spine-chilling scenarios.

His wife did not reply. The beats passed. Then Niharika began sobbing as if she were to be led to the gallows shortly!

'What's the status on the Shanti Villa tenants, Pol?' PSI Motkar asked, as soon as Pol and Angre walked into his cabin.

It was the kind of day when he had to be everywhere at the same time. Early morning, Motkar had first visited and discussed matters with the Excavation and Forensics teams at Shanti Villa, before they began digging up the rest of the plot. He would have to again drop by in the evening, or even earlier, depending on what fresh discoveries the team made as the day progressed. Motkar dreaded the thought of the plot throwing up more skeletons.

Equally important was the day-long interrogation of Niharika Das scheduled that day. And now, before that commenced, he had to get an update from Pol and Angre.

'We have managed to get in touch with most tenants, sir, and there is nothing suspicious or unusual to report so far,' Constable Pol said. 'Most seem to be ordinary folk, well-settled and at least appear above board.'

'I see. Did you ask them about any disturbing incidents during their stay or if they remember any reports of children going missing in the neighbourhood, back then?'

'Yes, sir. We did. Nobody seems to recollect anything like that,' Pol replied. 'Most of the tenants seem to remember their stay at Shanti Villa as pleasant and peaceful. They remember the senior Welde couple as being cordial but very particular about the rules the tenants were supposed to abide by. Some said that Shashank Welde would give them a list of dos and don'ts before agreeing to give them the house on rent. One of the rules was that tenants were strictly not to step into the lawns ever. In fact, one tenant told us and another confirmed that when the old couple travelled abroad to their son, they literally cordoned off the lawn and hung signs, as if to serve as a reminder to tenants, at all times.'

PSI Motkar felt his nerves tingling. Were the Weldes just being finicky, or did this not indicate that they wanted to eliminate even the remote possibility of anyone poking about the lawn for obvious reasons?

'I see. So even the children of the tenants would not be allowed to play in the lawns, I presume.'

'Sir,' the young constable Angre spoke before Pol did, then hesitated.

'Yes, Angre?'

'Sir, it's odd, but I noticed that almost all the tenants to whom the Weldes rented houses did not seem to have small children of school-going age at that time. They were either very young couples, who had no kids, or middle-aged people—bank managers or LIC officers or people like that who were posted in Pune away from their families. Then later, there were a few young working professionals. In all the tenants we have talked to so far, I came across just two couples who had children—one who had a baby born while they were tenants at Shanti Villa, and a couple who had a college-going son. So, neither the baby nor the college-going boy were likely to even try playing on the lawn.'

Motkar hadn't expected such an astute observation from the young constable. It meant he had applied himself to the job. Yet it was too early to give him a pat on the back.

'OK. We need to ask the house broker, Uttam Padwal, about this. Whether old man Welde actively refused tenants who had young children as well as about the lawn condition he imposed,' Motkar said. 'Any other insights or observations from the tenants? What did they have to say about senior Welde, his wife and the sister too?'

'Sir, most tenants described them as polite and formal but aloof. The old man would chat once in a while, but Mrs Welde almost never interacted with the tenants. The son, Sunit, came on a visit every two or three years, while Niharika Das and family dropped by for short stays every few months. That was the only time things were lively, most tenants said,' Pol replied. 'No one mentioned the sister Urmila, although one or two older tenants did remember her.'

Motkar felt disappointed. 'How many tenants have you not been able to contact, or are untraceable?' he asked.

'About four or five, sir,' Pol replied.

'How much more time are you going to require?'

'Two more days, sir, I think. If we still can't, then we'll have to try other ways to trace them. Maybe some have moved abroad …'

'What about the boys who were involved in some fracas? There was a police complaint and counter-complaint …'

'Sir, all that we know so far is that they were working for two companies of the same corporate group. The boys had given references from the HR department of their companies, along with office addresses, etc., not their residential addresses.'

'What about IDs?'

'Company ID cards ... We have contacted the companies concerned and they say they will take some time to get employee data because it's pretty old and neither of them is still employed in those organisations,' Pol replied.

'What are their names? Have you tried tracing them through their social media accounts?' Motkar asked.

Pol turned to the younger constable, as if indicating it was his turn to reply.

'Yes, sir, their names are Sambit Kumar and Kalpesh Mankad,' Angre said immediately. 'I have looked on Facebook and Instagram. I found Facebook accounts of quite a few people with those names, but none of them appear to be these two individuals ...'

'Have you tried LinkedIn? That's how ASI Zirpe traced one of the people she was looking for,' Motkar said. 'That's where you find profiles of most professionals.'

Angre nodded. 'I'll check it, sir.'

Motkar glanced at his watch. It was about time Niharika Das showed up. Why hadn't she? Policemen were supposed to keep suspects waiting, not the other way around. He felt mildly irritated.

'And, Pol, why haven't you been able to trace the police complaint about the incident between those fellows—Sambit, Kalpesh and a watchman from the neighbourhood?' he said with a mild reproach in his voice. 'Why is it taking so long?'

'Sir, there is something odd about it. Either there were no FIRs registered despite claims or perhaps the complaints were only treated as non-cognisable offences,' Constable Pol said, 'Also, there is no record of any chargesheets being filed after investigations, which strengthens the possibility that there were no FIRs in the first place.'

'Hmm … there is also a third and fourth possibility, Pol. One, that a case closure form could have been filed subsequently, if the parties decided to mutually withdraw complaints,' Motkar said. 'Or the complaints and related records could have gone missing deliberately. That's not unheard of.'

Constable Pol nodded. There were innumerable instances of old records, even evidence, going missing and the reasons ranged from police incompetence to corruption.

'I'll get them to check if there are any closure reports for which FIRs are missing,' he said. 'But to find FIRs that have completely disappeared all those years ago … it won't happen quickly, sir, given that it was a minor matter.'

'I know. You could also try and find out the names of the station staff and the officer in-charge in that period,' Motkar replied. 'If any one of them is still around, maybe we could jog their memories.'

Constable Pol was unconvinced that it would be of any help, but nodded nevertheless. Angre and he made their exit.

PSI Motkar cast a glance at the wall clock. There was still no sign of Niharika Das. Had she bluffed to him? She had called the previous morning and said she was reaching Pune that evening and would be at the Homicide Unit by 9.45–10 a.m. this morning. Where the hell was she, then? His boss wouldn't be too pleased if he reached and found that Niharika Das hadn't turned up for questioning.

Motkar clenched his teeth and began calling her number. Her phone was switched off. Motkar then began dialling her husband Anshuman Das's number. He was almost relieved to hear the rings. Anshuman Das's phone wasn't switched off but it wasn't answered either.

Motkar felt his anxiety grow. What was he to make of this? Had Niharika Das done a disappearing act, or was it just a delay arising out of nervousness or apprehension that people felt when appearing in front of the police? Why was her phone switched off, even though her husband's mobile wasn't? Just as he was deciding to call Anshuman Das again, his phone rang.

It was Niharika Das's husband calling. 'Hullo,' Motkar said, taking the call with alacrity. 'Mr Das, why isn't your wife here? Is she with you?'

'Hasn't Niharika reached your office?' Anshuman Das asked.

'What do you mean? Aren't you accompanying her? She was supposed to be here at 9.45 a.m. this morning. She called and told me she would be reaching Pune last evening,' Motkar said.

'Well, I am surprised. Let me try and contact her and get back to you,' Anshuman Das replied.

'Her phone is switched off, Mr Das. Or does she have another? Where is she staying? Rather both of you?'

'Well, Niharika was going to talk to her lawyer first. Maybe the lawyer advised her about something … I don't know. Let me try and get in touch with her or her lawyer,' Anshuman Das said rather tentatively and before Motkar could ask any more questions he hung up.

PSI Motkar chafed. There was definitely something wrong. Why was Niharika Das consulting a lawyer? Or had she gone into hiding or something? And if so, what did that mean? That she somehow knew the secret behind the skeletons discovered at Shanti Villa?

21

Rum had rarely given Saralkar a hangover and there was no reason to believe good old Old Monk would start inflicting one on him now. So, what explained that lousy, bilious, woozy, punishing feeling? As if neither standing, nor sitting, nor lying down would make the least difference to the sickly sensation he was experiencing. That it would simply be better if the human head were a detachable object, that could be kept aside for the day to let the rest of the body get by.

He had swallowed an antacid first, nibbled on the morning tea and biscuits that Jyoti had served, then slipped under the shower, taken his blood pressure medication, but none of it had helped in the least.

'What are you grinning at?' he asked his wife, who was giving him a knowing look.

'Nothing! You OK?' she asked, trying to keep a straight face.

'Fantastic!' he replied grudgingly, but even saying that seemed to worsen his condition. 'We got any cornflakes?' he asked.

It was his special hangover food, even though he had still not officially accepted he was suffering from one. Yet, the symptoms were close enough and cornflakes in milk was the only thing likely to make him feel better.

'No, it's a long, long time since you last had a hangover, so I hadn't stocked up,' Jyoti replied. 'But we'll have it delivered in no time.'

Saralkar groaned, while Jyoti was already dialling the provision store.

'It'll be here in five minutes,' she said after having finished ordering. 'And now that I know your hangover days are back, I'll make sure we don't run out of cornflakes ever again.'

'Shut up, Jyoti,' Saralkar said as his wife giggled.

He heard his mobile ring but made no attempt to take it. Instead, he said to Jyoti, 'If it's the CP on line, tell her I am dead.'

'It's Motkar,' his wife said, glancing at the caller ID.

For a few seconds, Saralkar baulked. Was Motkar calling because more skeletons had been found? It wasn't the kind of news he was feeling up to receiving in his present condition.

'You don't have to take every call, you know,' his wife said. 'Be kind to yourself sometimes.'

Her advice only prompted him to do the exact opposite. 'Hullo, yes, Motkar,' he said, bracing himself.

'Sir, morning! Niharika Das has not turned up for questioning. Her phone is unreachable and her husband told me she was first going to meet her lawyer,' Motkar said. 'Now ...'

'Slow down, Motkar,' Saralkar interrupted him, feeling greatly relieved that he wasn't calling to report more skeletons but about Niharika Das's non-appearance. 'So her husband's reachable but she isn't?'

'Yes, sir, and her lawyer just called a few minutes ago,' Motkar replied. 'Advocate Aradhana Shroff ...'

'Hmm,' Saralkar said. Advocate Aradhana Shroff was a well-regarded senior criminal lawyer. 'So, what did Advocate Shroff have to say?'

'Advocate Shroff wanted to first speak with you, sir, but I told her you were unavailable, so she finally deigned to speak to me,' Motkar said.

'Is that so? Well, where is her client?'

'Advocate Shroff asked me if her client is officially a suspect in this case because Niharika Das told her she apprehended arrest since we asked her to present herself within seventy-two hours,' Motkar continued. 'I told her that, in view of the fact that a second skeleton had been unearthed, lots of questions needed answers and hence she needed to be questioned because she was one of the owners.'

'And what was Shroff's response? Did she ask for an assurance that Das wouldn't be arrested or that her client should be questioned in her presence?' Saralkar asked.

He heard the bell ring and hoped the cornflakes ordered by Jyoti had arrived. In cornflakes with warm milk lay the antidote to his condition.

'Neither, sir. Advocate Shroff said her client was willing to be questioned through video conferencing but not in person. I asked her where exactly Niharika Das was. She responded by saying that she first needed our reply,' Motkar said. 'I said I'd have to check with you. What do you think we should do, sir?'

'Hmm. I'll call you back once I have had my breakfast, Motkar,' Saralkar replied after a moment's silence. 'I need to think this through.'

'Breakfast, sir?'

'Yes, Motkar. Cornflakes and warm milk! I know it's late and sounds strange but that's what I need. I'll call you soon.'

He hung up and gratefully accepted the bowl offered by his wife. Ten minutes later, he was feeling fifty per cent himself again. At least the itch to saw his head off had vanished. The cornflakes had worked.

'Bye,' Jyoti said as she got ready to step out of the house. 'See you in the evening and I hope you have learnt your lesson.'

He was too grateful to attempt a retort. He just gave a sheepish smile and dialled Motkar's number. 'Look, don't call Advocate Shroff back. Let's wait and watch what happens today. If we discover more skeletons, our case to question Niharika strengthens and it will get harder for her to deny appearing before us,' Saralkar said. 'Then we don't have to offer any assurances and she can go to court for anticipatory bail if she wishes to. But if we find nothing more today, then perhaps we can give a limited assurance and insist on her physical appearance before us.'

'Makes sense, sir, but what do I say to Advocate Shroff if she calls me again, before we find out the status?' Motkar asked.

'Tell her you have still not got a decision from me and that I am insisting on knowing Niharika's whereabouts.'

'OK, sir,' Motkar replied. 'Are you headed here now or Shanti Villa?'

'Neither, Motkar. DCP Khalap regained consciousness last night. I paid him a midnight visit but need to go again now. I also have to examine another lead that's come to light in the case,' Saralkar replied. 'Keep me posted. God forbid they find anything at Shanti Villa.'

He disconnected the phone on this note and looked at the missed calls and messages on his mobile. The CP seemed to have read the message he'd sent after getting back from hospital, updating her about DCP Khalap, but she had sent no remarks or instructions in response. PSI Rajguru had sent him a picture of the anonymous letter alleging incestuous relations between the Khalap siblings.

Saralkar hated reading attachments on the phone but he tapped on the picture and enlarged it. It was handwritten, with an attempt probably made to disguise the styling. The letter writer claimed to have heard about the incestuous relationship from Khalap's son himself. It seemed the consensual relationship had been established about a year ago, and Aditya claimed he and his sister, Pallavi, were in love. That they would frequently meet at the house of a friend of Aditya who remained unnamed.

The letter writer claimed that DCP Khalap's wife had somehow learnt about it and tried to counsel the children about how wrong it was and that if their father found out, it could lead to frightening consequences. Aditya had however said he would not be cowed down, and if his father came in the way, he would deal with it and not take it lying down. Without offering any proof, the letter writer suggested that the tragedy at the Khalap home was probably triggered by this incendiary, incestuous relationship.

Saralkar closed his eyes and regarded the contents of the letter in his mind. Was it a letter just written by some crank or by someone who genuinely had relevant information to share? In case it was the former, it was unflattering for Saralkar to note that a crank and he had shared suspicions along the same lines. It offered no solace that the crank and he might have arrived at the same thought, through differing routes—Saralkar through instinct and the crank through some poisonous psychological aberration.

If, on the other hand, the letter was from someone who genuinely thought it necessary to bring this information to the notice of the police, then it prised open a line of inquiry that Saralkar had pursued only half-heartedly so far.

What was sibling incest really? An impure, unacceptable perversion by two individuals of what was supposed to be a pure, non-sexual relationship? Or was it simply abuse and exploitation perpetrated by the older sibling—by transgressing the lines of love and affection and corrupting its nature? Or was it some emotional and physical accident of unnatural attraction that just happened between two siblings under certain conditions—something that was tainted in our perceptions but not theirs?

Saralkar had seen enough of human nature to know that everything about existence was deeply complicated and messed up. There was no point in delving into the rights and wrongs of the possible incest between the Khalap siblings, except whether it had a direct bearing on the murder-suicide in the Khalap household.

For instance, did the siblings shoot their parents and stage the murder-suicide? Or was it the issue of incest that had led to the flare-up that night at the Khalap house and not DCP Khalap's misdeeds? Or had one thing led to another and somehow culminated in the shooting?

Saralkar knew that as an investigator he had to satisfy himself with all lines of inquiry before reaching a final conclusion. It was time to confront the siblings on this delicate matter.

—

ASI Sanika Zirpe's phone buzzed. It was Constable Khot calling.

'Yes, Pol?'

'Madam, we have just traced one of the other maidservants who worked for the Weldes—Baidabai Ladkat. She's got a very interesting bit of information,' Constable Khot said.

Sanika Zirpe consulted the notes lying on her table. 'Baidabai Ladkat is the maid who had the reputation for lifting things—kleptomania, right?' she asked.

'Yes, madam, the same one, although we haven't asked her about that, naturally. She moved to the Katraj area many years ago and has now been running a vegetable vending business for long. The family also owns a small shop selling general items,' Khot said.

'So why are you calling from there? Why don't you get Baidabai here? Tell her there is nothing to be scared of and we will drop her back,' Sanika Zirpe said.

'Madam, she says she cannot leave the shop unattended. Her daughter-in-law only comes after lunch to take over from her while her husband and son are out at work,' Khot explained.

'Alright! What's the interesting bit of information she's got to share?' Zirpe asked.

'I'll put her on the phone, madam, so she can repeat what she told us,' Khot replied.

ASI Zirpe heard him speak to the woman, 'Baidabai, our madam is on the phone. Tell her about the boy.'

Sanika Zirpe's alertness spiked manifold the moment she heard the word 'boy'.

And old woman's scratchy voice now came on the line. 'Hullo …' it said gingerly. 'I am Baidabai Ladkat, madam …'

She paused, unsure whether to proceed.

'Hullo, Baidabai, this is ASI Sanika Zirpe. You worked for the Welde household many years ago, right?'

'Yes … yes, madam, but … but I had to leave, since my husband and I set up a vegetable stall in Katraj area,' the old woman replied haltingly.

'Do you remember Tayabai Mhaisal?'

'Yes … yes, but I haven't met her in a very long time,' the old woman answered.

'Never mind. Now go on and tell me what you told Constable Khot.'

Baidabai Ladkat cleared her throat. 'Well, Constable Khot asked me if I remembered any eleven-to-twelve year old boy who might have visited or frequented the bungalow back then and I … I remembered that, about the time I was going to leave, Welde madam employed a young boy who was to serve as a full-time help.'

Sanika Zirpe felt a chill run up her spine. 'Tell me more about the boy, Baidabai.'

'Welde madam told me that now that I was leaving, I should train the boy in tasks like sweeping, dusting, hanging clothes to dry, etc. She said she was going to need full-time help for light chores and tasks around the house and he would be staying in the small storeroom at the back of the house,' Baidabai said.

'Oh, do you remember his name and where he came from? And how old the boy was?' ASI Zirpe asked.

'He spoke only Hindi. I think he was from somewhere—UP, Bihar. I don't remember his name, but he seemed to be just about eleven-to-twelve years old,' Baidabai said.

'OK, what happened then? Did you train him?'

'Yes, for a few days, madam, although I wondered how a child that small could do all the work. No wonder he ran away in a month or two,' Baidabai said.

'What? How do you know that? Who told you?' ASI Zirpe asked.

'Welde madam herself told me when I went to visit her a few weeks later. I had borrowed money from her when we were shifting to Katraj. I had promised to return the amount in a couple of months,' Baidabai said. 'That's when I noticed no sign of the boy, but a new maidservant was in place, so I inquired. Welde madam told me the boy was always falling sick and avoiding work under some pretext. She complained he was very unhygienic and sloppy. So, one day, Welde sir gave him a walloping. He ran away the same night, and they thought it was good riddance.'

There was a certain ominous vibe to what Baidabai had just narrated.

'Are you sure of this, Baidabai?' ASI Zirpe asked.

'Sure of what, madam? I don't understand,' the old lady asked.

'That this eleven-to-twelve year old boy actually worked for the Weldes and then ran away? Because no one else has told us about this till now?'

'Why would I make something like this up, madam?' Baidabai said, sounding offended and hurt. 'I swear on my children, I met that boy, trained him and I have just told you what Welde madam narrated to me about him having run away! And if you don't believe me, I even have a small object that belonged to the boy.'

Sanika Zirpe's heart did a double flip. 'What object? How come?'

Baidabai Ladkat suddenly fell silent and ASI Zirpe heard Constable Khot's voice asking the old lady, 'What's wrong, Baidabai?'

She then heard what sounded like a brief wrangle between them and finally Constable Khot came on the line, 'Madam, I'll call you back. Just give me fifteen minutes ...'

'What happened, Khot? She was telling me something and stopped abruptly mid-sentence. She said she had something that belonged to the boy in her possession?'

'Yes, yes, madam, Baidabai said something inadvertently and got upset. Just give me some time and I'll call back with more information.'

ASI Zirpe sighed. 'Alright, but quick. Tell her she's got to talk, to help us! There is nothing else she has to worry about. We are not after her.'

But she realised that Constable Khot had already disconnected. Zirpe sat back in her chair. Was this the elusive breakthrough? Was this boy one of the skeletons they had found? She had to stop her thoughts running away with her, even as they tempted her into spinning theories. But she knew better than to do that. She had to first gather facts, find corroborating circumstantial evidence, and only then could any credible conjectures and suppositions emerge.

Fifteen minutes later, her phone rang. 'Yes Khot? What upset Baidabai?'

'Madam, I think we really might be on to something,' Constable Khot replied. 'Baidabai reconfirmed everything about the boy again and she's handed over the object she claims belonged to him.'

'What is the object?'

'It is a wooden spinning top!'

It took ASI Zirpe a few seconds to register. 'A wooden spinning top? You mean the toy that kids used to play with?'

'Yes, madam, exactly. Of course, kids rarely play with spinning tops these days, but it was once a very popular and cheap toy, especially in villages,' Constable Khot said.

Khot was right. Once upon a time, perhaps even thirty to forty years ago, spinning tops was a pastime, particularly for adolescents. Winding a thick thread around the body of the top, children would skilfully release it and watch it whirl around on the nail affixed to its base. The longer it spun, the faster it whirled, the more elated the child felt. It was indeed a toy of simpler times but much of human history was that of simpler times, which ended forever only with the coming of the digital age.

'So how come Baidabai has it, and why did she abruptly stop talking to me on the phone?' ASI Zirpe asked.

'Because she got flustered and ashamed, madam,' Constable Khot explained. 'She stole the top—her kleptomania was at play. She does not even remember how and when she did it, like with everything else she picks up even today. At least, she claims that. Back then Baidabai often got into trouble and would get accused of thieving. She said she did not know why she'd do it, but then someone counselled her to start returning things the moment she realised what she'd done. She says she'd decided to return the top to the boy too and carried it with her when she went to meet Mrs Welde, but learnt he had already gone.'

PSI Zirpe gave a gasp. It was unbelievable and sad—yet wasn't it Providence that the existence of this boy had come to light only because of a maid suffering from kleptomania who had picked and kept this toy? 'So, she kept the top all these years? That's a little hard to believe,' Zirpe said.

'Madam, it has become a fetish with her. All the things she has ever picked up, she either tries to return them. If she cannot do that due to a fear of repercussion, she keeps them in her trunks without ever using them,' Khot replied. 'She actually showed me the trunks and they are full of tiny objects and trinkets.'

'But how is she so sure she stole the top from that boy? After all, it's been over thirty years,' Zirpe asked. It was her job to be sceptical.

'She appears to be very sure, madam. Also, there is a roughly scratched name on the top surface. It is very hard to read but since the top has been lying unused I think we might be able to decipher what the name is, if we take a photo and enlarge it,' Khot said.

This almost seemed too good to be true. Were they really inching closer to identifying the victim? Again, she forced herself not to exult prematurely. 'OK, bring it over. We will give it to the Forensics team to see if they can make out what the name on it is,' Zirpe said and disconnected.

She felt a sudden surge of anger. What did it say about a family that tried to employ a child so young as a full-time house help? Even if the fact couldn't be judged by the standards of today, surely even thirty to thirty-five years ago, employing a child was a rather regressive idea for an educated middle-class family, wasn't it? Whatever the reason, whatever the excuses, it wasn't done!

But of course, the main question was: had they murdered and buried that unlucky child?

22

'I ALREADY TOLD YOU, SARALKAR, I AM BLANK! TOTALLY!' DCP Khalap said. His eyes did not meet the senior inspector's. Instead, he stared at a distant corner of the hospital room.

It was nearly impossible to prove with hundred per cent certainty that a man with a head injury could not have total loss of recollection about the traumatic event in which the damage was sustained. The human brain was a deeply complicated organ, with an intricate interplay of neurological and psychological factors that impaired memory.

'Your injuries are unlikely to have impaired your memory, doctors tell me,' Saralkar remarked patiently.

Khalap did not reply, nor did he shift his gaze.

'What do you remember?' Saralkar asked, then modified the question. 'What is the last thing you recollect?'

It was a question Khalap would have to answer, unless he intended to claim amnesia of his entire life.

DCP Khalap's eyes strayed towards Saralkar only briefly, as if trying to check his reaction without appearing to do so. 'The last memory I have is of me finishing my bath. I don't know what day it was ...' he replied.

It was either a genuine reply or a really clever one. Khalap had placed his last recollection so vague and in such an everyday activity that there was no challenging it or quizzing him further.

It could have been any day—the day of the mishap or even a week prior to that.

'I see. DCP Khalap, am I to understand that you have no recollection that you shot your wife and then attempted to commit suicide?' Saralkar said, finally deciding to take the bull by the horns.

Khalap's eyes were still averted, and his body made no movement, as if it knew it would probably betray him. 'No,' he replied.

'Hmm.' Saralkar waited. Wouldn't it be natural for even a man without memory to ask questions—seek details—when he was told he had committed grave crimes? Wouldn't he be anxious to know? Or was it more natural, in such circumstances, for the mind to try not to know and instead shut out what had happened?

All of Saralkar's instincts told him that DCP Khalap had chosen his line of defence—a denial of any recollection of his actions. Whether that was his psychological need after the ghastly deed or the most practical tactic to minimise responsibility and hence punishment, Saralkar was not yet sure.

He had to crack Khalap's veneer. 'DCP Khalap, I am going to narrate to you all that we have pieced together with the evidence we have gathered,' he said and began doing so. His eyes were riveted on Khalap, as Saralkar talked and walked around in a semi-circle from one side of Khalap's bed to the other and then back.

Khalap almost seemed to be holding his breath, never raising his eyes even to look in Saralkar's direction. His face was predictably impassive, but what Saralkar was really looking for were micro-reactions—giveaways that probably only highly trained spies learnt how to control, not normal people.

And he wasn't disappointed. The human face and body were not made of stone, even if they resolved to pretend they were. They were made of sinew and muscle that twitched with life, which could be subdued but never completely muted. Khalap, too, was made of the same material and some of the thirty-six trillion cells in his body confessed to what his conscious self wouldn't.

As Saralkar finished the narration, DCP Khalap closed his eyes. The first visible signs of emotion appeared on his face, as tears suddenly trickled down his shut eyes. Yet not a word or sound escaped his mouth.

'You do not recollect any of this? Not even in fragments?' Saralkar asked with a kind of gentle sharpness.

DCP Khalap shook his head slightly, his eyes still closed. Neither did he acknowledge his own tears by trying to wipe them.

'So, you don't admit to the acts?' Saralkar asked.

Khalap repeated the slight shake of head.

'Neither do you deny it?' Saralkar pressed on.

A couple of beats passed, then Khalap spoke, 'Yesterday you hinted my wife is still alive …'

It was Saralkar's turn to say nothing. Hearing no response, DCP Khalap's eyes opened and he looked at Saralkar, something he had been at pains to avoid before. Their eyes locked for a few seconds.

'Where is she? I want to meet her …'

Saralkar's mind searched for a smart response. He had played a bluff and Khalap was on the verge of calling it out. 'She is not in the condition to …' he replied.

'But … but you asked me if I wished to see her …' Khalap said, frowning.

Saralkar wondered whether there was any purpose to be served in continuing with the bluff. How long could he keep Khalap in the dark, given the fact that he probably knew his wife couldn't have possibly survived?

On the other hand, now that Khalap himself had survived, perhaps he could well be ready to believe she too had lived miraculously—that the doctors had also managed to save her. Perhaps that could nudge him to accept his crime, knowing her testimony would seal his fate.

'I didn't mean immediately,' Saralkar said.

'Has she spoken at all?' Khalap asked.

Saralkar decided the question would be best answered by non-verbal communication, given the situation. He nodded gravely.

'What has she said?' Khalap demanded.

Saralkar tackled his question with a counter question. 'How do you think I know what happened in such detail?'

DCP Khalap's shoulders slumped even as his watchful eyes tried unsuccessfully to be defiant.

'And of course, we have the testimonies of your two children,' Saralkar said adroitly.

Khalap blinked and his mouth opened reflexively as if about to say something. Then he looked away.

Was he going to capitulate and confess? Saralkar wasn't sure. It also struck him as strange that this man hadn't asked to see his children as yet. Saralkar had inquired with the doctors when he had arrived that morning. While Aditya and Pallavi had turned up to visit their father but were told they couldn't meet him just yet, the DCP had not expressed any desire to see his children.

Or perhaps it wasn't that strange after all. Why would a father feel up to facing the children whose mother he had shot?

A couple of minutes of silence followed, as if both Khalap and Saralkar were readying for the next round, figuring out the jabs and punches that they were going to exchange. Or even what they were going to duck out of the way of.

'DCP Khalap, I think the best course of action for you is the truth,' Saralkar said. 'It does not have to be recollected today, but the sooner the better.'

It was a warning, veiled as advice—a courtesy extended by one senior cop to an even more senior one.

Khalap refused to look at him but said, 'You can't force me to confess what I don't remember, Saralkar.' He raised his hands to his head, 'My head … is pounding. I can't take any more questions now.'

Saralkar regarded him carefully. 'If you don't wish to talk about the shooting, I have some other things to ask too.'

'What?'

'About Komal Raina and her charges against you,' Saralkar replied.

Khalap did not reply for a few seconds, then said, 'She can go to hell. I got my head blown off … It does not matter anymore.'

Saralkar was surprised by his attitude, wondering if it was another tactic. 'What does not matter?'

'The rape charges! That whore! I did nothing to her by force that I hadn't done before with her consent!' he said with a hitherto unseen viciousness. 'Anyway, you are not in charge of the rape inquiry, so why are you asking me about her?'

'Well, she seemed to be on your mind the night of the shooting. You sent your wife a message threatening to end your life because of her accusations and the consequent inquiry,' Saralkar replied.

A startled look had flashed across DCP Khalap's face and it went as quickly—as if DCP Khalap had genuinely forgotten he had sent such a message that night. 'Well, I already told you I do not recollect anything at all. Not a single thing that you narrated to me,' Khalap asserted.

'Komal Raina told me that you helped her escape imprisonment in a case. That your relationship began with that case,' Saralkar asked. 'What case was that?'

Khalap's entire demeanour was guarded now. He said nothing.

'Surely you haven't forgotten that too, DCP Khalap? Have you?' Saralkar asked.

'I … I don't know what you are talking about,' Khalap replied. 'If she told you that I helped her escape imprisonment, didn't she tell you what the case was?'

Saralkar grunted. He had to let it go for the moment. Khalap still seemed to have his wits around to block whatever Saralkar had thrown at him so far. 'One last question for today, DCP Khalap. Is it likely that your son and daughter had any role in the shooting?'

'Do you have a memory problem too, Senior Inspector Saralkar?' DCP Khalap unexpectedly let fly at him. 'How many times do I have to say I have no recollection of the events.'

Saralkar kept looking at him steadily even as Khalap glared back.

'Among your many troubles, the rape inquiry, the custodial death inquiry and the tension with your wife, did some serious issue relating to your children also arise?' Saralkar asked without blinking. 'Something that made the atmosphere at home even worse?'

Khalap continued glowering at him, trying to seem inscrutable. 'Children take sides because they have their own agenda,' he said gruffly. 'Mine too added fuel to the fire.'

'And what was your children's agenda?' Saralkar persisted.

'You are asking the question, so you probably know the answer, Saralkar,' DCP Khalap smirked. 'You won't get it from me!'

'DCP Khalap ...'

'Get out, Saralkar. Unless they have dismissed me from service, I'm still higher up than you in the police hierarchy,' Khalap replied curtly.

Saralkar stood looking at him quietly for a few seconds. He then said, 'DCP Khalap, I am giving you forty-eight hours to regain your memory on your own and come clean. After that, you will be shifted from here directly into my custody, and there I am going to cease to be as polite as I have been so far.'

PSI Motkar had heard his mobile ring twice, during his ride to Shanti Villa. He hadn't bothered taking the calls, since he hated talking on the phone in heavy traffic while on his motorcycle. About two years ago, he had taken a scary fall as his motorcycle skidded while he was talking on his mobile. It had been a miracle he hadn't been badly injured or fractured any bones.

Even more astonishing was the fact that, despite all the traffic behind him, no vehicle had run over him as he fell on the road. In fact, quite a few people stopped, lifted the bike off him, offered water and even a lift to a nearby doctor's clinic.

But he had taken the lesson to heart, especially when an elderly gentleman had mildly chided him about talking on the mobile while riding. 'That's no way to become a casualty in the line of duty, Inspector saheb,' the senior citizen had observed, as he handed Motkar his damaged phone, which he had retrieved from near the footpath.

Motkar had been wearing his uniform and hearing those words from the old pedestrian while dusting himself and checking for injuries had been his single most embarrassing moment. He had thanked the elderly gentleman and vowed never again to take a call while riding his bike. Whoever it was, they could wait—even if it was Saralkar!

As he alighted at Shanti Villa, he heard his mobile ring again, despite the din caused by the JCB at work. A sudden doubt fleeted through his mind. Could the urgent calls be from the Excavation team leader to intimate him about more bodies being found? His heart skipped a beat as he reached into his pocket for his mobile. Anyway, he was there now, to see for himself.

He was relieved to see it wasn't the Excavation team but Aradhana Shroff. Motkar decided that Niharika Das's lawyer could wait some more. Now that he was at Shanti Villa, his first priority was to confirm if any more bodies had indeed been found.

There were several reporters and camerapersons milling around, laying siege to the bungalow. Some of them swarmed over to him asking questions and updates. Motkar ignored them, even the familiar faces among them. He had nothing to tell them and it wasn't his job anyway.

The constables at the gate of the bungalow greeted him, and he quickly walked over to the cop overseeing operations and the leader of the Forensics team, both of whom were standing together. Neither had anything to report and Motkar felt incredible relief that nothing more had been found so far. Of course, that could change any moment, but the work had begun several hours ago and he reckoned if there had been more bodies, which had been Saralkar's unspoken fear, by now something would have emerged.

His phone buzzed again. It was Saralkar this time. 'Motkar, any more bones sticking out of the ground?' his boss asked.

The gallows humour was just a smokescreen. Motkar knew his boss was terribly apprehensive.

'Nothing more so far, sir,' he replied.

He heard Saralkar grunt with relief. 'How much area is left to excavate?' Saralkar asked.

'They'll probably take the rest of the afternoon, sir. We will know for sure by around 5–6 p.m.,' Motkar replied.

'OK, I am headed to the CP now. Anything else to report?'

'Niharika Das's lawyer has called me a couple of times, sir. I haven't taken her calls,' Motkar said. 'I'm calling back now and telling her what you instructed me to say.'

'She's tried my number too,' Saralkar said. 'Anyway, don't hesitate to call me immediately if something turns up at Shanti Villa. I'll take the call even if I am with the CP.'

'Yes, sir,' Motkar said, before the call disconnected.

The racket made by the JCB continued and Motkar reflected on the reporters and TV crews stationed outside. It was easy to brand them ghouls and some of them really were but others were just regular bread-and-butter reporters who had to be present where news was expected. Murder was news and the possibility of more bodies was potentially sensational breaking news.

Human beings were voyeurs by nature and TV channels were only feeding them their daily diet of misfortune that happened to hit other people's lives. People needed it to make their own lives less drab.

Motkar sighed inwardly at his musings, then dialled Senior Advocate Aradhana Shroff's mobile number. It was picked up by her assistant and promptly handed over to the senior advocate.

'I am still awaiting a response and an assurance for my client, Niharika Das, Inspector,' Aradhana Shroff said in a practised, peremptory voice she presumably used with policemen. It was a tone that seemed to suggest that the lawyer knew all cop tricks.

'I have not been able to get a reply from Senior Inspector Saralkar, madam,' PSI Motkar replied dryly.

'Have you really spoken to him?' the senior advocate asked.

'Of course, madam. He said he will call back and let me know.'

'Then why don't you remind him again?'

'Saralkar saheb does not need reminders, madam,' PSI Motkar shot back.

'Is that so? Well, tell him the onus is on you now. My client had offered to appear online!' Aradhana Shroff said.

'After first failing to appear before us in person, madam,' Motkar countered. 'Why don't you try calling Senior Inspector Saralkar directly, madam?'

'You think I haven't tried? He has not bothered picking up my calls,' the lawyer snapped.

'He is a busy man, madam,' Motkar replied. 'And if you do not mind, I am a little busy too. I'll call you back once I hear from Saralkar saheb.'

On that note, Motkar disconnected, happy at the way he had dealt with the formidable lawyer. Where, he wondered, was Niharika Das?

PSI Sanika Zirpe looked at the wooden spinning top. Its surface was scuffed and scraped at places, but the lacquer coating had not dulled all that much. The red and green coloured rings around the circumference were chipped at a few spots, but it was mostly intact.

The name had been carved roughly, unevenly between the red and green bands, possibly with a blunt knife or a screwdriver or something like that. Zirpe screwed up her eyes and stared at the letters closely. It was probably written in Hindi, but the alphabets used were far from clear.

'It's very difficult to read, madam,' Constable Khot said to her.

ASI Zirpe nodded, then held the top at a different angle and looked again to decipher the lettering. 'I think, the last two letters are "Ram",' she said tentatively.

She handed the top back to the constable, who took another look. 'You might be right, madam. Your eyesight is better than mine. So probably the boy's name ended with Ram.'

'That makes it no easier,' Zirpe said. 'It leaves us with hundreds of common prefixes that can possibly form a coherent name ending with Ram—Shantaram, Shivram, Rajaram! I can go on.'

'I am sure Forensics can figure it out or, as I said, even we can magnify the pic and manage to crack it,' Constable Khot said, suddenly brimming with confidence, having traced this important lead.

'Now we have to find someone who can corroborate what Baidabai told us about this boy,' Sanika Zirpe said. 'I think the most likely to know would be Phutane kaka, but more importantly, how did the boy land up at the Weldes? Who brought and introduced him to the family?'

Constable Khot nodded and said, 'So, if this boy with the top is one of the two skeletons, then does it mean they got another boy later on for housework and killed him too?'

ASI Sanika Zirpe gave a shudder and shrugged. 'It's a macabre thought, Khot, but let's leave the theories to Saralkar saheb. What we need right now is some information about the boy—his name, where he was from, did he have any family …'

She paused, as if something had suddenly struck her. What occurred to her was that if the boy had a family that they could manage to trace, then DNA testing could help establish the identity of the skeleton. All they'd need to do was to match the DNA of the buried body to that of a direct blood relative like mother, father or a sibling. Of course it depended on a number of factors, but it was quite possible.

Then again, she stopped herself from getting too far ahead and too excited.

23

'DOES NAVNATH SHINDE LIVE HERE?' THE OLD MAN ASKED AS soon as the inside door to the flat was opened.

The middle-aged woman who peered out through the grilles of the safety door inspected the stranger. 'No, my father-in-law stays nearby but my husband has just gone to pick him up. Who are you?'

'Navnath and I were colleagues before retirement,' Adinath Khubba said to Shinde's daughter-in-law. 'I have come all the way just to meet him. Can I wait for him inside if he is going to be here soon?'

The woman hesitated. She really couldn't say no. 'But you will be able to meet my father-in-law only for a few minutes.'

'A few minutes is all I need,' Khubba replied. 'Can I have some water? And I really need to sit down ...'

His manner was almost ingratiating. A vexed expression appeared on the woman's face, but she opened the safety door and let the old man in. She offered him a chair and went inside the kitchen to fetch water.

Adinath Khubba eased into the chair and felt relief. The body served a reminder every minute that it was long past its prime—that the wear and tear of ageing were real.

'Actually, my husband usually picks him up from his house and takes him directly to the hospital,' the woman said as she returned with a glass of water. 'But today he forgot to take my father-in-law's medical reports, so he's just coming back to collect them. I don't even know if father-in-law will come up with him.'

Just as she said that, the doorbell rang. A middle-aged man stepped in as the woman opened the door. His eyes fell on Khubba and a questioning look appeared on his face instantly.

'That's a colleague of father-in-law... he came looking for him,' the woman said almost guiltily, as if she expected her husband to be annoyed. 'I told him you are going to the hospital.'

'You are Shrikant, right? Navnath's son?' Adinath spoke addressing the man.

'Yes.'

'I am Adinath Khubba. Don't you recognise me, Shrikant?'

Recognition dawned on Shrikant's face. 'Oh yes, Adinath kaka. How are you?'

'I am OK. Where is Navnath? Why are you taking him to the hospital?'

Shrikant's face clouded. 'Father is in my car down below. He has cancer, kaka. I am taking him for chemotherapy. We have to rush there. I just came to collect his reports ...'

'Cancer? My God! Shrikant. I have come all the way. I need to meet Navnath for a few minutes,' Adinath Khubba said with a sinking feeling. He had gathered all his courage to come here. He couldn't bear the thought of going back without talking to Shinde.

Shrikant took the file his wife gave him, then said, 'Kaka, why don't you come with us to the hospital? Anyway it's a long wait. You and Appa can catch up while we wait our turn. I am sure seeing you will cheer him up.'

What Adinath Khubba needed to discuss with Navnath Shinde needed privacy. How was he to do that if Shrikant was going to be present? The next words from Shrikant's mouth provided an answer.

'In fact, I'll drop you both at the hospital, take a token and then quickly finish a small errand I have to run, while you wait with father. That way I don't have to leave him unattended and can finish the task I need to,' Shrikant suggested.

'Yes, yes, that's a good idea.'

'Come then, let's go. But there is a small request, kaka. Please don't talk about father's condition or anything upsetting,' Shrikant said. 'He just gets terribly distressed. You know how dreadful even the word "cancer" sounds.'

'I understand, Shrikant,' Adinath said, feeling quite depressed himself.

They left the flat and rode down in the lift. 'How's your health, kaka?' Shrikant asked.

'I'm OK,' Adinath Khubba replied. 'When you are young, you want to live till ripe old age. When you get old, you wonder if it's such a good idea.'

Before Shrikant could respond, the lift doors opened as they reached the ground floor. A car was parked right outside the building entrance.

'Come, kaka, father's sitting in the back.'

Adinath Khubba moved closer as Shrikant opened the car door.

'You have a surprise visitor, Appa! Guess who?'

Adinath Khubba was shocked to catch the first glimpse of Navnath Shinde, for inside sat a haggard old man, shrivelled beyond imagination, a far cry from the tall, strapping, well-built man he once was. His hair was gone, his face appeared drawn, pitiable, despondent, the eyes yellow and dully glazed.

It took a few moments for the flicker of recognition to show on Navnath's face, but it was a frown rather than a smile.

'How are you, Navnath?' Adinath Khubba asked.

'Adinath?' The voice that replied was hoarse and wary. The eyes looked at him apprehensively, flashing a quiet plea and a warning. 'How come … suddenly?'

'He's accompanying us to the hospital, Appa. You can chat and catch up while you wait there,' Shrikant said as he got into the car. Adinath climbed into the back seat beside Navnath, not an easy feat at his age, given the compact size of the car.

Navnath stared dumbly as Adinath sat back and squeezed his arm. 'Remember how they teased us mercilessly back then, calling us Prem Nath's sons,' Adinath guffawed and it even brought the ghost of a smile to Navnath's gaunt face.

The Prem Nath to whom Adinath was referring had been a swashbuckling hero of the 1940s and '50s. However, he later achieved much greater success in his second innings as a menacing screen villain in the 1970s.

'How are you, old friend?' Adinath continued, failing to keep the anxiety out of his voice. Navnath's condition wasn't going to make the discussion he'd come for any easier.

'See for yourself. I have cancer, you know,' Navnath said, his voice sounding as frail as he appeared. 'Life's passed a death sentence on me.'

Just as Shrikant and Adinath were about to chide him to not think or say such things, the old man broke into sobs.

'Are you sure they've found absolutely nothing?' Saralkar asked as he, Motkar and Zirpe gathered in his cabin.

'I was at Shanti Villa till 4 p.m., sir,' Motkar replied. 'There seem no sign of more bodies and it is unlikely, anything will be found in the patch that remains.'

Silence prevailed for a few seconds and the three officers stared at each other by turns, their minds trying to process the relief they felt, which was strangely mingled with slight disappointment.

'Well, that's quite an anti-climax,' Saralkar finally articulated the feeling. 'I sure am glad we don't have a Nithari on our hands, but I was counting on unearthing something helpful, even if it wasn't more bodies.'

'Should I contact Advocate Shroff now, sir? We can assure her that we won't arrest Niharika Das and ask her to present herself for the questioning tomorrow, with her lawyer in tow,' Motkar suggested.

'Hold on. Let me first figure out what to tell the media, which has probably been speculating sensationally all day,' Saralkar said. 'No more bodies is hardly the headline that's going to help us either while questioning Niharika Das or with furthering the investigation.'

'But isn't that the truth, sir?' Motkar said, even before he could stop himself.

Saralkar gave him a warning glare. 'You think I'm going to tell them we've found more bodies, is it?' he snapped. 'What we have to simply tell the media is that we have made several discoveries, which cannot be shared at the moment because it might jeopardise the investigation. We neither confirm nor deny finding more bodies. And most importantly, we issue an appeal through the media for witnesses to come forward or anyone who has any information to share about the Weldes, since these crimes are over thirty to thirty-five years old.'

He looked at both his subordinates. 'It makes sense from that point of view, sir, but at a later stage what are we going to claim as the discoveries made after digging up the plot?' Motkar said. 'And surely at some point in time we will have to admit that no more bodies were found.'

'Look, if we declare right now that we have found nothing, the media will lose interest because it is no longer sensational and all we get is egg on our face that all the hullabaloo was for nothing,' Saralkar explained. 'But we are still left with an unsolved case of two skeletons of two unknown, dead children in which we have made no progress. So, now that there is a media furore, why not use it to our advantage by keeping it in the news for a little longer and more importantly, invite the attention of witnesses. Somebody who may know something. It also helps us keep the pressure on Niharika Das and she might reveal critical information that she has held back so far.'

It was convoluted reasoning but Motkar saw the point his boss was making. He nodded.

Before Saralkar could speak further, ASI Sanika Zirpe cleared her throat and both men turned to her.

'Actually, sir, we have a new lead, even if it's not from the excavation,' she said trying hard not to sound either smug or self-important.

'What lead?' Saralkar asked.

ASI Zirpe quickly briefed them about Baidabai Ladkat's account of the Weldes employing an adolescent boy, his subsequent disappearance and how serendipitously she had stolen his spinning top and then kept it all these years.

Saralkar and Motkar heard her with mounting interest and when she produced the top, the senior inspector held and stared at it, as if he'd never seen one before. 'Good work, Zirpe, and give Khot a pat on the back from me.'

Zirpe felt as if she'd won a medal, for praise from Saralkar was rare.

'Niharika Das has got to know about this boy, Motkar,' Saralkar said. 'This lead is going to come in handy when we question her. Now, you can talk to Shroff and tell her she needs to appear tomorrow. Any other surprises we can plan for her?'

'Well, sir, Pol and Angre have also come up with some useful information on Welde's tenants,' Motkar replied. 'It seems old man Welde made it a point to warn tenants never to step on the lawn. It was a strict no-no. In fact, every time they travelled abroad to their son, Shashank Welde would physically cordon off the lawn and also put boards so that tenants would always know they were not supposed to enter the lawn.'

Saralkar's eyes shot up. 'You mean every tenant Pol or Angre spoke to mentioned that?'

'Yes, sir. Almost all of them recalled that oddity. What's more, Angre says the Weldes never rented their house to someone with small children, who might naturally play in the lawn. I have to double check with the broker, Uttam Padwal, if Welde made it a condition or actively rejected couples with small children.'

'Hmm. Old man Welde's aversion to tenants stepping on the lawn can either be ascribed to just eccentricity—people are peculiar—or it's a direct indicator of the dead bodies buried under it. Yes, that's a good point to grill Niharika about. So talk to Padwal. What else?'

'Sir, I had also asked Niharika Das to bring family photo albums of that period so that we might be able to get a good look at who formed their friends and family circle. You know, spot any individuals that we don't know about yet,' Motkar replied.

'Or perhaps even see if there are photos of eleven-to-twelve year old boys close to the family and check if any of them could be possible victims.'

'Needle in the haystack, shots in the dark—take your pick, but good thinking. We really have no choice but to also try some random methods to see if we hit something,' Saralkar said. 'When you speak to Advocate Shroff, tell her we want the photo albums delivered today, before the questioning.'

'Alright, sir! What if Advocate Shroff still wants to talk to you or has additional conditions?' Motkar asked.

'Tell her I have a meeting with the CP,' Saralkar said.

'I already told her that once, sir.'

'Well then tell her, the CP and I have gone out on a date,' Saralkar replied.

Motkar was too flabbergasted to react. He looked at Zirpe, who was trying hard not to laugh.

Saralkar, meanwhile, had picked up the spinning top again, holding it close and trying to decipher the name. 'I think the name scratched on this is Parshuram, though the letters are not well-formed and the spelling is also wrong,'

He thrust the top in Zirpe's direction. She took it from his hand, looking at her boss wondrously, as if he were a man blessed with super eyesight. Then she looked at the scratched letters and as if it were invisible ink becoming visible, she could now make sense of the carved scribble. She realised that if one read carefully, looking past the uneven, wobbly strokes, wrong accents and of course lettering mistakes that made the Devanagari script so prone to spelling errors, the name formed was indeed Parshuram.

Adinath Khubba and Navnath Shinde sat in the crowded waiting room, outside the Chemotherapy department. They were finally alone. Shrikant had found them places to sit and left for his errand, saying he'd be back in about half an hour. There were at least three patients ahead of Navnath, so a wait was clearly at hand.

'Have you been watching news on the TV lately?' Adinath Khubba finally broached the topic he had come all the way for.

Navnath looked up and studied his face. 'Yes, I guessed that's what brought you here,' he replied in a shaky voice.

Adinath patted his hand. 'His face flashes before me every single day.'

Navnath closed his eyes. 'I'm dying, Adinath. I'm scared of what lies on the other side. No chance of heaven awaiting us after what we did. The idea of hell scares me. Will he be waiting there to torture me?' He let out a pathetic whimper that spooked Adinath.

'Don't say such things, Navnath. We were just following orders … and … and we didn't strike the fatal blows,' he said, frantically trying to keep his voice down to a whisper.

Navnath gave a wretched sob. 'When three people thrash a pathetic wretch and he dies, it makes all three of them murderers.'

'No … no … no …' Adinath refuted his friend's words with intensity. 'We both had stopped … we had stopped … you and me … we didn't do it. He wanted to prove his manliness …'

Navnath sniffed, then sighed. 'We didn't stop him … we could have …'

'How could we have known? And even if we had … how could we?' Adinath protested.

They were silent for a minute or two, watching a patient being wheeled out of the Chemotherapy unit. Navnath Shinde shuddered.

'Twenty-five years … it's taken,' Navnath broke the silence. 'Why did we agree to hide the crime if we were not guilty too?'

'Because we were scared, Navnath, not guilty … we panicked … and … and you know why—because of his father! What were we going to do otherwise? What choice did we have?' Adinath argued.

Navnath said nothing for a few seconds. 'Well, that curse has got him too, hasn't it? You know about it, right? I'm dying … he's dying too …'

'I don't care what happens to him, Navnath,' Adinath said suddenly. 'They say if we repent for our sins in this world, God will have mercy … God will pardon us. You said you are scared of what awaits you, then should both of us not confess now that our crime has been unearthed?'

Navnath looked at him with disbelief. 'You mean … you mean we turn ourselves in?'

Adinath licked his lips. 'Yes … I don't have a minute's peace, Navnath. My conscience can't take the burden anymore …'

Navnath lowered his face into his open palms. 'I … I won't survive prison, Adinath … not in my condition. I don't even think I have too long to live. I'm scared as hell but confessing now would mean disgracing my son Shrikant and his family too … I can't do that …'

Adinath Khubba gazed at his shrunken, frail friend. 'I am shit scared of confessing all alone. I don't know what to do, Navnath … but I have to speak or I'll explode or go mad.'

'Adinath … Adinath …' Navnath croaked in alarm. 'Please … please do me a favour. Don't tell … don't confess till I die. I promise it won't be long …'

24

Niharika Das looked both intimidated and ashamed, as if she would burst into tears any moment. She had shown up as agreed, with Senior Advocate Shroff in tow, which surprised both Saralkar and Motkar. Unless the client was someone prominent, senior lawyers did not accompany them for preliminary interrogations. They usually sent juniors with instructions on how to safeguard their interests during police questioning.

'Maybe because the case is high-profile, sir, even if Niharika Das isn't,' Motkar had reasoned, as they kept the lawyer and her client waiting.

'Maybe,' Saralkar agreed sceptically. 'You lead the questioning Motkar. You are a gentleman, I'm not. I'll just fire ungentlemanly salvos in between. Zirpe, you shoot any additional questions about the lines of inquiry you have pursued, in case you feel we have not asked enough or skipped something.'

Both Motkar and Zirpe nodded. 'Have you had the time to go through the photo albums?'

'Just cursorily, sir,' Motkar replied. 'Perhaps we can take a look when we take a break.'

'OK,' Saralkar said. 'Call Niharika Das in now.'

Motkar nodded and went out to fetch Niharika Das. A minute ticked by, then two. Saralkar could hear the voice of

Advocate Shroff and guessed she was insisting on sitting in on the interrogation. Saralkar made his way outside.

'Senior Advocate Shroff, how are you?' he said, interrupting her argument with Motkar.

The formidable woman turned to him. Tall and slim, she was a rare combination of elegance and earthiness. Aradhana Shroff could be best described by boxer Mohammed Ali's quote—'Float like a butterfly, sting like a bee.'

'Not happy, Senior Inspector Saralkar,' she said.

'Madam, you know the rules. Your client faces the questioning alone. She can ask to consult with you anytime,' Saralkar said.

Aradhana Shroff snorted. She knew that legally, Saralkar was on solid ground, but a good lawyer had to try and do her best for her client.

'Everyone knows your subtle tactics to trick people into saying things,' she said. 'I want to guard against that happening to Niharika. She's more than a client. She's a friend.'

'We'll keep that in mind, madam,' Saralkar replied. 'Now let us do our job.'

Like a good lawyer, Shroff made a virtue of necessity. 'Alright Saralkar, do your job, but no sly attempts to get my client to self-implicate or to frame her, please.'

Saralkar did not react. He turned around and walked back into the interrogation room. Shroff, meanwhile, whispered some last-minute instructions into her sullen client's ears.

A minute later, Motkar walked in, followed by Niharika Das, who looked as if she was entering a chamber of no return. Plump, pretty-faced, still black-haired, fair, she was dressed in comfortable jeans and a half-sleeved, collared top. She glanced at all three officers, then fixed her gaze on Motkar who had also taken his seat.

'Where is her husband?' Saralkar leaned over and asked Motkar in a low whisper.

'I, too, am wondering, sir,' Motkar replied, in an even lower volume.

'Odd! If he's accompanied her to Pune, then why isn't he here?' Saralkar remarked. 'Anyway, let's start.'

As if a whistle had been blown, Motkar was off the mark immediately, 'Mrs Das, we have spoken earlier. Do you have anything to say before we start the questioning?'

Niharika Das exhaled, as if she'd been holding in her breath for several minutes. 'I know nothing. I am just shocked and horrified,' she said, her tone shaky and defensive.

'If you know nothing, why didn't you turn up yesterday as agreed?' Motkar asked.

She stared silently at the floor for a few seconds, then spoke, 'I … I had a panic attack … when I saw the news about the second skeleton,' She paused, as if reminded of the advice her lawyer had probably given her of answering to the point in the fewest possible words.

'Do you have any idea how the skeletons got there?' Motkar asked.

'No, I have no idea … who they are, how they got there … and … and how long they've been there …' Niharika Das said. She stole a glance at them, her gaze resting on ASI Sanika Zirpe as the most non-threatening, then her eyes returned to a neutral space.

'Your parents owned the bungalow plot since 1978. It is fairly certain the skeletons were buried around twenty-five to forty years ago, which means between 1985 to 2000 approximately,' Motkar said, taking slight liberties with the timeline. 'What do you have to say about that?'

Niharika Das had gone paler still. 'I don't know what you mean.'

'I mean what do you think this fact signifies?' Motkar shot back.

Niharika Das fidgeted with her response. 'Can I … can I speak to Aradhana … I mean Advocate Shroff?'

Saralkar cut in swiftly. 'If you are going to ask her whether you need to answer this question, then please note you don't need to,' he said. 'We will move to the next question. Is there anyone you can think of who might have killed and buried those in the lawns of your bungalow?'

Niharika Das shook her head. 'No … absolutely not! Why would anyone do that?'

'Motive, opportunity or spur-of-the-moment emotion is all it requires for one human being to kill another, madam,' Saralkar replied. 'Think hard.'

She looked uneasily at him, then shook her head. 'No, but as I already told Inspector Motkar, lots of people had access to the bungalow—servants, tenants and so on.'

Saralkar nodded. 'We will come to that. But even if there were people with access to the bungalow, digging up the lawn, burying a body and covering up the grave again is not something that can be accomplished in a jiffy. It leaves behind traces, unevenness of the earth. The lawn grass does not grow back immediately. All of it takes time. Burying a dead body is no mean feat. Could any of it have been done without your parents noticing?'

He paused and struck her with a glance, as if studying her reactions. Niharika Das drew in her lips, wetted them, and dabbed her forehead and mouth with her handkerchief. She was acutely aware of Saralkar's gaze. She turned to Motkar.

'I've already told PSI Motkar … and I think so has my brother Sunit … that my parents would often be away for months visiting him in the USA,' she replied, 'Three to four months is a long time … Maybe someone did something then.'

'But that was only after 1994, madam,' Motkar said. 'What about the period between 1985 and 1994? In that period, they didn't leave the bungalow for such long duration, did they?'

Niharika Das said nothing. She gave a distressed half shrug. The officers let the uneasy silence stretch for almost half a minute, which was a long time for anyone being questioned.

Then Motkar spoke again, 'So between 1985 and 1994, the residents of your bungalow were your parents, your aunt Urmila Welde, your brother Sunit and you. Correct?'

Niharika Das gave him a long, doubtful stare, as if she was being asked to sign a blank piece of paper. 'Yes,' she said finally.

'But I understand there were absences. Your brother Sunit was in a hostel for four years … you went to Mumbai for your MBA for two years. Right?'

Niharika Das nodded, as if reluctant to confirm because she knew where it was leading.

'Therefore, your parents and your aunt were the only ones here, throughout that entire period,' Motkar said.

'Yes,' Niharika Das replied, holding her breath again.

'Could it be possible then that your parents or your aunt were somehow responsible for the buried bodies?' Motkar asked, happy at what he thought was a deftly framed question.

Niharika Das's demeanour had undergone a change. There was a surge of anger now.

'How dare you talk such absolute rot about my parents?' she lashed out, her face red with anger, her eyes ready to pop. It looked like she'd start abusing them any minute now.

'Madam,' Saralkar said with mild sternness. 'Every suspect is likely to be someone's father or mother. We have to ask hard questions. We have to pursue unpleasant lines of inquiry and satisfy ourselves. Ordinarily, anyone on whose premises bodies are found become automatic suspects …'

Niharika Das was listening but hadn't stopped fuming. 'I need to talk to Aradhana … I want a break …'

Saralkar looked at her, let a few beats pass then said, 'Alright. Ten minutes! An interrogation isn't a picnic. Please be prepared for more such questions. We can't stop every time your feelings get hurt.'

Niharika Das stood up shaking, then walked out of the room briskly, as if she couldn't bear to breathe the same air as the policemen.

—

The internet was a curse. Whether you looked for things or not, things found you. Just as the Shanti Villa skeletons case somehow flashed on Rohidas Phule's mobile screen as a notification for a news update. How had it found its way there? He had not searched for it; he was not a news junkie. He certainly wasn't interested in crime updates or crime fiction or crime films. He wasn't attached to Pune in any way! Yet, there it was. Headlines that knocked his breath away.

It was nearly a week since that call from the police officer. He had already forgotten her name. Wasn't it Zirpe? Rohidas thought he had dealt with her and her questions rather well. He had been dismissive, like important men needed to be. He had admitted no recollection of having worked for the Weldes at their bungalow. Neither had he revealed that he remembered any of the other people the officer had mentioned—Namdev Phutane and that scumbag Bansi Vishwakarma. Of course, he remembered all of it, but he had left behind that poor, wretched existence long ago. Why would he feel any nostalgia for the days when he was a nobody?

But most importantly, he had managed to suppress his agitated reaction when she had hurled that curveball of a fact at him that a skeleton had been found buried in the premises of the Welde bungalow, even though it had triggered a rather uneasy memory. The memory of suddenly being asked one day to dig a deep trench in the lawn. Rohidas had been puzzled by the request but couldn't possibly turn it down. So, even while showing his willingness to do the task, he had inquired about the reason behind digging the pit.

The reply had been cagey and evasive. 'We need it for something important, Rohidas. Can you do it? It's urgent!'

Young Rohidas Phule had found it very strange. 'How big does it need to be?'

'About three to four feet deep and five feet wide. It needs to be done today. It should be easy for you. You are a gardener, Rohidas.'

'It's a lot of work,' Rohidas replied, still unable to understand why his employers would need such a trench pit.

'Come on, Rohidas. Haven't we always helped you whenever you needed money? We'll pay you well. Tell me, how much do you want?'

It was at that point in time that Rohidas suddenly felt uneasy, as if something wasn't quite right. He couldn't explain why. But the opportunity of earning a fast buck was very tempting in his straitened circumstances. He had thought briefly, then named a figure. What was even more odd was that he was instantly offered just a slightly lower figure, as if it was token bargaining, which he accepted with alacrity.

And yet doubts and misgivings continued to nag Rohidas, even as he set about digging the trench pit. He was an intelligent young lad, which explained why he had eventually risen so much in life. And it was the same intelligence that threw up questions in his mind. Especially because he was eventually made to dig a much deeper pit than what had been stated first and the driver Bansi Vishwakarma, whom he hated, also joined in to help with the task.

It was hard work and there was a strange silence as if they were all doing something that was best not spoken about. Task completed, Rohidas had gone home dog tired, with money in his pocket that was a kind of windfall. He had asked if he needed to come back the next day to refill the pit, but was told he should return two days later.

When Rohidas had returned two days later, he was surprised to see the crater completely refilled. It looked like an ugly rash by the side of the lawn. He was asked to rake and even up the surface, and to start covering it again with lawn grass.

That incident had come back to him in a flash when the policewoman had mentioned that a body had been found in the Welde bungalow. Perhaps it had always bothered him subconsciously, and maybe his mind had wondered if he had inadvertently helped hide something unsavoury. But that flash of recollection had turned into a sense of acute disquiet when the news item of the Shanti Villa case about another skeleton being found appeared on his mobile.

All of a sudden, it struck him that he had been made to dig that trench all those years ago to bury a body. That had to be it! Why else had he been asked to dig a pit that deep almost overnight? Why had he been paid a handsome amount for it and then found it covered up just two days later with no explanation for what purpose it had served? Why had someone else filled it up?

Scared and shocked, Rohidas Phule had no idea what he was supposed to do now as the realisation grew that all those years ago he had somehow helped in hiding a murder, that too probably of a child.

25

'My client has rights, Inspector Saralkar,' Advocate Shroff blazed. 'She doesn't have to answer your questions.'

'Well, the police have every right to ask questions, Advocate Shroff. You can't stop us from doing that,' Saralkar retorted calmly. 'We haven't forced her to answer any, but if she is going to get upset, angry and overwrought, that is her problem and yours, not ours.'

'Wouldn't you be upset if your parents or close family members were accused of murder, Saralkar?' Advocate Shroff asked.

'If skeletons are found in my parents' house, I would have no choice but to consider it a reasonable charge to be confronted with,' Saralkar replied. 'I thought as a good lawyer you would have advised your client on what the police might ask her.'

The moment he said it, he knew it was going to ruffle Advocate Shroff's ego but he didn't regret it. Her eyes flashed, her nostrils flared.

'I see, so now you are going to comment on …' she began.

But Saralkar quickly raised his hand and interjected, 'Advocate Shroff, all I meant was, you and I both know these suspicions about her parents are inevitable, as also the possibility that your client knew about it. So please just advise your client not to overreact. It's a waste of time. And, madam, I am not foolish enough to take cracks at you or raise your hackles. So, my apologies in case you felt I was doing that.'

Motkar, who was watching Saralkar, couldn't help admiring how shrewd and cunning his boss could be when he wanted to. He had planned both the insult and the instant apology.

Advocate Shroff shot Saralkar a grim look but Motkar could see she had been mollified. 'Alright, but some day, some case, I hope to roast you in court, Saralkar.'

He grinned. 'You have tried it a couple of times already, madam.'

She walked out to talk to her client and Saralkar looked at Motkar first, then Zirpe. 'Keep all your firepower ready. This time Motkar will begin, then you jump in, Zirpe. I'll just watch for a while. Understood?'

Both nodded, although unsure how long their irrepressible boss would simply watch before shooting his own questions. A few minutes later, Niharika Das walked in and took her seat. She was looking composed now, yet her nervousness was also palpable.

PSI Motkar gave her a few minutes to settle down, then said, 'Most of the tenants who lived at Shanti Villa have told us that your father specifically instructed them to never enter the lawns. Do you know why?'

Niharika Das replied defiantly, 'What's wrong with that? Every landlord has dos and don'ts for his tenants.'

'We understand Mr Shashank Welde also went to the extent of cordoning off the lawns and putting boards prohibiting anyone from stepping in, before your parents left on their US sojourns,' Motkar continued.

Niharika Das chewed on her lips. 'He wanted to make sure the tenants didn't break the rule deliberately or inadvertently,' she replied. 'He … he cared about the lawn …'

'You don't find it a bit extreme, in hindsight?'

'Not at all!'

'Isn't it more likely that he was so particular and touchy because he knew exactly what was buried under? Isn't that also the reason he built the two lawn platforms exactly above the two spots where the bodies were buried?' Motkar asked.

Niharika Das swallowed as if her throat had turned dry. 'I don't think so. My parents were good people.'

'Then why did your father specify in his will that the bungalow could not be sold for at least ten years after his or your mother's death?' PSI Motkar demanded and knew instantly from her expression that he'd caught Niharika on the wrong foot.

She gaped at him, at a loss of words, clearly not having expected the police to know this fact.

'We have a copy of your father's will, which is part of the development agreement you signed with the redeveloper and the indemnity bond signed both by your brother and you,' Motkar said. 'Your father probably didn't realise you would opt for redevelopment rather than outright sale …'

Niharika Das sat still, refusing to meet the eyes of the officers. 'I … I don't know why my father put that clause …' she finally said, still fumbling from the impact of the surprise question.

'Didn't you ask him why?'

'I hadn't read the contents of his will before he died …' Niharika lied.

'Your mother survived your father, didn't she? Surely, she would have known the reason. Didn't you ask her at least?' Saralkar interjected, before Motkar could speak.

She looked at him apprehensively, 'She … my mother didn't know. Neither did my brother.'

'It's a little difficult to believe your mother didn't know,' Saralkar smirked.

Niharika Das did not reply.

'What about the lawyer who made the will? Did your father not tell him the reason for such a clause?' Saralkar continued relentlessly.

'The lawyer too had no idea.' Niharika Das said.

'That's impossible,' Saralkar scoffed and came hard at her. 'Does the clause not indicate your father knew about the buried bodies and wanted to prolong discovery by another ten years at least?'

'But what proof do you have to keep hinting that my parents did it or had anything to do with those skeletons?' Niharika Das asked with genuine anguish. She glared at Saralkar not with anger but sadness.

'We will come to that too,' Saralkar replied and sat back, nudging Zirpe with a glance to take over the questioning now.

ASI Zirpe took the cue. 'OK, we spoke to some of the servants who worked at Shanti Villa. You might recollect you had given the name of Tayabai to my senior colleague, PSI Motkar, right?' Sanika Zirpe began.

'Yes,' Niharika Das replied, almost relieved that the woman officer was going to ask questions now.

'Now, among other things, Tayabai told me about an incident involving you.'

'Which incident?' Niharika Das asked warily.

'It seems when you were about ten or eleven years old, you had a pet parrot.'

Niharika Das visibly blanched. 'Yes,' she said in a hollow voice.

'What was the parrot's name?'

'We … we just called it Mithu!' Niharika replied.

'What happened to it?' Zirpe asked sharply.

'I … I don't remember,' Niharika Das said looking away. 'What does that have to do with anything?'

Zirpe let a few seconds tick by, then said, 'Tayabai told us that one day the parrot bit you. That the bite was deep and you bled a lot and you had to be taken to the doctor …'

'I don't remember. It was almost forty years ago,' Niharika Das said dismissively, her face expressionless.

'People usually don't forget such incidents,' Zirpe observed.

Niharika said nothing, just shrugged.

'Well, Tayabai told us that a few days later the parrot was found dead in its cage. Poisoned.'

'She's lying. Or imagining things,' Niharika Das snapped. 'Nothing like that happened. The parrot probably just died of natural causes or flew away or something.'

'Tayabai hinted that it was probably you who poisoned the parrot to avenge the bite,' Zirpe said, watching her carefully.

'How dare she tell such stories! How dare she make such an allegation?' Niharika Das said, erupting with fury. 'I didn't kill the parrot. I didn't poison it. How dare you accuse me?'

'We are not accusing you, madam. We are just asking you about the rumours Tayabai said she had heard,' Saralkar said, his voice rising above Niharika's. 'Please calm down, Mrs Das. No need to get worked up.'

But Niharika Das seemed almost beside herself with anger. 'What is the meaning of these questions based on what some maid said? And what does it have to do with the case?'

'We are simply trying to clarify with you the information we have received,' Saralkar replied.

'But why? Have you found a parrot's skeleton too? Are you also investigating its murder?' Niharika Das demanded.

Saralkar found himself momentarily speechless. 'OK, Mrs Das, point taken,' he conceded. 'Can we move on to the next question?'

Niharika Das, who was breathing heavily, looked away as if exhausted. 'I need water.'

Motkar quickly stood up, opened a plastic bottle kept on the side and poured it in a glass for her. She gulped it down.

ASI Zirpe gave her a few more seconds, then said, 'We also spoke to Namdev Phutane, the man who used to wash vehicles at your bungalow and in the neighbourhood.'

Niharika Das nodded absently, her mind probably still seething about the parrot episode. 'Yes, I only gave PSI Motkar all these names of people who worked for us long ago. I didn't know you would use it to …'

She glanced at Motkar, as if he had somehow betrayed her.

'Namdev Phutane recounted that your father had a Fiat at first and then bought a Maruti 1000 later on,' Zirpe said. 'Is that correct?'

'Yes. Why?'

'Phutane seems to remember that the Maruti 1000 met with an accident of some sort,' Zirpe said carefully. 'It seems the car suffered dents and front bumper damage in the incident. Can you confirm if something like this happened?'

Niharika Das frowned some more but this time as if she was quite bewildered. She shook her head. 'No, I can't recollect any car accident. My father was a careful driver and we used the car only within the city, never on highways or outstation trips,' she said.

'Did your father use the car to go to office and back every day?' Zirpe asked.

'Yes, his office was in Pune city, but he would often also go to the Pimpri-Chinchwad industrial area and Nigdi,' Niharika Das said.

'So, it's possible an accident could have occurred on his way to or from work, not in your presence?' ASI Zirpe said.

'Yes, but I would have heard my parents speak about such an accident or refer to it,' Niharika Das said. 'And if there were dents or bumps on the car, I would most certainly have noticed it.'

Zirpe felt that Niharika Das's response sounded authentic, not like she was trying to hide or evade facts. If the said accident had occurred then Niharika had no knowledge of it.

'But again, what is the relevance of this question?' Niharika Das asked the officers searchingly.

'Never mind, Mrs Das,' Saralkar intervened. 'Perhaps Namdev Phutane was mistaken. Let's move on to the other questions. We have a lot to cover.'

Niharika Das opened her mouth to speak but was overtaken by ASI Zirpe. 'Mrs Das, did your mother … rather your household ever employ full-time servants?'

'Full-time servants?'

'Yes, live-in servants?'

Niharika Das shook her head. 'No, why would we? We had servants who would come and go daily. We had maids for washing utensils and clothes and sweeping and mopping. My mother would do most of the cooking. My aunt helped sometimes and later we also had a cook to make chapatis. And then we had a gardener who would come every alternate day or so. My father also employed a driver after we bought the Maruti 1000, since he got promoted and had begun to go to other nearby towns frequently.'

'But our information says that your mother did hire a full-time servant at one stage,' Zirpe insisted.

'Who said so?' Niharika Das challenged.

'You had a maid, Baidabai Ladkat. She told us.'

Niharika Das's eyes clouded. 'That thief! How can you believe her? Either she's lying or mistaken.'

'Let me jog your memory then. Did you not hire a boy of about eleven or twelve, as a full-time help for a few weeks?'

Niharika's eyes widened, as if a long forgotten bell had gone off.

'His name was Parshuram. Do you now recall?' ASI Zirpe asked.

But Niharika's expressions had become furtive and frosty now. 'No, I don't recall any boy working for us,' she replied brusquely.

ASI Zirpe gave her a piercing stare. 'You don't remember this boy who worked and stayed in your house for a few weeks?'

'No, I don't. You've got wrong information,' Niharika replied.

'We have more than information, madam,' Saralkar spoke. 'We have evidence he worked at Shanti Villa.'

Niharika stiffened further. 'When was this? Maybe I had already left for Mumbai by then,' she said, trying to sound firm, but her voice lacked conviction.

'No, you were here. It was much before you left for higher studies,' Saralkar said.

'I am telling you I don't remember,' Niharika replied sounding evasive and annoyed. 'Maybe I was on vacation at my maternal grandmother's place in Nashik or a school or college trip. I don't know.'

Uneasiness seemed to be rippling all through her. Saralkar regarded her, then said, 'This time, you didn't ask us what the boy has got to do with the case …'

Niharika Das seemed to have frozen with fear, even as she was trying hard not to show it in her demeanour, which was a dead giveaway. 'What?' she croaked.

'Well, we think, one of the skeletons is that of this boy, Parshuram.'

An involuntary sound, halfway between a hiccup and a cry, escaped Niharika Das's lips and she looked ready to faint.

26

DCP Kuldeep Khalap reflected over the choices before him. The truth was an option, but not an attractive one, for it was grotesque and ugly without any redeeming feature. It could not be fixed, and the only hope lay in obscuring it and perhaps giving it a twist, while he still could.

Time was running out. He couldn't stall or foil forever. Any other cop perhaps, but not the Saralkar kind. He knew cops. He was a cop himself. He had lived and grown up among cops. He could smell cops that were real trouble from a mile.

That night had been a blur—a night of madness. A chain reaction of ghastly mistakes triggered by a terrible cocktail of provocation, fury and despair. A cathartic apogee with gruesome consequences simply because a firearm had been handy. Kuldeep Khalap cursed his luck. How different it would all have been if he hadn't lost his head and reached for his gun!

Why hadn't he died? The bullets should have done their job. One single bullet had killed his poor wife, hadn't it? He remembered the moment as if it were frozen in time—the look on her face as the bullet struck her. Like life and death were separated only by a switch. He had actually seen the life go out of her eyes as she crumpled and lay still.

Oh God, what a mess! What was he to do now that he had not died too? His problems had only multiplied. They were not going to vanish. Life was even harder than it had seemed that night. How was he to grapple with it? What would his father have done? He wasn't around to save him this time. Why couldn't he be more like that crooked, devious ruthless bastard who knew just how to be a bastard and enjoy it!

Despite Aradhana Shroff's vehement demand to stop the questioning and continue it the next day, Saralkar had not relented.

'She's not medically unfit to face questioning, just because she swooned, madam,' he said in response to Adv. Shroff's harangue.

'But look at the psychological toll it's taken, Saralkar! Heavens won't fall if the rest of the questioning is done tomorrow.'

'That's the language lawyers and judges use in the Supreme Court, madam, not in humble police stations,' Saralkar quipped. 'Why can't we continue with the questioning today? Does your client Niharika Das suffer from hypertension, diabetes, heart problems? I'm sure she doesn't or you would have already flagged it.'

'Look at her condition, Saralkar. You've knocked the wind out of her. She's not a criminal, dammit!' Adv. Shroff said, suddenly changing her tone from aggressive to reasonable, so that even the 'dammit' sounded like polite language. 'Who knows, she might even turn hysterical. You wouldn't want that, would you?'

Saralkar tut-tutted her. 'Is that what you are going to advise your client, Advocate Shroff? I am disappointed. I don't react well to hysterics.'

Shroff seemed to realise he wasn't going to budge. 'Alright then, but no more than forty-five minutes, now. Or I am going to dial some numbers and raise hell. She's a friend, I told you.'

Saralkar didn't react. He let her have the last word as she stomped off to prepare her client. He regarded both his team members. ASI Zirpe immediately asked him the question she was waiting to put, 'Should I press on about Parshuram, sir? Perhaps confront her with the spinning top too?'

Saralkar shook his head. 'She definitely knows about that poor boy but won't admit it today. The top has significance to us, but it might not rattle her. A corroboration by another servant might—or if we bring in Baidabai to confront her. But let's keep that for later. Let's shift the focus to her aunt instead.'

He turned to Motkar as if seeking his view. PSI Motkar nodded. 'You are right, sir. Niharika Das might not be expecting questions about her aunt just now and she'd shown lots of nervousness in sharing her contact details with us.'

'Right. By the way, have you checked up on Urmila Welde again, after you questioned her?' Saralkar asked.

PSI Motkar and ASI Zirpe exchanged glances. 'No, sir. You want me to send someone around to her place?'

'Yes. We need to keep a discreet watch for a few days.'

PSI Motkar was about to ask him why, but Niharika Das entered the room just then and took her seat. There was an uneasy alertness about her, as if she expected to be hauled over the coals.

Interrogation was a cruel process. It could sometimes be gentler if the police had the time to play a waiting game, but more often than not, the truth had to be dragged out by putting people through an ordeal—mostly psychological and unfortunately even physical many times.

'Let's talk about your aunt, Urmila Welde,' PSI Motkar began.

Niharika Das blinked as if she had got an out-of-syllabus question.

'When did she move in with your family?' Motkar asked.

'I … I don't know the exact year but—one or two years after we moved into Shanti Villa,' Niharika said. 'I was very little.'

'She was your father's younger sister?'

'Yes. Eight years younger.'

'Did your father and she have any other siblings? And are they still around?'

'My father was the oldest and Urmila Attya the youngest. There was one brother and one sister in between, but the brother passed away as a child—pneumonia or something—and the other sister died in a bus accident in the early 1970s. I don't know much about either of them.'

'I see. Was Urmila Welde unmarried?'

'Yes,' Niharika replied, then said in a flustered manner. 'She … she couldn't marry the person she wanted to … and decided to remain unmarried.'

'She was a working woman, right?'

'Yes, she worked in a bank.'

'How were relations between your parents and aunt?' Motkar asked.

Niharika Das hesitated just a second before she replied cryptically. 'Good. She was a family member.'

'Then why didn't she remain one after a few years? She started staying separately, didn't she?' Motkar asked.

Niharika Das went quiet for a few seconds, then shrugged. 'I … I don't know. I think my mother and she weren't getting along anymore. There was friction. So, my father helped her buy a flat.'

'What was the cause of the differences?' Motkar insisted.

Niharika Das looked at Saralkar, then away, then turned to Motkar defiantly. 'These are private matters. I don't want to answer the question.'

'How private and serious can it be that you cannot talk about it even twenty-five to thirty years later?' Saralkar interjected.

'It's just private and none of your business,' Niharika Das said with some heat.

Saralkar observed she still had spunk. 'Alright, why were you trying to prevent or delay us from questioning your aunt?' he asked.

Niharika Das immediately appeared on the back foot again. 'I … I already explained that to PSI Motkar. She's suffering from dementia. You must have seen her condition for yourself.' Niharika Das fumbled. 'I … I just didn't want her troubled.'

Saralkar was gazing at her cynically. 'Was that the only reason or were you scared she might tell us some family secrets … make some revelations?'

Niharika Das flinched. He could sense both fear and anger. 'Secrets? Revelations? What do you mean?'

She looked from one cop to another, but all three let the question hang there for a few beats without replying.

Then Motkar spoke. 'Urmila Welde told me a few things, which I hope you can shed some light on. For instance, when I asked her about your father, Shashank Welde, she made a strange remark that he was the worst brother one could ever have. Now why would she say that? Any idea? What went so wrong between them?'

Niharika Das had already started shaking her head when Motkar was mid-sentence. 'No … no … no … no … that is just her dementia speaking. Urmila Attya has no reason to say that. My father does not deserve to be spoken of like that.

You can't believe what a dementia patient says. Ask … ask any neurologist. They lose touch with reality. Everything is jumbled up and memories get twisted in their minds.'

A torrent of words spouted from her mouth as if she was trying to reverse-brainwash them. They watched her getting frantic and waited for her to say more. But she had reached out for the bottle of water, which had now been kept near her. Niharika put the bottle directly to her mouth and took several gulps.

PSI Motkar resumed the questioning. 'There were a few other startling things your aunt said. Can you help us make sense of it?'

'What?' she asked, as if her heart was sinking.

'When she learnt I was a policeman, your aunt stared at me and said, "Are you going to arrest me. I did it." Do you have any idea what she was referring to?' PSI Motkar asked.

Niharika Das had closed her eyes as if distraught. 'I don't know … Inspector … please … She's a woman who does not know what she thinks or says or sees anymore.'

'Hasn't she said something like this to you after she developed dementia?' Saralkar asked.

Niharika Das seemed to go silent as if thinking of an answer. 'She … just rambles … says all kinds of things. I … I … have no idea of what she means.'

It was definitely a half-truth or rather a half-lie. Saralkar was sure that Niharika had heard things from her aunt's mouth that were shocking and too terrible to contemplate.

'Could she have been telling the truth? Maybe about the murder of Parshuram?' Saralkar slipped in the question with devastating effect.

Niharika Das seemed to rock back like a boxer stunned by a punch she should have seen coming. She blinked, then looked searchingly at Saralkar, her eyes full of doubt. 'Did … did Urmila Attya …' she stuttered, on unsure ground. 'Are you telling me she mentioned … this Parshuram you keep bringing up?'

Saralkar was tempted to bluff but instead just gave her an icy smile. 'Madam, you can't answer questions with a counter-question. It's best you tell us what you know. Your aunt suffers from dementia, not you.'

Motkar had always admired the array of tactics and techniques his boss used while interrogating people. Here, for instance, what his boss had said carried little substance, but the way he said it and the tone he used appeared to turn Niharika Das into jelly.

'What … what do you mean?' she asked, shrinking into herself. 'I … I have nothing to do with any of this. I was just a school- or college-going kid back then.'

'Exactly what I am saying, madam. Don't let some misdirected sense of loyalty to your parents and aunt stop you from telling us the facts that you know of,' Saralkar said, pouncing on her panic. 'For example, admitting that you remember a boy called Parshuram had briefly worked for your parents as a live-in servant does not mean you are condemning them as murderers. Do you understand me?'

Niharika Das suddenly held her forehead in her palms and closed her eyes as if she was feeling dizzy again. Then she nodded very slowly. 'Yes, I remember the boy.'

Saralkar, Motkar and Zirpe exchanged quick glances, waiting for her to say more. But instead, Niharika Das stood up unsteadily and said, 'I … I can't answer any other questions today … I am going …'

She quickly turned around and scrambled towards the door, without waiting for permission to leave. But Saralkar did not try to stop her.

'Sir?' Motkar said. 'You are letting her go? I still need to ask her some questions about the other things Urmila Welde had said.'

'What?' Saralkar asked.

'That utterance about not sleeping with a policeman which she had suddenly blurted out,' Motkar replied.

'Hmm. It's OK. She's coming back tomorrow. Go, tell Shroff we want her here by 10 a.m.,' Saralkar replied.

Motkar nodded and rushed out of the room. Saralkar turned to Zirpe. 'Get started on the photo albums, Sanika.'

'Sister, are my son or daughter outside?' Kuldeep Khalap asked the nurse, who had just come to check his vitals and give him his afternoon medications.

The nurse gave him a wary look. 'We have been instructed to not answer any of your questions,' she replied.

'But it's just a simple question. What's the harm in replying?' DCP Khalap said.

'Sorry,' the nurse replied. 'Please ask Dr Kaushal when he comes for his evening visit.'

'OK, can you at least tell me whether my wife is now out of the ICU?' Khalap pleaded. 'Surely, you can tell me if she's recovered?'

The nurse frowned for a nano-second. 'I … I have to go,' she said and began walking away.

'But, Sister, the inspector told me I could see my wife today,' Khalap persisted.

The nurse threw a confused glance at him. 'I … I don't know anything about that.'

'At least tell me if she's OK? Please, Sister … She won't die, right?' Khalap implored in a quivering voice, calculated to generate sympathy.

The nurse hesitated, gave him one last anxious look, then opened the door and fled.

DCP Khalap reflected over her reactions and demeanour. All indications—her expressions, her body language, her tone—told him his wife was almost certainly dead and the nurse knew that.

Saralkar had clearly been trying to mislead him into believing his wife was alive, hoping to induce a confession.

27

ASI SANIKA ZIRPE HAD SPENT OVER TWO HOURS SCOURING THE photo albums submitted by Niharika Das. She'd had her first look at the faces of the dramatis personae—Shashank Welde, his wife Sheetal and sister Urmila. There were small square-shaped photos in black and white, probably taken prior to 1980, and then postcard-size colour photos taken after that.

All the pictures looked so quaint, as if not taken just thirty to forty years ago, but in a different era altogether. The clothes worn, the haircuts, the ambience, the objects, even the expressions of the people in them made it seem as if they belonged to a time far removed from the present. Had the world and India really changed so much?

Sanika was born in the mid-1990s, and perhaps that's the reason why everything in these photos looked so incredibly tacky to her eyes, as if scenes from some crummy period piece. The quality of the images got much better and suddenly appeared more modern after 1995.

She remembered some of her own old family photos. Perhaps it wasn't just life that had suddenly improved by leaps and bounds but also the technology to visually capture moments from it.

ASI Zirpe had also seen younger versions of Sunit Welde and Niharika Das—with family, with friends, with their respective spouses and children—at functions and get-togethers, trips and vacations. All members of the family seemed normal, their faces lit with different expressions and moods, but generally happy and relaxed.

But was it her imagination or did the parents and aunt of the siblings look ill at ease or grim or preoccupied in the albums of later years? Most certainly, there was a visible contrast between their expressions and demeanour in the older photos of the 1970s and early '80s and the pics of the subsequent years.

It's as if their smiles had vanished or become pasty. Their eyes appeared grim or wary as if they were only physically present, but far away mentally. Even in their photographs with their cute grandchildren, Zirpe could not spot any genuine happiness or pleasure on the faces of the Welde couple, which wasn't tinged with a vague preoccupation, as if their joy had been imprisoned by some larger anxiety.

Of course, it was possible she was reading too much into it. None of what she had observed could be remotely interpreted as proof indicating they were guilty of murder or even that there was something wrong within the family. There was no dearth of reasons why once-happy people or families could become sad—sickness, financial problems, strains in relationships, depression, tensions and so on. There was something very fragile and impermanent about human happiness and existence.

Anyway, her objective of looking through the photo albums was altogether different. It was to spot individuals of interest—people who had come into the ambit of the investigation so far and those that hadn't by either oversight, sheer coincidence or design.

ASI Zirpe had marked a few characters whose identities she needed to ask Niharika about—faces that had appeared in several photos. She had then gone through the albums carefully once more, to make sure she hadn't missed out on taking notes of any picture or any individual who roused her curiosity.

That's when her eyes fell on a photograph with a familiar face. It was a part of photos bunched together and kept loosely in an envelope, which was inserted in a pocket at the back of an album—photos that did not merit display either because they were not particularly well-clicked or because the people in them were probably of no great consequence to the family.

Sanika Zirpe had leafed through the photos earlier, but this particular photo had probably stuck to the previous one and had escaped her notice. She saw it only just now while browsing a second time. It was a photograph of three men standing by a guava tree on Shanti Villa lawns during some festive event.

They seemed to be helping in putting up decorative lighting, since one of them looked poised to step onto a ladder holding small bulb strings, while the second individual held the ladder and the third man just stood, with his hands on his hips.

The two men by the ladder were recognisable—Namdev Phutane and Rohidas Phule. Zirpe had no idea who the third man with his hands on his hips was, but wondered if it could be the driver, Bansi Vishwakarma. However, what caught her immediate attention was Rohidas Phule's neck. She almost couldn't believe her eyes. Where the hell was she going to find a magnifying glass? Would anyone in the department have one? Sounded so much like those old detective tales.

Sanika Zirpe scrambled out with excitement. She damn well needed to get a magnifying glass or something that blew up the image enough to confirm what hung around Phule's neck!

Saralkar's phone buzzed again just as he got off the call with CP Arundhati Kotwal, after updating her on the DCP Khalap's case. It was Inspector Rajguru calling. 'Yes, Rajguru?'

'Sir, the senior nurse, Sister Alka, has reported that DCP Khalap was fishing for information and asking questions about his wife's condition. He also asked if his children were waiting outside to see him.' Rajguru said.

'I see. I presume the nurse said nothing,' Saralkar replied.

'She didn't let anything on, sir.'

'Hmm.' Saralkar reflected. 'But I think he's figured out his wife is already dead. What he's unsure of is whether she gave some dying declaration or whether I am just bluffing that she's told us what happened.'

'There's one more development, sir. About Aditya and Pallavi,' Inspector Rajguru continued.

'What? Have you been able to confirm the incest rumour?' Saralkar asked.

'Yes, sir.'

'You have?'

'Yes, sir. At least two of Aditya's friends and one friend of the girl confirmed it,' Inspector Rajguru said.

Despite himself, Saralkar couldn't help feeling a little nauseated. One couldn't always force oneself to be broadminded about everything. 'Really?'

'But apparently there is a slight twist, sir. Both Aditya and Pallavi have claimed to their friends that they are not real brother and sister,' Rajguru explained. 'Each has told their friends that the other was adopted.'

Saralkar grunted. He had not seen that coming. 'I see. We need to get the facts, Rajguru—whether either of them has been legally adopted by the Khalaps. Check his personnel files. He's got to have submitted some paperwork to the department if either of his children are indeed adopted.'

'Yes, sir, I'll get after that. Do you also want me to question either of them?'

'No, hang on. Let's do that once we are sure and have documents in our possession to support this information,' Saralkar said. 'Meanwhile, there's one more thing that I want you to do.'

He quickly gave instructions to Rajguru.

Important people made everyone wait. It was one of the first lessons successful folk learnt, especially in India. Of course, all Indians were naturally adept at keeping others waiting, PSI Motkar reflected as he glanced at his watch again. He had already been there an hour.

Advocate Burjor Poonawala was undoubtedly a big shot—a much-in-demand lawyer specialising in commercial, civil and corporate law. Old man Welde had got his will made from him, which suggested that either Poonawala and he had been old acquaintances or that Shashank Welde had wanted legal drafting of a higher order than a normal will generally required.

'Inspector Motkar,' one of the lawyer's equally Parsi assistants said, appearing from nowhere. 'Advocate Poonawala will see you now.'

About time, Motkar thought to himself, as he made his way to Poonawala's well-furnished cabin. Inside sat a chubby, spectacled seventy-year-old man. He looked up superciliously as if doing the world generally—and Motkar personally—a gigantic favour.

He didn't hold out a hand. He probably didn't believe in shaking hands with anyone but moneyed clients.

Given his haughty, snobbish demeanour, Motkar was surprised by the first words out of the lawyer's mouth. 'Shashank Welde forgot to instruct me to add those two skeletons in his will,' he chuckled with unexpected dry humour.

So the man had obviously seen the papers or the news items about the Shanti Villa murder case on TV.

'Thank you for sparing your time, Advocate Poonawala,' PSI Motkar said.

'What choice did I have, Inspector,' the old man continued pleasantly. 'Sorry for keeping you waiting. I had a long conference call with a corporate client. That's a lot of money,' he said with a wink. 'Tell me, how can I help you, Inspector?'

Before Motkar could reply, Advocate Poonawala had already started talking again. 'Frankly, I don't know how I can, because I didn't know Shashank Welde personally. And I handled no other legal matter for him except this will. In fact, it surprised me he came to me at all for such a routine matter.'

'I see. Sir, did you eventually discuss what his purpose in seeking you out was?' Motkar asked.

'Well, if my memory serves me right, he had two major conditions that he somehow wanted included in the will,' Poonawala said. 'First, he wanted to put the condition that the property would not be sold by his heirs for at least twenty-five to thirty years. I told him that was inadvisable, totally impractical and unfair to his heirs. He argued that the ownership of the property would vest with his heirs, but since it wasn't an inherited property and he had built it with his own money, why couldn't he impose a condition that they retain it for twenty-five to thirty years?'

'Did he give a reason why he wanted to insert this condition?' PSI Motkar asked.

The old lawyer's eyes twinkled. 'Well, it's quite obvious now, isn't it? But no, Shashank Welde did not confide in me that he'd got two bodies buried under his lawns.' Poonawala chortled at his own humour. 'Anyway, jokes apart, when I asked him why, he gave me rather silly reasons. At first, he said he believed the property was auspicious and therefore needed to be retained in the family so that it could generate wealth for the next two generations. Then he said the house had been named after his mother and so he didn't want it sold to someone else. All of it sounded poppycock to my ears. But for the life of me, I did not suspect anything like this.'

He paused and smirked, 'When he kept insisting, I said I couldn't draw up a will with such an unreasonable clause because there was a chance that it might not stand the scrutiny of the law. I mean, the right to property includes the right to sell it.'

'But you did eventually make the will for him, sir,' PSI Motkar observed.

'Only after Welde agreed to reduce the period to ten years. He kept pestering me, so I also added a number of extenuating circumstances faced by the heirs like bankruptcy, life-threatening illness or damage to the bungalow structure, in which case the heirs could sell off the property earlier,' Poonawala said. 'I also added that the two heirs could approach me or my firm in such or other unexpected situations to waive off the clause, and we would arrange to facilitate the needful if we found adequate merit in their plea.'

'Oh, I see. So had Welde's son and daughter consulted you about the will, after his death?' Motkar asked.

The senior lawyer cast a shrewd glance at Motkar. 'No. I hear they smartly gave the property for redevelopment, which does not entail relinquishing title or selling the property. Probably their lawyer or the builder's lawyer showed them this loophole and advised them against approaching me for waiver of the period clause, although I wouldn't have objected. Their logic is right. They were doing nothing illegal since both heirs and the redeveloper were in agreement. No transfer of ownership was on the cards. There was no specific clause in Welde's will that barred redevelopment too. So, there was no need to make it public because who was going to object? The problem would have arisen only if one of the two heirs were not agreeable to the ten-year condition.'

Poonawala sat back and looked at his wristwatch. 'Poor siblings must be regretting it right now. Anyway, any other questions, Inspector? It's time I got home and had my precious evening tipple, you know.' He grinned. 'A drink a day keeps the doctor away.'

PSI Motkar smiled at the amused old Parsi. 'Just one last question, sir. You said Shashank Welde wanted to incorporate two conditions. What was the other one?'

'Ah! Welde wanted his sister to be made executor of the will, without informing her, or seeking her consent,' Poonawala said. 'Crazy idea. I told him, first, an executor was not needed, and second, his sister could not be appointed without her consent and knowledge. So, he again brought up that twenty-five to thirty year limitation on sale clause, saying his sister would effectively safeguard that. Then I learnt he and his sister were not on talking terms, so he wasn't going to inform her or seek consent. Eventually, Welde agreed to keep her out and instead, I inserted the clause of his heirs consulting me.'

Advocate Burjor Poonawala shook his head and said, 'Well, Inspector, I really cannot keep my whisky waiting any longer.' He stood up, smiled and thrust out his hand. 'Good night.'

PSI Motkar shook the old lawyer's hand, and accepted this polite dismissal. Some people had a knack for doing this, or maybe simply because he was an old man and a Parsi that Poonawala had managed to make it all sound courteous.

In any case, he had no more questions to ask. Also, if not a drink, at least dinner awaited Motkar at home and he was suddenly hungry. It had been a long day. He was dog-tired. Half an hour later, PSI Motkar was back home. He hit the bed another half an hour later, as soon as he had finished dinner.

It was when he woke up in the middle of the night to go to the loo that his groggy mind suddenly reminded Motkar of a task his boss had asked him to do. Motkar sighed. He was supposed to have checked in on Urmila Welde. How the hell had he forgotten to do that?

As he got back into bed, Motkar promised himself he would do it first thing in the morning, even before he brushed his teeth.

28

ASI Sanika Zirpe could barely contain her excitement. She had even considered calling up Senior Inspector Saralkar or at least PSI Motkar late the previous night when she had received confirmation that the amulet Rohidas Phule was wearing around his neck in the old photograph had enough visual similarity to the amulet that had been found with the first skeleton.

And while it would still need advanced technical analysis to decide whether it could be presented as evidence in a court of law, it could certainly be used to confront Rohidas Phule and interrogate him.

It was 8 a.m. now. Early, but not annoyingly early. Hopefully, her boss wouldn't mind. She hesitated, then decided it was well worth risking Saralkar's rebuke. She dialled his number. It took several rings for her call to be taken.

'Have they promoted you to Joint CP or something, Zirpe?' Saralkar's hoarse voice came over.

Zirpe bit her tongue. 'Sorry, sir. Did I disturb you?' she asked apologetically, expecting a barb or two to follow.

'Yes,' Saralkar replied. 'I presume you have good reason for it, Zirpe.'

'Yes, sir,' Sanika said hastily, took a deep breath and succinctly summarised her inferences related to Rohidas Phule's photo in the Welde family albums and the amulet found with the first skeleton.

'Hmm. You sure about it?' Saralkar asked.

'Yes, sir. We need to officially summon Rohidas Phule for questioning,' Zirpe said.

'OK. Run it by Motkar and get an email summons ready. We'll call Phule once I get to office,' Saralkar replied.

Sanika Zirpe could have kissed him. 'Thank you, sir,' she said before disconnecting.

DCP Kuldeep Khalap stirred to wakefulness. The pain from the bullet wound to his temple always hit him the hardest every morning at the moment of waking since regaining consciousness. It was as if his head reminded him afresh daily of the agony it had been subjected to. It was a blisteringly excruciating sensation that made him almost regret having survived.

He clenched his teeth, shut his eyes and fervently begged the hundreds of cells, nerves, blood vessels, shreds of flesh and bits of bones that had suffered injury to calm down. Minutes passed like hours before the gut-wrenching pain settled to a more tolerable level. Khalap opened his wet eyes slowly. You could call them tears of agony or just a bodily discharge to cope with the pain.

He realised it wasn't morning yet, probably dawn. But he needed to go to the toilet now, and his hand groped for the call bell. To his surprise, his fingers brushed against what felt like paper underneath the call bell.

He pressed the bell and pulled the paper to take a look. It felt like a thin square of tissue paper. Even in the darkness of the room, he could make out that there was something written on it. He reached out for the switch to the table lamp.

Scribbled on the tissue, in capital letters, were the words: 'WIFE NOT ALIVE.' Even before the message could register, he heard the night nurse opening the ICU room door. Khalap quickly tucked the paper under his pillow.

'Yes?' the night nurse asked.

'Toilet,' Khalap replied.

'I'll send the ward boy for the bedpan.'

'No more bedpan, Sister. I'd prefer using the toilet.'

The sister dithered. 'Are you sure?'

'Yes, I have been permitted since morning,' Khalap lied.

'OK. I'll fetch the ward boy to help you,' the sister said. 'Do you need anything else?'

'No.'

The nurse turned on her heels and left. Khalap pulled the tissue from under his pillow, smoothened it and read the words again. 'WIFE NOT ALIVE.'

He turned it over to see if anything else had been scribbled on the other folds of the tissue paper. Who had put the tissue paper by his side? Was it the morning nurse, Sister Alka, whom he'd asked the questions this morning? Or had she asked the ward boy to place it there during the night when no one would notice? But why? Sympathy? Or was it a service rendered for which she would claim the reward later, discreetly?

Or was it Aditya who had bribed the ward boy or the nurse to get the message across. He stared at the handwriting again. Was it Aditya's or Pallavi's? But why would his son write 'Wife' and not 'Mum'?

Just then, the door swung open and Khalap quickly crumpled the tissue into a ball in one of his fists.

'Bedpan, saheb? Or toilet?' the ward boy asked.

'Toilet,' Khalap replied. 'Were you here before?'

The ward boy shook his head. 'No,' he said as he began helping Khalap up. 'Should I also call sister in case you don't feel steady?'

Khalap gave him a long look, then said, 'No.'

—

PSI Motkar had already tried the number of Pushpa Sonawane, Urmila Welde's caretaker, twice with an interval of fifteen minutes. Both the calls had neither been taken nor returned. He looked at his watch. He would need to leave for work in another fifteen to twenty minutes. He hoped the caretaker would call back by then. Or would it be better to send LPC Patil, who had accompanied him earlier, to check up on Urmila Welde?

His phone rang just as he was mulling the question. Relieved, he reached out for his mobile only to realise it was Sanika Zirpe calling. 'Yes, Zirpe?'

ASI Zirpe wished him a good morning and crisply briefed him about Rohidas Phule's old photo she'd stumbled across wearing the old amulet, found with the first skeleton.

PSI Motkar felt an uncharacteristic twinge of envy. 'You are on a roll, Zirpe. First the top and now this amulet!' he said, trying not to sound the way he felt.

'Fell into my lap, sir,' Sanika Zirpe said modestly. 'Inspector Saralkar sir said I should run it past you. When will you be reaching office, sir?'

'Let's meet in forty-five minutes, Zirpe,' PSI Motkar replied and Zirpe hung up.

Motkar shook his head as if trying to get rid of the sudden blip of pettiness. It didn't behove him. He'd never been small-minded. Sanika Zirpe was a junior officer and much younger to him. She'd come into the Homicide department much later and all good investigation was a result of teamwork. So, he had no business entertaining envious thoughts.

He glanced at his watch and decided to call Urmila Welde's caretaker, Pushpa Sonawane, one last time. If not, he would dispatch LPC Patil to the house. His call was however picked up and Pushpa Sonawane's voice came on line. 'Hello, saheb?'

'PSI Motkar here. Didn't you see my missed calls? I have been trying to get in touch.'

'Sorry, saheb, I was just helping my sister-in-law with some chores,' Pushpa Sonawane replied.

'Your sister-in-law?' PSI Motkar asked, startled. 'You mean she's visiting you?'

'No, saheb. I am visiting her. I'm on leave for a few days.'

'You are on leave? So, who's with your patient … I mean … Urmila Welde?'

'The same lady who comes as a stand-by usually. Niharika madam has an arrangement with a spinster living nearby, who drops in a few times a day at Aaji's place, when I or the previous caretakers had to go on leave or attend to some personal work for a few hours.'

'Give me the lady's name and number,' Motkar said urgently.

Something had started buzzing in his brain.

'Just a minute, sir,' Pushpa Sonawane said. Motkar could hear the sound of clicking buttons and then she came on line again and gave him a number. 'Her name is Pramilabai.'

'OK. Since when have you been on leave?'

'Since day before yesterday. I had wanted to take a few days off and told Niharika madam. So, two days ago she made arrangements with Pramilabai and told me I could go,' the caretaker replied.

'Madam met you?'

'No, sir. She called from Goa.'

'I see. She didn't tell you she's here in Pune?'

'No, sir.'

'OK, I'll call you back if needed,' PSI Motkar said and disconnected.

He pondered briefly, then began dialling the number Pushpa Sonawane had given, but no one picked up. Motkar glanced at his watch. There was no time to waste. It was best to ask LPC Patil to rush to Urmila Welde's house.

The moment he saw the A4-size light brown–coloured envelope on his table, Saralkar knew it contained the forensic report on the second skeleton, sent in by the specialised central laboratory. The senior inspector wasted no time in slitting the envelope open.

The contents turned out to be no less jaw-dropping than the report on the first skeleton. Their assumption had yet again been flawed. The second skeleton wasn't that of another boy. It was of a man who must have been of around thirty-five or thirty-eight at the time of death.

The body had probably been buried anywhere between twenty-five to thirty years ago—approximately ten years after the burying of the first skeleton. It showed ample evidence of violence from head to toe. There was a crack in the skull, two ribs were broken, the nose was fractured and two front teeth had been knocked out. The left shin and three fingers of the right hand were shattered.

Saralkar shuddered. God had probably been absent as usual when this man had met his ghastly fate. Or maybe he was present but had his hands full with other things.

The senior inspector sat back and re-read the details, this time slowly. There was clearly no similarity between the deaths of the boy and this man. What the hell did it all mean? Why were a young boy and a man thirty-five killed and buried here ten years apart? The boy was in all probability Parshuram, but who was this man?

Killing an adolescent boy was completely different from murdering an able-bodied man in his prime. It was one thing to suspect the Welde couple of having killed a child—an act of violence not physically impossible for adults of their age. But could they have been capable of battering a thirty-five year old man to his death by themselves? Unless of course, it was done for them by hired goons. Somehow it was difficult to imagine such a scenario.

What could have been the motive? As he had observed to his team earlier, the reasons for killing a child were often very different from the motives behind killing an adult. So, the obvious and critical question was: were the two murders connected? If so, what explained the long gap between the two killings? Saralkar clicked his tongue. This case was far from over. In fact, it felt as if it was beginning all over again and getting even more complicated.

'Sir!'

Saralkar glanced up to find a pale Motkar lurch into his cabin. It took a lot to ruffle Motkar. Something else was up, Saralkar surmised.

'Yes, Motkar, what's the matter?'

Motkar seemed to shuffle and hesitate, as if bracing himself. 'Sir, Urmila Welde is missing from her home ...' he said finally.

Saralkar groaned. 'What? How did she go missing? And since when?'

'She's missing since yesterday afternoon, sir. Post lunch,' Motkar replied.

'But doesn't she have a live-in caretaker?'

PSI Motkar sighed and explained how the caretaker Pushpa Sonawane had gone on leave for three days and the standby arrangement with the neighbourhood spinster, Pramilabai, who would drop in at intervals through the day to check in on Urmila Welde.

'Pramilabai says she fed the old lady lunch, gave her medications yesterday, then went back to her house. When she returned to Urmila Welde's place around 5.30 p.m., no one opened the door, so Pramilabai unlocked it with a spare key,' Motkar said. 'The old lady was nowhere to be found, so Pramilabai panicked and began a futile search in the building and locality, asking people if they had seen Urmila Welde go out. Then she tried calling Pushpa Sonawane, the caretaker, whose number was unreachable. She then called Niharika Das. When she too didn't take the call, Pramilabai got franctic but didn't know what to do. When Niharika Das called back an hour later, around 7 p.m., Pramilabai informed her that Urmila Welde was missing.'

'And Niharika Das hasn't informed or filed a missing person complaint at the nearest police station in the area?' Saralkar asked.

'No, sir. I tried calling Niharika Das after I learnt about all this, but she hasn't taken my call. Anyway, she should be here soon, as was already scheduled,' Motkar said.

'Damn it, Motkar. Shouldn't you have checked on Urmila Welde from time to time, without me having to suggest that?' Saralkar said, suddenly losing his cool.

'Sir, honestly, only when you asked me to do so yesterday morning did I first think of how Urmila Welde needed to be kept an eye on …' Motkar admitted sheepishly.

Saralkar glared at him. 'It can't be a coincidence that Urmila Welde has gone missing now, just when Niharika Das is being grilled by us and is in town. When the needle of suspicion is pointing towards the Weldes and the discovery of thc identity of the servant boy,' he said. 'Could it be that Anshuman Das was not present here yesterday precisely to make Urmila go missing?'

Motkar looked at him, startled. 'Sir, you mean they whisked Urmila Welde away because she might be a witness to the crimes committed by Shashank Welde?'

Saralkar nodded. 'I don't know what to think, Motkar. There's been another development.'

'What, sir?'

Saralkar picked up the forensic report and gave it to Motkar. 'The second skeleton is not of a child, as we had hastened to assume. It's that of a man. About thirty-five years old. And he seems to have been battered to death and buried about ten years after the first victim.'

Motkar flinched and stared at Saralkar baffled. He began perusing the report.

'Perhaps it's time for me to retire, Motkar. I am getting too old for all this,' Saralkar groaned.

29

ADINATH KHUBBA HAD BROODED OVER NAVNATH SHINDE'S abject plea to him, to not confess till he passed away. He had given his word to Navnath reluctantly. But it was already weighing heavily on him. That voice people called their conscience had suddenly grown much too shrill to ignore. A secret he'd nursed for almost twenty-five years now simply deafened him with its screams, demanding to be let out.

Adinath had come to a decision. He would call Navnath's son, Shrikant, and ask to speak with Navnath. He would tell his old friend he was sorry that he found it impossible to keep his word any longer. He would ask Navnath to forgive him and beg to be released from his promise. And if Navnath still pleaded with him not to confess, he would have no choice but to refuse to oblige this time.

Yes, that was the only alternative. The ringing of his mobile intruded on his thoughts. He looked around for his spectacles and realised he'd forgotten where he had left them, as usual.

'Hullo,' he said, taking the call.

'Adinath kaka, this is Shrikant speaking. Navnath Shinde's son …'

Adinath gave a surprised gasp. 'Yes, yes, Shrikant. You will live for a hundred years. I was just thinking of your father and you. How's Navnath?'

'I am afraid there is bad news, kaka. Father passed away two days ago,' Shrikant replied. 'Sorry I couldn't inform you earlier. I was busy with all the arrangements and rituals.'

'Oh my God! Navnath's gone. So terrible to hear that,' Adinath said, shaken by the swiftness of it all. Had Navnath really had a premonition he was going to die soon, or was it something his body and soul sensed from inside, after being diagnosed with cancer? 'Did … did he suffer? Was he in pain?'

'No, kaka. Strangely, father died of a heart attack, not cancer, but doctors say he wouldn't have pulled on much longer in any case. It was a matter of weeks,' Shrikant replied.

'Oh? I am glad he was spared more suffering.'

'Yes, kaka, I called to also let you know that he's left something for you,' Shrikant continued.

'For me? What?' Adinath asked, surprised.

'It looks like a letter. He gummed and stapled the envelope, so I guess he wanted only you to see it,' Shrikant said, his voice tinged with slight resentment.

'Oh, is that so?' Adinath responded, wondering what message Navnath had left for him. 'Should I come over and pick it up from your home, Shrikant?'

'Well, I could have dropped it at your home, but I have guests here who'd come for the funeral and there are other … er … formalities and rituals I am going to be busy with.'

'Yes, yes, I understand. Shrikant, tell me what time I can come tomorrow?'

'No, you need not bother. I'll send the envelope over to you by Speed Post or courier,' Shrikant said. 'But kaka, I'm really curious about what is inside, if you don't mind. I mean, since the day you met him, father seemed extra restless—as if something was on his mind. My mother also told me he was quite disturbed.

In fact, my mother insisted we open the envelope ourselves but I didn't think it would be right to do so. Can you please tell me what the matter is, after you receive the letter?'

Adinath's heart was in his mouth. His blood had turned cold. What explanation was he going to give Navnath's son? Why hadn't Navnath just couriered or posted the letter to him directly, instead of giving it to his son?

'OK … OK …' he replied hoarsely, unsure of what else he could say.

'But I … I already told you, ASI Zirpe, I neither know nor recollect anything. I can't help you,' Rohidas Phule said, trying to sound exasperated and impatient. 'And I certainly don't have the time to come to Pune right now.' In reality, his heart was pounding.

Zirpe glanced at Senior Inspector Saralkar sitting right next to her, listening in on the telephone conversation distractedly. He hadn't spoken a word yet and looked preoccupied. Zirpe felt disappointed. She needed her boss to intervene decisively, not just listen passively.

He spoke just then. 'Mr Phule, this is Senior Inspector Saralkar. This is not a request. We are summoning you for questioning to Pune. We have evidence that you worked for the Weldes and that you have information related to the crime. If you refuse to cooperate, we will have to pursue official channels.'

There was no response from the other end for a few seconds, as if Rohidas Phule had been robbed of speech. 'Look … please, officer … Senior Inspector Saralkar, please understand I am a very senior executive of my company! Can't we have the interaction over a video call?'

'Please be here tomorrow, Mr Phule. ASI Zirpe will be emailing you a formal summons in the next five minutes,' Saralkar replied and ended the call.

He looked at a visibly elated Zirpe, got up without a word and strode towards the interrogation room, outside which stood PSI Motkar and Advocate Shroff.

'Niharika Das has got herself admitted to hospital, sir,' PSI Motkar said, as soon as Saralkar reached them.

The senior inspector scowled and glared at Advocate Shroff, who was looking rather defensive and uneasy. 'Has she acted on your advice, madam?' he asked edgily.

'I am a lawyer, not a doctor, Inspector Saralkar,' Advocate Shroff replied. 'I just came to know about it an hour ago. I have nothing to do with it. My … my client got admitted to the hospital in the middle of the night for food poisoning.'

'Food poisoning?'

'Here's the preliminary report from the hospital,' Advocate Shroff said, pointing to a letter she had handed over to PSI Motkar.

Saralkar took the letter from Motkar. It stated blandly that Mrs Niharika Das had been admitted to the hospital at 2.17 a.m., with vomiting and severe stomach cramps, a case of suspected food poisoning, and that while her condition was stable and nothing serious was diagnosed, she was being advised twenty-four hours of rest. She would be discharged the next afternoon after being kept under observation for a few hours.

'Convenient!' Saralkar snarled.

Advocate Shroff flushed. 'What's the big deal, Saralkar? It's just a question of a day. And it's genuine.'

'Really? Advocate Shroff, has your client told you that her aunt Urmila Welde has gone missing since last evening?' Saralkar said brusquely.

'What?'

'Yes. So I am pretty sure your client is going to extend her stay in hospital by hook or crook, to avoid answering inconvenient questions about her aunt's disappearance,' Saralkar said.

He turned to Motkar. 'Escort Advocate Shroff, find Niharika's husband Anshuman and bring him back. He will be questioned in place of his wife today.'

Constable Angre finally had his Eureka moment when he received a call from the HR Manager of the company in which the two young boys who'd rented Shashank Welde's house and got involved in a police complaint had worked back then.

'We've managed to retrieve records of Sambit Kumar Shastry and Kalpesh Mankad,' the HR Manager said. 'They worked at our Pune plant from 1999 to 2002, then Sambit Kumar was transferred to our plant in Hosur, where he worked till 2006. We are sending you his last known address, telephone numbers, as well as his relieving letter and experience certificate.'

'OK. And what about Kalpesh Mankad?'

'Kalpesh Mankad also worked in another group company till 2002. First in Pune, but then he was transferred to our Mandideep plant in MP. Unfortunately, Kalpesh died in an industrial accident at one of our ancillary units—a transformer blast while he was visiting the unit for some work. Two other people also died.'

'Oh! And who did he leave behind? Next of kin?' Angre asked.

'Compensation records show it was paid to his wife, Jalpa Mankad. I think he was just newly married,' the HR Manager replied.

'OK, so please send me contact details of surviving family members.'

Half an hour later, he had the details of both Sambit Kumar Shastry and Kalpesh Mankad's family. There was one landline number and one mobile number in the contact details of Sambit Kumar Shastry, who hailed from Bhubaneswar. Constable Angre realised that one of the reasons they had not been able to trace him was because in all the earlier documents they had, his name was mentioned as S. Sambit Kumar. The Shastry had emerged only now.

Angre immediately set about calling both numbers. The mobile number no longer belonged to Sambit Kumar Shastry or any of his family members. A man unrelated to him answered the call, although he too was from Bhubaneswar. Angre then tried the landline number and a recorded message told him to check the number he had dialled. Who retained landlines anyway?

Angre was about to turn to social media to search for Sambit Kumar Shastry with his full name, when it struck him that perhaps the landline could still be in service, but like in all cities and towns across the country in the last twenty to twenty-five years, perhaps the telephone numbers in Bhubaneswar too had added digits to their original numbers. Half an hour later he sat back, satisfied. He had actually managed to get the changed landline number.

He dialled it now and the rings actually started to pass at the other end. Even better, the phone was picked up by an old man. 'I am Sambit's father. He now lives in Dubai but you can call tomorrow, he is on his way to India and will be here …'

That's when Angre felt like a fully- clothed Archimedes.

Nurse Alka avoided Kuldeep Khalap's gaze as she walked into the room, behind Dr Kaushal and his assistant junior doctor. Constable Shaikh too had taken his position by the door, as he usually did when the doctor did his rounds, morning and evening.

She studiously seemed to avoid eye contact as the doctor examined Khalap, made his observations and gave instructions. Neither did she make any attempt to communicate when the doctors left and Shaikh stepped out while she stayed behind to take stock of the medication inventory available and those that needed to be replenished, added or changed.

Her extreme self-consciousness was evident. 'Thank you,' Khalap said cautiously.

She darted a quick look at him but returned no acknowledgement. Khalap pulled at the crumpled tissue paper he had hidden in his armpit and displayed it. The nurse's eyes suddenly became wary. She snatched it from his hands, rushed to the toilet and quickly flushed it down.

'You have true goodness of heart, Sister,' Khalap said looking at her. 'Will you please do something for me?'

The nurse seemed to turn pale and began hurrying away. 'Ouch. Nurse, I need help!' Kuldeep Khalap cried out, feigning pain.

Nurse Alka looked at him, hesitated, then took a few steps back. 'What's the problem? Should I get the doctor?'

'No! Can I have a painkiller?' He winked, then with his index finger indicated she come closer.

Nurse Alka was clearly very reluctant, but she stood by his bedside. 'I'll check with Dr Kaushal.'

Kuldeep Khalap suddenly whispered to her. 'I'll pay you twenty-five thousand rupees, Sister. I just need to get a message across to my family urgently. They are not letting me see anyone. Please … Just one call from your mobile.'

The nurse shook her head and stepped back. She began turning to leave when Khalap hissed, 'Sister, have a heart. I just want to make one call. If twenty-five thousand is not enough, I'll make it fifty thousand.'

Nurse Alka gave him a doubtful glance, then shook her head. 'Please, it's too risky. I'll lose my job. If the police find out I helped you, they'll arrest me too. The constable sits right outside and I've seen in *Crime Patrol*, they can trace anybody's calls.'

'No, no, Sister, listen, there is a perfectly safe way,' Khalap whispered. 'Get one of your family members—husband, son, sister, brother—anyone to go to my house. We'll fix a time. Once your family member reaches, they can give you a missed call. Then I'll go into the bathroom and call on your family member's phone from your mobile and speak to my son quickly. My son will pay you the money in cash, right after. He can even go to the ATM if he does not have it on him.

That way, the call would be between you and your family member and there would be no evidence whatsoever that you helped me. Understand? No risk at all, Sister.'

She looked at him wide-eyed and scared, then said, 'Let me speak to my … my husband.'

'Yes, but please hurry up. I don't have much time,' Kuldeep Khalap said. 'It needs to be done today or latest by tomorrow morning.'

Nurse Alka gave a non-committal nod and left. Kuldeep Khalap wondered what she would decide. Would the lure of the money work to persuade her to take the risk? Risk was often directly proportional to greed. The genius of greed was that it often masqueraded as need.

He hoped Nurse Alka and her husband needed the money enough to give in to greed.

'Exactly, why have I been randomly dragged here like this for questioning?' Anshuman Das asked haughtily as soon as he was led into the presence of Saralkar. He struck a defiant pose, looking annoyed. 'Is this the way? My wife is in hospital and you abruptly force me to come here?'

Saralkar glanced at him. Anshuman Das belonged to that breed of the educated upper-middle–class who believed the best way to deal with the police was to bristle and act offended.

'Weren't you concerned about your wife yesterday when we were questioning her?' Saralkar shot back with a sneer. 'She was here. Where were you?'

Anshuman Das lost some of his haughtiness and scowled uncertainly. 'What do you mean? Advocate Shroff was with her … So … so I didn't accompany Niharika, that's all.'

'I see. Where were you then?'

'I … I had some work.'

'What work? And where?'

Anshuman Das's frown turned darker. 'Why should I tell you about my whereabouts yesterday, or what work I had?'

'Why shouldn't you?' Saralkar challenged evenly.

It aggravated Das further. 'Because it is none of the police's business.'

'Suppose it is?' Saralkar said gruffly.

'Why? What for?' Anshuman Das asked angrily.

Saralkar paused and watched him fume uneasily. 'Because your wife's dear aunt, Urmila Welde, went missing yesterday.'

Anshuman Das blanched, as if caught totally unawares.

'Didn't expect us to know, did you?' Saralkar asked, his tone hardening.

Anshuman Das tried to recover. 'We were … going to inform you … but … but …'

'When were you going to tell us? And why didn't you file a missing person's complaint last evening, knowing she suffers from dementia?' Saralkar said, raising his voice.

Anshuman Das seemed at a loss of words. 'We … we … you see, Inspector, too many things happened … my wife got food poisoning … my brother-in-law Sunit arrived from the USA and we thought … we should first try and look for Urmila Attya ourselves …'

'Your brother-in-law Sunit is here?' Saralkar asked with surprise. 'Since when?'

'Yes … Sunit arrived yesterday morning. Because Niharika told him about how the whole ordeal was taking a big toll on us … so he decided to come to be by her side …' Anshuman Das said.

A sudden suspicion struck Saralkar. Could Anshuman Das and Sunit Welde together be behind Urmila Welde's disappearance? Could they have whisked the old lady away? Taken her someplace where the police wouldn't find her, then claim she had gone missing? Because Urmila Welde knew something about the buried bodies that would indict Sunit and Niharika's parents?

Saralkar decided he needed to corner this man to get to the truth. 'Mr Das, stop lying and start speaking the truth. What have you done with Urmila Welde? Where is she?'

'What are you saying, Inspector? I have no idea … You think I … I have anything to do with her disappearance? That's crazy! Why would I?'

Saralkar raised his hand sternly. 'Your mobile was active yesterday at the location Urmila Welde stays in, as per call data records. Now what do you have to say to that?'

Anshuman Das looked stunned and he slumped into the chair. 'No … no it can't be,' he said, desperate disbelief spreading across his face. 'I … I was nowhere in that area … I swear …'

'Then how did you phone get there, Mr Das?'

Ashuman Das's baffled face suddenly changed expression. 'I … I had given one of my phones to Sunit to use, since he does not have a local sim card … Maybe …'

He hesitated and stopped.

'Ah!' Saralkar said. 'Is that so? Could it be that your brother-in-law came to India with the express intent of curing his aunt permanently? Of freeing her from her sufferings? Perhaps your wife and Sunit mutually agreed that was the only solution.'

Anshuman Das gave him a dazed look. The bluff about his mobile number had worked, Saralkar realised. How fortunate it hadn't crossed Anshuman Das's mind that the police had only one number of his, not the other one he had only just revealed.

'I suppose Sunit's in the hospital with your wife, right?'

Anshuman Das nodded. 'Yes. But you … you are completely mistaken, Inspector! How can you suggest my wife and brother-in-law have harmed Urmila Attya in any way?' he said wretchedly.

'Not just them. You too! All of you are under suspicion,' Saralkar remarked. 'Unless we find the missing old lady safe and sound.'

30

'REVIVE THE BASTARD,' THE ASI SAID. HE NEITHER SWAYED ON his feet nor was his speech slurred, but he couldn't possibly be sober, the constable reckoned.

It was well past midnight. 'Saheb, you've already taught him a solid lesson,' he said nervously.

'He's already pissed in his pants a few times,' the other constable chimed in with more flattery. 'Another round with you and he'll start shitting bricks, saheb.'

The ASI smirked and shook his head. 'You know what my father says, right? Stop battering them not when their bones break, but when your fists start complaining.' He chuckled and rumbled with laughter.

It didn't amuse the two constables, but they joined in the laughter.

'Go … revive him,' the ASI said again. 'My fists aren't complaining yet …'

'Why am I here, Inspector? Please don't forget I am an American citizen,' Sunit Welde said with that slight affectation of manner that many NRIs displayed. It probably wasn't something they did consciously but had acquired after staying abroad for so long.

'So?' Saralkar asked.

'Nothing, except please don't try to take liberties with me that you may be accustomed to taking with Indian citizens.'

Saralkar gave him a long steady look. There was apprehension lurking behind that impertinence. 'Such as?'

Sunit Welde let out an irritated sigh. 'We both know what I am talking about, Inspector.'

Saralkar gave him another smug look. 'How come your aunt disappeared right after you landed in India?' he asked.

'What's that supposed to mean? That I had something to do with it?' Sunit Welde asked, offended.

'It's a possibility that we are considering,' Saralkar said with a nod.

'On what basis? Why would I make her disappear?'

'Mr Welde, I am the cop. I ask the questions,' Saralkar said in a tone that sought to put Sunit Welde in place. 'Understood?'

Sunit Welde blinked, then looked away.

'Now, tell me—was this trip to India a planned one?' Saralkar asked.

'My sister Niharika called me up three days ago. She sounded very disturbed. I realised I needed to be here to support her because she's been bearing the brunt of this terrible ordeal alone for weeks now,' Sunit replied.

'I see. Were you concerned about her or about the family secrets tumbling out?'

'Of course I was concerned about Niku. She's my sister,' Sunit snapped. 'And what family secrets? We know nothing. We are just as shocked and bewildered about this ghastly matter.'

Saralkar narrowed his eyes. 'You say you came over to support your sister but neither you nor her husband Anshuman accompanied her here for questioning yesterday?'

Sunit Welde frowned. 'I landed in Mumbai early morning, and by the time I reached Pune by road, it was 11.30 a.m. I was dog-tired, so I ate something and slept. I asked Anshuman if we should come here to be with Niharika, but he told me Advocate Shroff was with her and had advised against it.'

'Hmm. So then you went to visit your Urmila Attya?' Saralkar said.

'What? No, I did not pay any visit to my aunt's place …' Sunit said vehemently.

'Then please explain why your mobile was active at the spot for about half an hour?' Saralkar asked, using the same bluff he'd played with Anshuman Das.

'What are you talking about? I wasn't even carrying my mobile when I went out,' Sunit countered.

'You were carrying your brother-in-law's mobile, right? That's the one I am talking about,' Saralkar retorted sharply.

Sunit seemed momentarily at a loss for words. 'Yes, I had Anshuman's mobile with me but I don't even know where my aunt lives, so how could I be there?'

'Then how did the mobile get there? And if you were not there, where were you?'

'I was in the Koregaon Park area with a friend …'

'So, give us the contact details of this friend and we will check out your alibi.'

'Alibi? What are you talking about, Inspector? I have not abducted my aunt, damn it,' Sunit Welde flared up. 'Why would I do that?'

'So that she does not spill family secrets about the two skeletons found in Shanti Villa.'

Sunit Welde threw back his head in exasperation. 'Do you have any proof of all your suspicions and these allegations?'

Saralkar's mobile buzzed, just as he was about to respond. It was Inspector Rajguru again. He took the call and listened. 'Yes, OK. Let it proceed as discussed,' he said shortly then disconnected, and turned to Sunit again. 'Give us details of the friend you claim you were with yesterday,' he repeated.

Sunit Welde hesitated. 'I … I cannot. That would put my friend in an awkward position.'

'Why should that be so?'

'That's none of your business. It's a personal matter,' Sunit Welde said.

'That means you are without an alibi,' Saralkar emphasised and let it sink in. 'Tell me, you also told Inspector Zirpe that you were not on good terms with your aunt. Why is that?'

Sunit flushed. 'What's that got to do with anything? Some family members just don't get along. That's all!'

'True. But I'd like to know if something happened—some incident or problem—that led to the estrangement?' Saralkar persisted. He had been watching Sunit's expressions and was sure that the man bore an active dislike for his aunt.

'I am not obliged to tell you that, Inspector.'

'You are. Your aunt is missing and I think you may have had something to do with her disappearance,' Saralkar asserted impatiently. He was getting irritated with Sunit Welde's refusal to part with information.

'To hell with your suspicions! What are you going to do if I don't answer your questions,' Sunit Welde suddenly blurted out.

He glared at Saralkar defiantly.

The door of the interrogation room flew open and PSI Motkar rushed in. 'Sir,' he said and quickly whispered something into Saralkar's ear.

Saralkar listened, his eyes not leaving Sunit Welde. Motkar finished and rushed out of the room, as hastily as he had come.

'I'll tell you what I'm going to do, Sunit Welde, American citizen. I might decide to arrest you right away, because your aunt's dead body has just been found,' Saralkar remarked and watched Sunit Welde congeal and baulk.

'I can't bear to live here anymore,' Pallavi remarked with a shudder. 'I get the creepy feeling that Mum's watching us all the time. I remember that look on her face the first time she caught us.'

She covered her face with her hands.

Aditya watched her grapple with shame. 'We have nothing to be ashamed of, Pallavi. I'll rent a small flat and we'll move into it as soon as I get a job. I have sent in a lot of applications.'

She sniffed and looked up. 'But you've still to complete your MBA.'

'Getting a job is a priority right now,' Aditya said. 'We don't know what is going to happen with Papa and in case he gets convicted ...'

His sentence was cut short by the sound of the doorbell. Both Aditya and Pallavi looked at each other. Who could it be? Then Aditya got up from the sofa they were sitting on, walked across the hall and opened the door.

A slim, middle-aged man stood outside, looking warily. 'Are you Aditya Khalap?' he asked.

'Yes. Who are you?'

The man licked his lips and spoke in a low voice as if afraid of being overheard. 'My wife, Alka, works as a nurse at the hospital. Your father is not being allowed to meet or contact you, so he requested my wife to help. I am supposed to give a missed call on her number now, so that your father can call back from her mobile and talk to you, without anyone knowing. Can I come in?'

Aditya looked at him with doubt and disbelief. 'What? How do I know you are telling me the truth?'

The man shuffled uneasily. 'Look … I'll dial my wife's number and when your father calls back you can see for yourself if it's him speaking.'

Aditya gazed at him, then glanced at Pallavi who was staring apprehensively. 'OK, come in.'

'So, what has finally been determined as the cause of death?' Saralkar demanded.

'Sir, it's complicated. The doctor reckons she died by drowning, but the skull and other injuries she sustained could have killed Urmila Welde anyway,' Motkar explained.

Saralkar tapped the table with his knuckles. 'And they don't think the injuries were inflicted on her by an assailant?'

'No, sir. They think the injuries are consistent with a fall from the bridge,' Motkar replied. 'Urmila Welde was either pushed or thrown down into the river, from the bridge. Since there was very little water depth in the river—hardly a foot or two—she hit the river bed, suffered the injuries, lost consciousness and died due to drowning, since her face was underwater. If she hadn't drowned, the injuries were anyway severe enough to be fatal.'

'What a way to die!' Saralkar grunted. 'Are there any signs of a scuffle—any scratches on the body, signs of hands or feet being bound?'

'Too early to say, sir. Even this prima facie opinion of cause of death is subject to post-mortem confirmation that will be conducted tomorrow morning,' Motkar said.

A strange, restless expression spread itself on Saralkar's face. 'It's at times like these that I get the urge to resort to third degree, Motkar,' he mumbled angrily.

'You mean with the Das couple and Sunit Welde, sir?' Motkar asked hesitantly.

Saralkar nodded grimly.

'But, sir, all we have is conjecture, not even circumstantial evidence to suggest they could have done this to the old woman,' Motkar said.

'I know that very well, Motkar. That's precisely why I won't indulge my urge to beat it out of them,' Saralkar snapped. 'Anyway, do we have any leads at all? Did you grill the standby caretaker lady from the neighbourhood again?'

'Yes, sir. Pramilabai said she was contacted by Niharika Das two days ago asking her if she would be able to look after Urmila Welde since the regular caretaker, Pushpa Sonawane, was going on leave. Pramilabai said she was ready as per their usual arrangement—spend the night at Urmila Welde's home, give her breakfast and morning medication, bathe her, then go back to her own house for about two hours,' Motkar said. 'She'd come back around 1.30 p.m., give the old lady lunch and afternoon medication, wait till Urmila Welde settled in for a siesta, then go back to her own home. She would usually return around 5–5.30 p.m., check everything was fine, give the old lady tea, take her for a quick walk, then make her a light dinner like soup and rice. After that, Pramilabai would go home for about an hour, and then return to give Urmila Welde her medication and sleep there for the night.'

'Where was the caretaker's house?' Saralkar asked.

'Just two lanes away, sir. Less than five hundred metres.'

'But then instead of all this to and fro, why wouldn't she just spend the whole day at Urmila Welde's home?'

'Sir, that's because it seems this Pramilabai does some tailoring work from home on a contract basis, so she had to be at home doing her job for a few hours.'

'Did you have all that checked out?'

'Yes, sir.'

'So, there was no practice of locking Urmila Welde's door from outside?' Saralkar asked.

'No, sir.'

'Isn't that strange? I mean the old lady could just walk out and get lost, couldn't she?'

'Yes, sir, but it seems Urmila Welde had never attempted any such thing. She just needed someone to look after her,' Motkar said. 'Generally speaking, she would be alright and this standby arrangement with Pramilabai went without a hitch, if it were a question of a few days. Moreover, she was used to Pramilabai … or at least did not look upon her as a stranger.'

'I see,' Saralkar said. 'So you don't think this Pramilabai had a hand in the disappearance?'

'No, sir. I doubt it.'

'Are you sure she wasn't hand-in-glove with the Das couple in arranging Urmila Welde vanishing?'

'No, sir,' Motkar said. 'It's very unlikely.'

'What kind of lock did the flat door have? Normal latch lock?'

'Yes, sir.'

'So, no one could just open and enter? She would have to let them in or someone would have to have the key?' Saralkar asked.

'Yes, sir. Pushpa Sonawane usually had two keys, one of which she gave to Pramilabai, the standby caretaker, before going on leave.'

'Hmm. It stands to reason that Niharika Das must also have one additional key to the flat with herself as a precaution, in case the caretaker misplaced or lost the keys, and given the fact that caretakers kept changing every few months, right?' Saralkar surmised.

Motkar nodded slowly, 'Yes, sir. Although of what practical value would a spare key be in an emergency, if it was in Niharika Das's possession in Goa?'

'True. Perhaps Niharika Das left the spare key with someone in Pune—a friend or acquaintance,' Saralkar said. 'We need to get a confirmation that a spare key exists, because that is what might have been used to gain entrance into the flat if Urmila Welde was whisked away or abducted.'

Motkar made a quick note.

'What else, Motkar? Any witnesses who saw Urmila Welde with anyone or getting into a car with someone?' Saralkar asked.

'No, sir. We have been scouring the neighbourhood, but no one's come forward so far.'

'No one even saw an unknown visitor come into the building that day or a stranger seen loitering nearby?' Saralkar asked.

Motkar shook his head. 'Sir, the worst part is the locality is such that there are no CCTVs around in the vicinity, so there's no way of checking if she left with someone. We've circulated her photo and description, but no leads have come in yet.'

Saralkar drummed his fingers on the table, baffled. 'How about the bridge from which she might have been pushed?

There's got to be CCTVs around somewhere leading up to that bridge. There's got to be some footage of how she got there and who was with her.'

'We are checking the footage, sir,' Motkar replied.

'Damn it, Motkar. How did we manage to let the one person who might know the secrets of this case first vanish and then die like that?' Saralkar said, suddenly angry.

They were both silent for a few seconds, incredibly disappointed with themselves.

'Have you searched Urmila Welde's flat?' Saralkar asked.

'No forensic leads, sir,' Motkar replied.

'No, not just that. Search her belongings. Turn her house upside down,' Saralkar said.

'To look for what exactly, sir?'

'I don't know, Motkar. There's got to be something,' Saralkar said, almost sounding desperate.

Motkar gaped at his boss. He had never seen Saralkar look and sound so frantic. Perhaps even sharp minds sometimes needed a chance breakthrough to rally their efforts.

Saralkar's phone buzzed, breaking that momentary brooding silence. 'Yes, Rajguru!'

'Sir,' Inspector Rajguru said, 'DCP Khalap's son Aditya is here. He says he wishes to retract his earlier statement and give a new one.'

'I see. I am on my way,' Saralkar replied wearily, disconnected, then turned to Motkar. 'By the way, did you check all the numbers that Niharika Das made and received calls from, over the last month?'

'Yes, sir, I have already initiated that,' Motkar replied.

'OK. Keep me posted. I might be occupied with the Khalap case even tomorrow morning,' Saralkar said, giving him a world-weary look and trudged out of the room.

Motkar slumped in his chair. He himself was feeling no less careworn. Saralkar hadn't said it in so many words but Motkar had to admit to himself that it had been remiss of him not to have arranged for a discreet watch on Urmila Welde. As an experienced officer, why had it needed a prod from his boss to realise the significance of Urmila Welde to the investigation? That if anyone was likely to have known the secrets of Shanti Villa, it would have to be her, and for that reason alone she needed to be safeguarded.

And now she was dead—a helpless, old woman suffering from dementia, who had fallen down one hundred feet into a shallow and filthy riverbed, broken her skull and other bones in her frail body, then drowned to death. Hardly a death she deserved. Or did she? Whatever it was, she had carried her secrets to her grave.

'Sir,' Angre peeped at him through the half-open door.

'Yes, Angre?'

The young constable floated into the room. He seemed all aflutter, the expressions on his face animated. 'Sir … yesterday I managed to trace the two young professionals, Sambit Kumar and Kalpesh Mankad, who'd stayed as tenants at Shanti Villa in 1999–2002,' Angre said, words tumbling out.

'Yesterday? So why have you taken so long to inform me?' Motkar asked, readying to rebuke him.

'Sorry, sir, but there was nothing noteworthy to report yesterday and … you … you seemed terribly busy both days,' Angre said.

Motkar rolled his eyes. 'So have things changed today?'

'Yes, sir …' Angre said breathlessly. 'While Kalpesh Mankad died in an industrial accident many years ago, Sambit Kumar Shastry is based in Dubai but, as luck would have it, he's visiting his family in India. I called up today to speak to him, as his father had suggested yesterday. And Sambit Kumar told me something very interesting, sir.'

Angre paused as if he was narrating a dramatic story.

'Go on …'

What Angre told him intrigued PSI Motkar. 'That certainly sounds odd, Angre. I'd like to hear it again from Sambit Kumar himself. Call him up. But well done!'

'Yes, sir,' Angre beamed and dialled Sambit Kumar Shastry's number.

31

Aditya Khalap sat hunched forward on a wooden chair, his elbows resting on his knees, his palms clasped together, fingers interlocked, raised towards his mouth, tapping at his lips. It was as if he had undergone a personality transformation since Saralkar had last questioned him.

He looked up as Saralkar walked in with Rajguru. Gone was the seething anger and blaze in his eyes. It had been replaced by anxiety and sadness.

'What's this I hear, Aditya? That you want to change your earlier statement and all the things you told me last time?' Saralkar asked.

Aditya nodded. 'Yes, I wish to withdraw my statement, saying my father shot my mother …'

Saralkar sat down and looked at him grimly. 'What do you mean? If he didn't shoot your mother, who did?'

Aditya shook his head, clearly troubled. 'I mean, it did not happen the way I said it did.'

'So, were you lying to me?' Saralkar asked sharply. 'You know that's an offence.'

'No … I … I was angry with my father for all the upheavals in our lives—the rape, the custodial death, the inquiries. I blamed him for my mother's mental state and agitation … and held him responsible for all that happened that night … her death,' Aditya said, his voice lifeless and flat. 'But now that it is clear he has no memory of anything, it is not fair of me to have stated that he killed my mother.'

'Fair?'

Aditya nodded. 'Yes … my mother did not die trying to stop my father from shooting himself …'

He paused and took a couple of breaths as if preparing to launch himself into a difficult task.

'Actually she … she grabbed the gun and threatened to shoot him … it was then that he tried to snatch the gun from her in self-defence … and … and … she … my mother got shot in the scuffle.'

Aditya stopped, as if his mouth had suddenly gone dry and his tongue had scalded.

Saralkar and Rajguru looked at each other. Inspector Rajguru raised his eyebrows and began reaching for his pocket. Saralkar gestured to him to wait, then turned to Aditya. 'And how do you know this? What you told us earlier was based on what you claimed to have heard happening inside their locked bedroom. You also said this is exactly what your father also communicated to you before he shot himself?' Saralkar asked.

Aditya hesitated, then looked at him straight in his eyes. 'Because … because I … I saw it with my own eyes. I was witness to it.'

Saralkar scoffed at him. 'Now you are telling me you were inside your parents' bedroom when everything happened?'

Aditya shook his head. 'No … I had run to the back of the bungalow to try and see what was happening and intervene by talking to them through the sliding grille doors that opened on the flowerbeds behind their bedroom.'

Saralkar was startled. This was exactly what he had suspected. 'Go on.'

'But the grille doors were bolted and the sliding glass windows were drawn close and jammed, so I could not enter. I tried in vain to stop my parents by pleading and asking them to calm down but they were both in a very … very edgy, dangerous mood … and it all just spun out of control,' Aditya said. 'I couldn't do a thing. My mother attacked father, there was a scuffle and then the gun went off … She fell back limp and he was so overcome that he was convinced he had killed her … he started muttering that he was going to kill himself … I begged him not to. Then I ran to the car, got the jack and tried to break down the bedroom door as I said but it was too late … I heard him shoot himself … That is what actually happened …'

Saralkar regarded him for a few seconds, without saying a word. 'Aditya, how do I know you are telling me the truth now? Maybe you are lying just to save your father?' he said finally.

'Sir, I lied earlier. I am telling you the facts now. You can confirm with … with Pallavi,' Aditya replied.

'Was she also present when you were looking in through the sliding window grilles? Did she also witness everything?' Saralkar asked.

'No, no, I had narrated everything I had seen to her that night …' Aditya replied. 'I am not making it all up. You can ask her.'

'I see. What exactly is your relationship with your sister, Aditya?' Saralkar decided it was time to get to the bottom of the matter.

Anxiety leapt into Aditya's eyes. 'What?'

'Pallavi and you are not related by blood, right? She's not your real sister. She's adopted, correct?'

Aditya's eyes had widened with fear and he had turned unbelievably pale. He looked speechless.

'You love each other not as brother and sister but romantically. You are in a relationship,' Saralkar said as gently as he could, but his tone had an undercurrent of firmness that would brook no nonsense.

Deep, stormy emotions bubbled under the dazed expression on Aditya's face. He was clearly shaken that the secret that made them most vulnerable was known to the police.

'It's not a crime, legally or morally. We can't help feeling the way we do,' he said in a hollow voice, as if scared and defiant at the same time but looking for assurance.

Saralkar didn't want to debate that aspect right now. His reasons for bringing up the topic were entirely different. He shrugged, 'That might be so, but it is definitely a crime to give false evidence, which helps acquit someone guilty of murder. That's exactly what you are doing to safeguard Pallavi, right?'

Aditya regarded him warily.

'Today, you spoke to your father on phone, Aditya. A call made from a nurse's phone to her husband's mobile. We know all about it. During the call, your father threatened you to retract whatever you had told the police earlier and record a fresh statement absolving him. He asked you to testify that your mother attacked him and she died in the scuffle, while he was just trying to defend himself,' Saralkar said, then paused and looked at Inspector Rajguru.

'The telephone conversation was recorded,' Inspector Rajguru said addressing Aditya. 'Your father can clearly be heard warning you that even if he remained in custody or was eventually sentenced to jail, he would get Pallavi eliminated through his underworld contacts at some point in time—if not now, then a year later. That he would find both of you wherever you went and ensure she died, if you didn't change your statement like he wanted, because she wasn't really his blood. He knew all about your romantic involvement with Pallavi. Probably your mother had learnt about it first, a few days before the shooting—all of which had added to the tension at home.'

Aditya suddenly lost his composure and began sobbing. His body shuddered as he dipped his face into his palms and let all his defences dissolve. Both cops let him cry. It had been a well-laid trap they had set for DCP Kuldeep Khalap and they were glad he had fallen into it.

Saralkar had reckoned that Khalap would be desperate to establish contact with his son or his lawyer after the senior inspector had said he would be moved to jail from hospital, after the forty-eight-hour deadline. It had helped that Constable Shaikh had established a good rapport with Nurse Alka and Inspector Rajguru had persuaded her to play her part the moment Khalap had first sought her help in confirming whether his wife was alive. They had planted the tissue paper note and Khalap had jumped to the conclusion that it was Sister Alka trying to unobtrusively help. Her reluctance and hesitation, even after he lured her with money, had only convinced him further she could be trusted.

It had worked out even better because Khalap himself had worked out a plan that he believed was safe—in a way setting up his own trap.

Aditya had quietened down. 'He'll kill her … he'll kill Pallavi someday, if I don't stick to the account I just gave …' he pleaded with Saralkar. 'He's a killer. He's killed earlier …'

'You mean the custodial death inquiry?' Saralkar asked, pricking his ears.

'No … even before that … when he was younger … I wasn't even born then. All of it came tumbling out just before the shooting. That's why he had gone so crazy, so berserk because he thought all his past sins were suddenly catching up with him,' Aditya said. 'He was just freaking out. He was drunk half the time … Just before the rape inquiry announcement, I had also told my mother about Pallavi and me, when she … er … came upon us together one day … and an ugly confrontation had erupted. He even threatened to kill us both in the name of honour or to kill himself. Our house was a cauldron like I told you.'

'I see. So now tell us, were you really an eyewitness to what happened between your parents that night or are you making this version up because of your father's threats today,' Saralkar asked.

Aditya shook his head. 'I can't risk putting Pallavi's life in danger. My father will kill her if I don't do as he says.'

'What makes you think that you father is going to be less of a danger to Pallavi and you if he gets away with not being convicted for your mother's murder, but for causing accidental death or killing in self-defence?' Saralkar said to him. 'And look, if you go ahead with a false testimony to help him, you too can be charged, convicted and imprisoned for abetment to his crime. Then what will happen to Pallavi? Where will she go? She has not even finished her studies. How will she earn? What kind of a life will she lead? Remember, we have the recording of the telephone conversation with your father.'

Aditya clutched his forehead and closed his eyes. 'I am scared.'

'You haven't done anything to be scared, Aditya,' Saralkar said. 'Your best bet is to testify about what actually happened. And to provide all other information that you may have of any crimes DCP Khalap has committed in the past.'

Aditya didn't raise his head. 'He's my father.'

'Yes, but he's done what he's done and is now asking you to conceal a heinous crime. Not only that, he's forcing you to concoct a false testimony which vilifies your mother as the aggressor and has threatened to kill Pallavi, whom you love and who still happens to be his adopted daughter,' Saralkar said. 'Are these the actions of a good father?'

He let a few beats pass for Aditya to sift through his thoughts and let the implications sink in. Love, fear, loyalty were emotions that produced strange outcomes because convoluted logic often masqueraded as convincing rationale.

'Much more happened that night,' Aditya finally spoke. 'When my mother went into the bedroom, as I said, things calmed down at first. Pallavi went to her room and I hung around in the outside room, waiting a little longer to make sure things were really alright. Then just before sleeping, I went to Pallavi's room to check if she was OK. We sat whispering and discussing things. Around fifteen minutes later, by some rotten coincidence, just as I stepped out of Pallavi's room, my parents' door opened and father came out, probably for water or something. As soon as he saw me, he lost his temper and began raging, saying the most vulgar things about us and that he would not allow such things under his roof. I tried to explain that Pallavi and I were just talking, but it only fuelled his rage. He seemed to be even more drunk. My mother also woke up and came out to intervene. But his anger only escalated and he began calling Pallavi a slut and a whore. That's when I could stand it no more and told him he had no right to lecture us on morals and honour and such stuff. I even said something like I would forget he was my father if he uttered another filthy word about Pallavi.'

Aditya paused as if the scene was replaying right in front of his eyes. 'I should've known just how disturbed he was but I couldn't help responding like that. It incensed him further and he turned on his heels into his room. What came out of his mouth next chilled us all. He said he was going to get his gun and shoot Pallavi dead. I couldn't believe my ears. My mother followed him inside, pleading with him, and just as she shut their bedroom door, she shouted to me to bolt it from outside.

I was stunned, then panicked. I quickly bolted their bedroom door from outside, then rushed to Pallavi's room and told her to lock her door and stay inside. I could hear my parents' raised voices. I ran to the back of the house, as I said, to see what was happening. The grille door was bolted, and the sliding windows were jammed, but through a gap in the curtain I could see that my father and mother were physically grappling. My father was telling her to let him go—that he was going to shoot Pallavi, as she was the root of all our current misfortunes. He was completely out of control. Then he said he would shoot the entire family and then himself. My mother was calling him a coward, and that he had gone mad.'

Aditya stopped and gasped, then began sobbing. 'I … I was a coward too … I should've tried to talk and reason with my father through the windows or attempted somehow to enter the room by shattering the glass or gone back into the house to break open their bedroom door. Instead … I just froze and watched … scared and dreading my fate and Pallavi's. And then the gun went off. My mother let out that blood-curdling scream I will never forget. She slumped to the ground. There was blood all over and it jolted my father out of his frenzy. He just stood like a statue gazing at her dead body, then the rest happened exactly like I had said in my first statement. He eventually turned the gun on himself.'

'I see. So, he didn't come after you or Pallavi? He realised that he had injured your mother fatally and decided to kill himself too?' Saralkar asked.

'Yes, I was horrified by all that I had seen him do, but the last thing I wanted was for him to shoot himself as well. I told him a couple of times that my mother might still be alive, but he kept saying she was dead and that he had killed her,' Aditya said. 'I did my best to dissuade him from killing himself, but …'

'OK,' Saralkar said. 'Now Inspector Rajguru is going to take down your fresh statement. Is there anything else you have been hiding or keeping from us? If so, now is the time to tell.'

Aditya stared at him for a few seconds, then shook his head. 'Why doesn't telling the truth make me feel any safer, sir? Why do I feel sure my father will eventually get Pallavi and me?'

Yet again, the young man had asked him a question with no easy answers. 'No, he won't,' Saralkar replied. 'Trust me!' He hoped the words he had uttered wouldn't turn out to be empty.

32

Rohidas Phule had read every word of the typed statement carefully and made several corrections, almost as if meticulously editing an essay. He removed his spectacles and handed back the paper to ASI Zirpe. 'Please rectify these errors and I'll sign the statement.'

Sanika Zirpe glanced through the corrections. Phule hadn't backtracked on anything he'd stated, nor tried to introduce ambiguity. Instead, he'd added more clarity or inserted detail. She nodded and called the constable who'd taken down and typed the draft. 'Get me a final copy with corrections, for signatures.'

She'd been dismayed that morning to find that neither Saralkar nor Motkar were in a position to join her in interrogating Rohidas Phule, who had turned up as summoned. She would have to handle it all on her own. But ASI Zirpe had realised almost at once that the man in front of her had been considerably softened by the terse, peremptory manner in which Saralkar had spoken to him the previous day.

Rohidas Phule had come with his wife, not his lawyer, which was a good sign. Any other man in his position could easily have thought it safer, especially because he could afford one. But he had chosen not to, which probably meant Phule believed there could not be anything potentially incriminating against him.

Zirpe had borrowed her boss's brusqueness and wasted no time in first showing Phule his photo along with others, found in the Welde family albums. No sooner had he acknowledged that it was him, Zirpe had produced blow-ups of the amulet, around his neck in the pic and the broken piece found with the first skeleton. Upon being asked what had happened to the amulet he wore, Rohidas Phule was unable to recall precisely but vaguely remembered having lost it while at work back then.

Zirpe had promptly revealed that it had been found with the first skeleton of the small boy. A stunned silence had followed as Rohidas Phule fidgeted and fiddled with the metal strap of his wristwatch, clicking it open, then shutting it.

Finally, he cleared his throat and out tumbled the story of having been urgently requested to dig a trench by Shashank Welde, being offered a surprising amount of money for it, and doing the task in the company of Bansi Vishwakarma, the driver. Phule had also narrated the misgivings and doubts that had arisen in his mind subsequently, but having found no concrete reason to believe he had inadvertently helped in committing a crime, he had completely forgotten about it.

'And yes, it's likely my amulet got lost that same evening, while digging the trench,' Rohidas Phule concluded. 'I have a vague recollection of realising that it was missing from around my neck that night when I went for bath. However, I cannot be sure since it was so long ago.'

He paused, then leaned forward emphatically, 'But ... please understand, I had no role to play if a crime had been committed, nor did I have an inkling that I was being asked to hide such a deed ... although later I did feel a little uneasy and puzzled.'

He paused again and trembled just a little. 'God forgive me if I was remiss in asking questions about what I had felt was a strange request by Welde saheb, but it was beyond my imagination … back then … that … that a man of his status … of his kindness and quality … would kill and bury someone … that too a child …'

He stopped and shook his head in disbelief. 'I still find it hard to believe.'

'I see. What about his driver, Bansi Vishwakarma? We understand you did not get along,' Zirpe asked.

Rohidas Phule grimaced. 'Rotten fellow. Rogue. Obsequious to the Weldes, and totally boorish with me and the other … er … servants. Can't believe I was once in the servant category. That's why I feel no nostalgia for those times.'

Zirpe nodded. 'Did he by any chance maintain contact with you later or maybe bump into you somewhere …'

Rohidas Phule shook his head. 'Never. Thank God. I moved out of the working-class orbit. I wouldn't be surprised if he's still remained a driver.'

'Do you remember any details about him? His native place, family details or any other thing he may have mentioned or bragged about?'

Rohidas Phule thought for a moment. 'He was from some small town in Bihar. That's all I remember.'

'Alright. Do you at all recollect a small boy called Parshuram who was briefly employed by the Weldes as a live-in servant?' Zirpe asked.

Something like a flash registered in Rohidas Phule's eyes. 'Oh my God … was it that boy?' He looked at Zirpe with complete horror. 'I swear I did not remember him at all before this moment when you mentioned him … My God … but … but he was … if I remember correctly … from Vishwakarma's village or something. He'd brought the boy to work.'

Zirpe sat up. 'Are you sure?'

'Yes. He was. Now I remember the boy had a habit of plucking guavas and vegetables from the garden surreptitiously. I would get enraged … I told madam and sir too … Anyway, he was gone after a few weeks … I heard he was found unsuitable and packed off back to his village … My God … you mean he … he was … it's his skeleton?'

'Most likely,' Zirpe said.

'Poor kid. But … but it was Vishwakarma who told us the boy was packed off to the village …' Rohidas Phule said.

Sanika Zirpe's heart was pounding. 'Mr Phule, I need you to add this information to your statement as well. Will you do that?'

'Of course!' Rohidas Phule said, without dithering even one bit.

'Good morning, Kuldeep Khalap,' Senior Inspector Saralkar said, as he entered the hospital room accompanied by Inspector Rajguru and Constable Shaikh. 'I said I'd be back after forty-eight hours and here I am. Your discharge papers are ready and so is the CP's sanction to place you under arrest.'

A storm seemed to descend over Kuldeep Khalap's face and he stared at Saralkar with quiet fury. It was as if he couldn't trust himself to speak lest profanities flew out of his mouth.

'Fuck you, Saralkar!' he finally snarled. 'I'll make you pay for this!'

'You are just adding to your list of crimes, Khalap. Rape, murder, attempted suicide and now threatening a police officer,' Saralkar said and gestured to his team. 'Rajguru, Shaikh, take Kuldeep Khalap into custody.'

'How dare you? You are going to fall flat on your face, Saralkar … and I promise, I'll make you regret this,' Khalap said clenching his teeth, seething with anger.

'How? You have done such a fantastic job of implicating yourself by making that call to your son, Khalap,' Saralkar said. 'In one stroke you have provided evidence that you were faking loss of memory and that you didn't shoot your wife by accident or in self-defence.'

Khalap's face had assumed an expression of deadly bafflement. 'You bastard. You set me up?'

'Oh no! I merely created conditions so that you could set yourself up. As they say, *vinaash kale vipareet buddhi*! You cooked your own goose,' Saralkar chuckled grimly. 'Thanks to you, anyone listening to the recording will recognise what a thoroughly despicable and vicious policeman you are. It's probably something you yourself realised momentarily after you killed your wife, which is why you were disgusted enough with yourself to try and end your life too.'

Khalap's glare seemed to lose its fire. 'Who told you to save my life? Only so that you could try, convict, punish and humiliate me?'

'There's no pleasure in taking a man down, Khalap, especially a fellow cop,' Saralkar said. 'You survived. You could've tried to redeem yourself. Instead, you made pathetic attempts to escape guilt by threatening your own children with their lives? Shame on you!'

Khalap sneered. 'You have zero understanding of human nature, Saralkar. I am what I am. I am what I have become. It's my nature … in my genes! And show me one human being who wants to be punished for the wrongs he's committed. Even a good cop like you! As for me, if you knew all the things I've done.'

He paused and gave Saralkar a cynical look, 'As I said, you should have let me die … I shot myself in a moment of true regret and self-loathing, but that moment and sentiment is gone now, because I am alive. Self-flagellation is a very transient state of mind and even more rarely does it drive one to the point of self-annihilation. The survival instinct is far stronger and ever present.'

As always, human nature both marvelled and dismayed Saralkar. Moreover, criminals spouting wisdom always drove him up the wall. 'You are half-way to becoming a philosopher, Khalap,' he smirked. 'In prison, I am sure you'll come to more profound conclusions soon, like good is simply the inability to be bad and bad is just being yourself. But save it all to regale fellow prisoners in jail. Your son told me you were also worried about another crime of yours being unearthed, that you have killed before. Somehow, I get a feeling that I might nail you for that old crime too. Very soon!'

Kuldeep Khalap reddened visibly, and for the first time in his life, Saralkar got the uncanny feeling he had spoken something intuitively, without the slightest idea why he had said it. Even more inexplicably, it had rattled Khalap, as if confronted with a truth Saralkar himself hadn't found out yet.

Eknath Khubba tore open the sealed envelope gingerly, as if scared he would clumsily tear what was inside too. It had been sent by courier as Shrikant had said he would.

A smaller envelope lay inside, on which Eknath's name was scrawled. There appeared no signs that Shrikant had tried to open it and check the note Navnath had sent his friend. Eknath took a deep breath and slit open the smaller envelope. His fingers pulled out the folded note written by Navnath.

Dear Eknath,

Every day I feel death getting nearer. Maybe tomorrow. Maybe day after. Thank you for honouring my request of waiting till I'm gone. I can't stop you after that, but why don't you let sleeping dogs lie? Isn't it futile and too late?

Yet, if you choose to confess, I beg you to leave me out of it. As I said, I don't want my son, my wife, my family to know about what we did. Keep my secret safe with you, my friend. Goodbye!

Navnath

Eknath felt a lump rise in his throat. The burden of their sin now felt crushingly heavier than ever. There was nothing to stop him any longer, from doing the right thing. And yet a kind of moral torpor and lack of resolve seemed to grip him. Where was the restlessness of spirit and soul that had propelled him all these days? In its place a pitiful wretched dilemma crept over him. Would he really feel better if he went ahead and confessed? Would it do any good at all? Or would it be futile as Navnath had written?

He put on the television to distract himself. Not two minutes later, his dilemma stood resolved.

'Sir, we've finally found CCTV footage of Urmila Welde,' Motkar said. 'She was seen at a traffic crossing, about a kilometre from her house around 3 p.m. on the day she went missing. She was alone and was likely holding papers in one hand. She was seen asking pedestrians something. Most of them shrugged or shook their heads, then one lady gestured as if giving Urmila Welde directions. About fifteen minutes later, she was again spotted entering the area's post office and went inside. The CCTV footage inside the post office was not working, so we don't know what she did inside. Later, she is seen leaving the post office. No papers can be seen in her hands then. We checked the layout of the post office. There is a post box right outside the door but it cannot be seen on the outside CCTV. It's possible she posted a letter.'

Saralkar's eyes narrowed. 'You mean Urmila Welde left her house on her own? You are sure there wasn't anyone with her, behind her, ahead of her?'

'No, sir. Although there are no CCTVs near her house from which we could possibly get footage showing her leaving her house or walking out of her lane. But from that crossing onward, she was definitely alone. Even at the post office,' Motkar replied.

'What did the post office staff say? Which counter did Urmila Welde go to? She could have sent a registered letter for all we know.'

'Sir, one of the lady clerks vaguely remembers that Urmila Welde inquired about stamps, but it was past 3 p.m., so the stamp sale was closed,' Motkar said.

'But if she was desperate, she could still have dropped the letter in the post box without stamps. Earlier the practice was to collect the postage from the receiver, I think, if there was inadequate postage or no stamps on the envelope. Do they still follow that?' Saralkar wondered. 'Have you spoken to the sorters? They might remember an unstamped envelope that day or next morning. It's even likely they might remember the address or the postal code it was sent to.'

Motkar shook his head. 'I have already checked, sir. None of the sorters present remember, even though it's rare to find letters without postage.'

Saralkar clicked his tongue. 'OK, what about later? How did she reach the bridge? Any CCTV footage?'

'Yes, sir. We concentrated on CCTV footage near the Holkar bridge. We are still piecing together where she went from the post office or the route she took. We need some more time for that, but she can be seen approaching the Holkar bridge about three hours later. It was already dark but she came from the Khadki Cantonment side,' Motkar explained. 'Again, no one was with her. She passed the Ordnance factory, then it is not possible to make out very clearly from the images but in the flash of vehicle lights, she can be seen standing alone, about halfway across the bridge, staring at the riverbed. Then one can spot very hazy movement where she was standing and a minute or two later when some cars pass by, she is no longer visible anywhere—either walking or standing.'

'What do you mean? How long was she standing there? And you are absolutely sure there was no one else?' Saralkar asked.

'She was standing there for about fifteen to seventeen minutes. Many vehicles and a couple of pedestrians crossed the bridge but it's unlikely anyone tried to attack or push her,' Motkar replied. 'It was dark, so we can't be absolutely sure, but the least we could have seen in the footage was some sort of a scuffle or some suspects running away from the spot. Nothing like that appears. We will try and enhance the footage though.'

Saralkar stared at him. 'How is it possible? You mean she either jumped on her own or lost her balance and fell from the bridge? That she wasn't pushed or killed?'

Motkar shook his head slowly. 'Sir, one thing is certain. Whenever we've spotted her in CCTV footages so far—at the crossing, the post office and at Holkar bridge—she is alone. No one was with her. As we identify more CCTV footage along the way she took, we will be looking for signs of someone being with her. And of course, we need to figure out why she took three hours to get to the bridge, which cannot have been more than an hour's walking distance from the post office.'

'We also need to talk to her neurologist and ask her if a person in Urmila Welde's stage of dementia is capable of all that she has been seen doing,' Saralkar said. 'Also why would she jump? Could she be capable of suicidal thoughts or could she have suffered hallucinations that it wasn't a river but something else into which she decided to jump because of her condition?'

'Yes, sir. It also means our theory that Niharika, Anshuman Das and Sunit Welde could be involved comes to nought.'

'I know, I know, Motkar. But let's not extend the benefit of doubt to them just yet. We need to have a full picture of what happened to Urmila Welde first,' Saralkar said. Then, he turned to Zirpe, 'OK, what else have we got? Zirpe, what did you wring out of Rohidas Phule?'

ASI Sanika Zirpe had been waiting for her turn patiently and she quickly took Saralkar and Motkar through Rohidas Phule's statement.

'You think he knew nothing about the child's murder or suspect that he was being asked to dig a grave not a trench?' Saralkar asked.

'Yes, sir. And Phule readily accepted that the amulet was probably his and he could well have lost it while digging the pit,' Zirpe said.

'Hmm,' Saralkar said thoughtfully. 'So Phule's amulet falls into the grave and it's too small to be noticed in the soil, especially at night-time. The unclothed body of the boy Parshuram is lowered into the grave by the murderers, and the amulet lies right beneath it when the pit gets covered by the earth. Over time, the body decomposes into a skeleton, and the amulet gets stuck to the skeleton's underside. But how did it end up in the ribcage?'

The three officers were silent, pondering the little puzzle. Then Zirpe said, 'Sir couldn't that have happened when the skeleton got dug up or during retrieval of the bones?'

'Or maybe the body of the boy was laid face down and once the flesh was gone, the amulet slid into the ribcage because it wasn't exactly underneath but beside it?' Motkar offered.

Saralkar nodded and shrugged. 'There's got to be a logical explanation, which experts might be able to provide. I am inclined to go with Zirpe's explanation. Anyway, you said Phule stated that Bansi Vishwakarma was the one tasked with helping him dig the pit?'

'Yes, sir,' Sanika Zirpe said. 'But the most important thing Phule said was that Vishwakarma was the one who had got the boy for the Weldes as a live-in servant in the first place. Parshuram was his distant relative.'

Saralkar punched his left fist into his right palm. 'Then this driver would obviously have known something had happened to Parshuram. The Weldes wouldn't have been able to keep it from him. Moreover, if he helped in digging the grave, then possibly he was also in on the attempt to hide the crime,' the senior inspector said. 'Why the hell have we not been able to trace him yet? Somebody's got to know something about Bansi Vishwakarma. If he was working as a driver, he must've had a licence issued here or in his home state.'

'Sir, how do we trace a licence issued thirty or thirty-five years ago when we are not even sure of his home state?' Motkar said.

'Maybe he got it renewed here in Maharashtra or got a fresh one if his profession continued to be driving. Maybe he owns a taxi in his own name? Have you tried any of it?' Saralkar said. 'I want results in forty-eight hours, Motkar, Zirpe. Don't you realise, if we trace this man, we could crack the case.'

Both Motkar and Zirpe nodded.

'OK, sir,' Motkar said. 'And two more things to report. First, Angre managed to track down the last tenant we had not been able to locate. A person called Sambit Kumar Shastry. He stayed as a tenant in one of Welde's houses from 1999 to 2002 with one of his colleagues, Kalpesh Mankad. This Shastry told us a very strange thing. About half way through their tenancy, one day, early morning, Urmila Welde came to him with an odd request. The Welde couple was abroad with Sunit. They had left about a month earlier. The tenants of the other house were also away on a short trip somewhere, so only Urmila Welde was in the bungalow below and these two young men in the flat upstairs.

Urmila Welde asked the boys to vacate the flat for three days, saying some urgent work needed to be done. She would not explain what but said her brother had said that they would pay for the hotel stay of the two boys for the three days. The boys tried to plead that they would be inconvenienced. She just told them to do as she requested. So, the boys finally relented and checked into a hotel near their office, a few kilometres away. When they returned three days later, they could see no work done but the lawn was covered with empty gunny bags and some big stones were placed on it. They were left wondering about it but soon forgot the incident.'

'When was this?' Saralkar asked, all agog.

'Sambit Shastry says it happened sometime in late 2000, November or December.'

'Did they speak to Shashank Welde about it after he came back from the USA?'

'Yes, he says they did and Shashank Welde said there was something really urgent that had come up but gave no explanation.'

'Which means, this was probably when the second body was buried. And yet the Weldes were away in the USA and only Urmila Welde was here at that time. Means what? She killed a man? And who helped her bury him?' Saralkar asked. 'Does not make sense.'

Again, the trio were quiet for a few seconds. The air was thick with bafflement.

'This is simply maddening,' Saralkar growled. 'What was the other thing you wanted to tell me, Motkar?'

'Sir, the other thing was you had asked me to check what numbers DCP Khalap had called and received calls from on the day of his wife's death. I realised they hadn't checked WhatsApp calls, so I had asked one of the constables to check for calls about three to four days leading up to the shooting,' Motkar replied. 'I was startled to find that Niharika Das is listed as a contact and Khalap and she exchanged calls two days before the shooting. His call history shows that they had spoken a couple of times even two months ago.'

'What? How in the world do Kuldeep Khalap and Niharika Das know each other?'

'No idea, sir. So should I ask Niharika Das, or do you want to put that question to DCP Khalap now that he's in custody?'

'No. Ladies first!' Saralkar quipped.

33

'He's not breathing, saheb,' Constable Khubba said.

Panic seized him as he squatted beside the still, limp body of the man.

'What?' the ASI barked, the information still not registering in his alcohol addled brain. 'The bastard must be pretending. I'll show you. Watch how he sits up squealing now.'

The officer walked into the cell and landed a kick to the prone man's groin.

Constable Khubba stared at the ASI horrified, as the prone man's body remained unresponsive, neither jerking nor writhing. Nor did he hear a moan or a sound of pain.

'Saheb, we need to rush him to a doctor,' he said frantically.

In response, the ASI landed a flurry of agitated kicks to the body, then stopped and tottered on his feet a little. 'Where is Navnath?'

'He's outside, grabbing a smoke, I think,' Eknath replied.

'Get him quick. He knows how to revive these fuckers when they fall unconscious,' the ASI said hoarsely.

Eknath scrambled to his feet and shot out of the cell to fetch Navnath.

The ASI stared at the man in his late thirties he had thrashed over a couple of hours now. His father had said he would definitely reach by 1 a.m. when he had started from Kolhapur around 8 p.m. 'Soften the arsehole by the time I get there,' had been his father's instructions.

Eknath and Navnath strode back into the cell.

'Ah, Navnath, this guy's unconscious! See what's wrong and fix it …' the ASI said and left the cell.

Navnath quickly bent down and began examining the man. A chill ran down his spine and he exchanged a glance with Eknath.

'Saheb,' he called out to the ASI, 'he's not unconscious. He's … he's probably dead … or dying … we need to call a doctor.'

'Tchah!' the ASI said savagely. 'Don't talk rubbish, Navnath. Pour some water on him.'

Navnath looked at the sozzled officer and realised the futility of arguing. 'Get some water, Eknath,' he said to his colleague.

Eknath left the cell again. The ASI and Navnath waited in uneasy silence. The night was quiet but the clamour in their minds was just beginning. Eknath was back with a bucket and a bowl.

'That's better,' the ASI said. 'Splash it on his face.'

Eknath did as he was told.

'Some more,' the ASI barked.

The man continued to lie still with no reflex movement whatsoever.

The ASI now started shaking. 'How the hell could he have died? He's not bleeding much and we didn't really thrash him too much, did we? he said, regarding the two constables.

Navnath had turned pale. 'Saheb, I told you to go easy … to stop,'

The ASI glared at him, his fury wrestling with fear. 'Are you saying I killed him, you smart arse? If he's really dead how do you know it's not your blows that proved fatal or Eknath's?' he raged at both the constables. 'Don't you dare try and put it all on me, motherfuckers!'

'But, saheb,' Eknath protested. 'I … we just slapped him a couple of times but you …'

'Shut the fuck up! My father will be here soon. He'll know what to do …' the ASI said, then spat out profanities at them.

Eknath and Navnath regarded each other, looking for answers in the nightmare of a scenario that was unfolding. Just then, they heard a vehicle drive in and halt outside the chowki.

'Stay here,' the ASI said. 'I think it's my father.'

He ran out of the cell, leaving the two constables with the prone man.

'What are we going to do if he's dead, Navnath?' Eknath asked. 'Will a case be filed against us? Will we be imprisoned and lose our jobs?'

'Don't talk like that. Pray for him to stay alive,' Navnath fumbled as he replied. 'Otherwise we'll be ruined.'

'We should tell the saheb's father what really happened. That we didn't cause this man's death … his own son did,' Eknath said.

'Fat chance he'll accept that. What if he turns around and says we did it? No, just keep quiet and play along. Saheb's father is a retired senior policeman. I'm sure he'll want to protect his son … and that means we'll be protected too,' Navnath replied.

They fell silent trying to hear father and son murmuring in undertones outside. 'I told you to soften him, not kill him, you fool,' the older man's slightly raised voice reached their ears.

'I didn't hit him that hard, Baba. There isn't even much blood … take a look,' the ASI said.

'There's something known as internal bleeding. You are too drunk to realise how hard you went at him,' the senior retired policeman replied.

'But …'

'Shut up. Let me take a look at him first,' the older man snapped. 'Where's the cell?'

'Inside there …'

And then Navnath Shinde and Eknath Khubba heard both father and son walk towards the cell.

—

'So, you were wrong to accuse my brother and husband for Urmila Attya's disappearance and death, right?' Niharika Das said angrily. 'They are no longer suspects, correct?'

Senior Inspector Saralkar was in no mood to indulge her, although she had a right to be angry. 'Let's say, as of now, we don't have any evidence against them,' he replied.

'And you won't find any because we had nothing to do with it,' Sunit Welde fumed. 'Just admit you were wrong, Inspector, and damn well apologise.'

'It's my job to suspect everyone who might have a prima facie motive, Sunit Welde,' Saralkar said wagging a finger at him. 'Nothing changes the fact that your aunt went missing and was found dead in extremely suspicious circumstances. Until we establish beyond doubt how that came about, you will remain suspects. Is that clear? And don't forget that two skeletons were found in a bungalow owned by you, built by your parents.'

He threw a sweeping glance at the three of them—Sunit, Anshuman and Niharika. Then, he added, 'Now, Mrs Das, tell me how you know a policeman named DCP Kuldeep Khalap?'

Niharika Das's brow furrowed at the mention of the name but she didn't look flustered. 'I don't know him well, but we talked to each other a few times,' she replied.

'What about?'

'Well … he had got in touch with me after my parents passed away last year. He came over to offer his condolences when I was in Pune. He told me his father was a friend of my father,' she paused and turned to Anshuman and Sunit. 'Remember I told you he made an offer to buy Shanti Villa?'

'Oh, that fellow. Yes, I remember,' Anshuman replied.

Sunit piped in, 'Right, you asked me if I recollected if Papa had had a friend called Chandrakant Khalap.'

'Kuldeep Khalap offered to buy Shanti Villa?' Saralkar asked.

'Yes. He said he'd always liked our bungalow and the locality,' Niharika Das said. 'He also offered a fantastic price. Very tempting. But at that time, we were still not sure what we were going to do about the property. Sunit and I briefly discussed the matter but thought it was too soon after our parents' death to make a decision. So, I told Khalap that we were not selling the bungalow. He then said, any time we decided to sell, I should get in touch with him and he'll offer a better price than any other buyer. After that he would call up randomly after every three or four months and inquire if we had made the decision to sell.'

Saralkar felt his imagination starting to run wild. 'And how come you spoke about two weeks ago around the time the first skeleton was found?' he asked.

Niharika Das suddenly looked uncomfortable. 'Actually, I just called him because he was from Pune Police and I wanted to check if he could help in any way, since he claimed his father was my father's friend,' she replied.

'Help in what way, Mrs Das?'

'I mean … I … we were so shocked by the discovery of the skeleton … that I just thought it would be good to get in touch with DCP Khalap in case we might need some help in … in … dealing with the matter,' Niharika Das said. 'Isn't that what most people do when they face trouble with the police? Try and see if they know anyone with influence who might help.'

Saralkar grunted inwardly. She was right. It was a way of life in India to try and use one's contacts to sort things out. 'Do you remember the date you contacted Khalap?'

'I can check my call log if you want,' Niharika Das offered.

'Never mind,' Saralkar said. He knew already that they had spoken two days before Khalap had shot his wife and himself. 'How did he react when you spoke to him?'

'Well, it was quite unpleasant,' Niharika Das said. 'The moment I told him what had happened, he just flew off the handle. He said why hadn't we just sold the bungalow to him when he was ready to pay whatever price we wanted. He called me and my brother foolish for having given the bungalow for redevelopment and that such a problem would never have arisen if we had sold the bungalow to him. Then he just abruptly cut the call. His outburst was so unexpected I didn't know what to think.'

She paused and looked at both her brother and husband, who were staring at each other with consternation. It was Anshuman who suddenly spoke. 'Wait a minute. This name DCP Kuldeep Khalap … I have heard it or seen it recently in the news. Isn't he the same cop who shot his wife and almost blew his brains out? He was accused of rape or something else too.'

The senior inspector nodded. 'That's right. This conversation your wife had with him was just two days before he did it.'

'What? But … but … what are you implying? I mean …' Niharika Das spluttered.

'Nothing, I'm not implying anything, Mrs Das,' Saralkar replied. 'Tell me, did he at all ask you for any details, like how many skeletons were found?'

'Well, I just said a skeleton because only one had been found then, but now … now that you ask …' she stammered, as if something had struck her. 'Khalap, I remember, kept saying skeletons, as in plural, every time he said the word during the conversation.'

'Hmm,' Saralkar responded, his brain in complete overdrive now, generating theories by the minute, improvising, finessing, pondering. 'One last question, Mrs Das,' he finally said. 'Did you mention your Urmila Attya to DCP Khalap in any of your conversations over the last year?'

Niharika Das frowned. 'I am not sure … I think I may have mentioned her when Khalap came to meet me after my parents passed away.'

'OK,' Saralkar nodded, getting up to leave. 'How come none of you mentioned a driver named Bansi Vishwakarma who worked for your father when we asked about your servants?'

The siblings looked at each other. 'Oh, that fellow. I was mostly studying out of Pune when he worked for my father,' Sunit Welde said. 'But yes, he did teach me to drive the car …'

Niharika Das shrugged. 'He was OK, but I had totally forgotten about him. Why? What about him?'

'It seems the little boy Parshuram was his nephew or distant relative,' Saralkar said, watching their reactions but none of them had expressions other than mild surprise. 'Any idea when Vishwakarma left the job, where he went or where he was from exactly?' he asked Sunit. 'You said he taught you to drive the car?'

Sunit Welde's eyebrows arched. 'Unbelievable, but I think I remember having seen Vishwakarma's driving licence. Just give me a minute to recollect. It was issued from a place with an unusual name.'

'Unusual? How? I am told he was from Uttar Pradesh,' Saralkar prompted to confuse him.

'No … no … he was from Bihar … yes, the RTO was Daltonganj,' Sunit Welde said, brightening up. 'It stuck in my mind because of the English name … very quaint and unusual.'

'Daltonganj?' Saralkar said. 'There's actually a place by that name in India?'

'Oh, I am sure of that,' Sunit Welde said.

Saralkar quickly did a Google search for the name and was surprised that there indeed existed a place called Daltonganj in undivided Bihar. He glanced at Sunit Welde, 'Daltonganj was renamed Medinipur and is a part of Jharkhand, which was carved out of Bihar in 2000. The town was renamed in 2004, so you are right, his licence would have mentioned Daltonganj on it.'

'I hope you trace him now so that at least he can confirm that the boy Parshuram is alive and my parents will no longer be suspected of wrongdoing,' Niharika Das remarked with feeling.

'On the other hand, perhaps he might confirm the exact opposite,' Saralkar countered.

—

PSI Motkar regarded the thin, wiry and bespectacled old man sitting in the waiting area of the Pune Homicide Unit. Constable Pol had told him that the man had walked in fifteen minutes ago and claimed to be a former constable. He had said he had some important information to share about the Shanti Villa case.

'I am PSI Motkar. Saralkar saheb is not in office,' Motkar said approaching the old man.

The old man stood up and saluted Motkar—something only a former constable was likely to do when face to face with an officer.

'I am Eknath Khubba, saheb. I retired as Senior Constable a few years ago. You can check my record, sir,' the old man said, furnishing an old ID and rattling out his buckle details.

'I see. Please come with me,' PSI Motkar said leading him into his room. 'Tell me, what information you wished to share about the Shanti Villa case.'

The old man suddenly looked as if all his breath had been sucked out of him. He took a few seconds to compose himself. His face had reddened and his eyes were moist. 'It's a long … long story,' he stuttered. 'Can I please have some water and tea, saheb?'

PSI Motkar looked at his state and body language and was intrigued. 'Sure,' he replied, hoping Eknath Khubba wasn't some retired cop gone crazy.

He quickly dialled the canteen on the intercom and ordered water and tea. 'It'll take a few minutes. Why don't you start telling me what you know,' he said to Eknath Khubba.

The old man seemed to start breathing again. He nodded. 'Of the two … skeletons you have found, one is that of a man, isn't it? The … the first one was of a boy … but the other one is of a man, no?'

It startled Motkar. How did this old man know that? They had been careful not to let the media know that the second skeleton hadn't turned out to be that of a child. 'Why do you say that?' he asked Khubba.

The old man took out a handkerchief from his pocket and wiped his sweat. 'I … I know who it is and I know how the man's skeleton got there. And who put him there.'

The way it was said sent a chill down Motkar's spine. 'Tell me everything.'

Eknath Khubba stared at him, blinking his eyes, as if revving up his courage for the final push. 'The skeleton is … is that of a man called Bansi Vishwakarma. He died in a police lock-up, around twenty-five years ago, in November 2000, killed by a police officer called Kuldeep Khalap … whom you have placed under arrest yesterday for killing his wife and attempting suicide.'

'What?' Motkar exclaimed, trying to process the information. 'How do you know this?'

'I … I was there when it happened … and we … er … I helped bury Vishwakarma's body in the lawns of the bungalow in which it was found …' Eknath Khubba said, his voice tremulous. He paused, then removed a bunch of papers from his shirt pocket and handed it over to PSI Motkar. 'Please read my detailed statement.'

The canteen boy arrived with the tea and water just then. Eknath Khubba downed the water in just two three gulps and reached for the tea.

PSI Motkar watched him with disbelief and began reading the statement, deeply intrigued.

Saralkar parked his vehicle, locked it and walked into the roadside restaurant. He was neither particularly hungry nor in need of tea. He just needed to sit and sift through the thoughts zipping around in his brain.

'Get me a cup of tea and a plate of sabudana khichdi,' he said to the waiter, without glancing at the menu.

'No sabudana khichdi, sir,' the waiter replied.

'What? Then get sabudana vada.'

The waiter shook his head. 'No sabudana vada either.'

'You ought to be ashamed of yourself,' Saralkar said with indignation.

'There are other items on the menu, sir,' the waiter persisted.

'Just get the tea,' Saralkar said dismissively and returned to his thoughts.

What earthly reason could Kuldeep Khalap have had for wanting to purchase Shanti Villa for a higher than market price? And why would he have started frothing at the mouth after being told about the discovery of the skeleton? What was the damn connection? He had claimed his father had been Shashank Welde's friend. But if that was so, wouldn't Niharika or Sunit have had at least a fleeting prior acquaintance with him if that was so?

Unless? Saralkar's mind had already thrown up a sinister theory, but now was the time to examine whether it ought to be investigated further. The waiter arrived with the tea. Saralkar took a sip and the taste met with his approval.

'Get one more cup after ten minutes,' he told the waiter and took another sip.

Kuldeep Khalap's father, Chandrakant Khalap, had been a police officer too, till 1995. Saralkar had checked that out when the CP had mentioned it earlier. Assuming, he had been friends with Shashank Welde or known him, could it be possible that Welde had turned to the senior Khalap for help to cover up Parshuram's murder? It wasn't far-fetched at all, but even assuming Chandrakant Khalap had helped Shashank Welde, and

Kuldeep Khalap knew about this, why would he get so disturbed on hearing about the skeleton's discovery?

It couldn't have been his father who had killed the boy. So why the hell would it bother Kuldeep Khalap so much? Unless? Saralkar froze!

It was the buzz of his mobile that pulled him away from the bizarre theory his mind was suggesting. 'Yes, Motkar?'

'Sir, you need to get here right away,' Motkar said, the excitement in his voice way higher than usual. 'I have a walk-in witness, a former constable who knows at least one important part of the story of the Shanti Villa murders.'

He quickly summarised what Eknath Khubba had narrated.

'I'm on my way, Motkar,' Saralkar said, quickly gulping down his cup as he contemplated the eerie similarity between what he had just heard and the theory his brain had been in the process of cooking.

'Cancel the second tea,' he hollered to the waiter and reached into his wallet to pay for the first one.

The waiter wasn't amused.

34

'At around 9.30 p.m., our saheb ASI Kuldeep Khalap reached the police chowki on his motorcycle with Bansi Vishwakarma,' Eknath Khubba said. 'Both were slightly drunk. The man asked our saheb what time senior Khalap saheb was reaching. Kuldeep saheb said he'd be there by around 11.00 p.m.'

'Kuldeep Khalap told you his name and why he was there?' Saralkar asked.

'Not at first. He just took us aside and whispered that the man with him was blackmailing someone important and that he was first going to try and make him see reason. If the man still played hardball, then we would have to give him our special treatment, which, as you well know, sir, meant … er …' Eknath Khubba faltered.

'Yes, go on …' Motkar said with a nod.

'Kuldeep saheb told us to finish our pending tasks and deal with petty matters, while he dealt with this man. Just a little later, we got a message on the wireless about some minor fracas nearby, so I left to look into it, while my fellow constable stayed behind at the duty desk.'

'Who was this other constable with you?' Saralkar asked.

Eknath Khubba paused. 'I … I don't remember his name, sir,' he lied. Navnath's request needed to be honoured as far as possible.

'OK, carry on,' Saralkar said, getting the distinct feeling that in an otherwise truthful-sounding account the old man had just fibbed.

Eknath Khubba cleared his throat. 'When I returned an hour later, I heard the sounds of a thrashing in progress in the lock-up. My colleague said Kuldeep saheb was personally whacking the guy with gusto. Usually, saheb would leave the special treatment to us constables first and came in only later, but not this time. My colleague told me the fellow was drunk and spoke in Hindi, not much Marathi. He had heard the man say Kuldeep saheb would regret he had laid a hand on him.

I asked Nav … er … my colleague what it was all about and he said he wasn't sure. All that he had gathered was that the man's name was Bansi Vishwakarma and that the matter involved Kuldeep saheb's father.

I soon got to know more since Kuldeep saheb called me inside the lock-up and told me to strip the fellow to his underpants and collect all his belongings. This wasn't very unusual, so I went in. Vishwakarma had taken a fair amount of beating, but put up a struggle as Kuldeep saheb and I stripped him. Kuldeep saheb landed a few more punches on him, then took a break. We left the cell and Kuldeep saheb had another peg. I asked him what exactly the matter was. He wouldn't say much but hinted that Vishwakarma was trying to blackmail senior Khalap saheb.

For the next two hours or so, Kuldeep saheb would take either me or the other constable to the cell, beat the guy up then rest for a drink. Both of us were very concerned now, so we tried to dissuade Kuldeep saheb from continuing the assault. But he said he was going to teach the guy a lesson for daring to blackmail his father.

Vishwakarma was already in a bad state and begging for mercy by now … he said he had a heart problem but instead of calming saheb down, it made him angrier.'

'Didn't you get to talk to Bansi Vishwakarma and find out more?' Saralkar interrupted. 'Surely you must have needed to take him to the toilet or give him water in between?'

Eknath Khubba nodded. 'Yes … yes, I'll come to that. My colleague … did get a chance to talk to him. Nav … er … my colleague told me Vishwakarma said he'd helped senior Khalap hide a crime several years ago, but wouldn't say what. He later begged me also to tell Kuldeep saheb he wouldn't cause any trouble and didn't want any money. I heard him begging Kuldeep saheb to spare him.'

'Didn't you two constables do anything when Vishwakarma told you all this?' Saralkar asked angrily.

Eknath Khubba hung his head as if in shame. 'I have asked myself this question thousands of times since that day,' he said. 'But, sir … honestly … we tried our best to tell Kuldeep saheb go easy on him … but how exactly could we have stopped an officer? We thought senior Khalap saheb would be here soon and stop his son … Nav … er … we both didn't even participate in the thrashing after a while. One more thing, sir … Kuldeep saheb was thrashing Vishwakarma around but … but didn't seem to be inflicting the kind of injuries that could turn fatal …'

'Bullshit! Do you know his skeleton shows injuries to his head, ribs and limbs? He died, didn't he?' Saralkar snapped.

'I know that, saheb … I am saying we didn't realise just how bad his injuries were …' Eknath Khubba said. 'Otherwise we would have told Kuldeep saheb to stop instead of just hinting and nudging that it was enough or to let it go …'

'So, what led to his death eventually? Did Kuldeep Khalap launch a particularly brutal attack on him?' Motkar asked.

'Not really, saheb. I won't lie. Both my colleague and I stopped joining in the beating. I mean we would go into the cell with Kuldeep saheb, who would land a couple of tired kicks and punches on Vishwakarma and we would only pretend to rough him up,' Eknath Khubba said. 'The last time this happened, Vishwakarma just lay exhausted and whimpering, but didn't look any worse or wasn't unconscious. But fifteen minutes later, I went back in to check, and my heart skipped a beat for he didn't seem to be breathing.'

The old man paused and looked at Saralkar and Motkar, then said in a hollow voice, 'There didn't seem to be any profuse bleeding, no vomiting … nothing … but I just knew Bansi Vishwakarma was dead …'

Constable Angre took one glance at the envelope and letter forwarded from Pune Police HQ in a plastic zip-lock evidence pouch and his eyes popped out. He picked up the zip-lock pouch with its contents and flew up the stairs, two storeys up. He peeped into PSI Motkar's room and found it empty. Angre proceeded to ASI Zirpe's room and was relieved to see her there.

'Madam,' he said as he knocked and entered, 'HQ has forwarded this. It is probably the letter which the old lady, Urmila Welde, was seen posting.'

Sanika Zirpe was too surprised to react. She reached inside her drawer, slipped on a pair of evidence-handling gloves and took the zip-lock bag from Angre. Inside, she could see an open envelope and a folded bunch of handwritten pages. On the envelope, the address was Pune Police HQ, Murder Squad, Pune 411001, written in the same unsteady scrawl. She removed the letter, which was scribbled on notebook paper, and flipped cursorily through the pages. On the last page was the name and signature of Urmila Welde.

She began reading the letter. The handwriting was an inconsistent scrawl, as if it had been written at different times, with different pens. What unfolded seemed a little like diary entries—a scrambled, rambling account of events that had occurred between twenty-five to thirty-five years ago. It was incoherent and difficult to follow in places, surprisingly sharp and crisp on some pages—incidents strung together in a haphazard and random manner. It wasn't necessarily sequential and was going to require a lot of figuring out to piece it all together to decipher the timeline of what happened when.

Yet, it potentially answered the vital question of how two corpses came to be buried under the lawns of Shanti Villa.

'Senior Khalap saheb told us in no uncertain terms that we had no choice but to do as he said. We were totally spooked,' Eknath Khubba continued. 'Senior Khalap saheb left after giving us specific instructions on how Kuldeep saheb and we were supposed to dispose of Vishwakarma's various belongings. An hour later, he was back and got us to load the body wrapped inside a car tarpaulin, into his car's dickie. He told me to stay behind at the chowki since it could not be left unmanned, while Kuldeep saheb and the other constable went with him.

They returned about one and a half hours later. Senior Khalap saheb told us that we would have to come back the following evening. He took a look at all the cleaning up that had been done, checked out all the details and again warned us against betrayal. We completed our shift and went home in the morning. I asked my colleague where the body had been disposed of.

That's when Nav ... er ... I mean my colleague told me they had left the body in the bathroom of a bungalow. The next day, Navnath and I ...' Eknath Khubba spluttered to a halt and went red in the face as he realised he'd let Navnath's name slip out of his mouth.

'You might as well tell us the full name of the other constable now,' Saralkar said to him.

'He's dead, sir. He was not just a colleague but a friend. He wanted me to keep his name out of it, lest his family comes to know about it if this gets splashed in the media,' Eknath pleaded. 'Vishwakarma's death weighed heavily on his conscience too.'

'When did he die?'

'Last week, sir. He had cancer. When I met him and told him I needed to confess, he asked me to wait till his death. And so, I am here now, or I would have come forward a fortnight earlier.'

'I see. What triggered this confession?' Saralkar asked.

'It had been building up for a long time, saheb, but when news came about Kuldeep saheb's suicide attempt and the discovery of the skeletons at Shanti Villa, I thought it was a sign from God, from life, that it was time to tell the truth,' the old man said. His voice cracked a bit.

'Although late, what you have done is right,' Saralkar said, trying to sound encouraging. 'Go on, tell us what happened the next evening.'

Eknath Khubba sniffed and nodded. 'Navnath and I reached the Shanti Villa bungalow that evening. Navnath had already been there the previous night. It was already dark. Senior Khalap saheb was already there, but Kuldeep saheb wasn't. The body was still in the bathroom but placed on two or three ice-blocks, which Khalap saheb seemed to have got from somewhere. A big pit had been dug in the lawns. I have no idea who Khalap saheb had got these dug by.

Only a middle-aged woman seemed to be staying in the bungalow. She seemed to be a bundle of nerves, as if she could go to pieces anytime.

Senior Khalap saheb told her to keep watch outside. Around 11 p.m., everything was quiet and the locality seemed to be asleep. Khalap saheb led us to the bathroom. The body had begun stinking despite the ice blocks. Khalap saheb explained to us that we had to bury the corpse in the pit. Both Navnath and I broke into a sweat and started asking questions. He told us to shut up, that he knew what he was doing and that the less we knew the better. He told us to trust him and just do as he said. I still asked him to answer why Kuldeep saheb wasn't there, and why we were doing the dirty work in his absence.

Senior Khalap saheb said it would look odd if Kuldeep saheb was not on duty whereas he had created a trail that he'd sent both of us out on some official work. This was necessary to create proper alibis for all of us. Navnath and I were finally convinced.

The body was stiff and heavy, but between the three of us, we managed to shift it to the pit and drop it inside. We then began shovelling in the heaps of mud lying on the sides, back into the pit. After about three hours, we managed to cover it completely. Over the next two days, Navnath and I went to the bungalow by turns to complete the levelling, then covered the area with gunny bags. Every time we went to the bungalow the woman was there, but we didn't speak to each other except if we needed something.'

'You mean you don't know who exactly she was?' Motkar asked.

'No, not at that time, sir. Senior Khalap saheb didn't tell us and we hadn't spoken to her,' Khubba said. 'But of course, Navnath and I began wondering and over the years we did try and find out as much as we could without being nosy. Even Kuldeep saheb remained tight-lipped and didn't try to discuss anything with us later, then eventually got transferred and rose in the ranks.

For months and years, we dreaded that some relative of Bansi Vishwakarma might appear one day, make inquiries or lodge a missing complaint, but nothing like that happened. Nobody seemed to bother that a man had disappeared.

Then about ten years later, I was again posted under Kuldeep saheb. His father had passed away recently and I don't know what came over him, but he told me the entire backstory about senior Khalap saheb, Bansi Vishwakarma and Shanti Villa ...'

'And what was that? Saralkar prompted.

The old man sighed. 'Can I please take a short break, saheb? I need to ... er ... go to the toilet.'

'OK,' Saralkar said.

PSI Motkar opened the door of the room and summoned a constable to accompany Eknath Khubba.

'Sir,' ASI Sanika Zirpe almost gate-crashed into the room a few moments later, even before Motkar could take his seat.

'Yes, Zirpe?'

'Sir, the letter Urmila Welde posted has found its way to us,' she gushed. 'She addressed it to Police HQ and it's been forwarded to us.'

'What? She wrote to us?' Saralkar asked.

'Yes, sir. It's very jumbled, but she's basically narrated all the facts about the Shanti Villa case.'

'Really?' Saralkar glanced at Motkar quizzically. 'Wasn't she suffering from dementia? Can a person in that condition be capable of ...?'

The three officers looked at each other perplexed, then Sanika spoke, 'As I said, sir, the letter's confusing and jumbled, but comprehensible.'

'And you have managed to extract the gist of it?' Saralkar asked.

'Yes, sir, Angre and I've read it a few times in the last two hours and made notes. Can I brief you now or should I do it after you finish interrogating the old man?' Zirpe asked.

'No, let's hear it. Motkar, what do you say?'

'Yes, sir. I'll just ask Pol to take Khubba into the other room when he's back from the toilet and give him some tea and stuff,' Motkar said and left the room.

Saralkar took the zip-lock pouch and stared at it. 'Did you check the postmarks?'

'Yes, sir. It was posted from the post office she was seen entering. The postmark date also matches with the CCTV footage we have,' ASI Zirpe said.

Saralkar handed the zip-lock pouch back to her as Motkar entered the room.

'OK, Zirpe, tell us what you have gleaned from Urmila Welde's letter.'

35

ASI Sanika Zirpe's detailed summary of Urmila Welde's letter

'Sir, she confirmed that the first skeleton is that of Parshuram, the live-in servant boy, who was an orphan and a distant nephew of their driver, Bansi Vishwakarma. It seems Sheetal Welde, Shashank Welde's wife, was not finding Parshuram very useful after a few weeks. The boy was barely eleven and would often make mistakes, break things or was unable to do the chores given to him. It was also becoming a problem because Parshuram was also prone to do things he wasn't supposed to, like plucking guavas and tomatoes from the garden. Sometimes, he would also sneak out and play truant. They were thinking of discontinuing his employment and asking Vishwakarma to send him back.

It appears, sometime in November 1990, both Sheetal and Urmila Welde were alone at home for a few days. Shashank Welde was travelling for work, and Sunit and Niharika had gone on a trip with their maternal grandparents.

Late one night, there was a power cut, which was quite common those days. Urmila Welde was woken up by urgent pounding on the door of her room. It was her sister-in-law begging her to open up. Since there was no power, she too was scared but opened the door to find Sheetal hysterically telling her that something horrible had happened.

Sheetal said she'd heard sounds of someone prowling in the bungalow premises and then enter the house. Being pitch dark, since even the streetlights were off, she had panicked and grabbed the wooden cloth beater from her bathroom and silently opened her bedroom door. She hadn't been able to find the torch. As she tiptoed towards the phone in the hall, Sheetal said she suddenly felt someone's presence, as if the prowler was about to attack her. So, she screamed and began swinging the cloth beater wildly in sheer panic. She said she heard it hit a shadowy form and lashed again at it blindly, then began running towards her sister-in-law's room. She collided with someone and both fell down. That's when she said she heard moaning, like that of a child.

She got up, groped her way to the kitchen and lit a candle. Another shock awaited her. Sheetal Welde realised that the child Parshuram was lying injured on the floor. He didn't seem to be conscious and there was some bleeding. To her eyes, he looked dead. A fresh wave of panic hit her and she rushed to wake Urmila up, who was a deep sleeper. She had heard nothing till she had been awakened by Sheetal pounding on her door.

Urmila calmed Sheetal down, then they looked for the torch she had in her drawer and both went outside to examine the situation. The boy was still lying unconscious, but he was breathing. Urmila realised that although there was not a lot of bleeding visible, one side of his head and face were caked with blood and swollen. The hair was sticky with blood. It looked like at least a couple of blows of the cloth beater had struck him on one side, when Sheetal had swung it around in panic.

The power was still not back and they tried to revive the boy by splashing water and holding onions by his nose to sniff.

Urmila suggested they take him to the doctor or a hospital. But how were they going to do that? It was 2.30 a.m. Neither of the two knew how to drive a car, and trying to get an auto-rickshaw was impossible and unsafe. Then they toyed with the idea of waking up a neighbour or calling an ambulance, but Sheetal became hysterical, fearing a police case. So, Urmila decided to try some first aid.

The women set about cleaning the boy's wounds with Dettol, applied antiseptic cream and saffron paste. They bandaged him and shifted him to his tiny room at the back of the house and hoped he would regain consciousness soon. Urmila and Sheetal also cleaned up the drawing room and the blood.

That's when they noticed a few guavas and tomatoes scattered on the floor. A small steel bowl also lay on the carpet, its contents—salt and powdered chilli—spilled out. It suddenly struck them that for some godforsaken reason, Parshuram had crept out into the garden to pluck some guavas and tomatoes. Maybe he had been hungry or simply unable to go back to sleep because of the power cut. He had entered the house to get some salt and chilli from the kitchen, since he knew where it was kept. It was his movements that Sheetal had probably heard and mistaken for a prowler's. When Sheetal had stepped out of her room, the poor boy was just trying to avoid being discovered. In the darkness they had collided into each other, or Sheetal had tripped over him as he tried to get out of her path.

By this time, Sheetal and Urmila were exhausted and went back to sleep, hoping things would be alright in the morning since Shashank was anyway expected back the next day. They figured he would know what to do. Since he was well connected, perhaps they would take Parshuram to a doctor he knew, if necessary.

Sometime around 6 a.m., Urmila woke up and decided to take a look if the boy was doing better. She realised the swelling on the side of his face and head had increased, his breathing was laborious, and he was shaking and shivering. Parshuram was also moaning and mumbling. She thought she heard him asking for water. So, Urmila woke Sheetal up and told her she needed to hold the boy up, while she gave him water and probably an analgesic to ease his pain. Sheetal was a little reluctant but both went to the boy and attempted to make him swallow the analgesic tablet and drink water.

They gave him a few sips and then placed the tablet in his mouth and poured a little more water to wash it down his throat. The boy coughed and began flipping and convulsing. They tried to turn him around in case the tablet and water were choking him, but Parshuram's convulsions and coughing only increased and then he suddenly went still.

When both women realised that the boy had died right in front of their eyes, a blame-game erupted. Sheetal accused Urmila of having triggered Parshuram's death by giving him the analgesic tablet and water. Urmila was shocked and countered that the boy had probably suffered brain injury because of Sheetal's blows, and that death was a result of that. She had only given water because she had heard him moan for it.

They raged and argued for a while about the tablet having caused choking. Urmila lamented having not thought of crushing the tablet and mixing it with water, but pointed out that Sheetal had not suggested it either. But then the enormity of inadvertently having killed Parshuram sank in. They had no idea what to do. They wrapped the boy up in a bedsheet and locked his door, waiting for Shashank to return.

When he reached home around 9.30 a.m., they told him what had happened. Shashank Welde was completely shaken by the events—that his wife and sister could well be held guilty of murder. His first instinct was to take the boy to a friend's hospital to ascertain if he was really dead and then to the police. But Sheetal simply went to pieces, pleading with him that she didn't want to go to prison. She begged him to save her. She blamed Urmila for Parshuram's death again. She said the boy had been alive even after getting injured but died only when Urmila insisted on giving him the tablet and water. This led to another round of recriminations between Urmila and Sheetal.

Completely at a loss of what to do, Shashank toyed with the idea of approaching a police officer he was acquainted with, Senior Inspector Chandrakant Khalap, who was posted at the Deccan Police Station. The cop had a reputation of being a fixer. Shashank had been introduced to him by a lawyer friend a few years ago and they had stayed in touch. After beating around the bush, Shashank finally took Chandrakant Khalap into confidence about the ghastly events that had unfolded at his home.

Chandrakant Khalap asked him many searching questions about the child and how he came to be working as a servant with them. Khalap told Shashank bluntly that if the crime was reported his wife would definitely be convicted of non-culpable homicide and his sister as an accomplice. They were guaranteed a jail sentence, even if the best lawyers defended them.

Shashank begged him for help to get them out of the situation. Chandrakant Khalap told him he had an idea of how to cover-up the matter but a lot of things would need to be managed, including the driver, Bansi Vishwakarma, who would come asking questions sooner or later or demand his pound of flesh. The cover up would require a lot of money and Shashank and his family would have to do exactly as Chandrakant Khalap instructed them to.

Shashank was desperate and agreed. They drove to Shanti Villa. Chandrakant Khalap had a thorough look at everything then outlined his plan. Parshuram's body would have to be buried on the Shanti Villa premises under the lawn. A deep pit would have to be dug under some pretext and would later be covered up. Bansi Vishwakarma would have to be roped in and be a part of the whole thing, so that he too would be an accomplice to the crime and destruction of evidence.

And that's what was finally done. Chandrakant Khalap and Shashank Welde first tackled the driver. After an initial show of shock and reluctance, Bansi Vishwakarma agreed to keep quiet, spread the rumour that Parshuram had run away and also help in burying the body. In return, they agreed on a sum to be paid to him—some of it immediately and the rest over two to three years, while he still worked with them.

Shashank Welde got their gardener, Rohidas Phule, to dig a pit under the pretext of urgently needing a trench dug. He, along with Bansi Vishwakarma, dug it that evening.

The actual burying of Parshuram's body was done late at night by Bansi and Shashank, supervised by Chandrakant Khalap. The pit was then covered up by Bansi Vishwakarma, part of it the same night and the rest of the task was completed the next day. All the boy's belongings were disposed of exactly as instructed by Khalap.

Bansi Vishwakarma continued working as driver for Shashank Welde and family for two more years, collected all his money and left the city. The shadow of the dark secret haunted the Weldes and affected their lives deeply. The fear of their secret being revealed at any time and their guilt weighed heavily on all of them. They, of course, didn't dare tell even Niharika and Sunit. It was too ghastly and shameful.

Things, however, took a turn for the worse when Senior Inspector Chandrakant Khalap began dropping in at the Weldes' home every few weeks. He'd started taking an interest in Urmila Welde, and his behaviour with her soon turned increasingly suggestive and borderline lecherous. He began openly propositioning her.

Urmila was both livid and terrified. She turned down his advances, but when she realised he wasn't going to stop, she told her brother Shashank, who had already noticed it. He hesitantly spoke to Chandrakant Khalap, but the cop told him bluntly he fancied Urmila and wanted a sexual relationship with her, either by consent or force.

Urmila, Shashank and Sheetal had a massive showdown, with Urmila flaying her brother for not being man enough to stand up to Khalap. The worst part was Sheetal ranted at Urmila that they had provided her a roof to live under all her life. Shashank had paid for his younger sister's higher education and made her a part of the family, taking care of her household expenses and her every need and luxury. It was time she repaid her brother's family, especially because Parshuram had died only because of her actions.

Throughout his wife's outburst, Shashank was quiet and this disturbed Urmila greatly. But she was even more outraged when Shashank later talked to her alone and begged her to give in to Chandrakant Khalap's demand for sexual favours. He asked her what if Khalap somehow leaked their secret and implicated them if she refused. All three of them could be jailed.

Urmila was appalled that her brother was asking her to oblige Khalap. But eventually, she also caved in to the pressure and became Chandrakant Khalap's mistress for about a year. It didn't last long, and only because Khalap quickly lost interest in Urmila. However, it left Urmila feeling violated and demeaned. She also hated the fact she was too weak and didn't have the courage to remain firm.

Her relations with her brother were strained, and Sheetal and she totally stopped talking to each other after a few more flare-ups. During this time, there was also an unfortunate occasion when her nephew Sunit, who was quite fond of his aunt, chanced upon Khalap and Urmila's intimacy. It shamed Urmila and led to Sunit's estrangement from her.

With the passage of some more time, things changed a little. Chandrakant Khalap retired from the police force, Sunit moved abroad to study and Niharika got married. While fear still lurked at the back of their minds, it appeared like the danger of being discovered was receding.

Meanwhile, Shashank Welde added another floor to his bungalow and began letting out the two flats to tenants. He was very particular about the tenants he chose and ensured no one even set foot on the lawns.

Then, out of the blue, almost ten years after Parshuram's death, Bansi Vishwakarma turned up again at Shanti Villa. Shashank and Sheetal Welde were abroad visiting Sunit, and Urmila was all alone here. Vishwakarma told her he needed money urgently for medical treatment. Urmila didn't believe him and didn't know what to do. She told him Shashank was out of India but Vishwakarma said she had to somehow arrange the sum he demanded, because it was a question of his life. He said, if not cash, surely, she could give him her or Sheetal's jewellery worth that sum. Otherwise, he was as good as dead if he didn't receive treatment. Having nothing to lose, he would not hesitate to reveal everything about Parshuram's death. He said he would be back the next day and also gave her the phone number of the lodge where he was staying.

Urmila was stupefied. She made an ISD call to her brother in the USA and told him everything. Shashank told her not to panic and said he would speak to Chandrakant Khalap who, although retired, would know exactly how to take care of the matter. She got a call from Khalap an hour later and he assured her he would handle the driver. He took all details from her about what Vishwakarma had said and his contact details at the lodge. Khalap told her he was in Kolhapur and was leaving for Pune right away.

Urmila later learnt from Chandrakant Khalap that he had immediately called up his son, ASI Kuldeep Khalap, who was posted in Pune to track down Bansi Vishwakarma at the lodge, ply him with liquor and dinner, and lure him for a meeting with his father at his police chowki. Once there, Kuldeep Khalap was to just soften the driver up by using mild third-degree, so that he would be amenable to settle for a far lesser amount than he was demanding.

Urmila Welde waited anxiously till around midnight for further news. Then she went to sleep and was woken up first by a call from Chandrakant Khalap around 2 a.m. He visited her half an hour later. He was grim faced and told her things had gone horribly wrong, then took a quick look around the bungalow.

He then told her that Bansi Vishwakarma had suffered a heart attack while being roughed up and had died. They needed to repeat exactly what they had done with Parshuram's body—bury Bansi Vishwakarma in the lawns of Shanti Villa. Urmila Welde was stunned by this new complication and suffered an anxiety attack. But Khalap calmed her down. Together they called up

Shashank in the USA. Khalap explained what had occurred and that they had no choice but to bury Vishwakarma's body under the Shanti Villa lawns. Shashank also panicked but agreed. He told Urmila that they would have to co-operate.

Urmila was a bundle of nerves, but she pointed out that while one tenant was away, the tenants of the other flat were there. How were they going to dig a pit and bury Vishwakarma's body under such circumstances? Shashank Welde came up with the idea that in the morning, before they left for office, Urmila should approach the boys with the request that they needed to shift to a hotel for a couple of days because some urgent work needed to be undertaken at the bungalow. That Shashank would bear the cost of their hotel stay and deduct it from the next month's rent. Chandrakant Khalap agreed it was a good idea and so it was decided.

Khalap left and returned around 3.30 a.m. with two constables and quickly hid Vishwakarma's body in the guest room. Urmila Welde's blood ran cold but she had to keep her presence of mind. Around 7 a.m., Khalap arranged for ice blocks to be delivered, which were placed in the bathroom. He and his son, Kuldeep, then managed to shift Vishwakarma's body onto the ice slabs. It was all horrible but Urmila was by now in a kind of zombie-like daze.

She played her role in getting the tenants to move to the hotel in the morning. When that was done, Chandrakant Khalap got two men to dig the pit in the lawn. Urmila asked no questions about who they were. She thought they looked like goons but they could well have been ordinary labourers who had no idea why they were digging the pit. That whole day she kept feeling she was about to have a nervous breakdown. She was alone with a dead body, the labourers were digging outside and Khalap kept dropping in.

After dark, the two constables returned and Bansi Vishwakarma's body was buried under Chandrakant Khalap's supervision. Urmila Welde was now almost in a state of utter collapse. Over the next few days, she was in a state of terror. The two constables came back twice to level the lawns, and Chandrakant Khalap came by to reiterate that she needed to keep her wits around and told her what to say if some day someone turned up making inquiries about Bansi Vishwakarma.

None of it helped Urmila because she was alone except for the two tenants who came back two days later. A little later, she was seized with the irrational fear that Bansi Vishwakarma's ghost would start haunting her and the bungalow. She felt she would go crazy. Fortunately, Shashank Welde cut short his US visit and returned about a week later, as soon as he got a ticket, even as Sheetal stayed back with her son.

Once her brother was back, Urmila fell seriously ill, then decided she just couldn't bear to stay at Shanti Villa any longer. She told Shashank she wanted to break off ties with them and shift elsewhere because she was a nervous wreck after the second ordeal.

Shashank Welde understood Urmila was at the end of her tether. He helped her find a place.'

'That's more or less where Urmila Welde's account ends, sir,' ASI Sanika Zirpe said. 'She says she pulled herself together, kept in touch with Niharika and Shashank Welde off and on, but generally kept her distance from the Weldes and Shanti Villa. She then abruptly shifts to the present. She says she knows her dementia is getting bad and that she's paid a heavy price mentally because of all that happened and crippling guilt. She has a few kind words to say only about Niharika. Then she ends by saying she has had enough of life and wishes to die.'

Zirpe paused. There was pin-drop silence in the room as Saralkar and Motkar chewed on what they had just heard.

'This can't be anything but the truth, can it?' Saralkar finally said. 'The second part of her account about Bansi Vishwakarma dovetails with what Eknath Khubba has told us, and the first part sounds plausible—that the unfortunate boy, Parshuram, met his death at their hands. This is something we had clearly suspected. Our investigation also seemed to point in the same direction, and Rohidas Phule also confessed to being asked to help dig a trench.'

'Yes, sir,' Motkar said. 'And this can be considered a kind of confessional suicide note …'

'Hmm! Does Urmila Welde's post-mortem report indicate death by suicide? What injuries were sustained?' Saralkar asked. 'The CCTV footage shows no one was with her and that she posted the letter on her own, not under coercion. Yet, it brings us back to the question—can a person suffering from acute dementia write a letter this lucid and take their own life? It's baffling and we have to get an expert opinion. Also, most importantly, we need to trace Bansi Vishwakarma's family—son, daughter, brother, sister—and ascertain the second skeleton is his through DNA testing. What's going to be more difficult is that, if Parshuram was his distant nephew and an orphan, whose DNA are we going to test his remains against?'

36

Saralkar regarded Kuldeep Khalap's crestfallen face—a twisted expression pasted across it to camouflage his desperation. The senior inspector had just confronted him with all the evidence against him in the Shanti Villa case.

'You did not solve the case, Saralkar,' Kuldeep Khalap said with a mocking snarl. 'You were just lucky that … that fool Eknath had an attack of conscience and walked into your office to confess.'

Saralkar nodded. 'You are right. It was plain luck. But who said luck is the monopoly of murderers like you, who escaped justice for almost twenty-five years after killing Bansi Vishwakarma?'

'I didn't kill the bastard. He died of heart failure because I knocked him around a bit,' Kuldeep Khalap said. 'My father should have told me he had a serious heart problem … that it wasn't just a pretext to ask for money.'

'Eknath has testified you kept thrashing him in short bursts, drinking and enjoying it because the man had rubbed you the wrong way with some remarks,' Saralkar replied. 'You killed him. His injuries were pretty bad—broken ribs and teeth, head concussions, broken knuckles. What do you call that? A mild beating?'

Kuldeep Khalap looked away. 'He was a blackmailer who had kept quiet about his nephew's death—and was an accessory to it.'

'And what about your father? Wasn't he an accessory too?'

Kuldeep Khalap went quiet for a few seconds. 'He was what he was and I am what I am, I already told you. Blame it on our genes.'

'Well, there's enough evidence to convict and punish you for your crimes, Khalap—your wife's death, Bansi Vishwakarma's murder and yes, I have also dug around and identified the case in which you helped Komal Raina, the woman you raped, get away with murder five years ago. She overdosed her son, Ashit, who was suffering from haemophilia, didn't she? And you helped turn it into a case of accidental death, right?' Saralkar said.

Khalap's face had turned white as he tried to control his fear. 'Damn you, Saralkar …'

'Sir, isn't it bizarre the kind of strange phenomena that occur in this world—in the human mind, body and all aspects of human existence,' PSI Motkar observed. 'I mean this condition called paradoxical lucidity in dementia patients which explains how Urmila Welde behaved like a normal person that her neurologist explained—getting out of her house, finding her way to the post office and then deciding to end her life!'

'Yes, Motkar. I had no idea that this is observed in the case of some patients suffering from acute dementia for years—that they suddenly behave normally again, regain their memories and cognitive skills, often a few days or weeks before their deaths,' Saralkar said. 'It's fascinating that it happens and that science still does not know exactly how or why. Didn't the neurologist say that they also call it "terminal lucidity" because in most cases, death follows within days or weeks?'

'I wonder when Urmila Welde wrote—or started writing—her account, sir?' Motkar said.

'The neurologist said that she had probably started lapsing into brief periods of lucidity in the last few months and something in her mind prodded her to write about these most traumatic events that affected and shaped her life,' Saralkar explained. 'So she most likely penned things down over a period of few months. And when full lucidity returned, perhaps a few days ago, she decided she was going to confess and end her life. Of course, the dementia specialists are studying the letter and have been talking to her full-time caretakers from over the last one year. We should have a clearer picture in the next few days, which will help us present this as evidence.'

Both were quiet for a while, then Saralkar spoke, 'Kuldeep Khalap was right. We could crack the case only because Eknath Khubba came forward and Urmila Welde penned her account and posted it to us, courtesy her paradoxical lucidity.'

'But, sir, you set a trap for Khalap in the murder-suicide case. That's why we got him in the first place,' Motkar observed.

'Hmm,' Saralkar grunted and turned thoughtful again. His phone buzzed and the senior inspector squinted at it. 'The CP,' he said, made a face and then took the call. 'Yes, madam.'

His expressions didn't take long to turn into surprise, then consternation and even shock. At that very moment, ASI Zirpe entered the cabin after a knock, her face serious and disturbed.

Saralkar held up his hand, then concluded his call with the CP, saying, 'I'm on to it, madam.'

He looked at Motkar, then Zirpe with a scowl. 'I know what you have to report, Zirpe! How come the CP knows about it before me?'

'I don't know about that, sir. I just got the news.'

'What news, sir?' Motkar asked.

'Kuldeep Khalap gave the slip to the police cordon led by Inspector Rajguru, inside the courthouse. He had been taken there for extension of his judicial custody,' Saralkar said grimly. 'He ran out of the court premises, straight into the middle of the road and jumped in front of a truck.'

'What?' Motkar stared.

'That's right, sir. He committed suicide.'

Motkar looked at Saralkar with disbelief. 'Sounds almost like an encounter, sir,' he muttered.

Saralkar shuddered, 'It's certainly going to be hard for Pune Police to explain, Motkar. Terrible optics! I am so glad we were nowhere near when Khalap decided to do what he did. Thank God for small mercies!'

'Should I proceed to the spot, sir?' ASI Zirpe volunteered.

Saralkar nodded and Sanika left. A thoughtful, weary silence reigned for a few minutes.

'Sir…?' Motkar said pricking the silence. 'Can I ask you something, if you don't mind?'

'What?'

Motkar hesitated. 'Just wanted you to clear up a personal mystery, sir?'

Saralkar looked up at him alert, as if on his guard. 'What personal mystery?'

Motkar's face became straighter than usual. 'What is your first name, sir? No one seems to know.'

Saralkar stared at him, his gaze belligerent. 'Why do you want to know?'

Motkar cleared his throat. 'Just curious, sir. I have been working with you for so many years …'

Saralkar looked away. Motkar was sure he had taken offence as seconds ticked away.

'It's Adhokshaj,' Saralkar finally said, turning to him defiantly. 'Ever heard of the name? Know what it means?'

Motkar shook his head, unable to hide his surprise. 'No, sir. It's unusual …'

'Odd is what you really mean. A mouthful. At school I was teased like hell. No wonder I grew allergic to it and have kept it under wraps ever since,' Saralkar said.

Motkar wished he hadn't broached the topic at all. 'I'm sorry if I ….'

Saralkar shook his head and grinned wryly. 'It's OK. It's said to be one of Vishnu's names, you know. It's got an enviable meaning.'

'Please tell me, sir.'

'Adhokshaj means one who cannot be measured or diminished,' the senior inspector replied. 'Impressively abstract, eh!'

Motkar smiled. Saralkar winked.